SEX CRIMINALS

THREE THE HARD WAY

MATT FRACTION
CHIP ZDARSKY

THOMAS K
EDITING

DREW GILL
PRODUCTION

LAUREN SANKOVITCH
MANAGING EDITOR

IMAGE COMICS, INC.
Robert Kirkman – Chief Operating Officer
Erik Larsen – Chief Financial Officer
Todd McFarlane – President
Marc Silvestri – Chief Executive Officer
Jim Valentino – Vice-President

Eric Stephenson – Publisher
Corey Murphy – Director of Sales
Jeff Boison – Director of Publishing Planning & Book Trade Sales
Jeremy Sullivan – Director of Digital Sales
Kat Salazar – Director of PR & Marketing
Emily Miller – Director of Operations
Branwyn Bigglestone – Senior Accounts Manager
Sarah Mello – Accounts Manager
Drew Gill – Art Director
Jonathan Chan – Production Manager
Meredith Wallace – Print Manager
Briah Skelly – Publicity Assistant
Sasha Head – Sales & Marketing Production Designer
Randy Okamura – Digital Production Designer
David Brothers – Branding Manager
Ally Power – Content Manager
Addison Duke – Production Artist
Vincent Kukua – Production Artist
Tricia Ramos – Production Artist
Jeff Stang – Direct Market Sales Representative
Emilio Bautista – Digital Sales Associate
Leanna Caunter – Accounting Assistant
Chloe Ramos-Peterson – Administrative Assistant
IMAGECOMICS.COM

FOR CHIP
BECAUSE LOOK, chum, seriously
if I get this book back from the printer
and I see you dedicated it
to someone else than me
I'M JUST SAYIN
we're entering murder-suicide territory
help me chum
help me help us
help

MATT

To Sex Criminals Volume Two.
You taught me so much.
I couldn't have done
Sex Criminals Volume Three
without you.

CHIP

11
MANIME

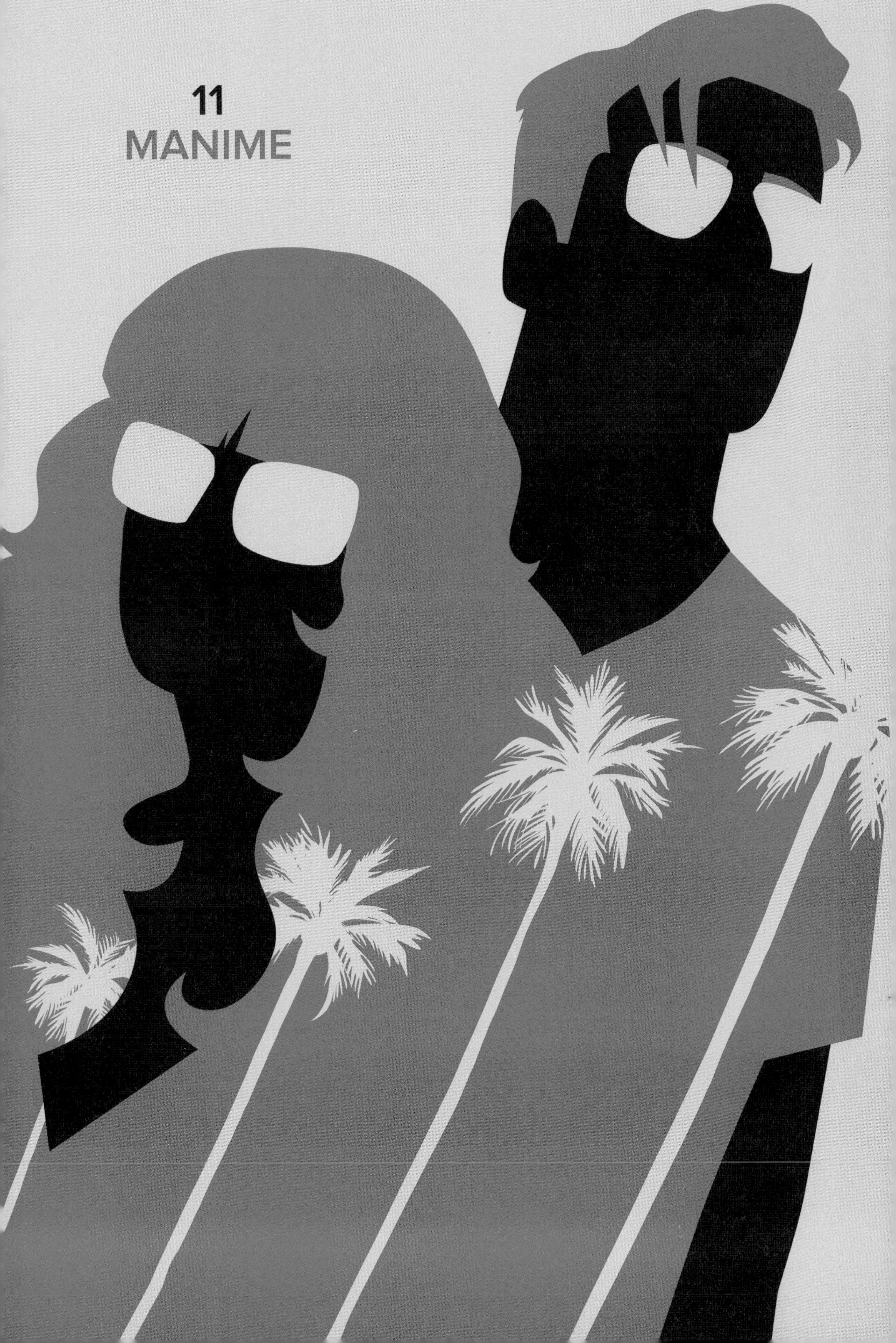

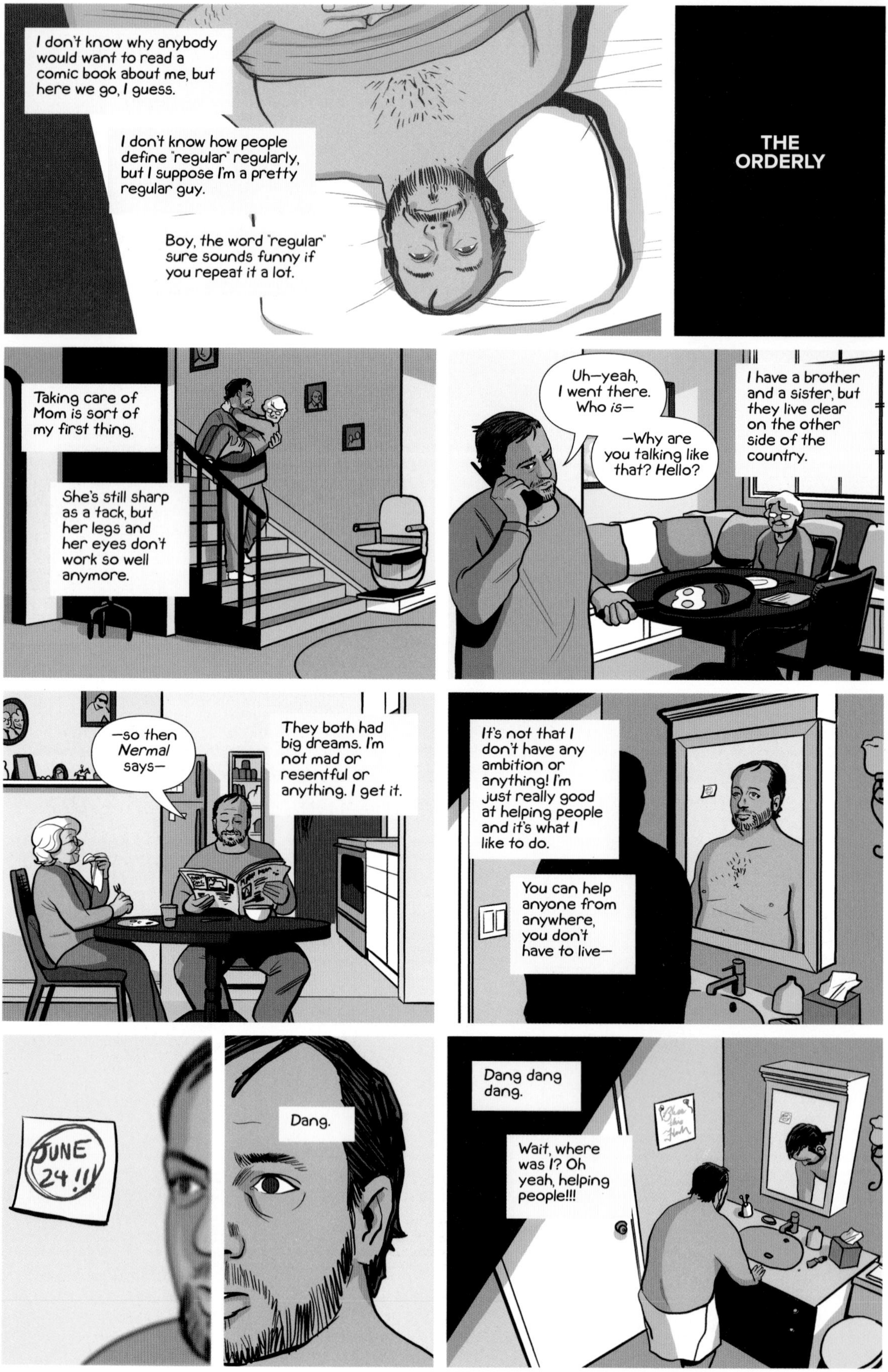

I don't know why anybody would want to read a comic book about me, but here we go, I guess.
I don't know how people define "regular" regularly, but I suppose I'm a pretty regular guy.
Boy, the word "regular" sure sounds funny if you repeat it a lot.
THE ORDERLY
Taking care of Mom is sort of my first thing.
She's still sharp as a tack, but her legs and her eyes don't work so well anymore.
Uh—yeah, I went there. Who *is*—
—Why are you talking like that? Hello?
I have a brother and a sister, but they live clear on the other side of the country.
—so then *Nermal* says—
They both had big dreams. I'm not mad or resentful or anything. I get it.
It's not that I don't have any ambition or anything! I'm just really good at helping people and it's what I like to do.
You can help anyone from anywhere, you don't have to live—
JUNE 24!!
Dang.
Dang dang dang.
Wait, where was I? Oh yeah, helping people!!!

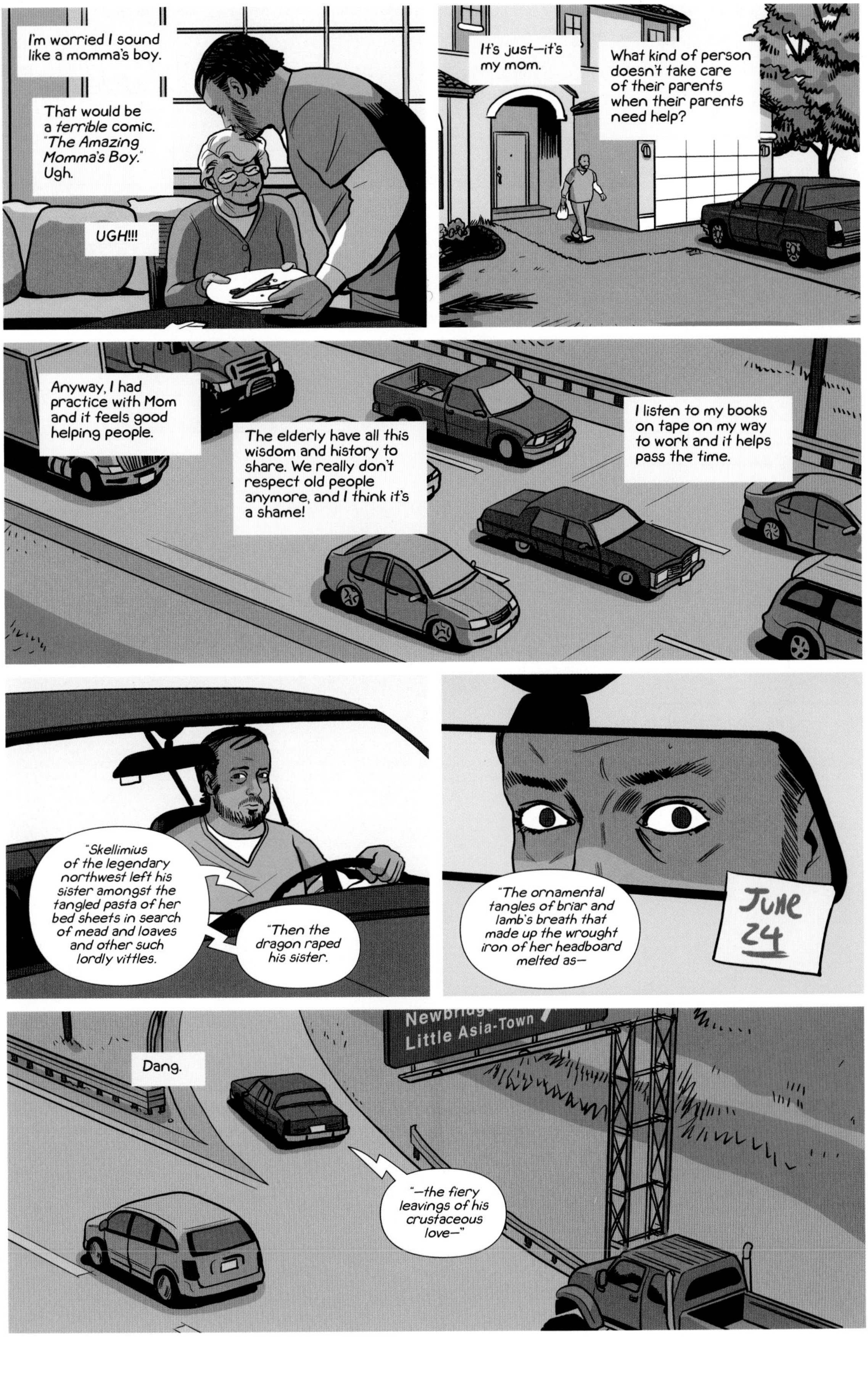
I'm worried I sound like a momma's boy.
That would be a *terrible* comic. *"The Amazing Momma's Boy."* Ugh.
UGH!!!
It's just—it's my mom.
What kind of person doesn't take care of their parents when their parents need help?
Anyway, I had practice with Mom and it feels good helping people.
The elderly have all this wisdom and history to share. We really don't respect old people anymore, and I think it's a shame!
I listen to my books on tape on my way to work and it helps pass the time.
"Skellimius of the legendary northwest left his sister amongst the tangled pasta of her bed sheets in search of mead and loaves and other such lordly vittles.
"Then the dragon raped his sister.
"The ornamental tangles of briar and lamb's breath that made up the wrought iron of her headboard melted as—
June 24
Little Asia-Town
Dang.
"—the fiery leavings of his crustaceous love—"

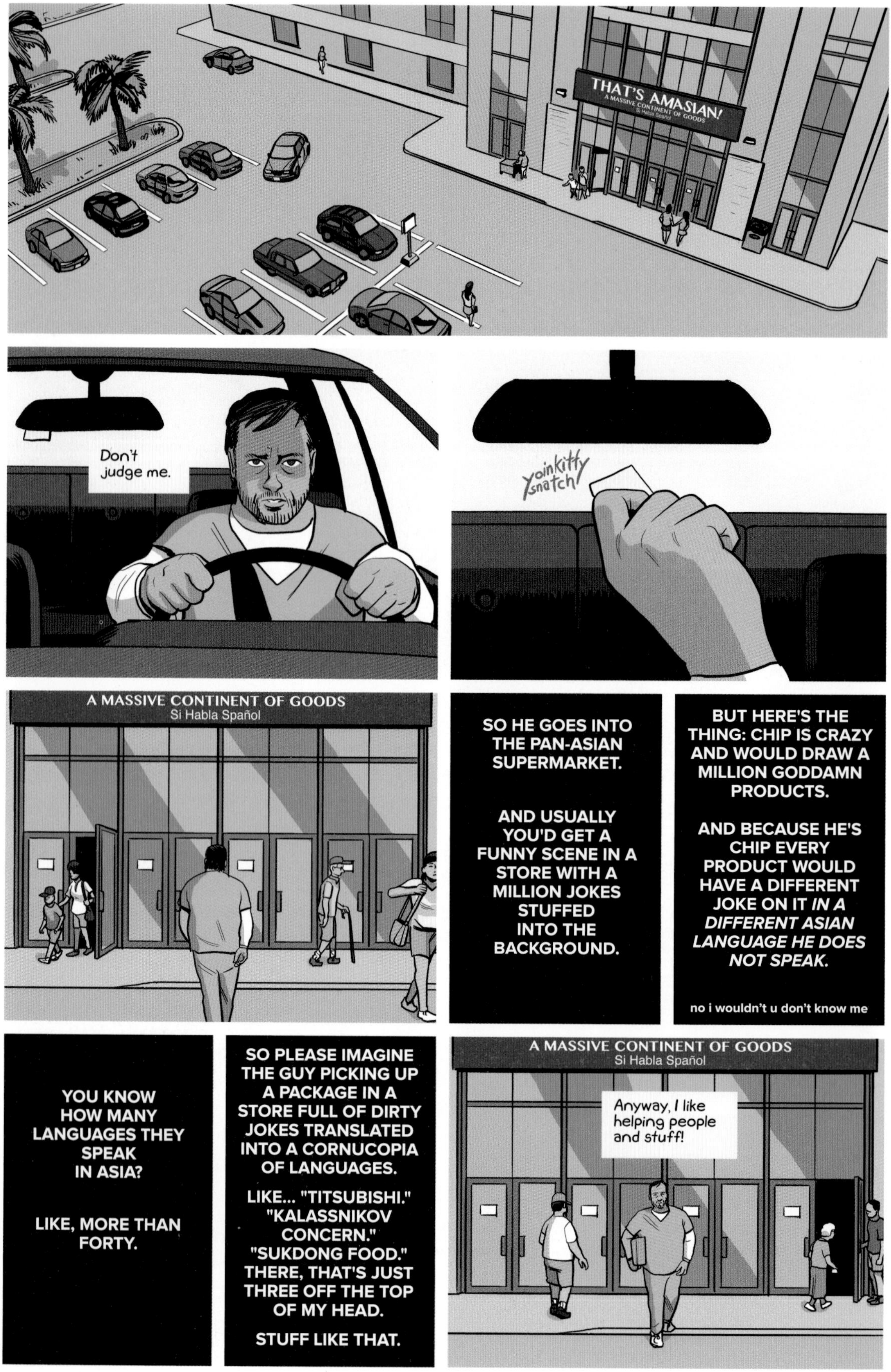
THAT'S AMASIAN!
A MASSIVE CONTINENT OF GOODS
Si Habla Spañol
Don't judge me.
yoinkitty snatch!
A MASSIVE CONTINENT OF GOODS
Si Habla Spañol
SO HE GOES INTO THE PAN-ASIAN SUPERMARKET.
AND USUALLY YOU'D GET A FUNNY SCENE IN A STORE WITH A MILLION JOKES STUFFED INTO THE BACKGROUND.
BUT HERE'S THE THING: CHIP IS CRAZY AND WOULD DRAW A MILLION GODDAMN PRODUCTS.
AND BECAUSE HE'S CHIP EVERY PRODUCT WOULD HAVE A DIFFERENT JOKE ON IT *IN A DIFFERENT ASIAN LANGUAGE HE DOES NOT SPEAK.*
no i wouldn't u don't know me
YOU KNOW HOW MANY LANGUAGES THEY SPEAK IN ASIA?
LIKE, MORE THAN FORTY.
SO PLEASE IMAGINE THE GUY PICKING UP A PACKAGE IN A STORE FULL OF DIRTY JOKES TRANSLATED INTO A CORNUCOPIA OF LANGUAGES.
LIKE... "TITSUBISHI." "KALASSNIKOV CONCERN." "SUKDONG FOOD." THERE, THAT'S JUST THREE OFF THE TOP OF MY HEAD.
STUFF LIKE THAT.
A MASSIVE CONTINENT OF GOODS
Si Habla Spañol
Anyway, I like helping people and stuff!

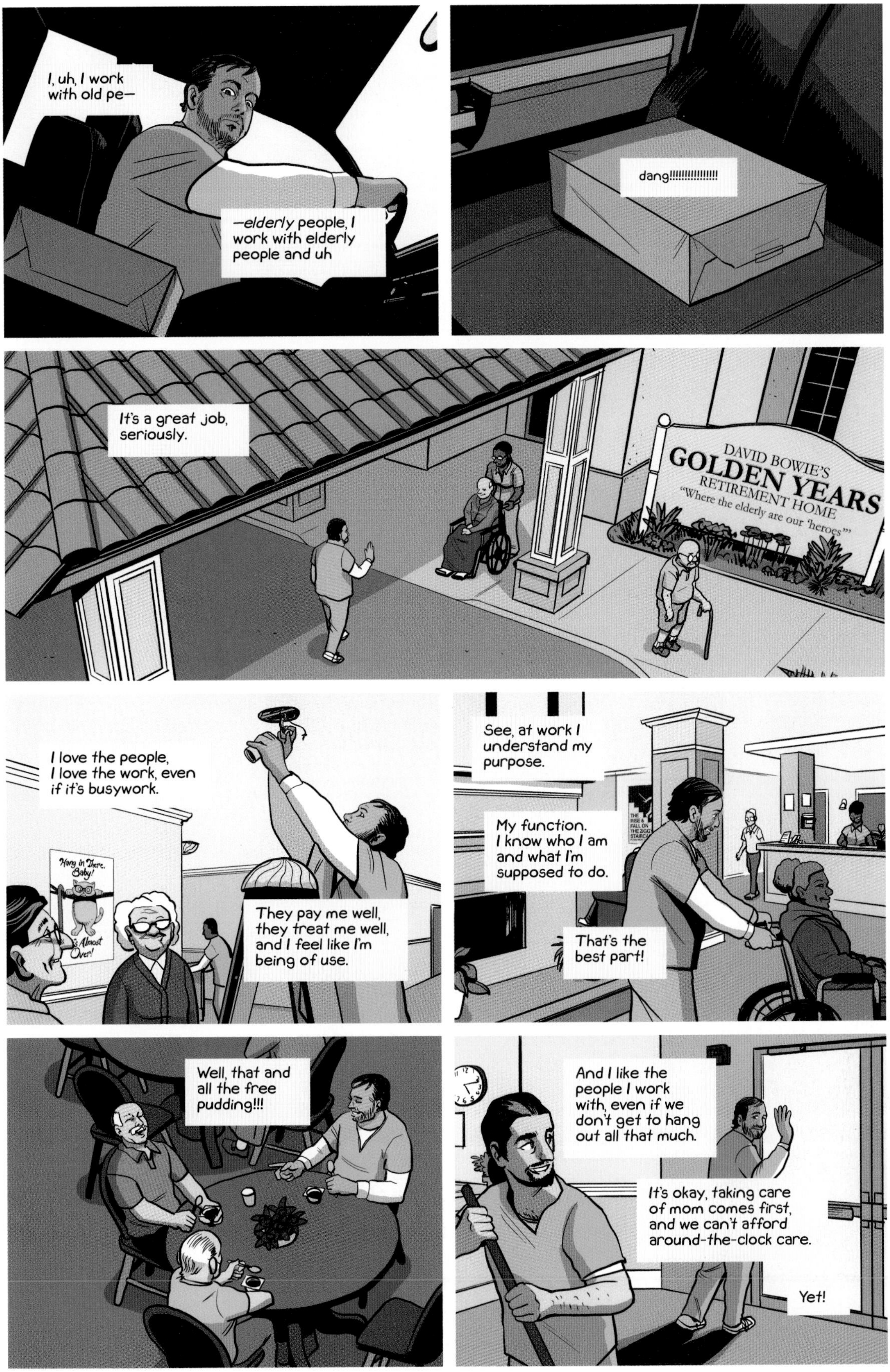
I, uh, I work with old pe—
—*elderly* people, I work with elderly people and uh
dang!!!!!!!!!!!!!!!
It's a great job, seriously.
DAVID BOWIE'S
GOLDEN YEARS
RETIREMENT HOME
"Where the elderly are our 'heroes'"
I love the people, I love the work, even if it's busywork.
Hang in There, Baby!
They pay me well, they treat me well, and I feel like I'm being of use.
See, at work I understand my purpose.
My function. I know who I am and what I'm supposed to do.
That's the best part!
Well, that and all the free pudding!!!
And I like the people I work with, even if we don't get to hang out all that much.
It's okay, taking care of mom comes first, and we can't afford around-the-clock care.
Yet!

"—still smoldered on the charred ruins of his sister's body, the scent of scorched pork and sweet firewood smoke filling his bedchambers—".

Our evening routine is like the morning, just in reverse!

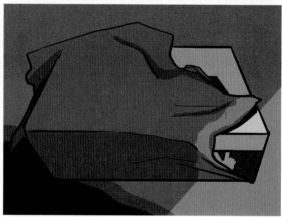

マスク！

グッド倍！ 楽しい！

Mom sleeps like a baby, so once she's out...

...Once she's out, the nighttime is my time.

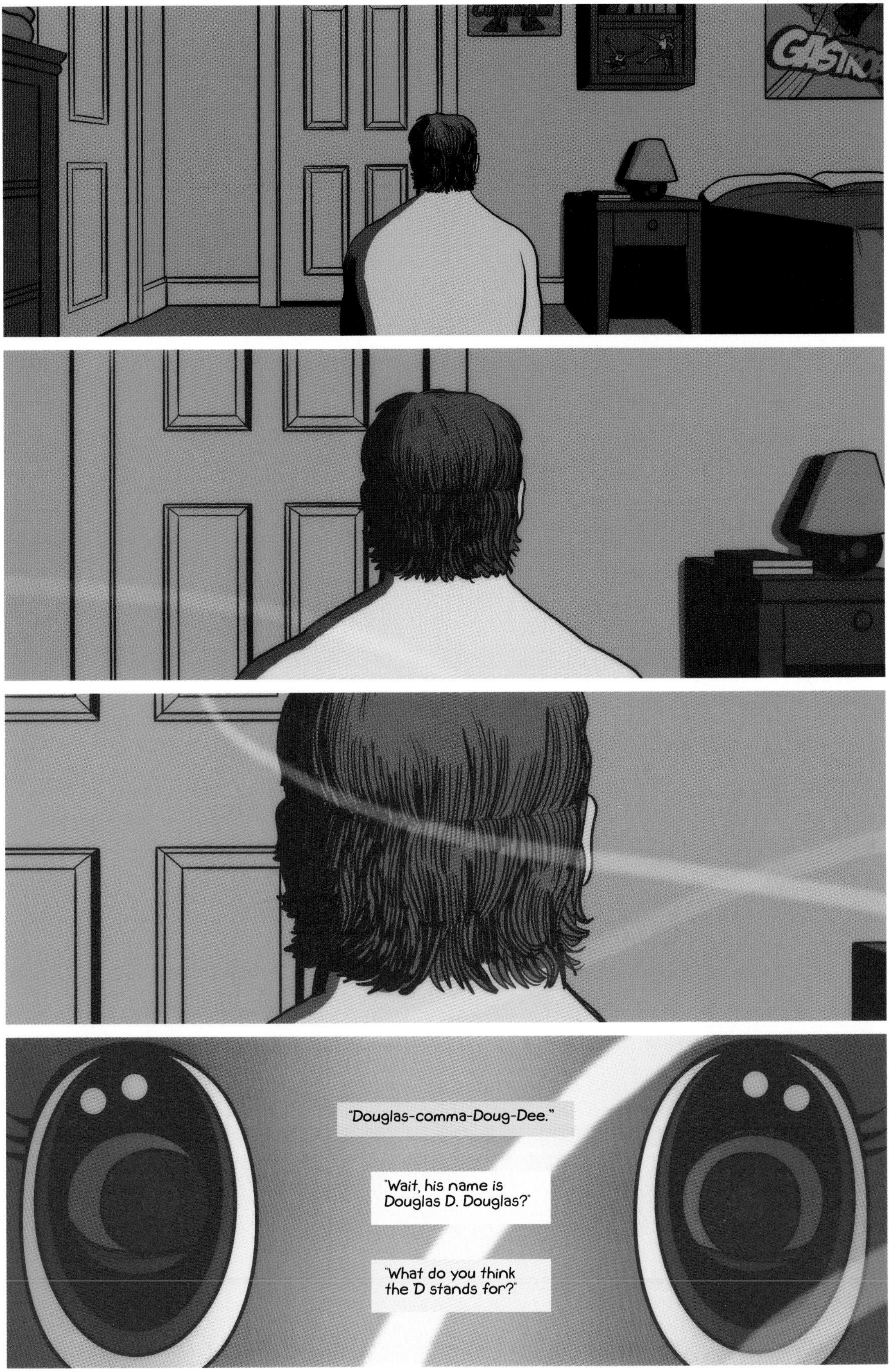
"Douglas-comma-Doug-Dee."
"Wait, his name is Douglas D. Douglas?"
"What do you think the 'D' stands for?"

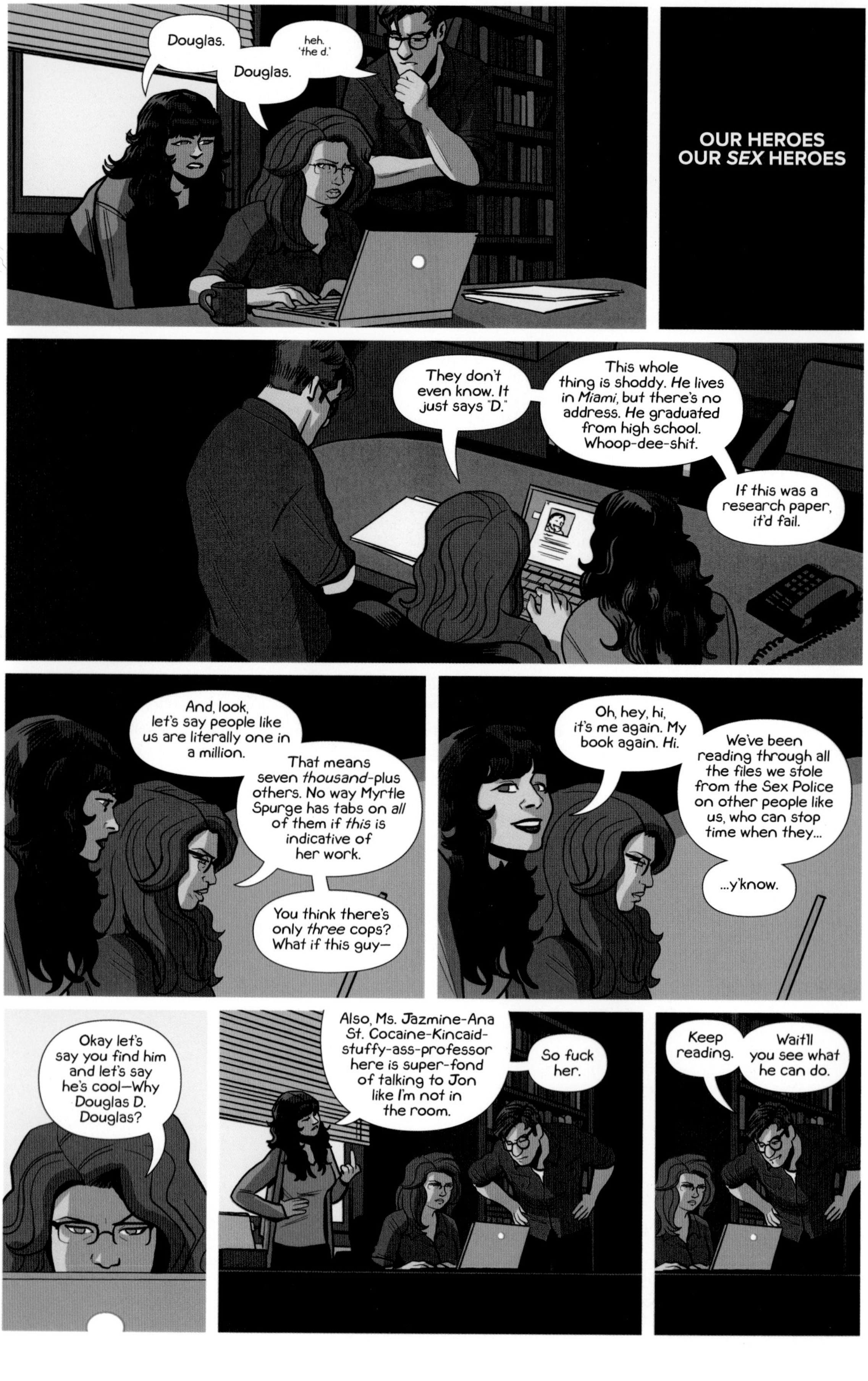

Douglas.
Douglas.
heh. 'the d.'
OUR HEROES
OUR *SEX* HEROES
They don't even know. It just says "D."
This whole thing is shoddy. He lives in *Miami*, but there's no address. He graduated from high school. Whoop-dee-shit.
If this was a research paper, it'd fail.
And, look, let's say people like us are literally one in a million.
That means seven *thousand*-plus others. No way Myrtle Spurge has tabs on *all* of them if *this* is indicative of her work.
You think there's only *three* cops? What if this guy—
Oh, hey, hi, it's me again. My book again. *Hi.*
We've been reading through all the files we stole from the Sex Police on other people like us, who can stop time when they...
...y'know.
Okay let's say you find him and let's say he's cool—Why Douglas D. Douglas?
Also, Ms. Jazmine-Ana St. Cocaine-Kincaid-stuffy-ass-professor here is super-fond of talking to Jon like I'm not in the room.
So fuck her.
Keep reading.
Wait'll you see what he can do.

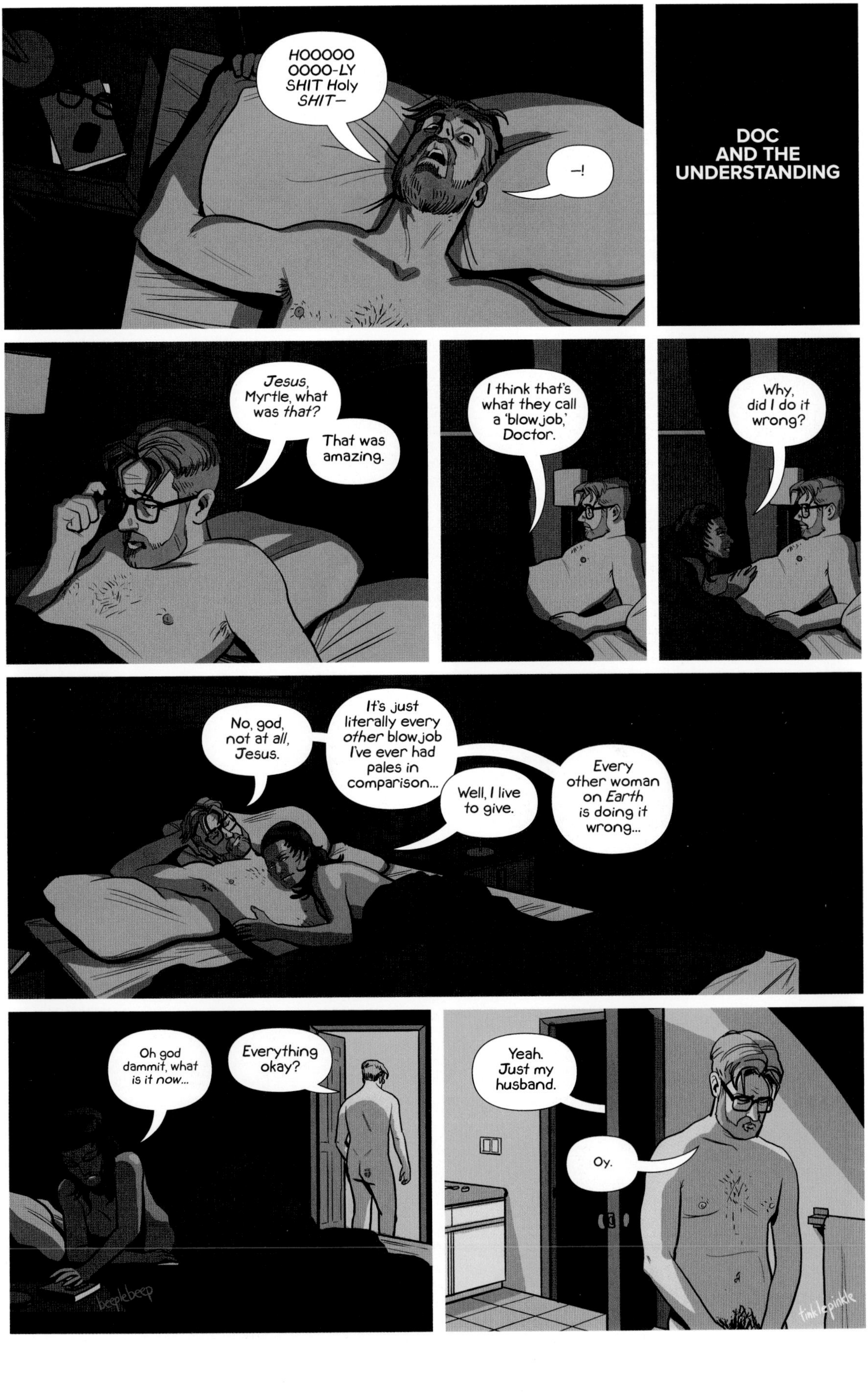
HOOOOO OOOO-LY SHIT Holy SHIT—
—!
DOC AND THE UNDERSTANDING
Jesus, Myrtle, what was that?
That was amazing.
I think that's what they call a 'blowjob,' Doctor.
Why, did I do it wrong?
No, god, not at all, Jesus.
It's just literally every other blowjob I've ever had pales in comparison...
Well, I live to give.
Every other woman on Earth is doing it wrong...
Oh god dammit, what is it now...
beeplebeep
Everything okay?
Yeah. Just my husband.
Oy.
tinklepinkle

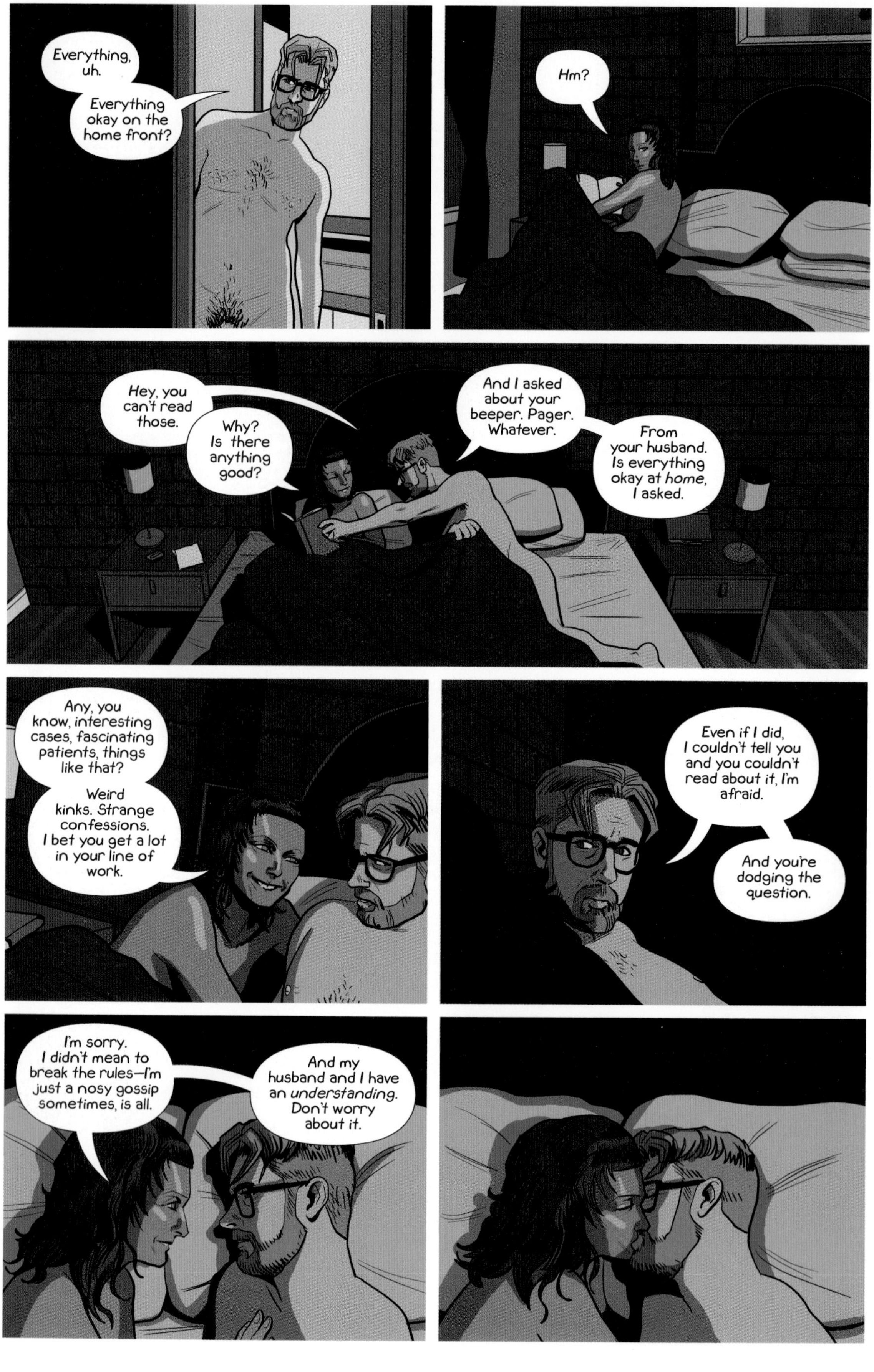
Everything, uh.
Everything okay on the home front?
Hm?
Hey, you can't read those.
Why? Is there anything good?
And I asked about your beeper. Pager. Whatever.
From your husband. Is everything okay at *home*, I asked.
Any, you know, interesting cases, fascinating patients, things like that?
Weird kinks. Strange confessions. I bet you get a lot in your line of work.
Even if I did, I couldn't tell you and you couldn't read about it, I'm afraid.
And you're dodging the question.
I'm sorry. I didn't mean to break the rules—I'm just a nosy gossip sometimes, is all.
And my husband and I have an *understanding*. Don't worry about it.

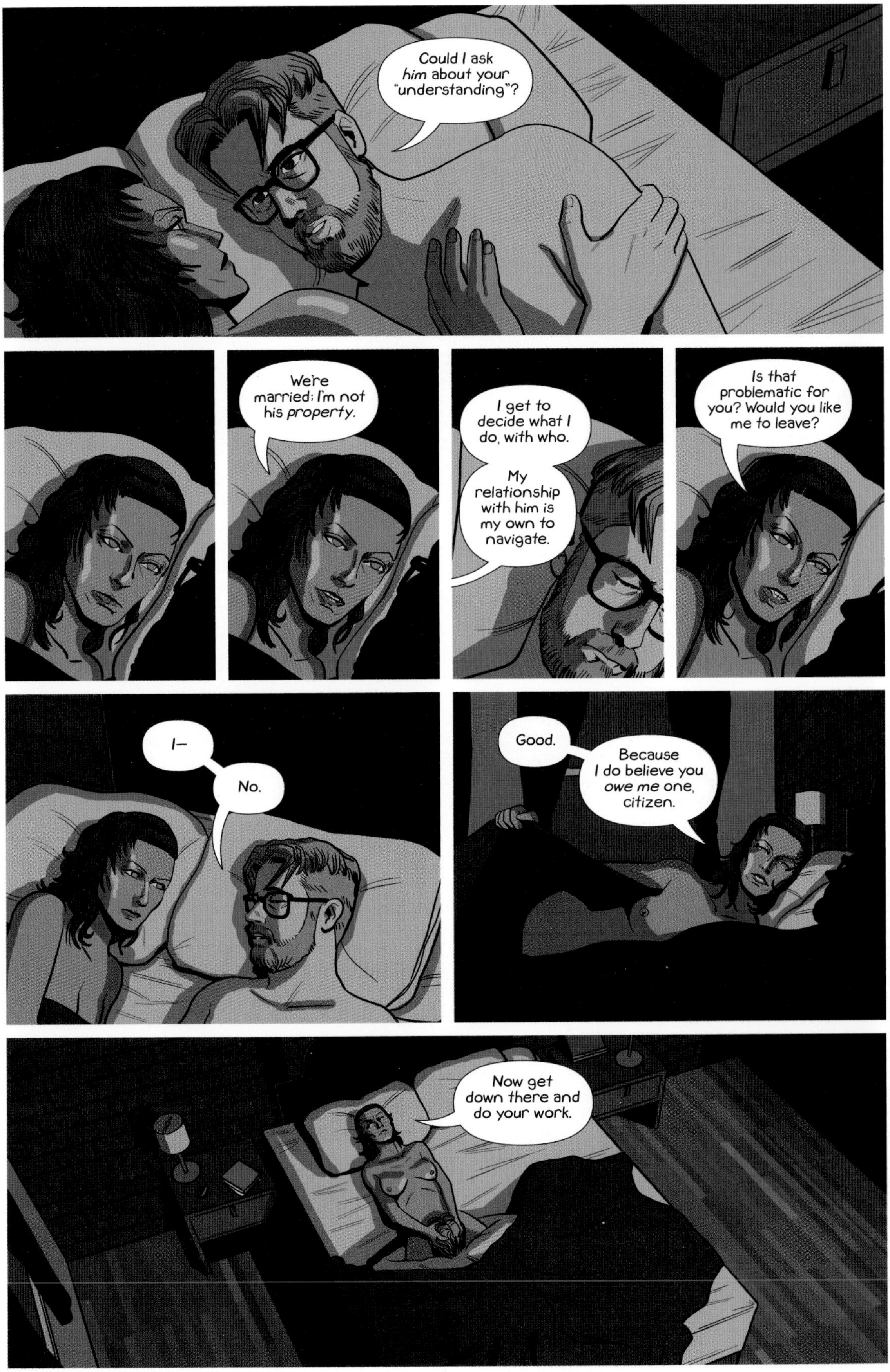
Could I ask *him* about your "understanding"?
We're married; I'm not his *property*.
I get to decide what I do, with who.
My relationship with him is my own to navigate.
Is that problematic for you? Would you like me to leave?
I–
No.
Good.
Because I do believe you *owe me* one, citizen.
Now get down there and do your work.

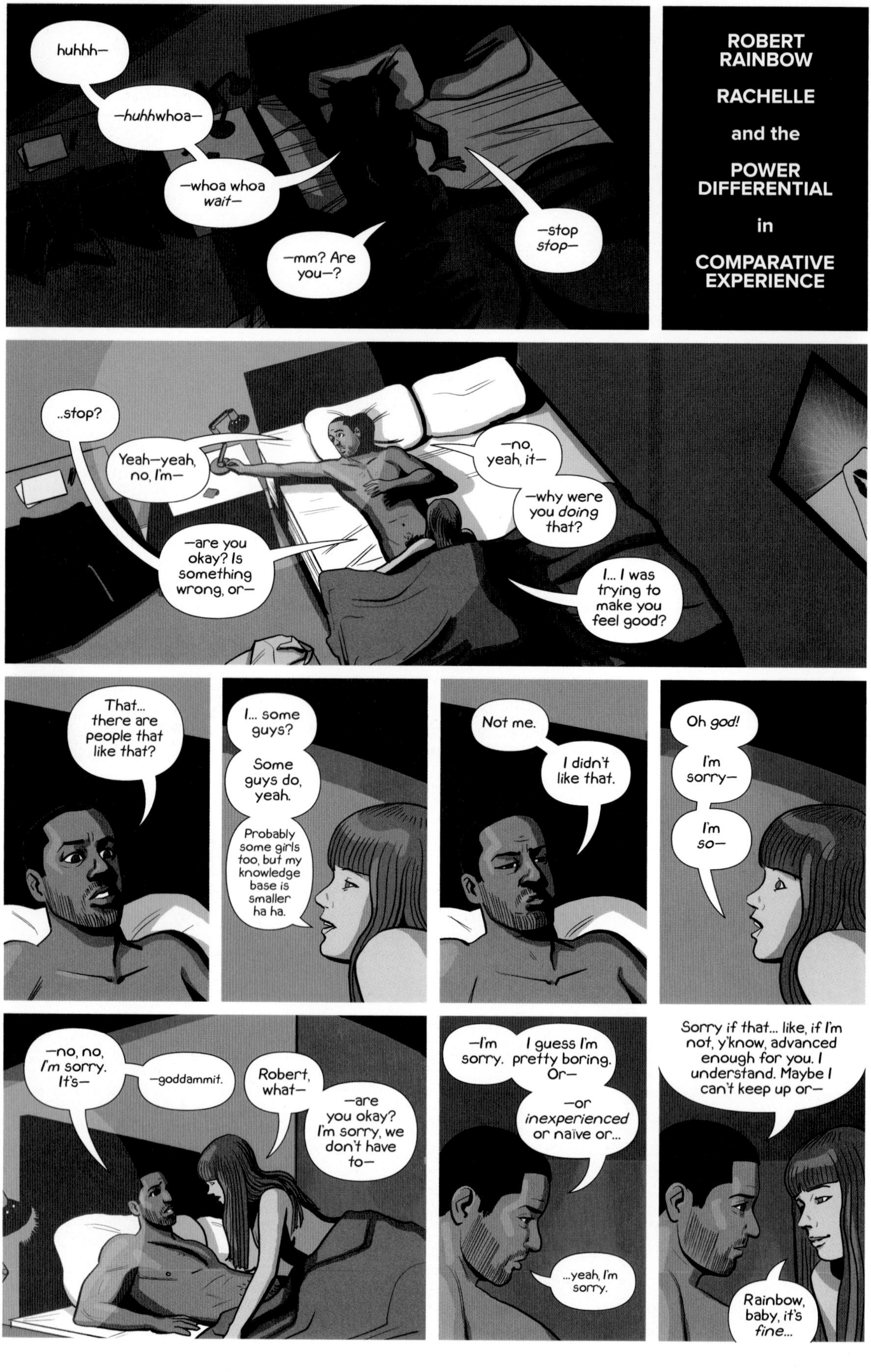
huhhh—
—*huhh*whoa—
—whoa whoa *wait*—
—mm? Are you—?
—stop *stop*—
ROBERT RAINBOW
RACHELLE
and the
POWER DIFFERENTIAL
in
COMPARATIVE EXPERIENCE
..stop?
Yeah—yeah, no, I'm—
—are you okay? Is something wrong, or—
—no, yeah, it—
—why were you *doing* that?
I... I was trying to make you feel good?
That... there are people that like that?
I... some guys?
Some guys do, yeah.
Probably some girls too, but my knowledge base is smaller ha ha.
Not me.
I didn't like that.
Oh *god!*
I'm sorry—
I'm *so*—
—no, no, *I'm* sorry. It's—
—goddammit.
Robert, what—
—are you okay? I'm sorry, we don't have to—
—I'm sorry.
I guess I'm pretty boring. Or—
—or *inexperienced* or naïve or...
...yeah, I'm sorry.
Sorry if that... like, if I'm not, y'know, advanced enough for you. I understand. Maybe I can't keep up or—
Rainbow, baby, it's *fine*...

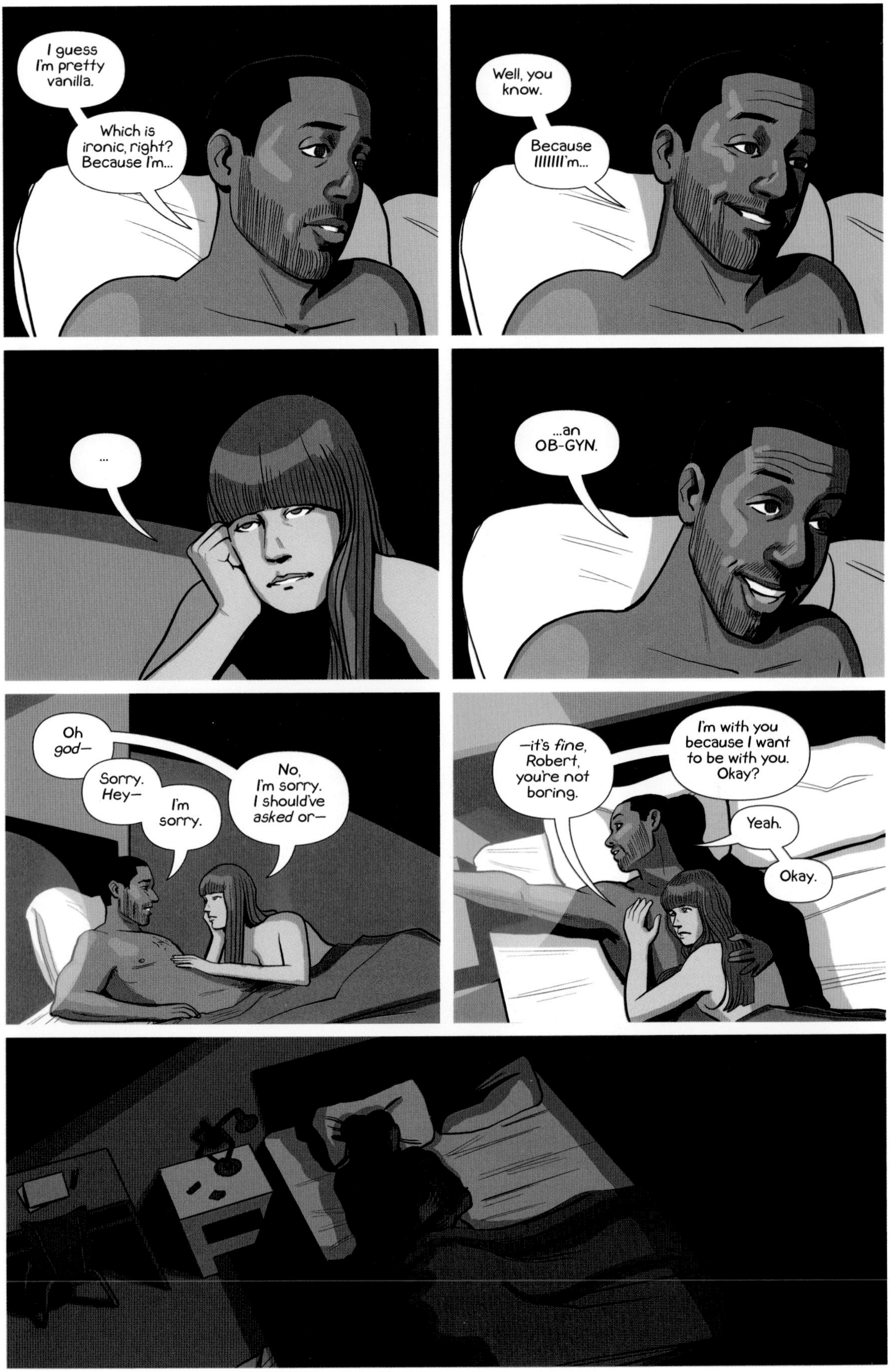
I guess I'm pretty vanilla.
Which is ironic, right? Because I'm...
Well, you know.
Because IIIIIII'm...
...
...an OB-GYN.
Oh *god*—
Sorry. Hey—
I'm sorry.
No, I'm sorry. I should've *asked* or—
—it's *fine*, Robert, you're not boring.
I'm with you because I want to be with you. Okay?
Yeah.
Okay.

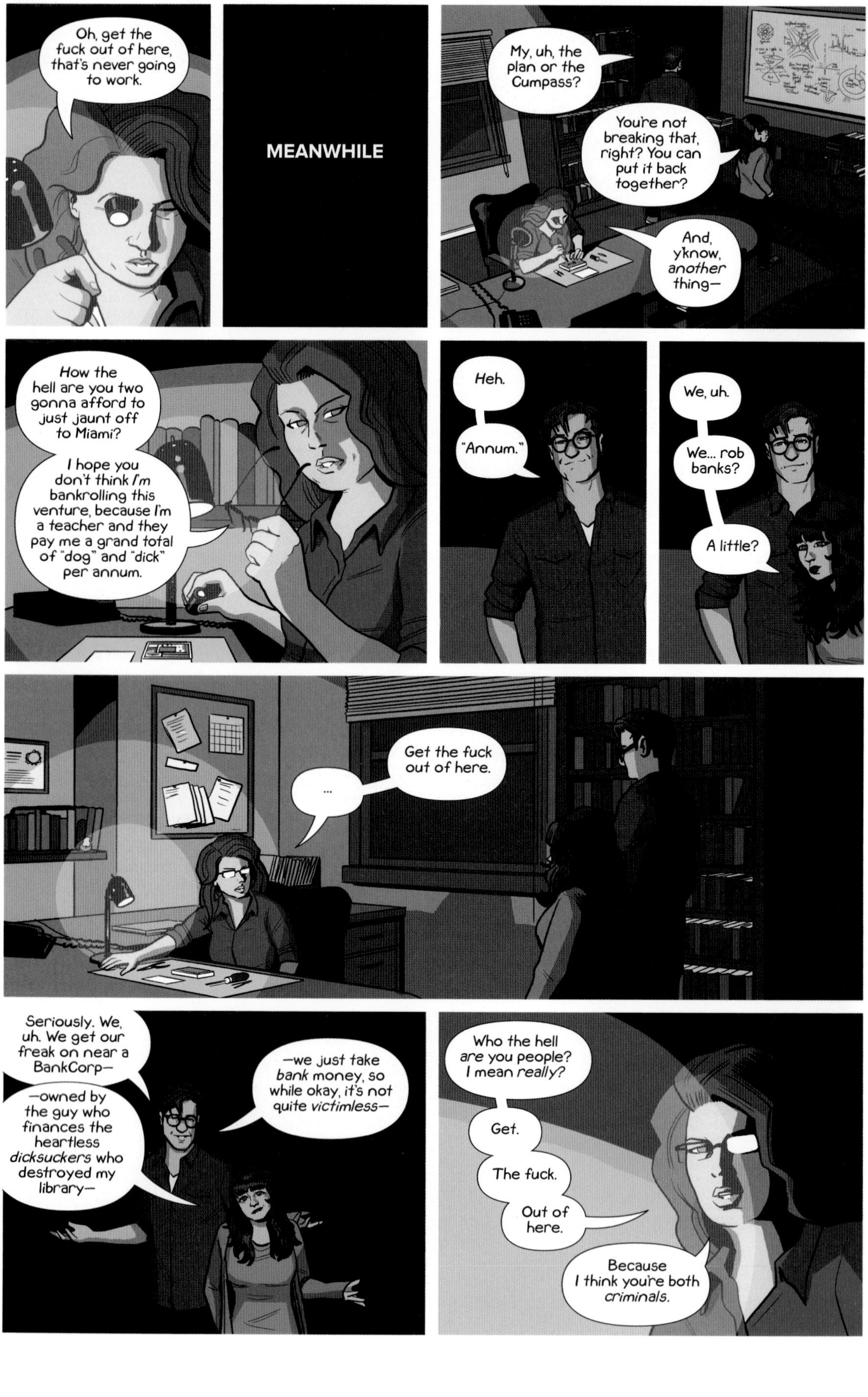
Oh, get the fuck out of here, that's never going to work.
MEANWHILE
My, uh, the plan or the Cumpass?
You're not breaking that, right? You can put it back together?
And, y'know, *another* thing—
How the hell are you two gonna afford to just jaunt off to Miami?
I hope you don't think *I'm* bankrolling this venture, because I'm a teacher and they pay me a grand total of "dog" and "dick" per annum.
Heh.
"Annum."
We, uh.
We... rob banks?
A little?
Get the fuck out of here.
...
Seriously. We, uh. We get our freak on near a BankCorp—
—owned by the guy who finances the heartless *dicksuckers* who destroyed my library—
—we just take *bank* money, so while okay, it's not quite *victimless*—
Who the hell *are you people*? I mean *really*?
Get.
The fuck.
Out of here.
Because I think you're both *criminals*.

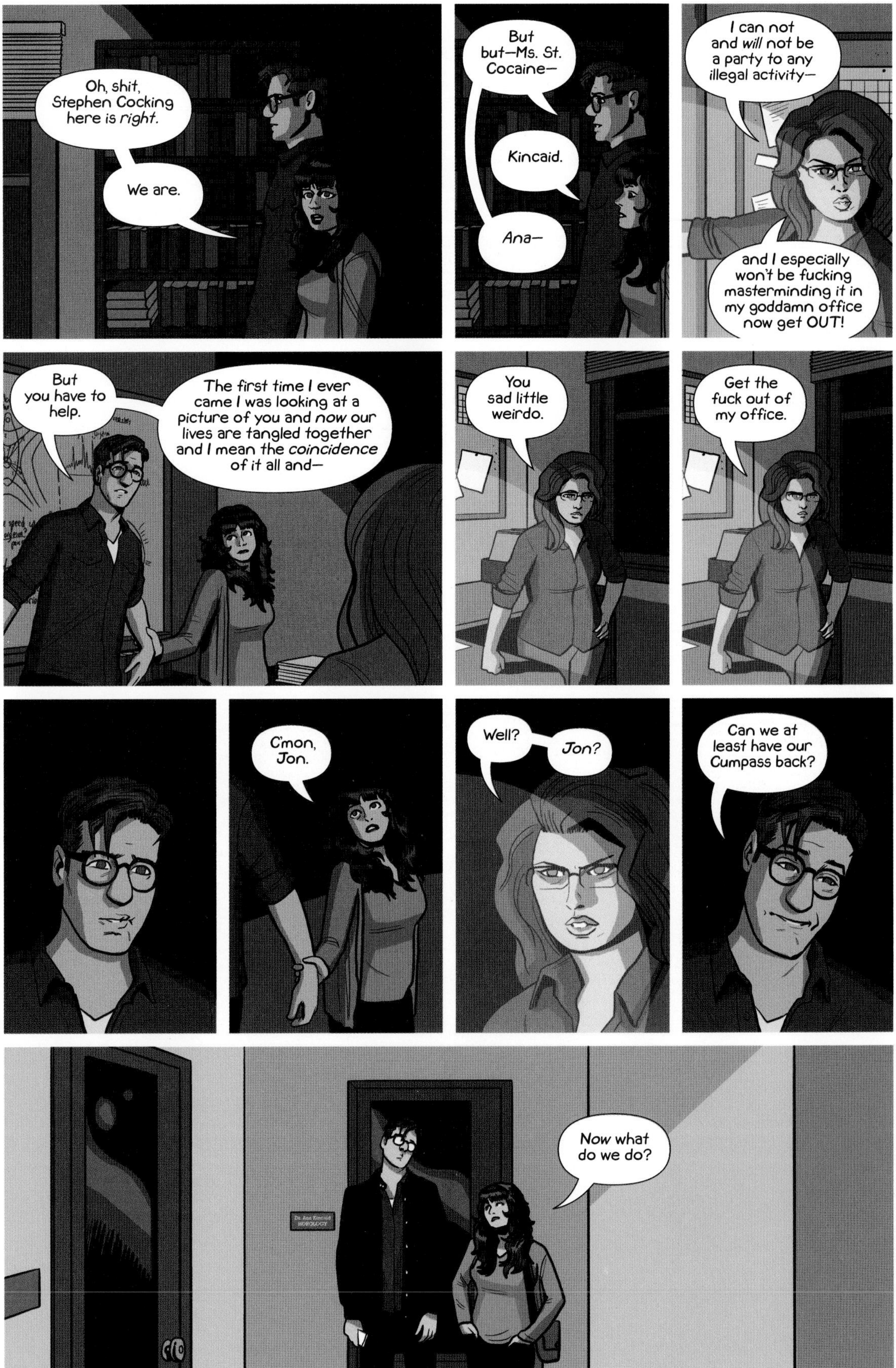
Oh, shit, Stephen Cocking here is *right*.
We are.
But but—Ms. St. Cocaine—
Kincaid.
Ana—
I can not and *will* not be a party to any illegal activity—
and I especially won't be fucking masterminding it in my goddamn office now get OUT!
But you have to help.
The first time I ever came I was looking at a picture of you and *now* our lives are tangled together and I mean the *coincidence* of it all and—
You sad little weirdo.
Get the fuck out of my office.
C'mon, Jon.
Well?
Jon?
Can we at least have our Cumpass back?
Now what do we do?

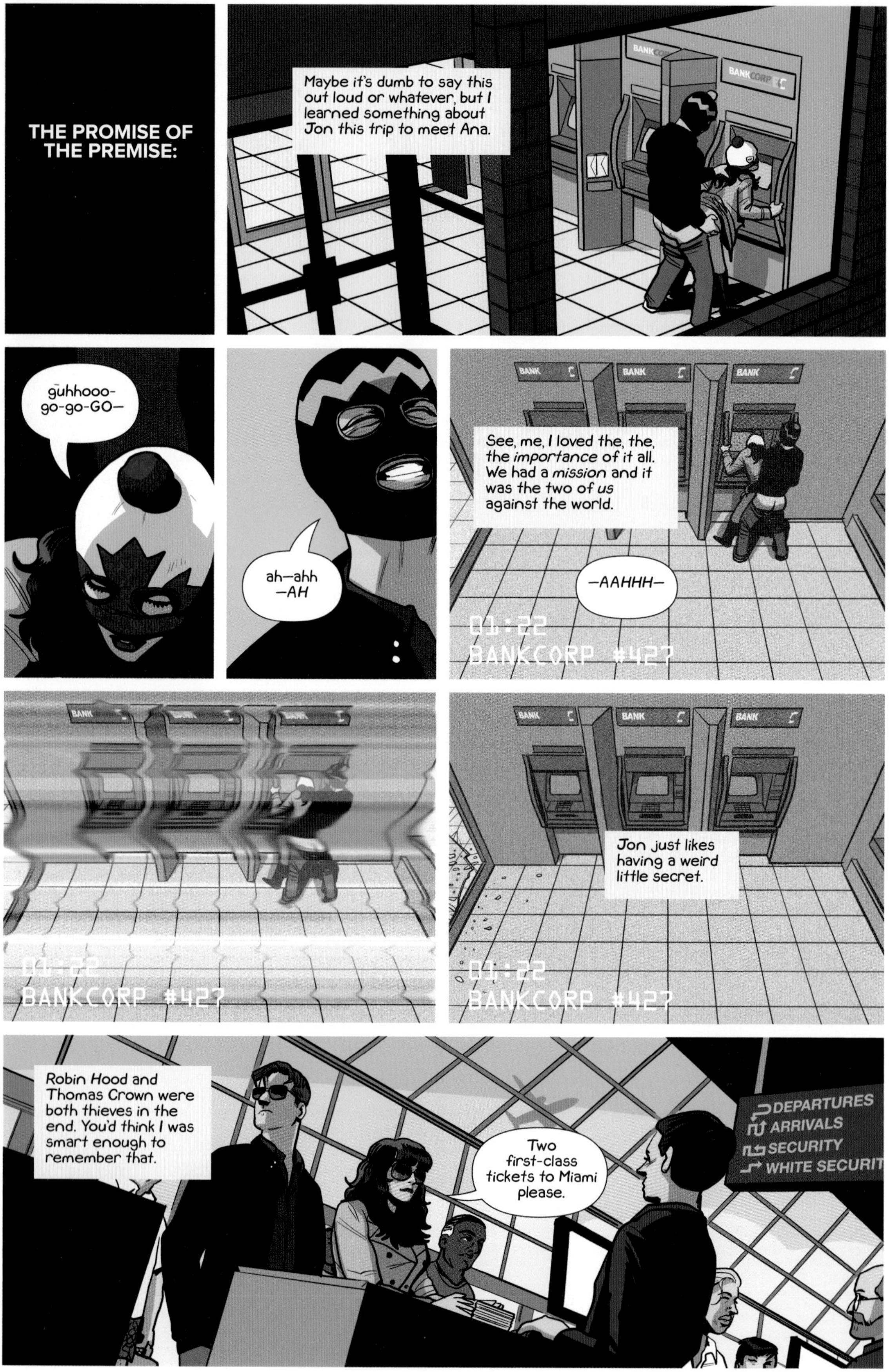
THE PROMISE OF THE PREMISE:
Maybe it's dumb to say this out loud or whatever, but I learned something about Jon this trip to meet Ana.
guhhooo-go-go-GO—
ah—ahh —AH
See, me, I loved the, the, the *importance* of it all. We had a *mission* and it was the two of *us* against the world.
—AAHHH—
01:22
BANKCORP #427
01:22
BANKCORP #427
Jon just likes having a weird little secret.
01:22
BANKCORP #427
Robin Hood and Thomas Crown were both thieves in the end. You'd think I was smart enough to remember that.
Two first-class tickets to Miami please.
DEPARTURES
ARRIVALS
SECURITY
WHITE SECURIT

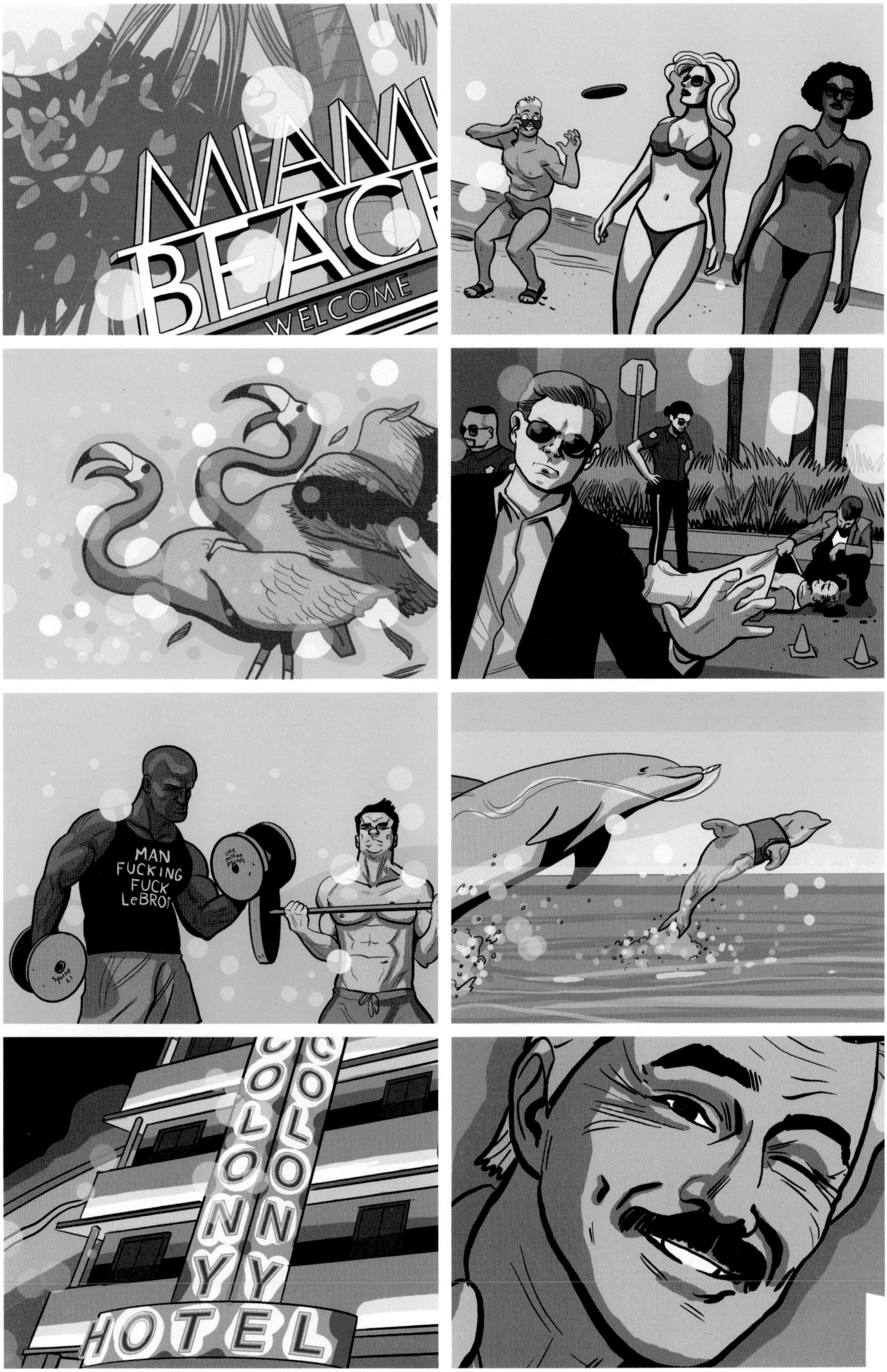
WELCOME
MAN
FUCKING
FUCK
COLONY
COLONY
HOTEL

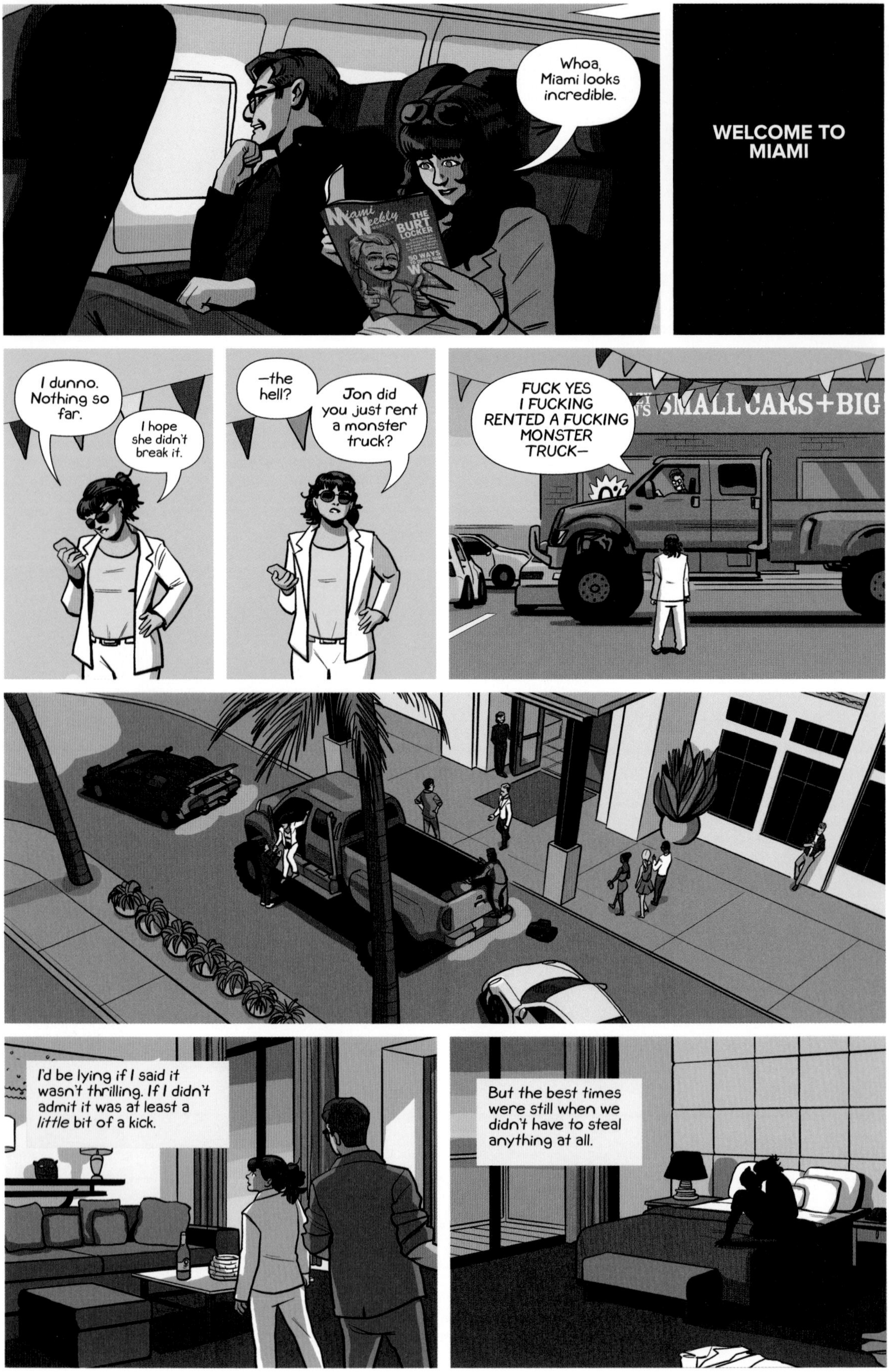
Miami Weekly
THE BURT LOCKER
Whoa, Miami looks incredible.
WELCOME TO MIAMI
I dunno. Nothing so far.
I hope she didn't break it.
—the hell?
Jon did you just rent a monster truck?
SMALL CARS + BIG
FUCK YES I FUCKING RENTED A FUCKING MONSTER TRUCK—
I'd be lying if I said it wasn't thrilling. If I didn't admit it was at least a *little* bit of a kick.
But the best times were still when we didn't have to steal anything at all.

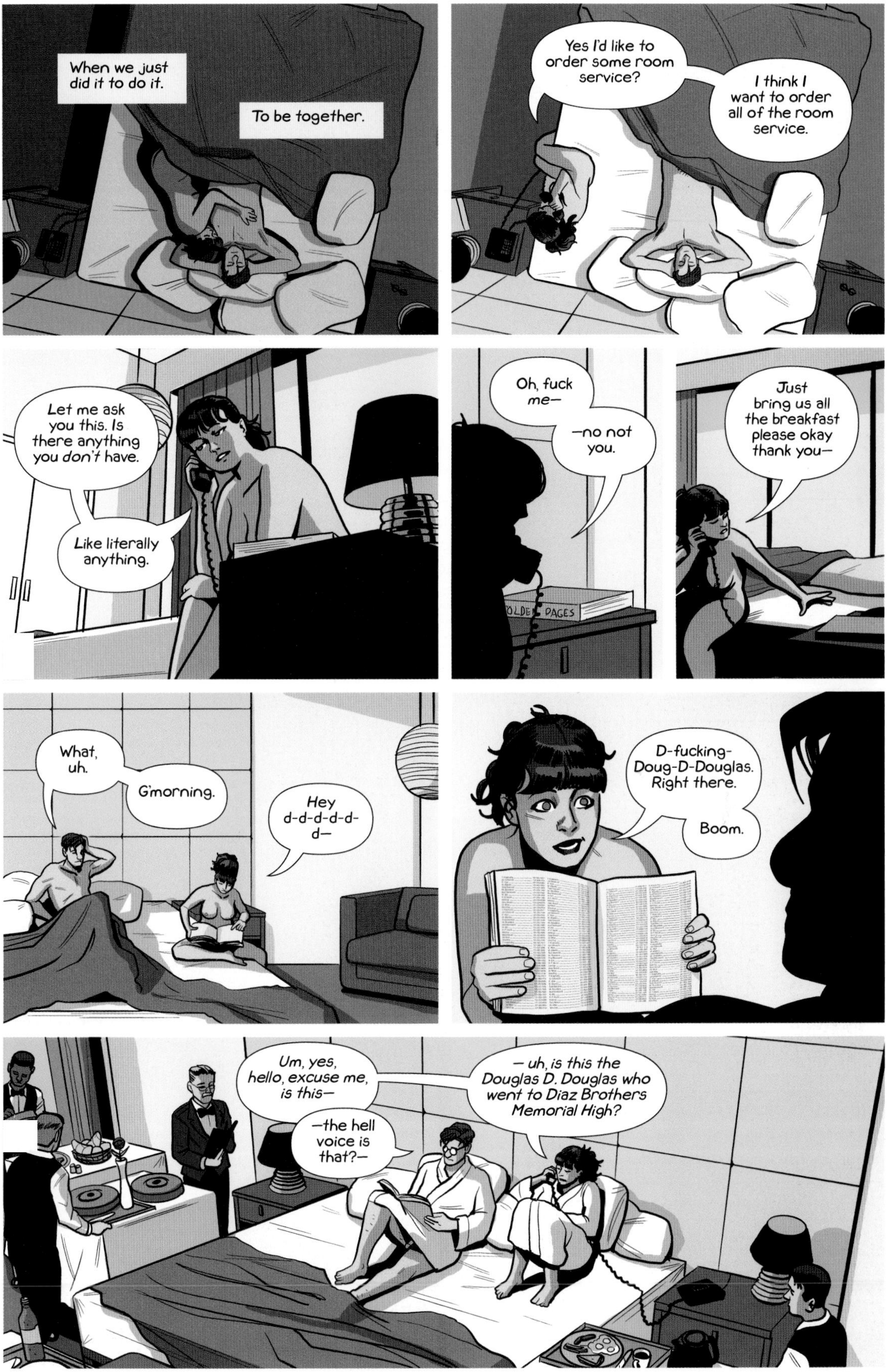
When we just did it to do it.
To be together.
Yes I'd like to order some room service?
I think I want to order all of the room service.
Let me ask you this. Is there anything you *don't* have.
Like literally anything.
Oh, fuck *me*—
—no not you.
GOLDEN PAGES
Just bring us all the breakfast please okay thank you—
What, uh.
G'morning.
Hey d-d-d-d-d-d—
D-fucking-Doug-D-Douglas. Right there.
Boom.
Um, yes, hello, excuse me, is this—
— uh, is this the Douglas D. Douglas who went to Diaz Brothers Memorial High?
—the hell voice is that?—

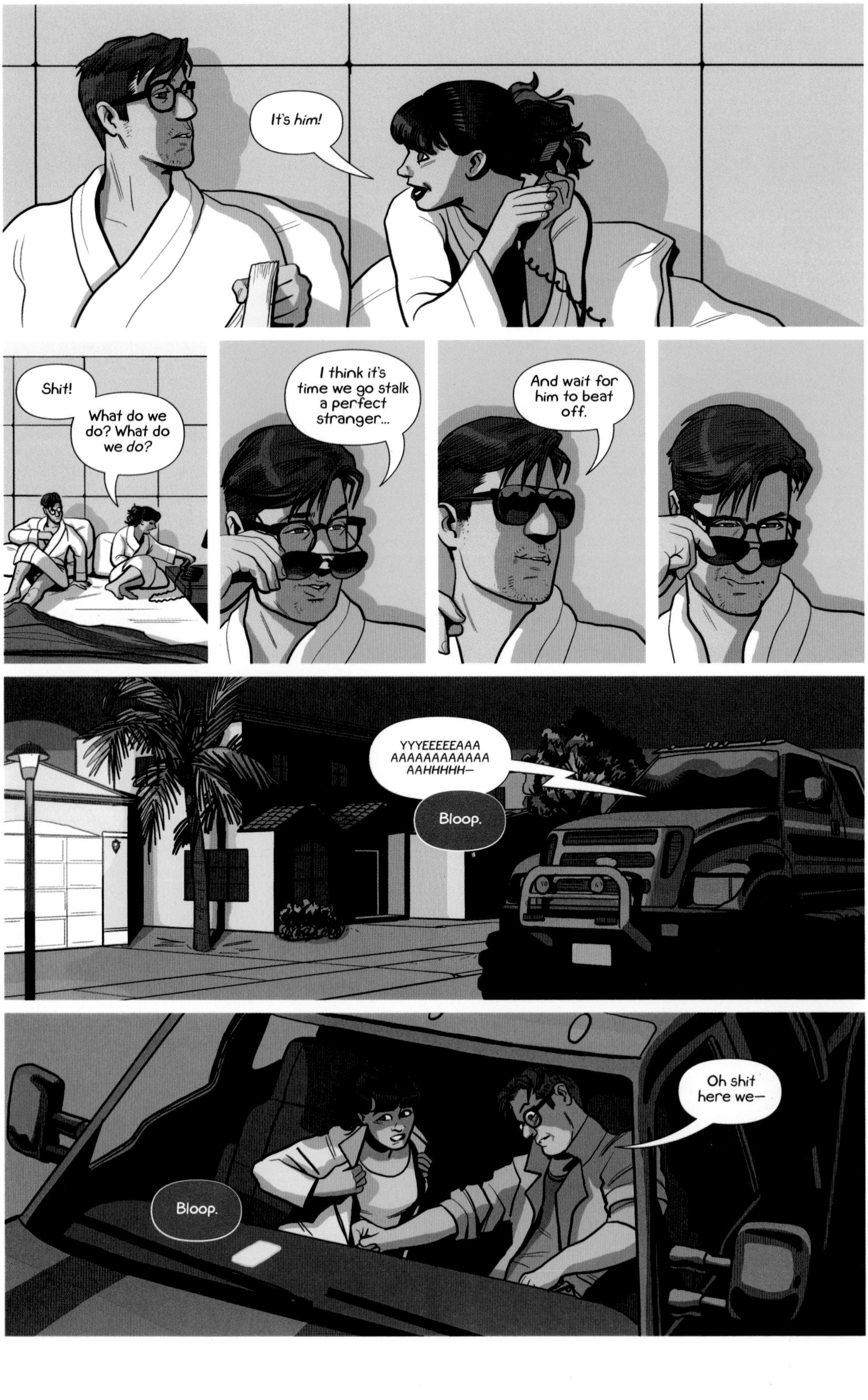
It's *him!*
Shit!
What do we do? What do we *do?*
I think it's time we go stalk a perfect stranger...
And wait for him to beat off.
YYYEEEEEAAA AAAAAAAAAAAA AAHHHHH—
Bloop.
Oh shit here we—
Bloop.

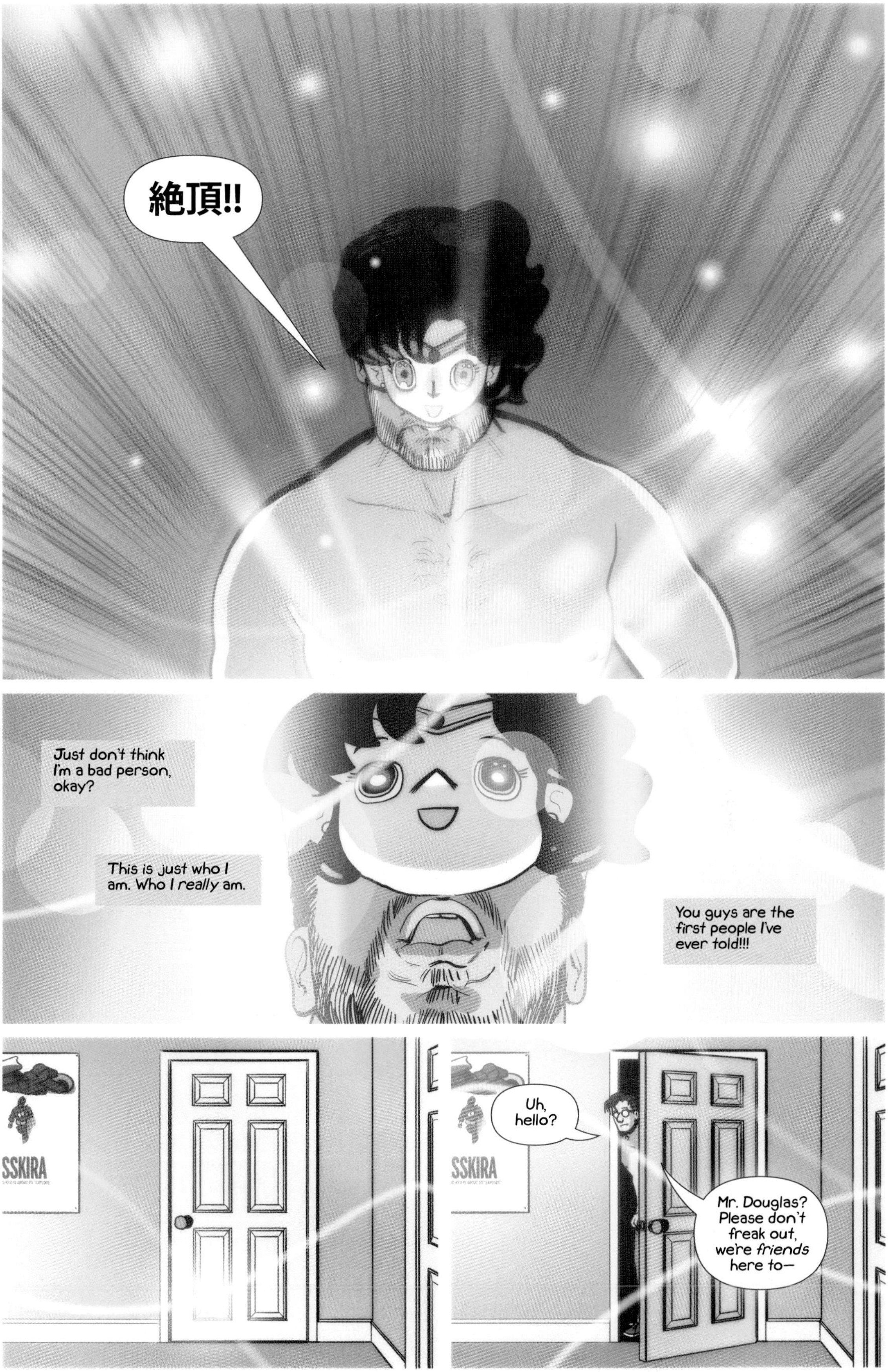
絶頂!!
Just don't think I'm a bad person, okay?
This is just who I am. Who I *really* am.
You guys are the first people I've ever told!!!
SSKIRA
SSKIRA
Uh, hello?
Mr. Douglas? Please don't freak out, we're *friends* here to—

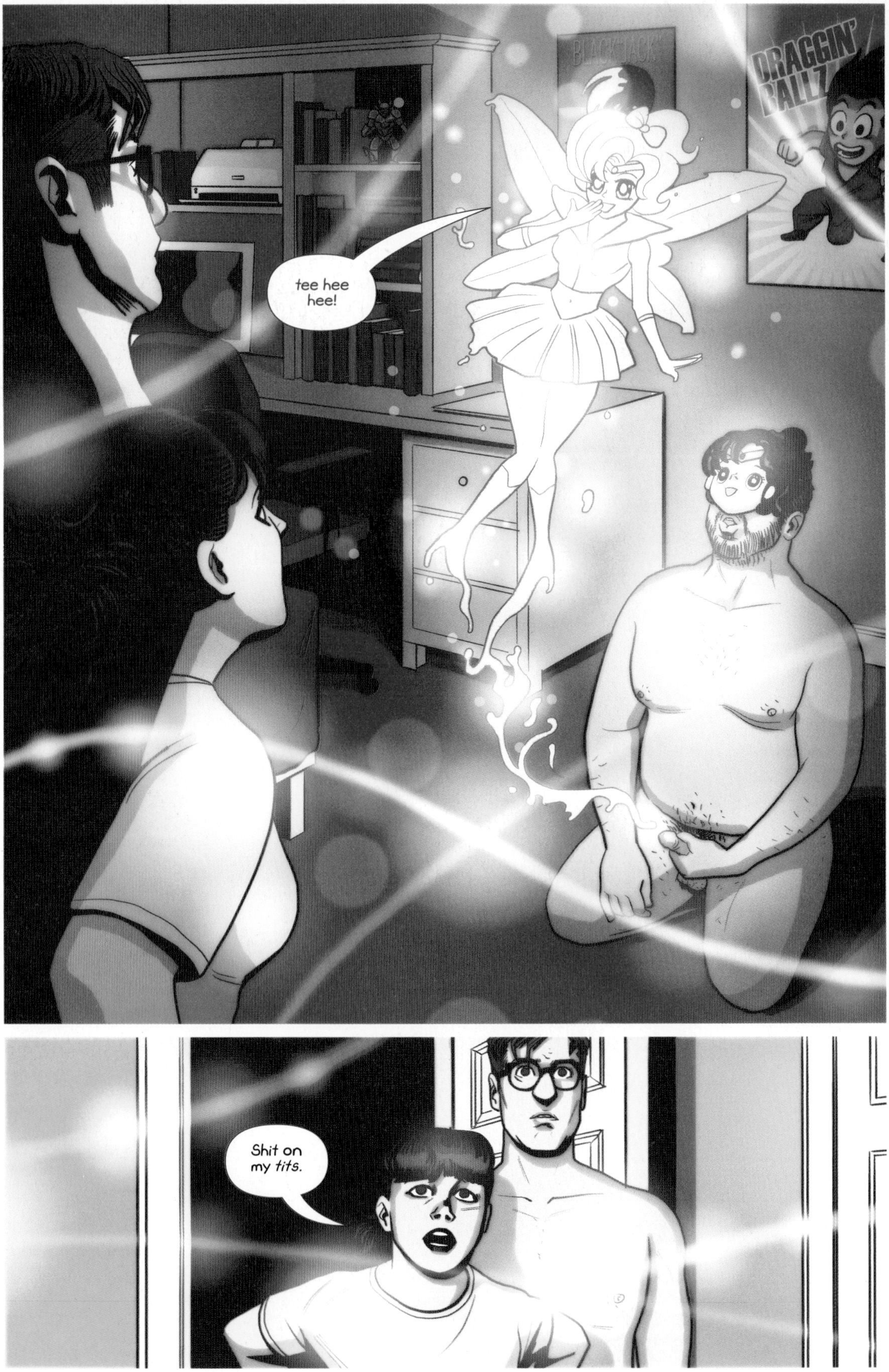
DRAGGIN' BALLZ
tee hee hee!
Shit on my *tits*.

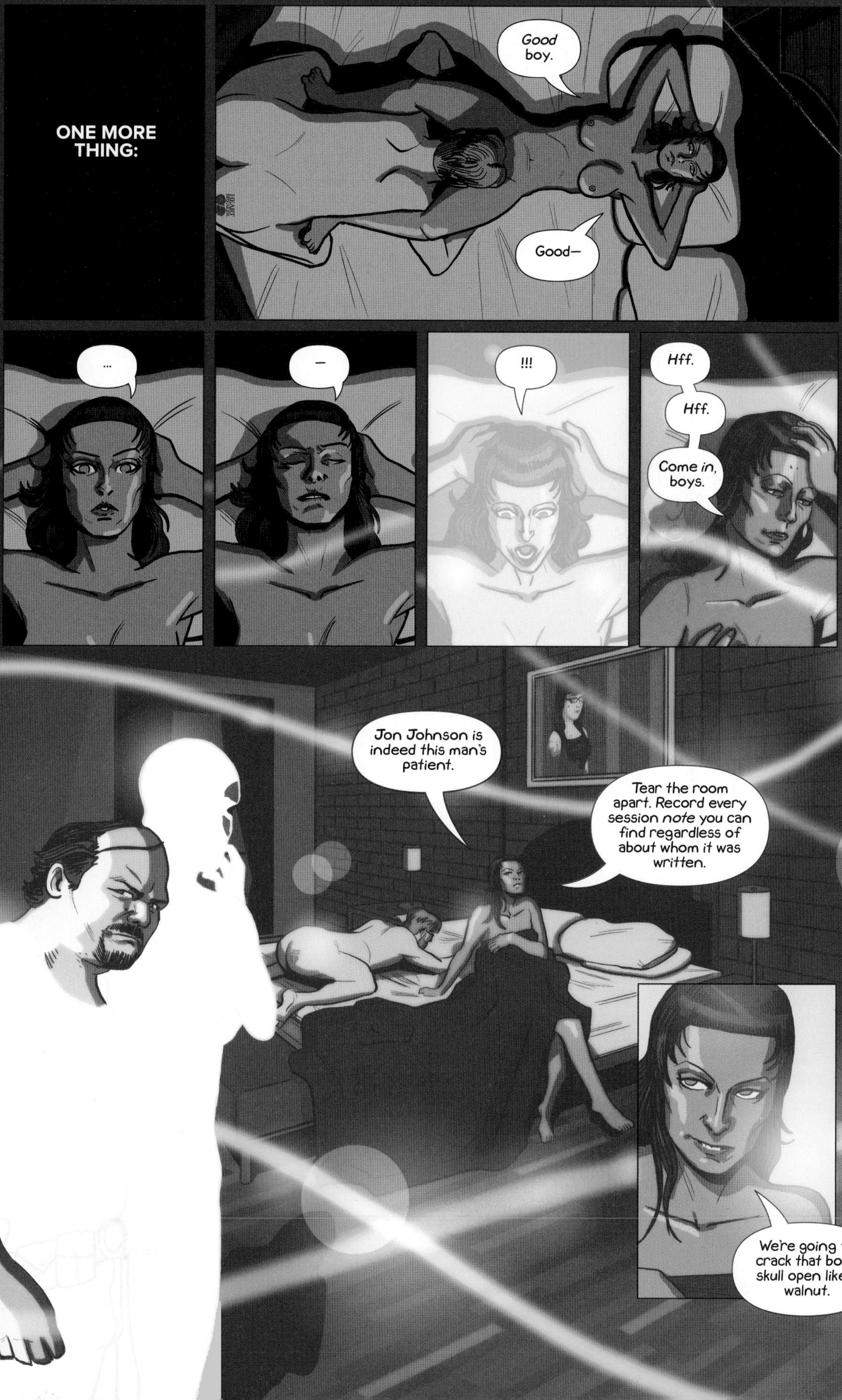
ONE MORE THING:
Good boy.
Good—
...
—
!!!
Hff.
Hff.
Come *in*, boys.
Jon Johnson is indeed this man's patient.
Tear the room apart. Record every session *note* you can find regardless of about whom it was written.
We're going to crack that boy's skull open like a walnut.

12
WE THINK IT'S THE FLUIDS THAT KEEP GETTING US BANNED ON iTUNES AND ANDROID

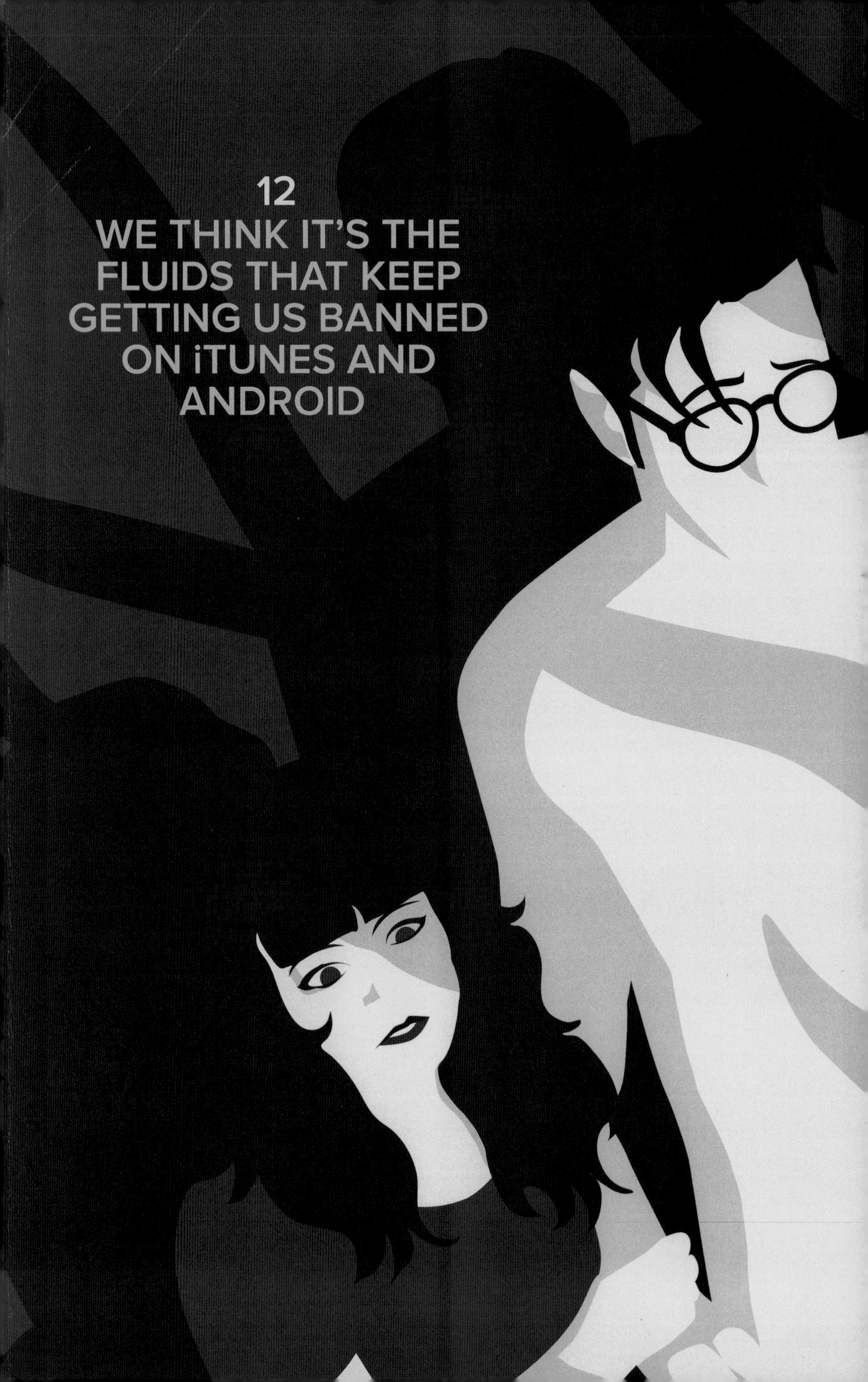

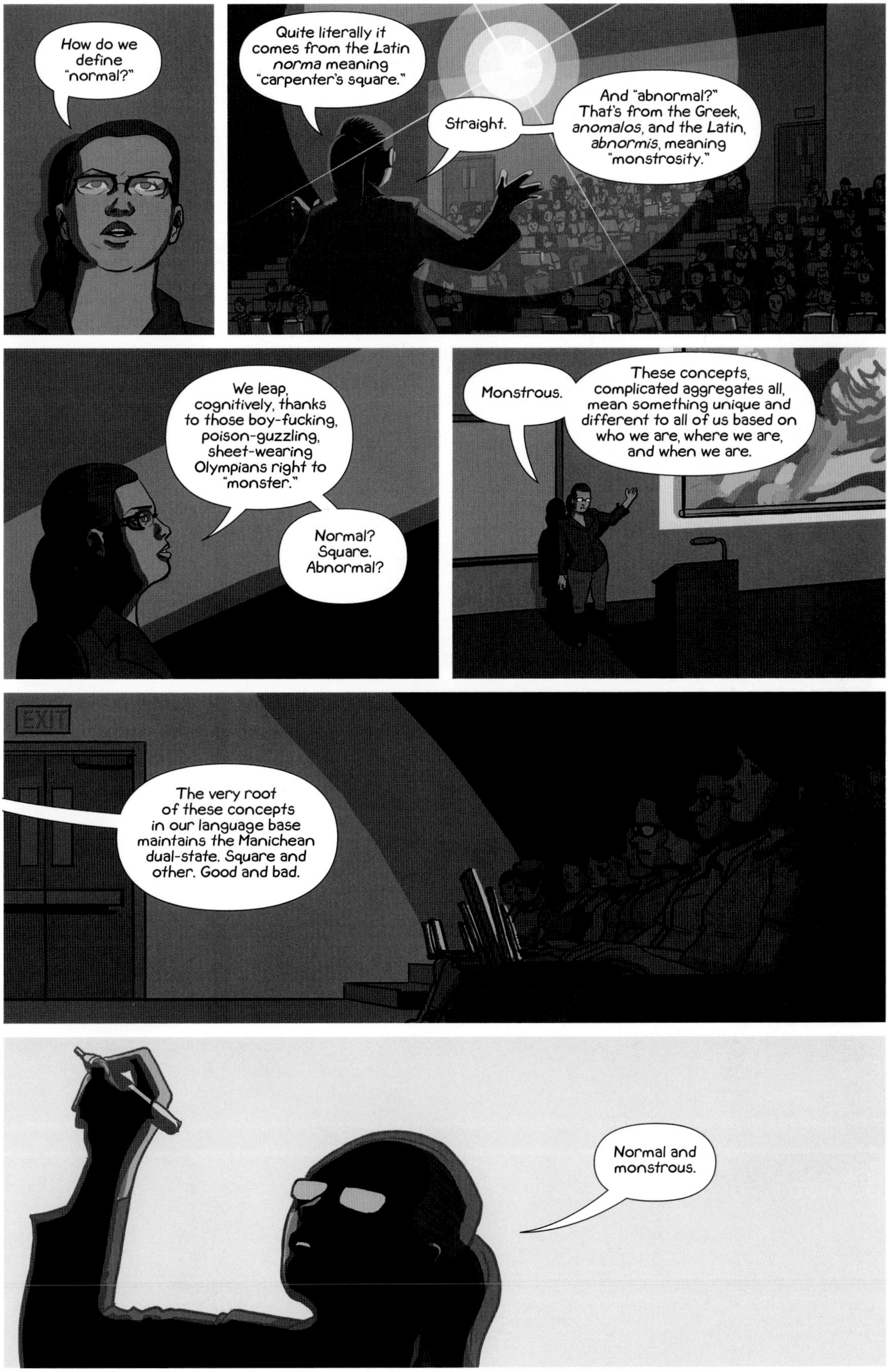
How do we define "normal?"
Quite literally it comes from the Latin *norma* meaning "carpenter's square."
Straight.
And "abnormal?" That's from the Greek, *anomalos*, and the Latin, *abnormis*, meaning "monstrosity."
We leap, cognitively, thanks to those boy-fucking, poison-guzzling, sheet-wearing Olympians right to "monster."
Normal? Square. Abnormal?
Monstrous.
These concepts, complicated aggregates all, mean something unique and different to all of us based on who we are, where we are, and when we are.
EXIT
The very root of these concepts in our language base maintains the Manichean dual-state. Square and other. Good and bad.
Normal and monstrous.

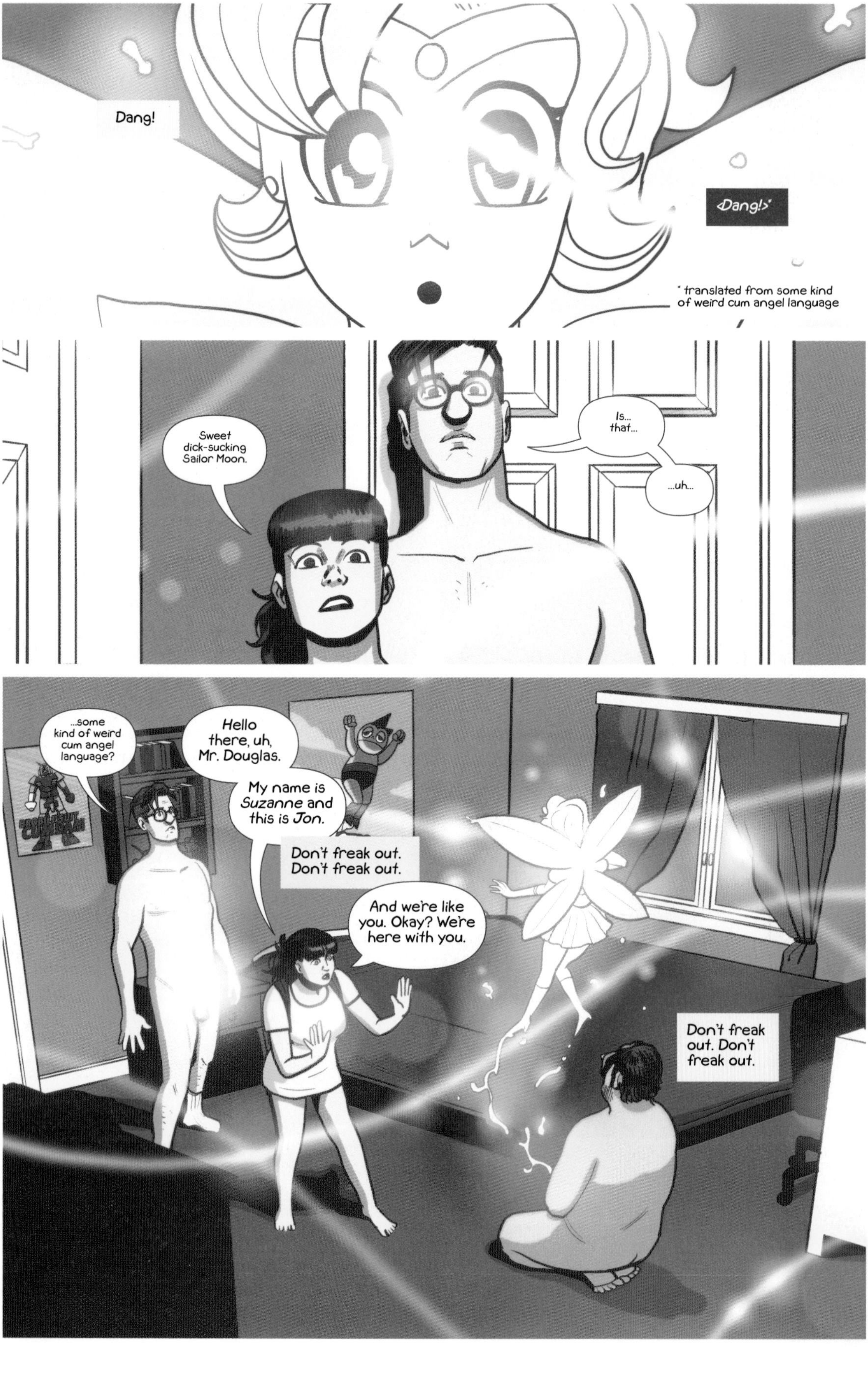
Dang!
<Dang!>*
* translated from some kind of weird cum angel language
Sweet dick-sucking Sailor Moon.
Is... that...
...uh...
...some kind of weird cum angel language?
Hello there, uh, Mr. Douglas.
My name is *Suzanne* and this is *Jon*.
Don't freak out. Don't freak out.
And we're like you. Okay? We're here with you.
Don't freak out. Don't freak out.

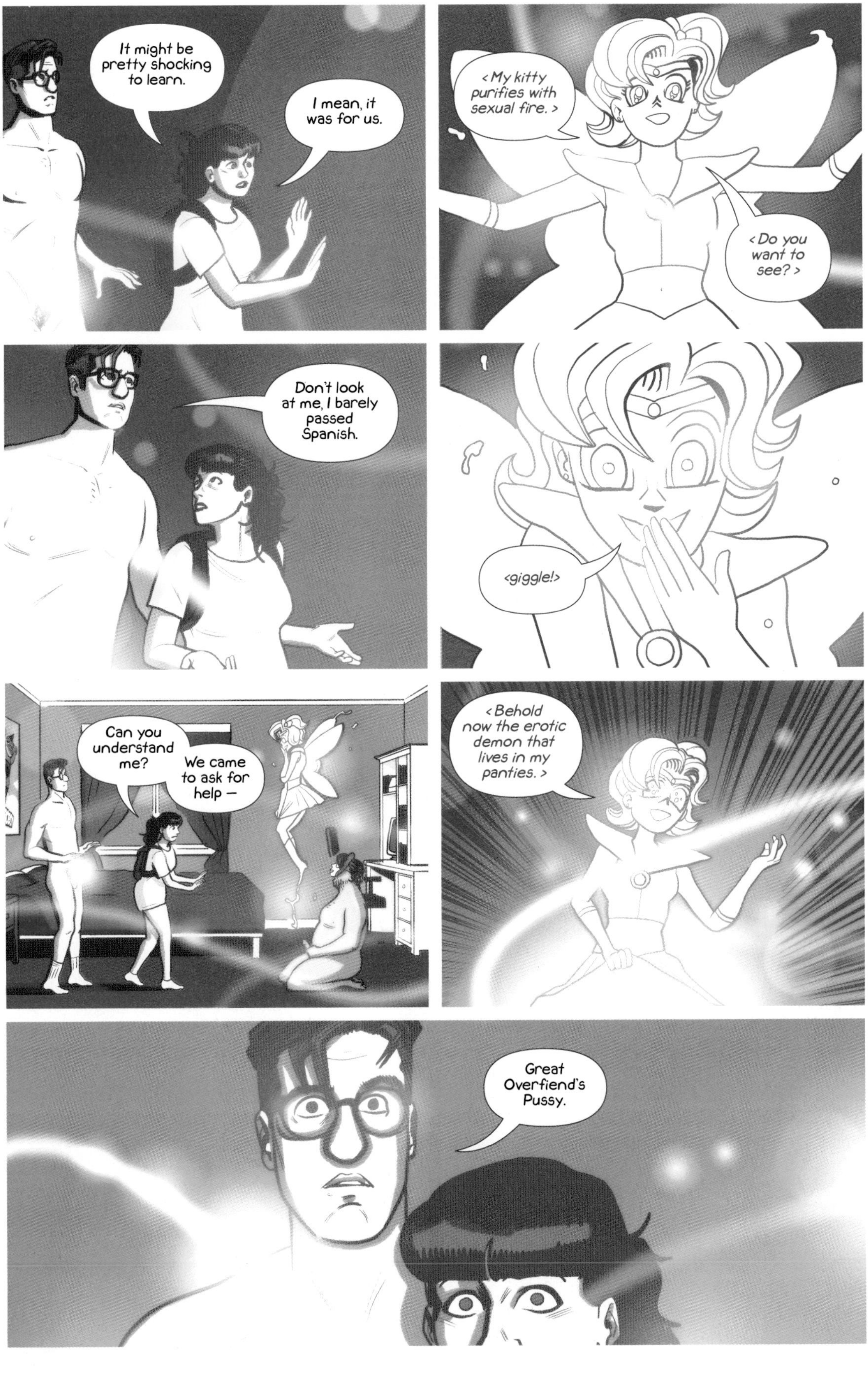

It might be pretty shocking to learn.
I mean, it was for us.
< My kitty purifies with sexual fire. >
< Do you want to see? >
Don't look at me, I barely passed Spanish.
<giggle!>
Can you understand me?
We came to ask for help —
< Behold now the erotic demon that lives in my panties. >
Great Overfiend's Pussy.

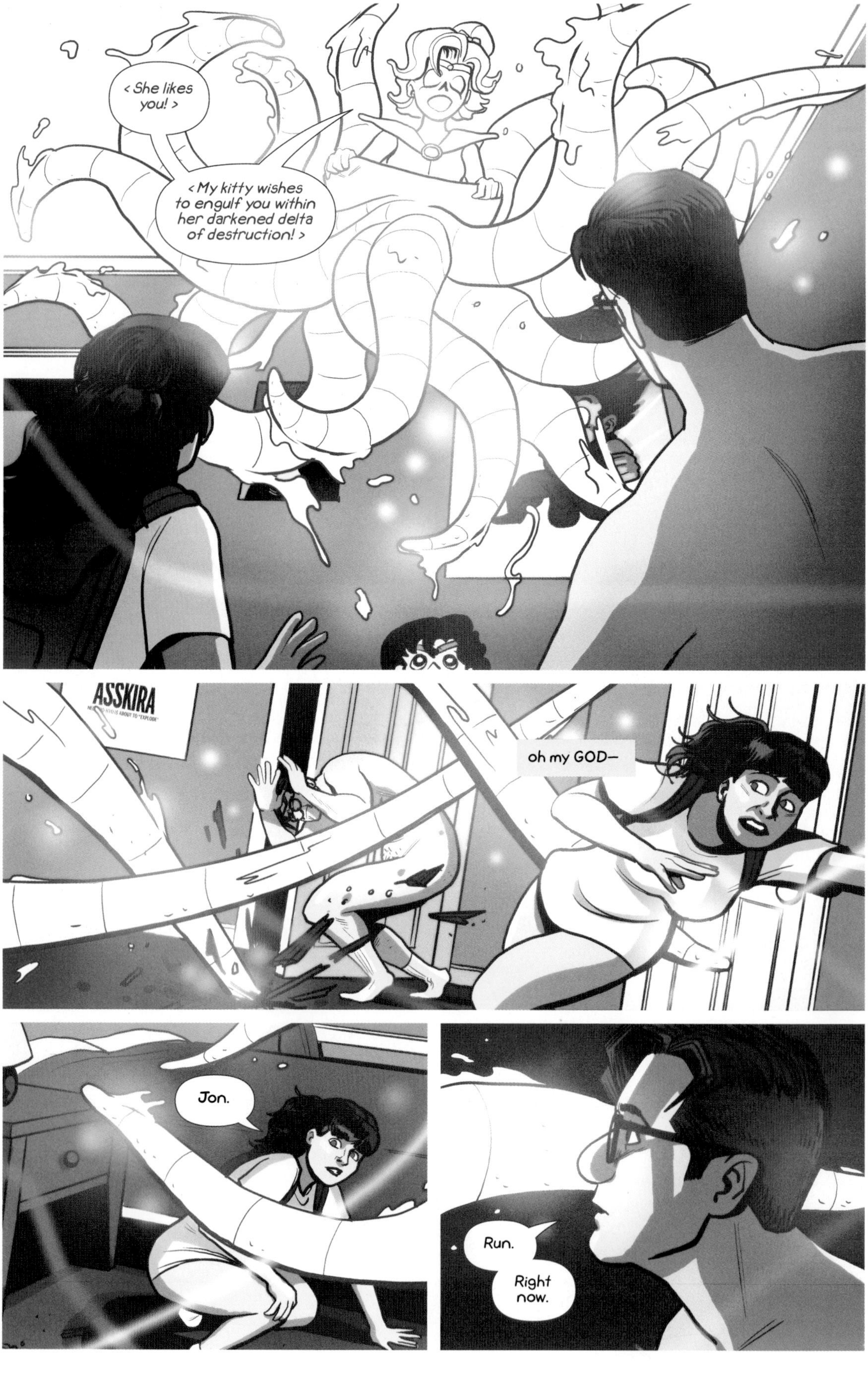
< She likes you! >
< My kitty wishes to engulf you within her darkened delta of destruction! >
ASSKIRA
oh my GOD—
Jon.
Run.
Right now.

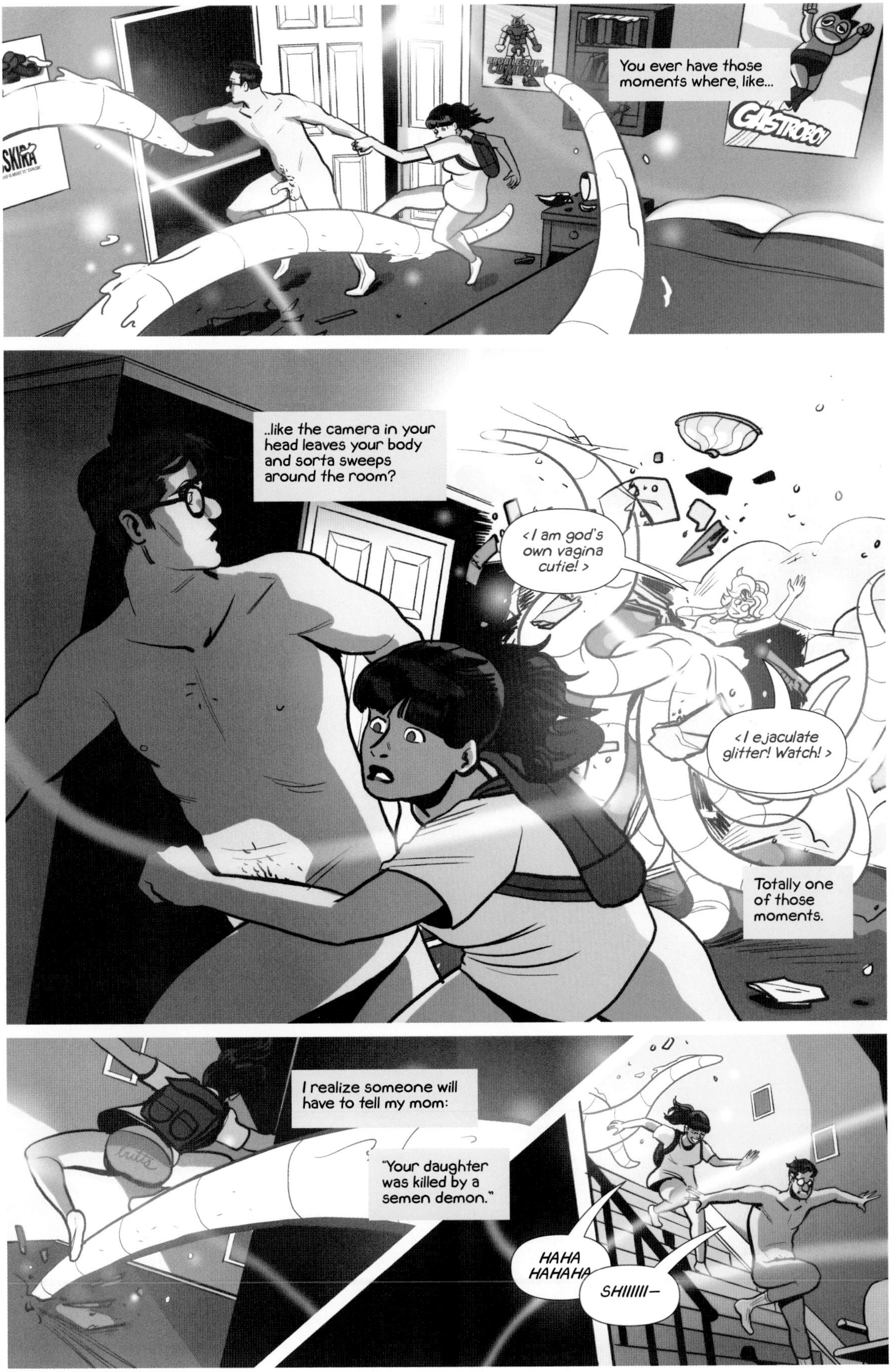
You ever have those moments where, like...
GASTROBOY
..like the camera in your head leaves your body and sorta sweeps around the room?
< I am god's own vagina cutie! >
< I ejaculate glitter! Watch! >
Totally one of those moments.
I realize someone will have to tell my mom:
"Your daughter was killed by a semen demon."
HAHA HAHAHA
SHIIIIII—

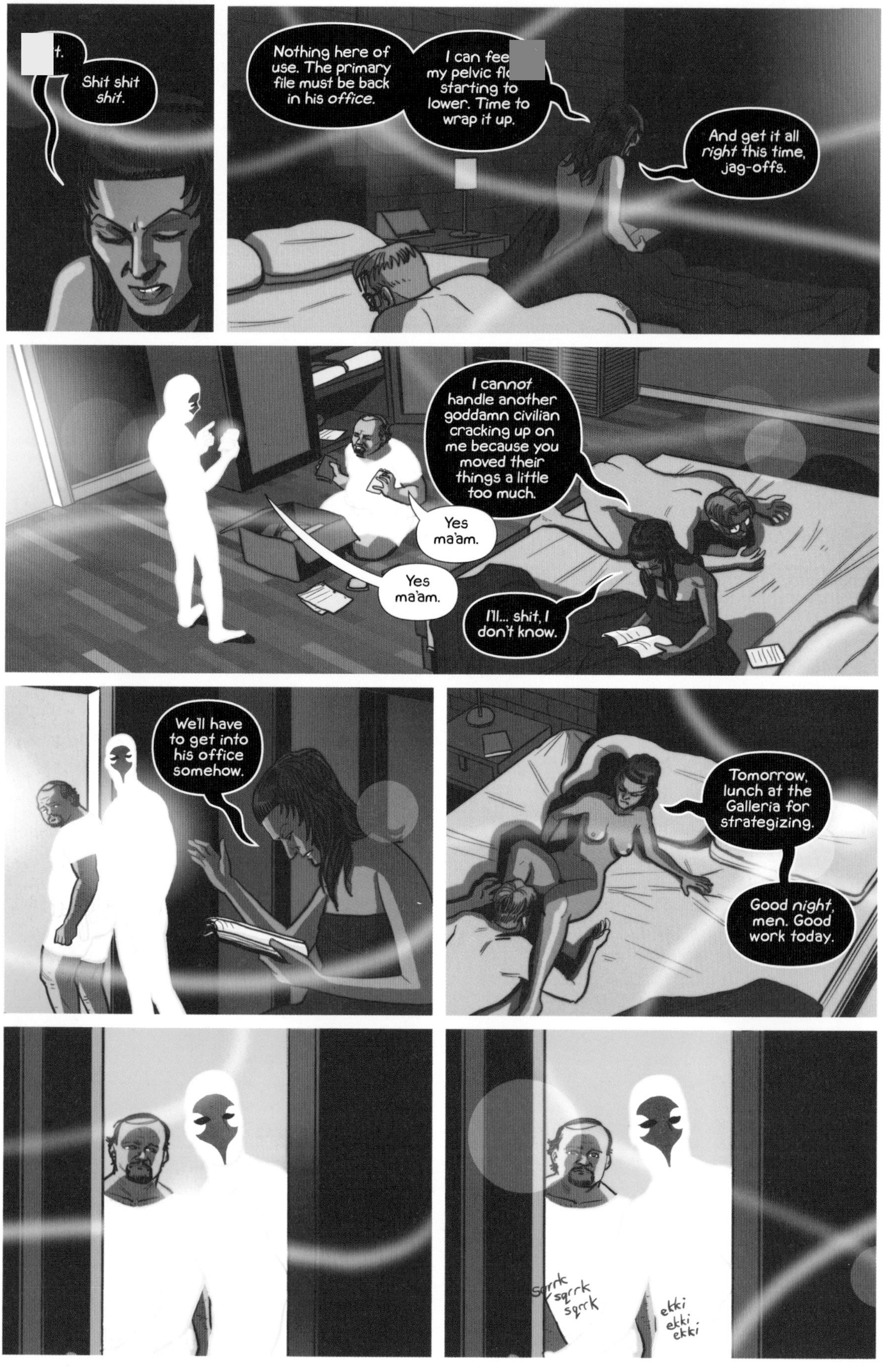
t.
Shit shit *shit*.
Nothing here of use. The primary file must be back in his *office*.
I can fee my pelvic flo starting to lower. Time to wrap it up.
And get it all *right* this time, jag-offs.
I *cannot* handle another goddamn civilian cracking up on me because you moved their things a little too much.
Yes ma'am.
Yes ma'am.
I'll... shit, I don't know.
We'll have to get into his office somehow.
Tomorrow, lunch at the Galleria for strategizing.
Good *night*, men. Good work today.
sqrrk sqrrk sqrrk
ekki ekki ekki

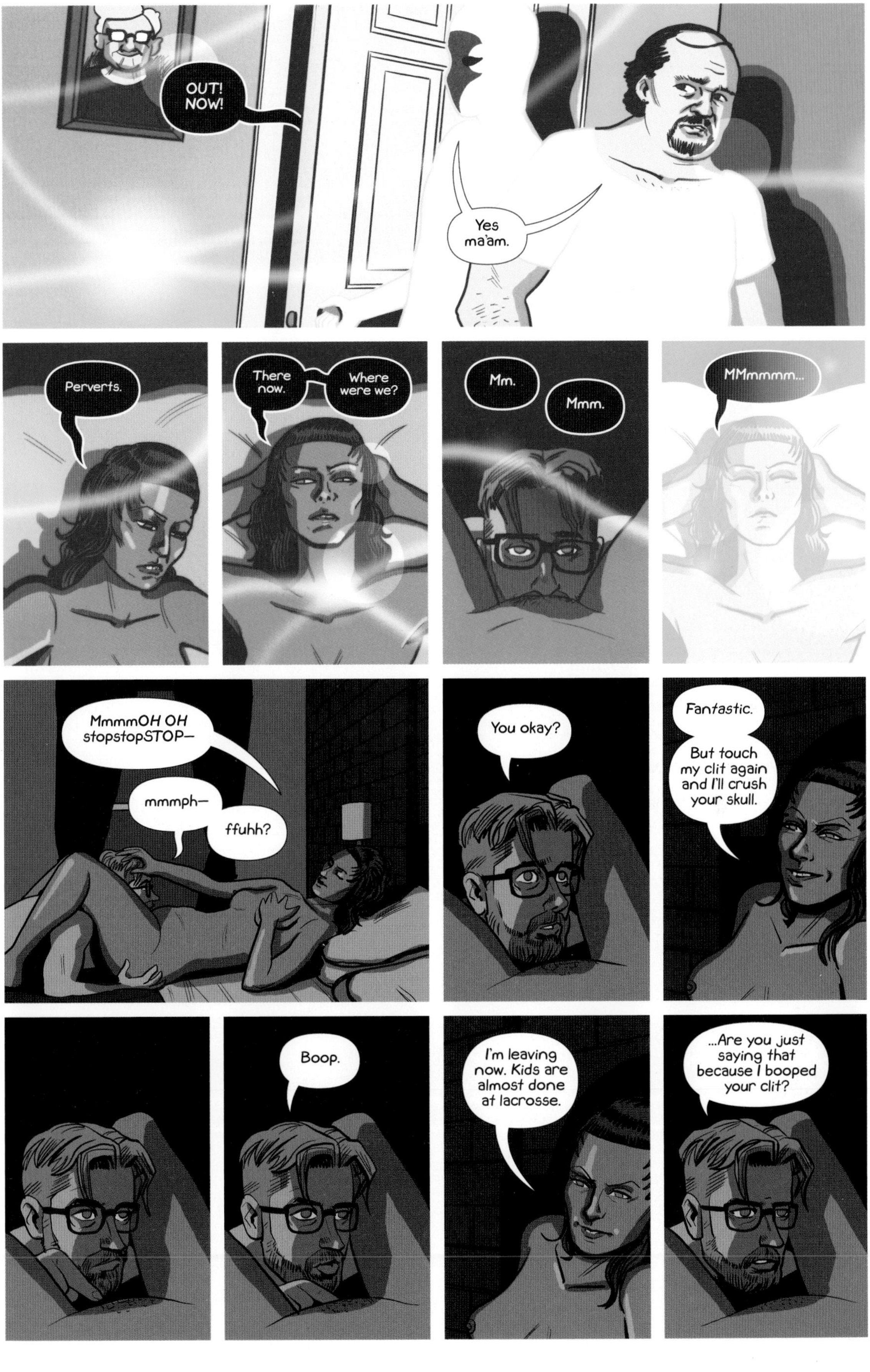

OUT! NOW!
Yes ma'am.
Perverts.
There now.
Where were we?
Mm.
Mmm.
MMmmmm...
MmmmOH OH stopstopSTOP—
mmmph—
ffuhh?
You okay?
Fantastic.
But touch my clit again and I'll crush your skull.
Boop.
I'm leaving now. Kids are almost done at lacrosse.
...Are you just saying that because I booped your clit?

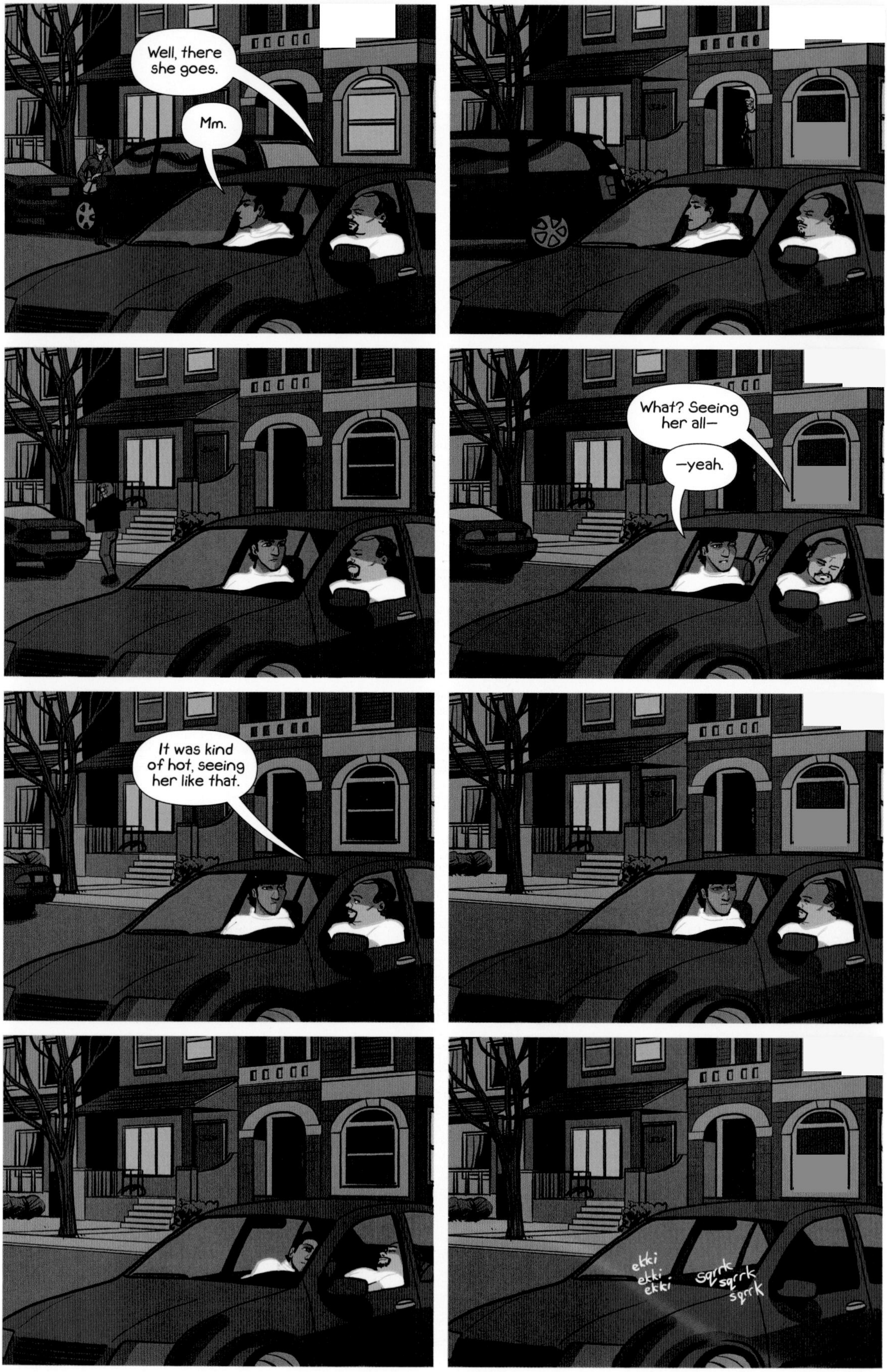
Well, there she goes.
Mm.
What? Seeing her all—
—yeah.
It was kind of hot, seeing her like that.
ekki ekki ekki
sqrrk sqrrk sqrrk

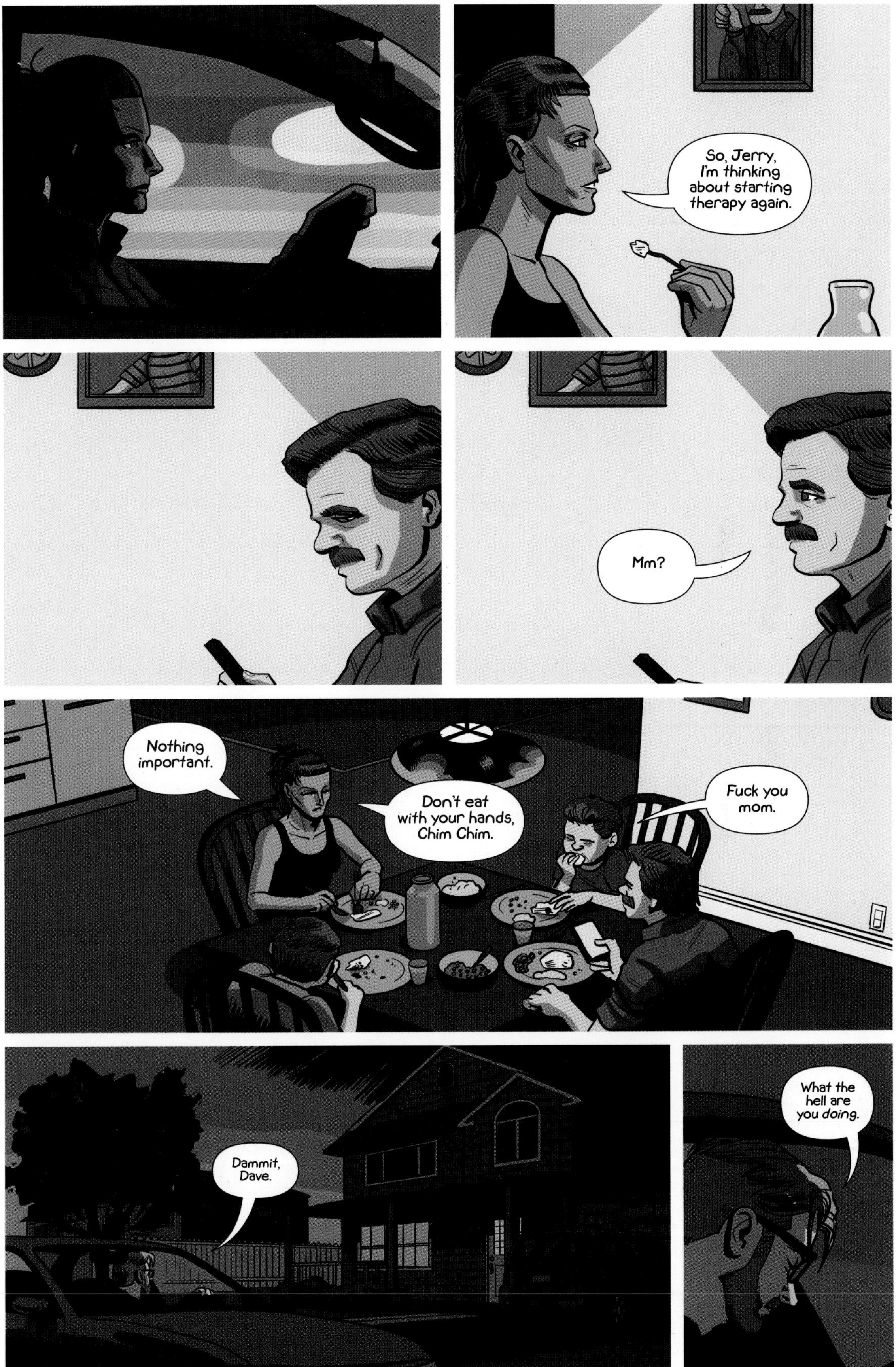
So, Jerry, I'm thinking about starting therapy again.
Mm?
Nothing important.
Don't eat with your hands, Chim Chim.
Fuck you mom.
Dammit, Dave.
What the hell are you *doing*.

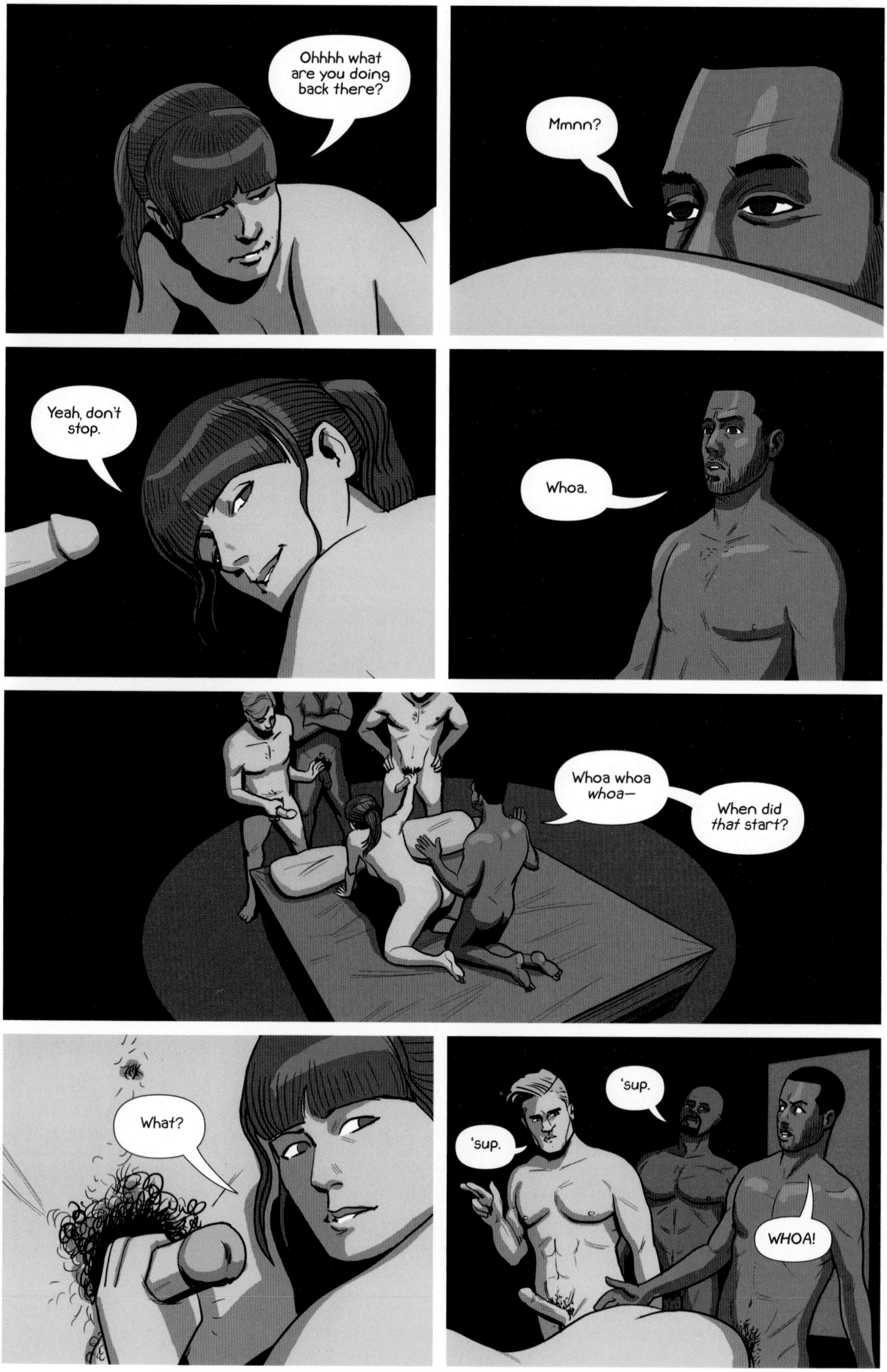
Ohhhh what are you doing back there?
Mmnn?
Yeah, don't stop.
Whoa.
Whoa whoa whoa—
When did that start?
What?
'sup.
'sup.
WHOA!

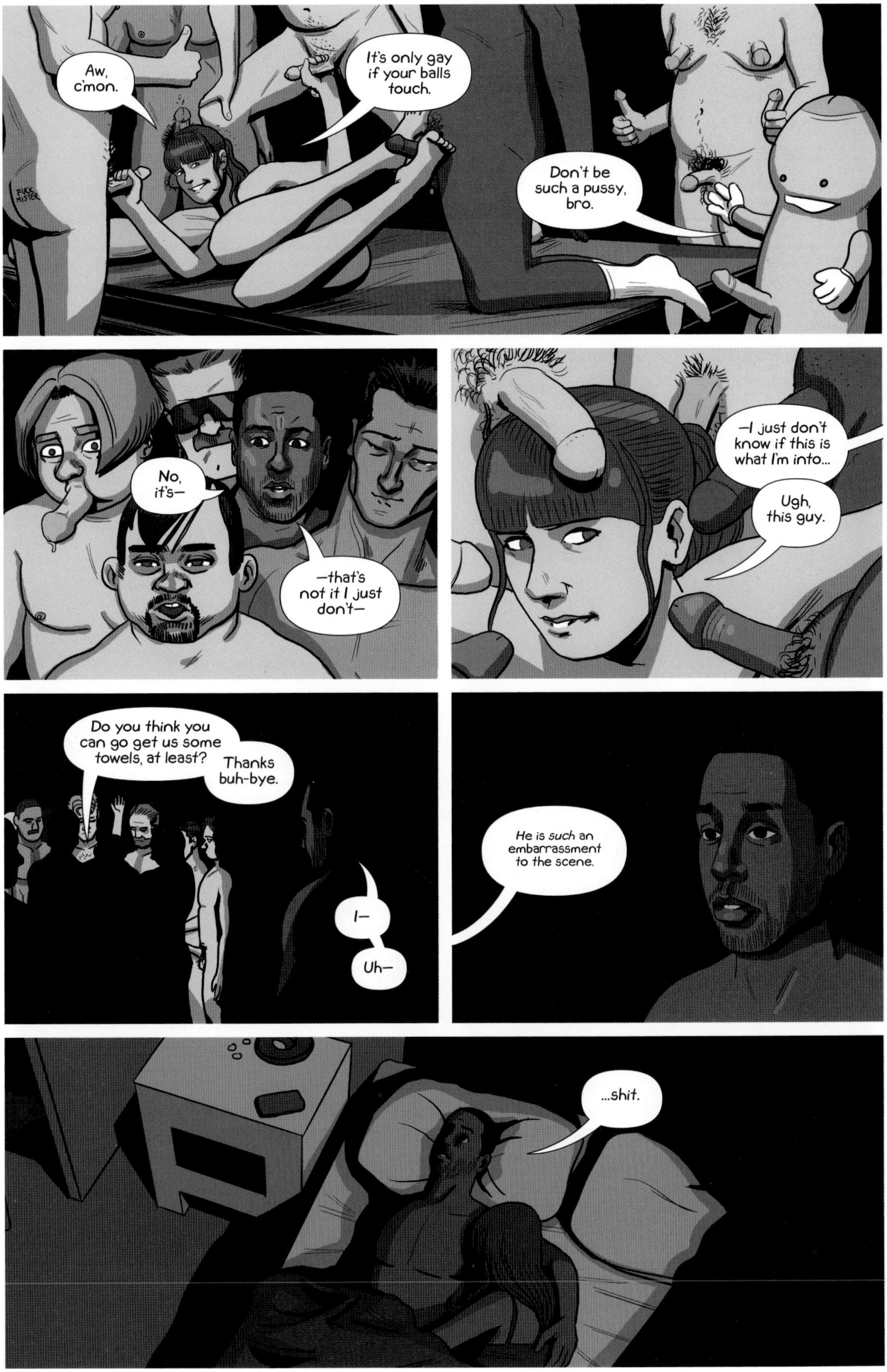
Aw, c'mon.
It's only gay if your balls touch.
Don't be such a pussy, bro.
No, it's—
—that's not it I just don't—
—I just don't know if this is what I'm into...
Ugh, this guy.
Do you think you can go get us some towels, at least?
Thanks buh-bye.
I—
Uh—
He is *such* an embarrassment to the scene.
...shit.

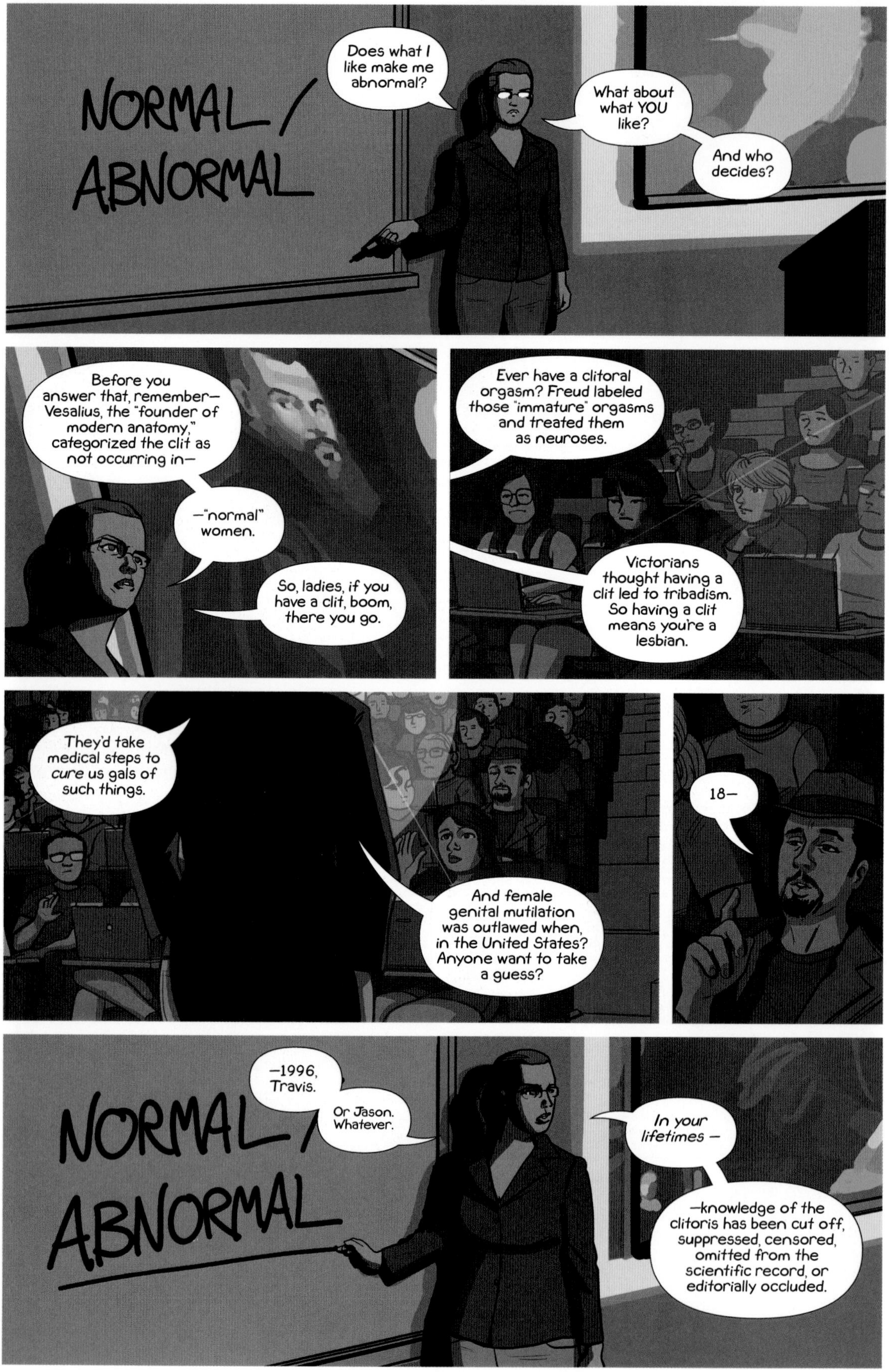
NORMAL / ABNORMAL
Does what I like make me abnormal?
What about what YOU like?
And who decides?
Before you answer that, remember— Vesalius, the "founder of modern anatomy," categorized the clit as not occurring in—
—"normal" women.
So, ladies, if you have a clit, boom, there you go.
Ever have a clitoral orgasm? Freud labeled those "immature" orgasms and treated them as neuroses.
Victorians thought having a clit led to tribadism. So having a clit means you're a lesbian.
They'd take medical steps to *cure* us gals of such things.
And female genital mutilation was outlawed when, in the United States? Anyone want to take a guess?
18—
—1996, Travis.
Or Jason. Whatever.
NORMAL / ABNORMAL
In your lifetimes —
—knowledge of the clitoris has been cut off, suppressed, censored, omitted from the scientific record, or editorially occluded.

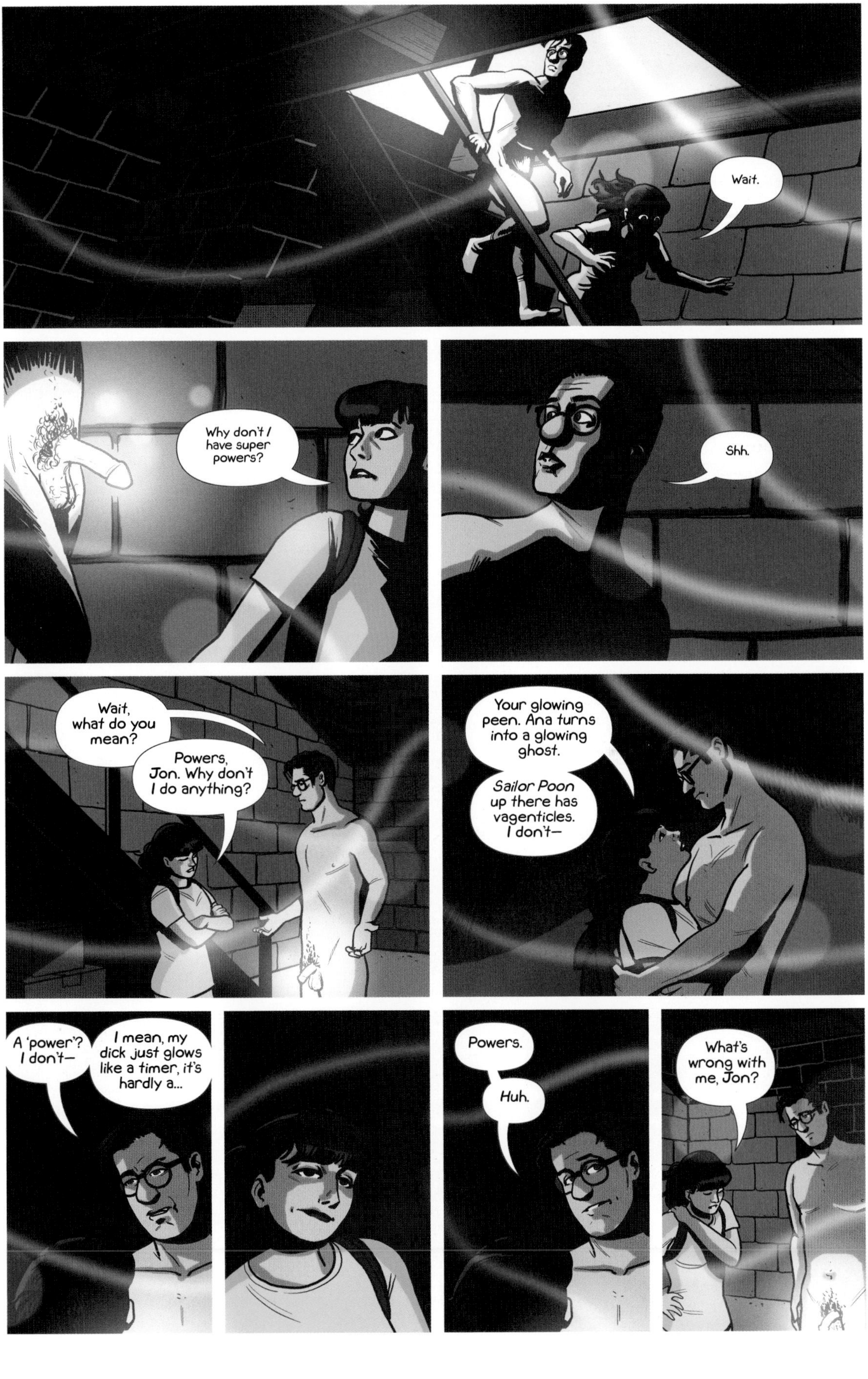

Wait.
Why don't I have super powers?
Shh.
Wait, what do you mean?
Powers, Jon. Why don't I do anything?
Your glowing peen. Ana turns into a glowing ghost.
Sailor Poon up there has vagenticles. I don't—
A 'power'? I don't—
I mean, my dick just glows like a timer, it's hardly a...
Powers.
Huh.
What's wrong with me, Jon?

Imagine, men, if your own *anatomy* remained mysterious.

It was only 1981 when Professor Emeritus Beverly Whipple and—

—some guy, I don't know—

—even coined the term "G-spot." And it's been misused, misinterpreted, and sold to women ever since.

And yet in 2012 the Journal of Sexual Medicine said, *quote:*

"Objective measures have failed to provide strong and consistent evidence for the existence of an anatomical site that could be related to the famed G-spot."

So the very truth of what Drs. Whipple and Perry found, that anterior wall stimulation of the vagina causes some women great amounts of pleasure...

...some, ehn. Some, not so much...

...is that the clitoris isn't solely the center of the female orgasm.

In other words, this thing that you shouldn't have causes this other thing that you shouldn't have.

So we've seen the female orgasm and its anatomical associates turned into a marketing ploy, a checklist item, or a magazine listicle.

THIS SEASON'S HOTTEST ORGASMS YOU'VE GOT TO TRY

Politics, history, philosophy, and language have turned a woman's orgasm into a morphological place you either have or don't, can find or can not.

A destination rather than a journey. A noun rather than a verb.

10 ways SPRUCE U your clit

SEX UP YO SEX WITH EX

ABNORMAL

And, lastly, before you categorize yourself, remember please that "hysteria"—

—womb fury—

—was only removed from the DSM in 1980.

Yet another thing that makes half the population "abnormal."

Monstrous.

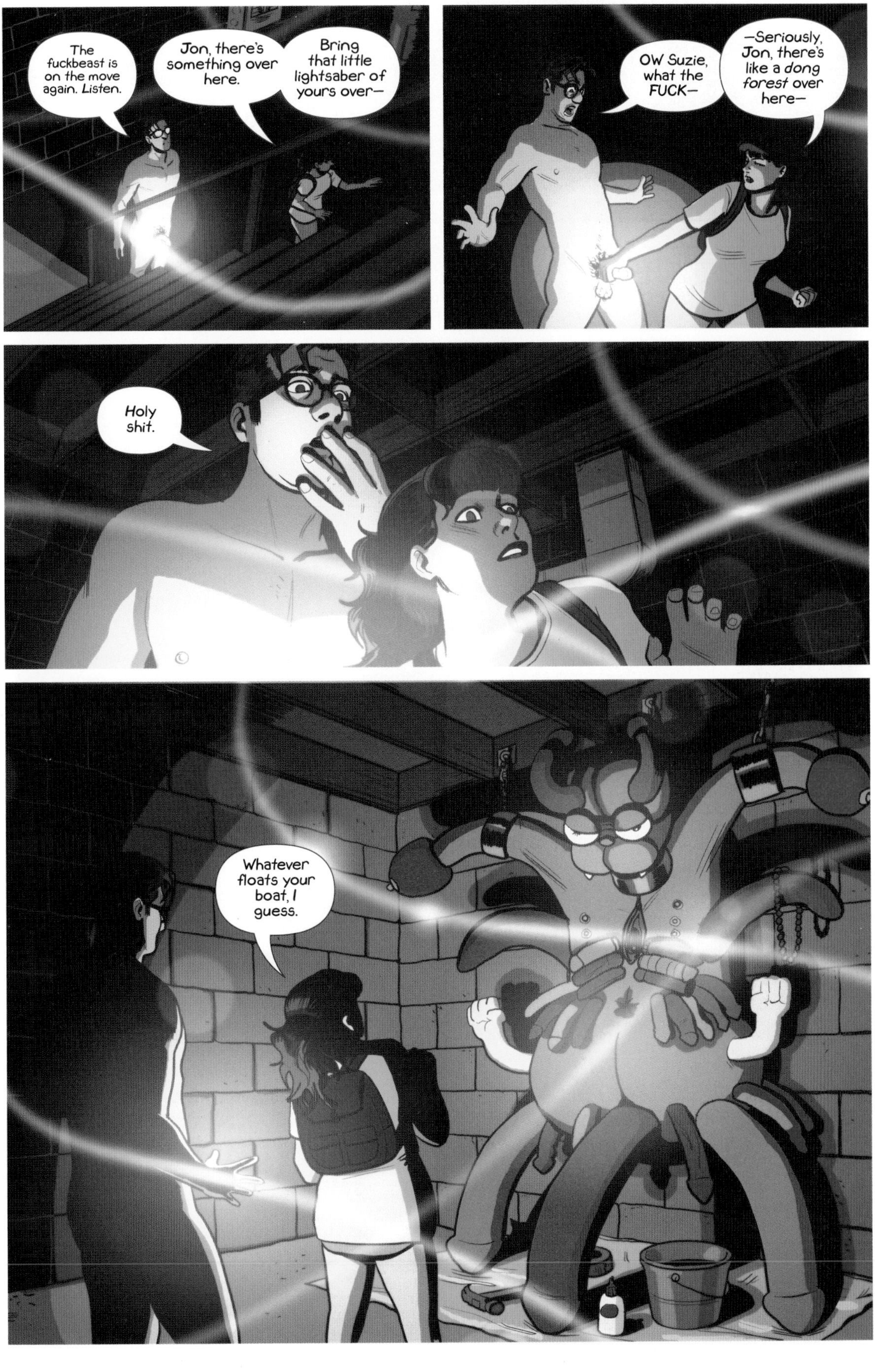
The fuckbeast is on the move again. Listen.
Jon, there's something over here.
Bring that little lightsaber of yours over—
OW Suzie, what the FUCK—
—Seriously, Jon, there's like a *dong forest* over here—
Holy shit.
Whatever floats your boat, I guess.

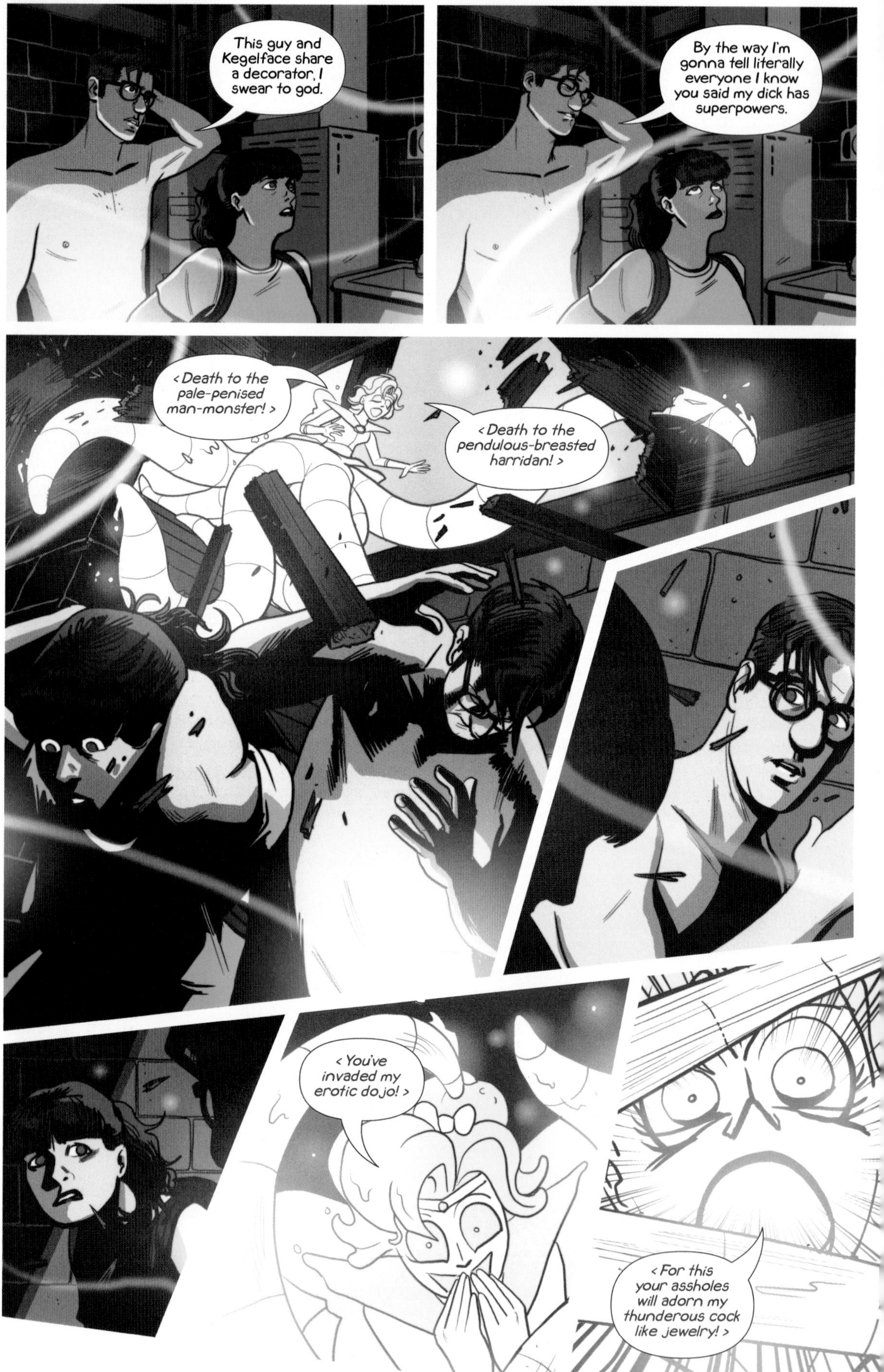
This guy and Kegelface share a decorator, I swear to god.
By the way I'm gonna tell literally everyone I know you said my dick has superpowers.
< Death to the pale-penised man-monster! >
< Death to the pendulous-breasted harridan! >
< You've invaded my erotic dojo! >
< For this your assholes will adorn my thunderous cock like jewelry! >

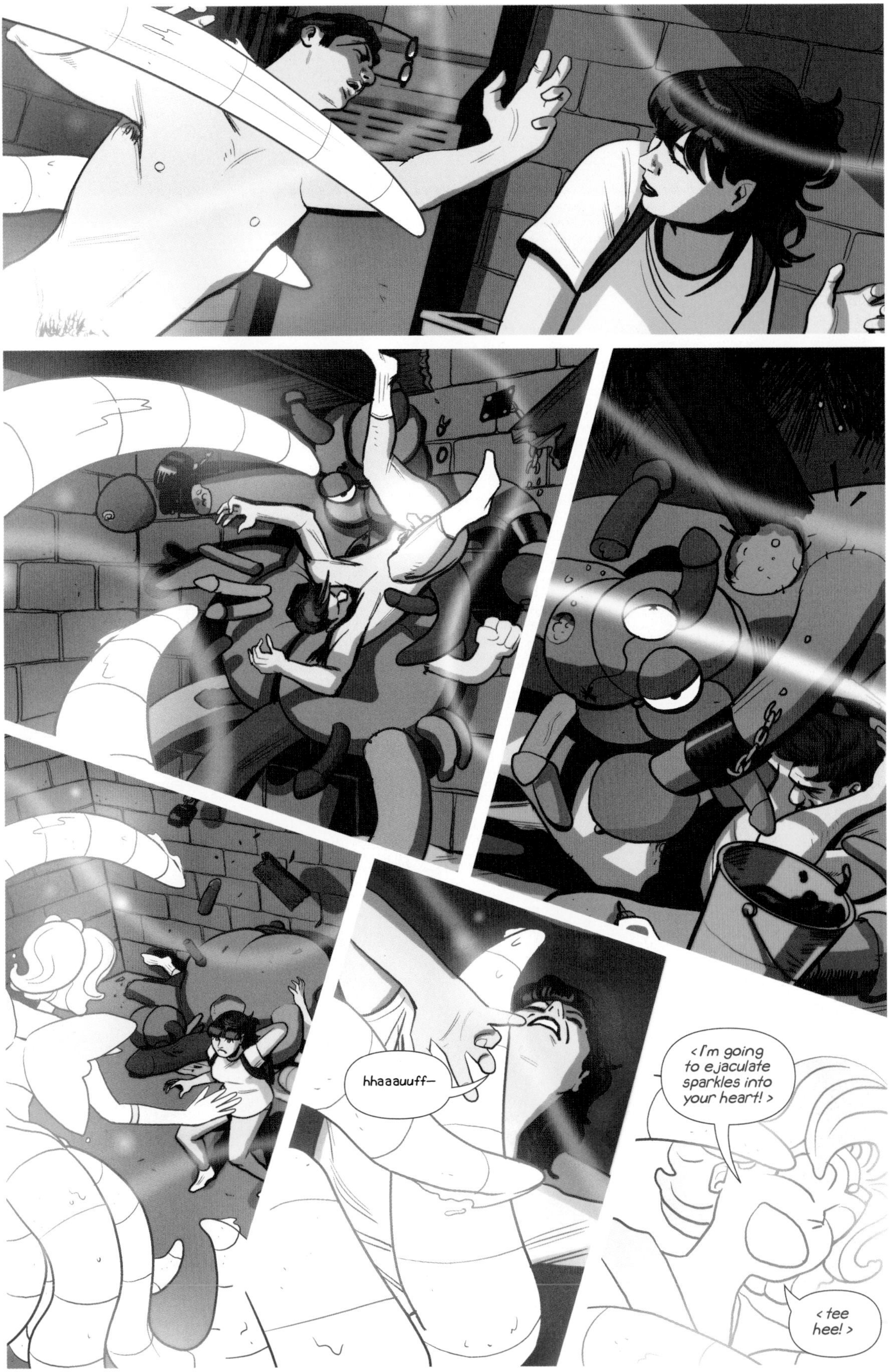
hhaaauuff—
< I'm going to ejaculate sparkles into your heart! >
< tee hee! >

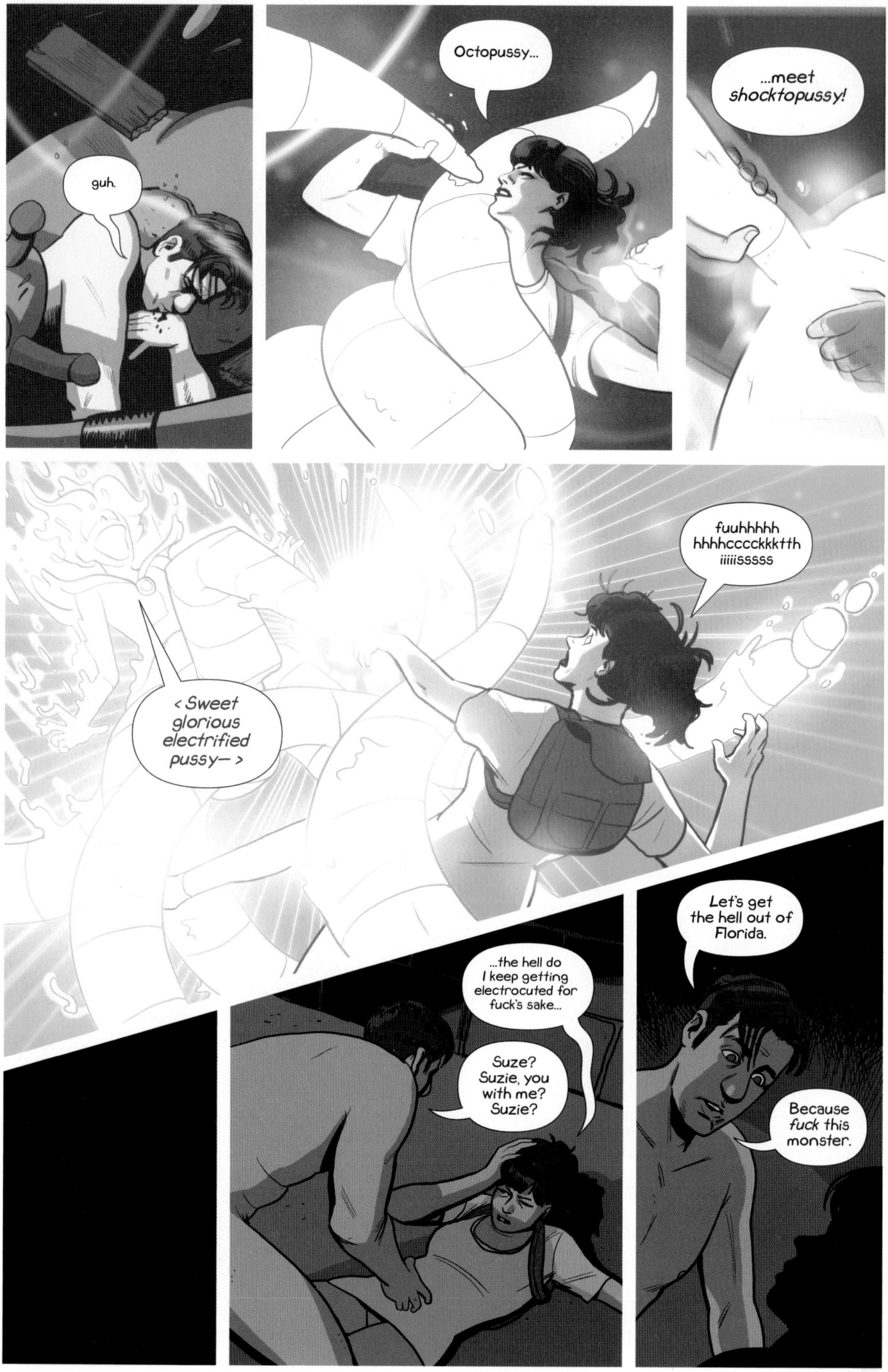
guh.
Octopussy...
...meet shocktopussy!
fuuhhhhh hhhhccccckkktth iiiiissss
< Sweet glorious electrified pussy— >
...the hell do I keep getting electrocuted for fuck's sake...
Suze? Suzie, you with me? Suzie?
Let's get the hell out of Florida.
Because fuck this monster.

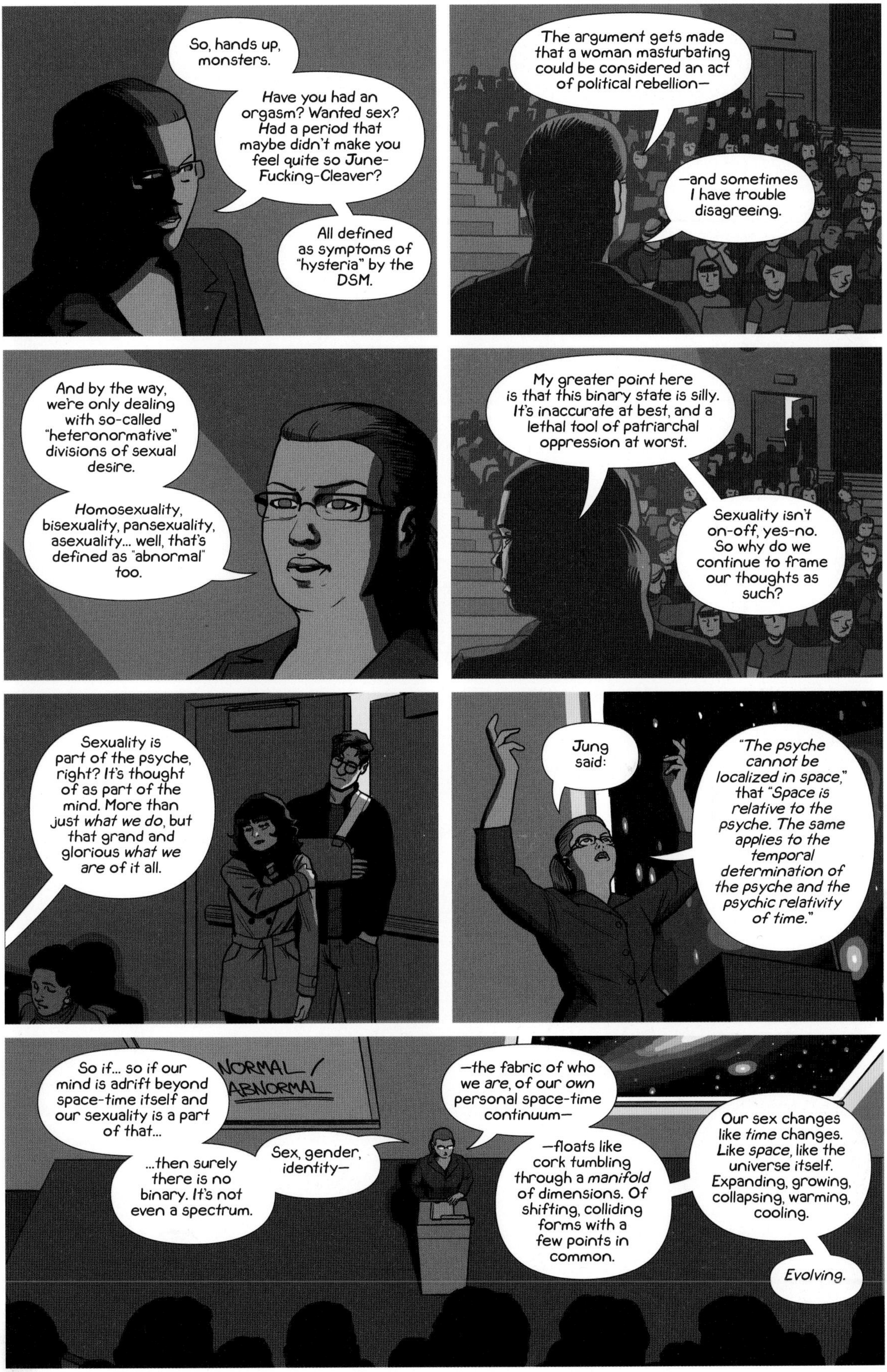

So, hands up, monsters.
Have you had an orgasm? Wanted sex? Had a period that maybe didn't make you feel quite so June-Fucking-Cleaver?
All defined as symptoms of "hysteria" by the DSM.
The argument gets made that a woman masturbating could be considered an act of political rebellion—
—and sometimes I have trouble disagreeing.
And by the way, we're only dealing with so-called "heteronormative" divisions of sexual desire.
*Homo*sexuality, bisexuality, pansexuality, asexuality... well, that's defined as "abnormal" too.
My greater point here is that this binary state is silly. It's inaccurate at best, and a lethal tool of patriarchal oppression at worst.
Sexuality isn't on-off, yes-no. So why do we continue to frame our thoughts as such?
Sexuality is part of the psyche, right? It's thought of as part of the mind. More than just *what we do*, but that grand and glorious *what we are* of it all.
Jung said:
"The psyche cannot be localized in space," that *"Space is relative to the psyche. The same applies to the temporal determination of the psyche and the psychic relativity of time."*
NORMAL / ABNORMAL
So if... so if our mind is adrift beyond space-time itself and our sexuality is a part of that...
...then surely there is no binary. It's not even a spectrum.
Sex, gender, identity—
—the fabric of who we *are*, of our *own* personal space-time continuum—
—floats like cork tumbling through a *manifold* of dimensions. Of shifting, colliding forms with a few points in common.
Our sex changes like *time* changes. Like *space*, like the universe itself. Expanding, growing, collapsing, warming, cooling.
Evolving.

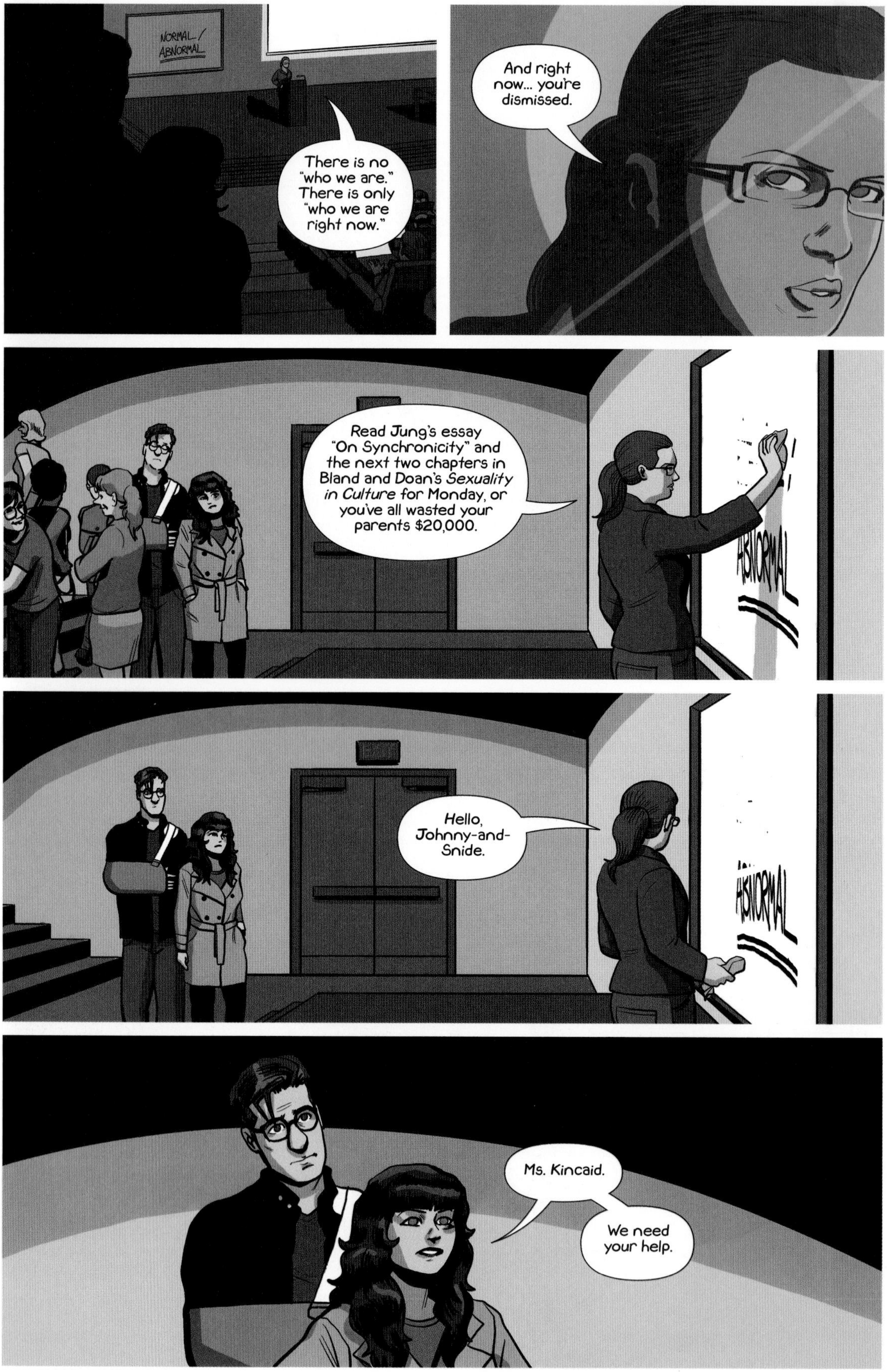
NORMAL / ABNORMAL
There is no "who we are." There is only "who we are right now."
And right now... you're dismissed.
Read Jung's essay "On Synchronicity" and the next two chapters in Bland and Doan's *Sexuality in Culture* for Monday, or you've all wasted your parents $20,000.
ABNORMAL
Hello, Johnny-and-Snide.
ABNORMAL
Ms. Kincaid.
We need your help.

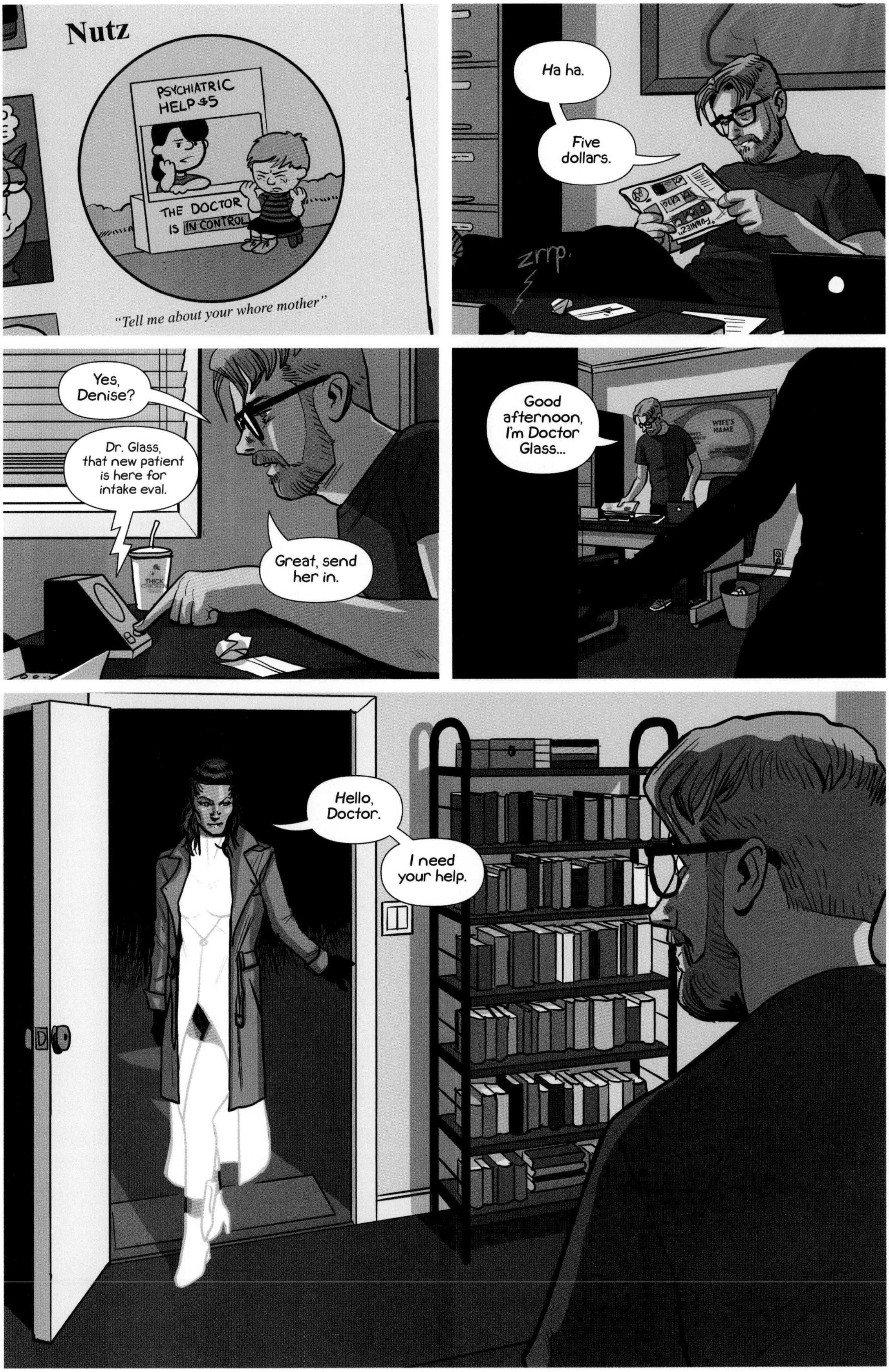
Nutz
PSYCHIATRIC HELP $5
THE DOCTOR IS IN CONTROL
"Tell me about your whore mother"
Ha ha.
Five dollars.
FUNNIES
zrrp.
Yes, Denise?
Dr. Glass, that new patient is here for intake eval.
Great, send her in.
THICK CHICKEN
Good afternoon, I'm Doctor Glass...
WIFE'S NAME
Hello, Doctor.
I need your help.

13
BACE

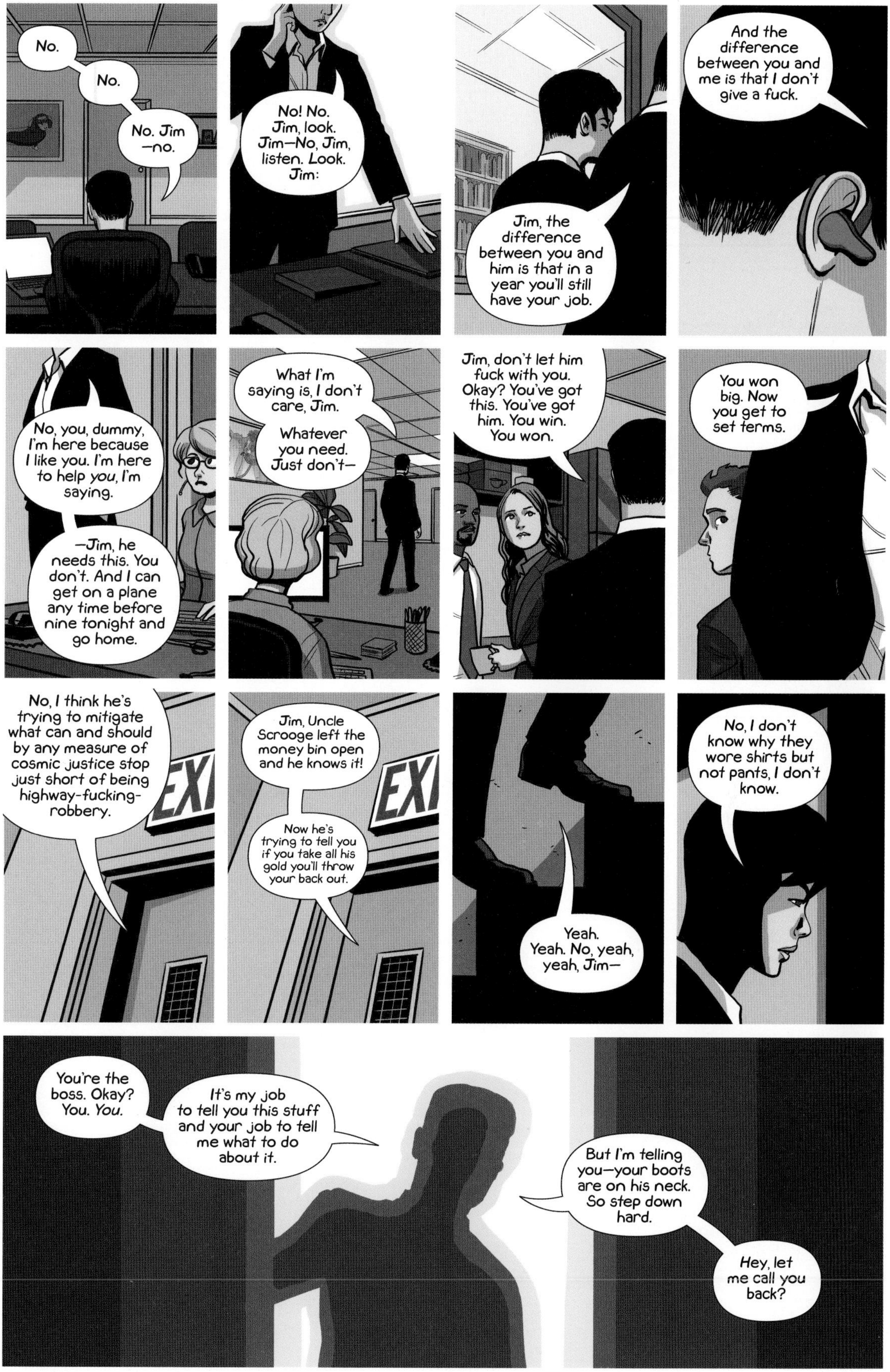
No.
No.
No. Jim —no.
No! No. Jim, look. Jim—No, Jim, listen. Look. Jim:
Jim, the difference between you and him is that in a year you'll still have your job.
And the difference between you and me is that I don't give a fuck.
No, you, dummy, I'm here because I like you. I'm here to help *you*, I'm saying.
—Jim, he needs this. You don't. And I can get on a plane any time before nine tonight and go home.
What I'm saying is, I don't care, Jim.
Whatever you need. Just don't—
Jim, don't let him fuck with you. Okay? You've got this. You've got him. You win. You won.
You won big. Now you get to set terms.
No, I think he's trying to mitigate what can and should by any measure of cosmic justice stop just short of being highway-fucking-robbery.
EXI
Jim, Uncle Scrooge left the money bin open and he knows *it*!
Now he's trying to tell you if you take all his gold you'll throw your back out.
EXI
Yeah. Yeah. No, yeah, yeah, Jim—
No, I don't know why they wore shirts but not pants, I don't know.
You're the boss. Okay? You. *You.*
It's my job to tell you this stuff and your job to tell me what to do about it.
But I'm telling you—your boots are on his neck. So step down hard.
Hey, let me call you back?

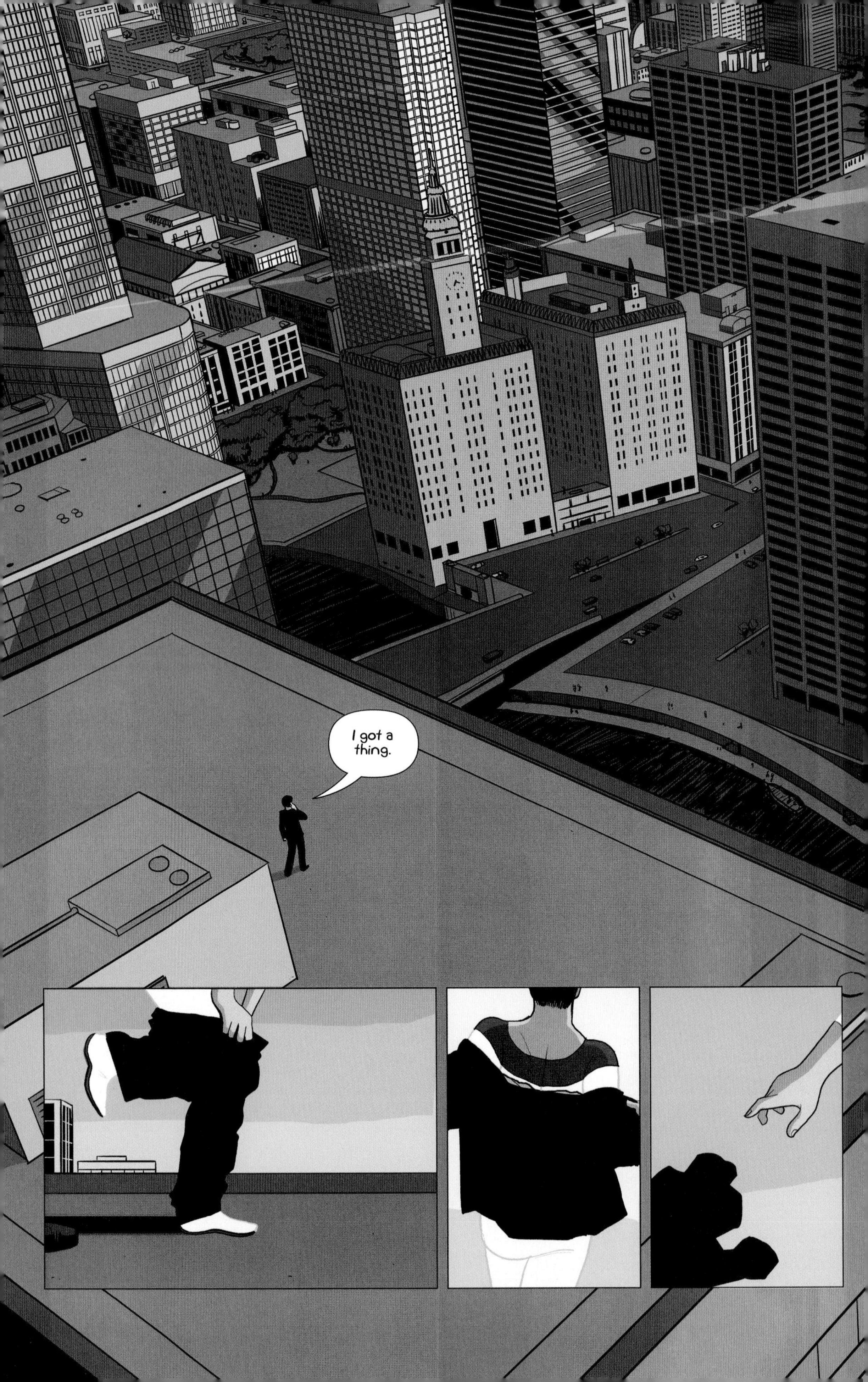
I got a thing.

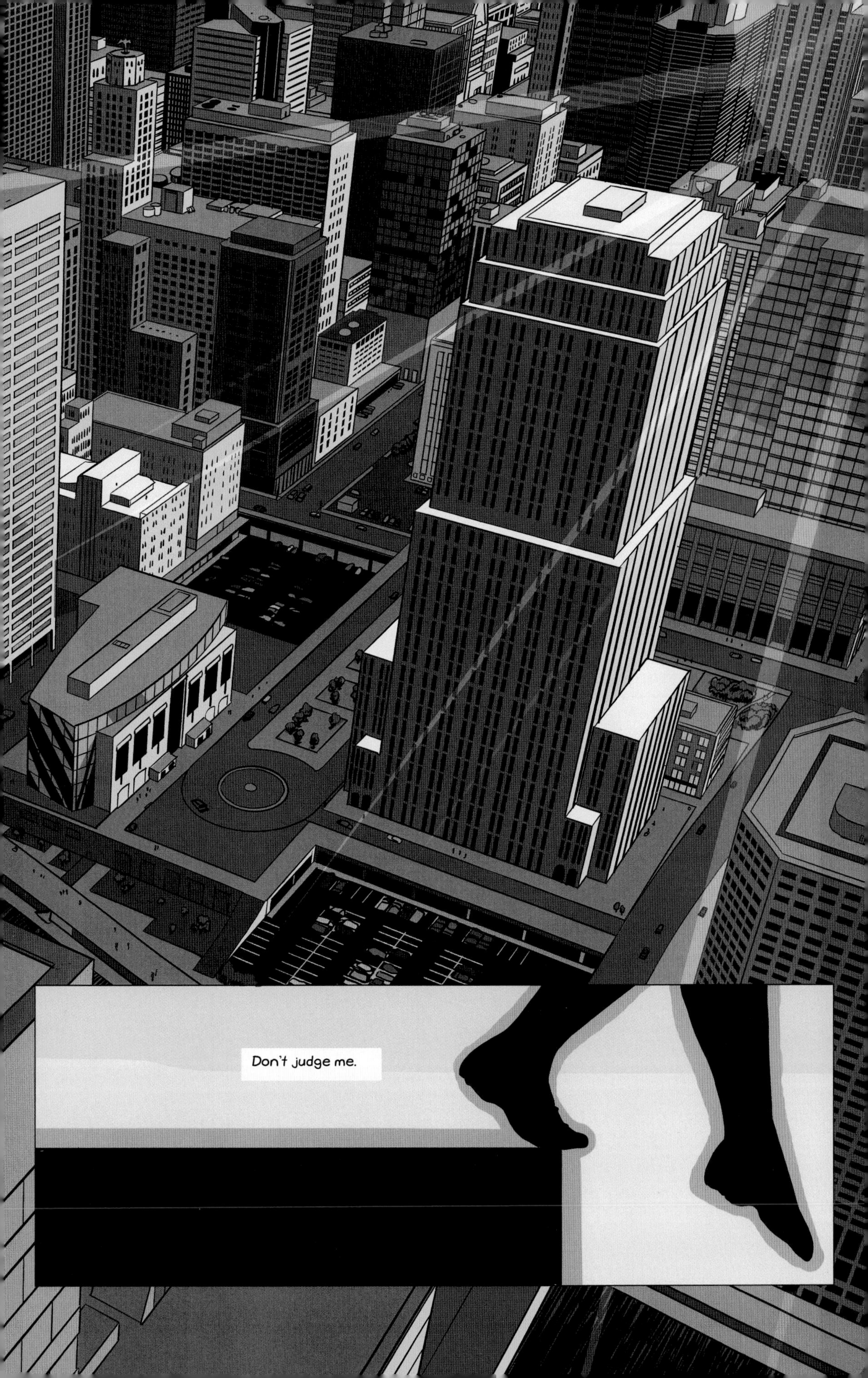
Don't judge me.

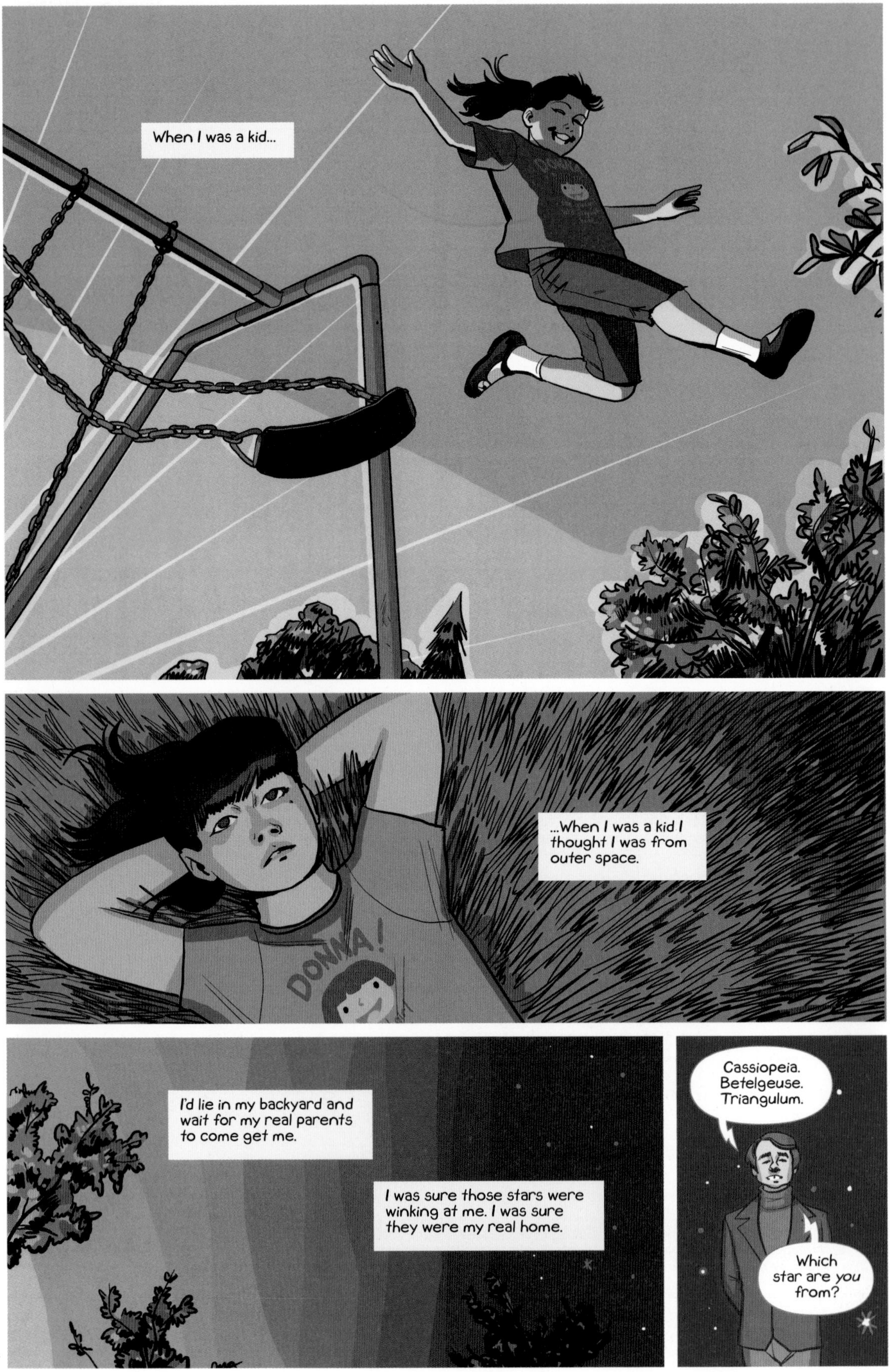

When I was a kid...
...When I was a kid I thought I was from outer space.
DONNA!
I'd lie in my backyard and wait for my real parents to come get me.
I was sure those stars were winking at me. I was sure they were my real home.
Cassiopeia. Betelgeuse. Triangulum.
Which star are *you* from?

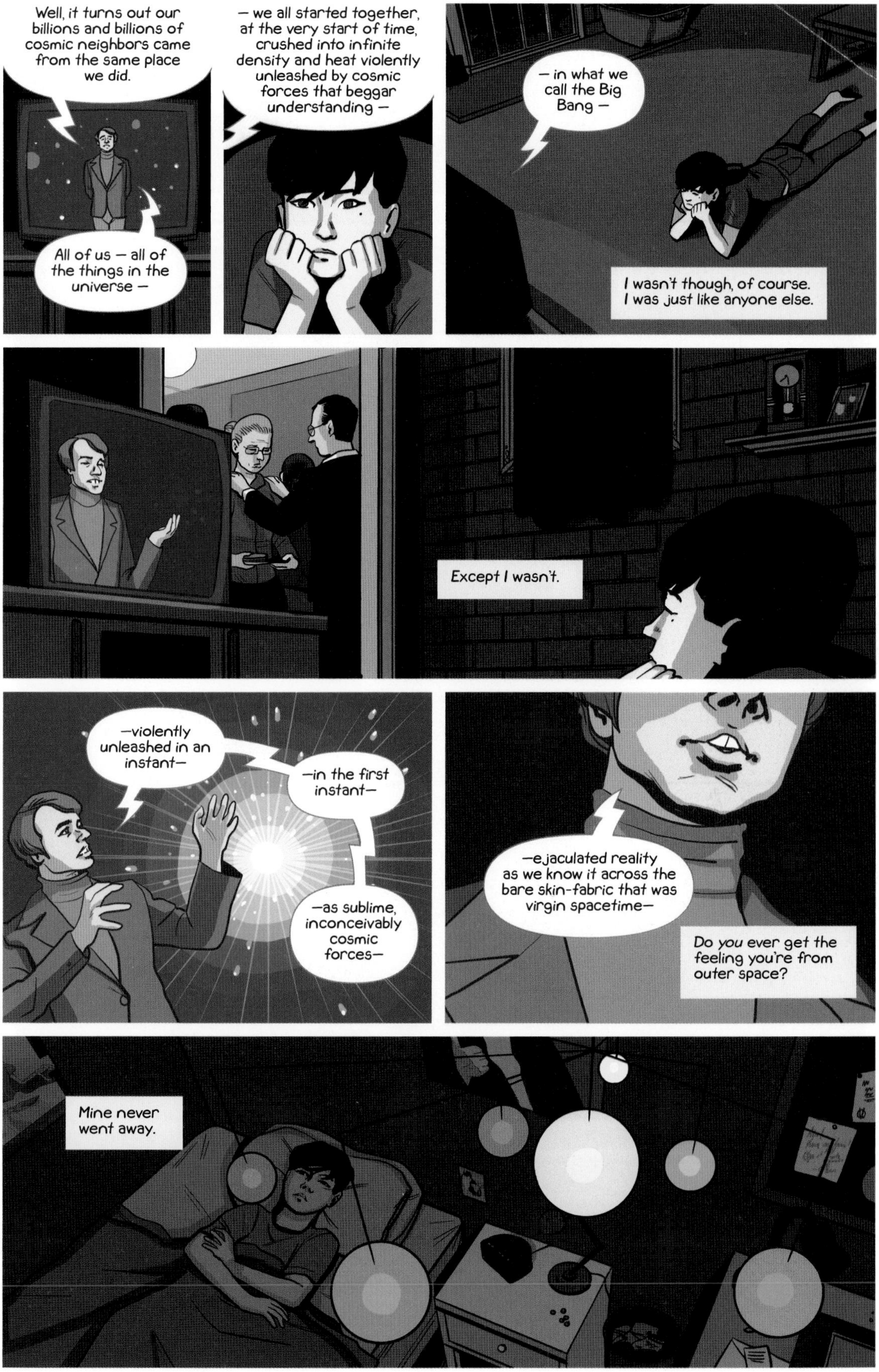
Well, it turns out our billions and billions of cosmic neighbors came from the same place we did.
All of us — all of the things in the universe —
— we all started together, at the very start of time, crushed into infinite density and heat violently unleashed by cosmic forces that beggar understanding —
— in what we call the Big Bang —
I wasn't though, of course. I was just like anyone else.
Except I wasn't.
—violently unleashed in an instant—
—in the first instant—
—as sublime, inconceivably cosmic forces—
—ejaculated reality as we know it across the bare skin-fabric that was virgin spacetime—
Do *you* ever get the feeling you're from outer space?
Mine never went away.

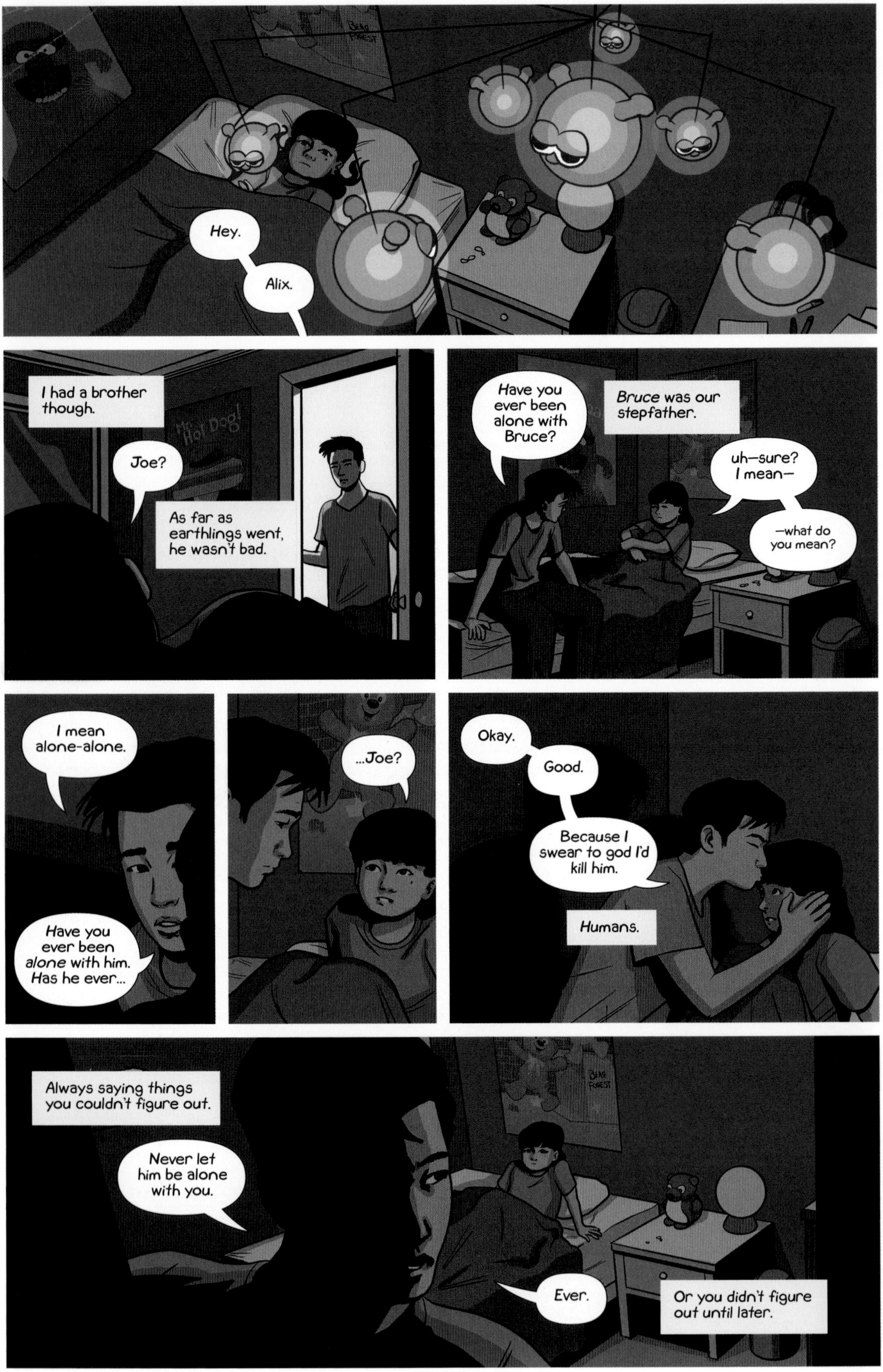
Hey.
Alix.
I had a brother though.
Joe?
As far as earthlings went, he wasn't bad.
Have you ever been alone with Bruce?
Bruce was our stepfather.
uh—sure? I mean—
—what do you mean?
I mean alone-alone.
Have you ever been *alone* with him. Has he ever...
...Joe?
Okay.
Good.
Because I swear to god I'd kill him.
Humans.
Always saying things you couldn't figure out.
Never let him be alone with you.
Ever.
Or you didn't figure out until later.

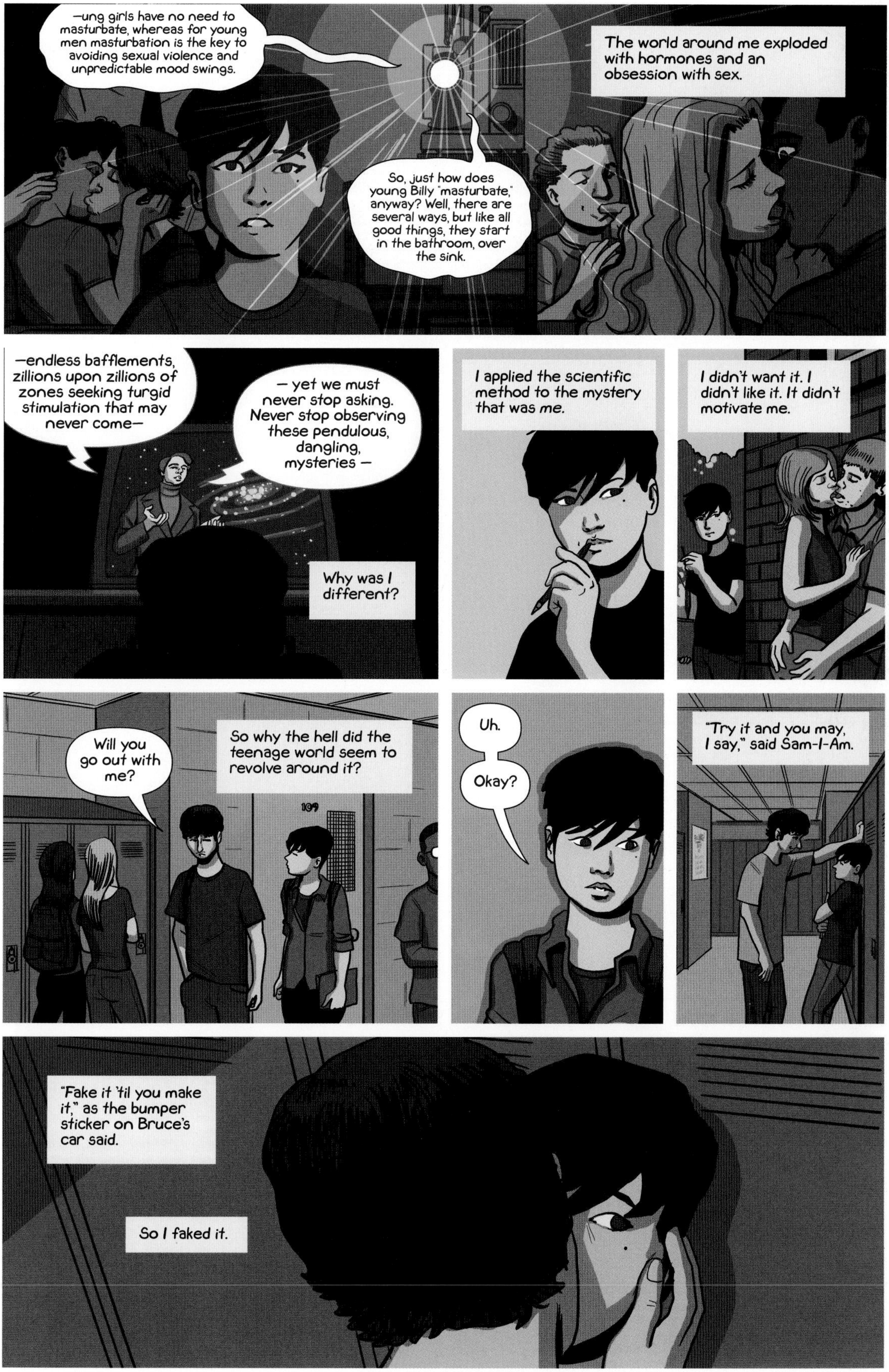
—ung girls have no need to masturbate, whereas for young men masturbation is the key to avoiding sexual violence and unpredictable mood swings.
The world around me exploded with hormones and an obsession with sex.
So, just how does young Billy "masturbate," anyway? Well, there are several ways, but like all good things, they start in the bathroom, over the sink.
—endless bafflements, zillions upon zillions of zones seeking turgid stimulation that may never come—
— yet we must never stop asking. Never stop observing these pendulous, dangling, mysteries —
Why was I different?
I applied the scientific method to the mystery that was *me.*
I didn't want it. I didn't like it. It didn't motivate me.
Will you go out with me?
So why the hell did the teenage world seem to revolve around it?
Uh.
Okay?
"Try it and you may, I say," said Sam-I-Am.
"Fake it 'til you make it," as the bumper sticker on Bruce's car said.
So I faked it.

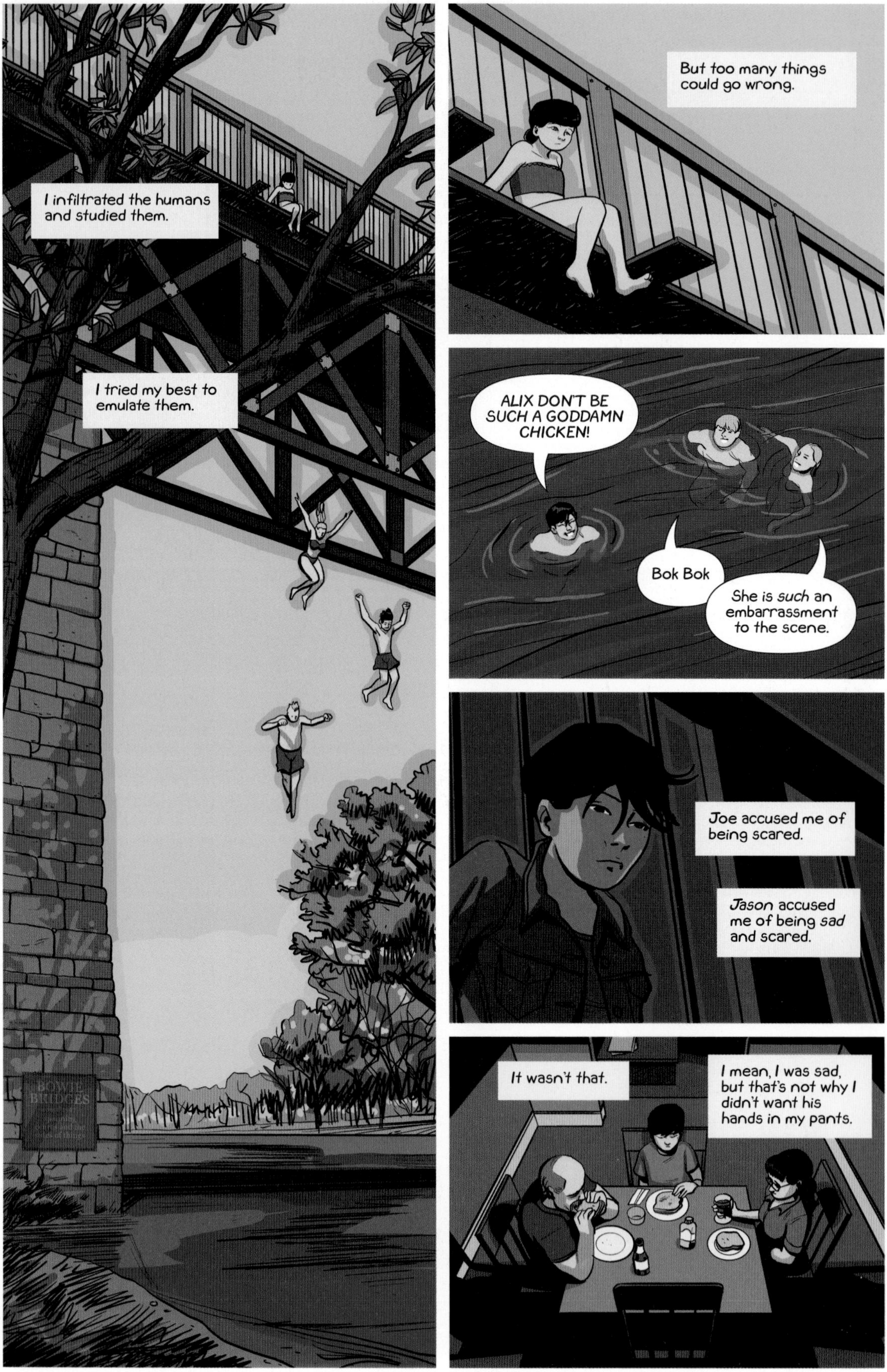
I infiltrated the humans and studied them.
I tried my best to emulate them.
BOWIE BRIDGES
But too many things could go wrong.
ALIX DON'T BE SUCH A GODDAMN CHICKEN!
Bok Bok
She is *such* an embarrassment to the scene.
Joe accused me of being scared.
Jason accused me of being *sad* and scared.
It wasn't that.
I mean, I was sad, but that's not why I didn't want his hands in my pants.

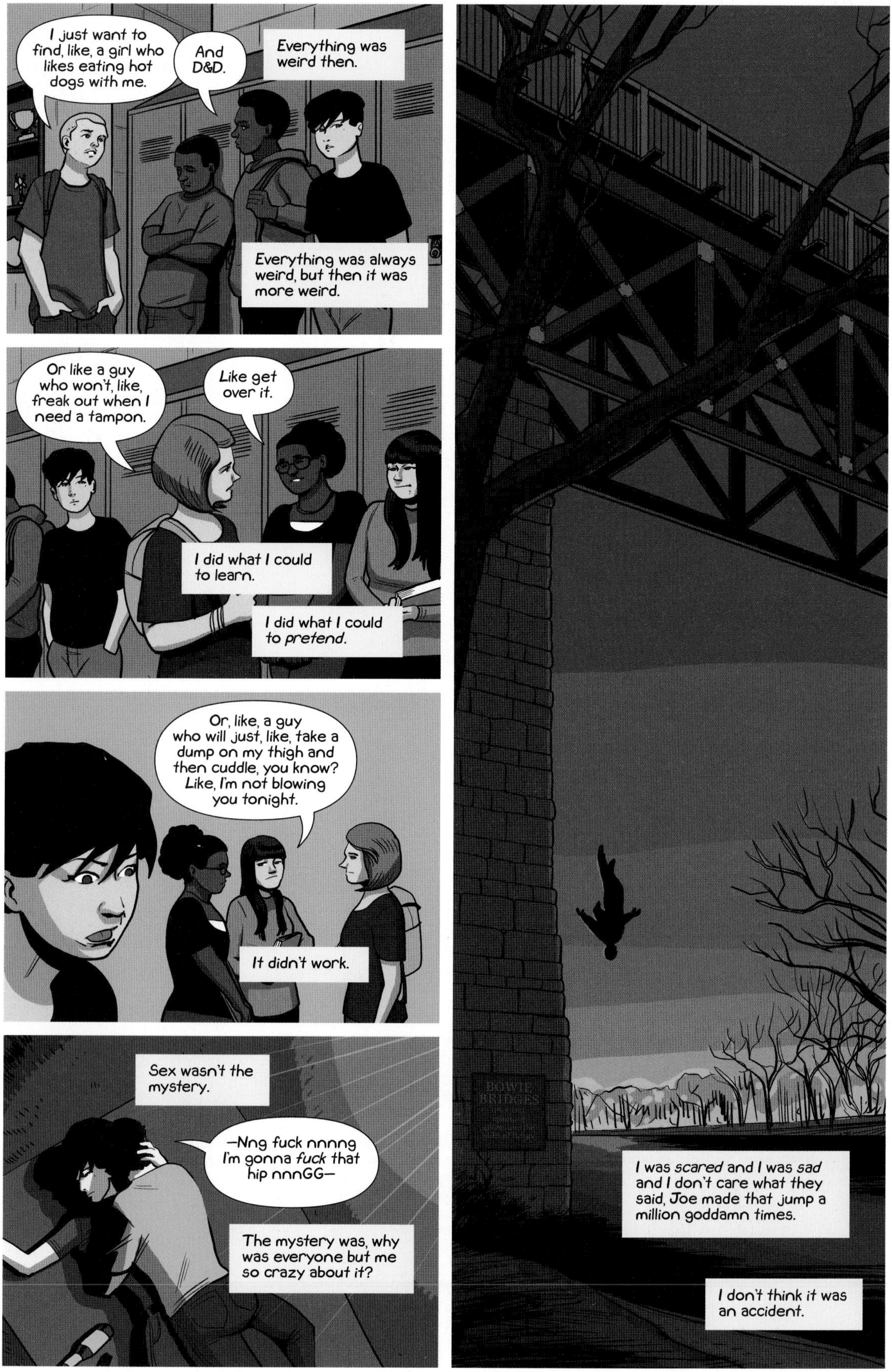
I just want to find, like, a girl who likes eating hot dogs with me.
And D&D.
Everything was weird then.
Everything was always weird, but then it was more weird.
Or like a guy who won't, like, freak out when I need a tampon.
Like get over it.
I did what I could to learn.
I did what I could to *pretend*.
Or, like, a guy who will just, like, take a dump on my thigh and then cuddle, you know? Like, I'm not blowing you tonight.
It didn't work.
Sex wasn't the mystery.
—Nng fuck nnnng I'm gonna *fuck* that hip nnnGG—
The mystery was, why was everyone but me so crazy about it?
I was *scared* and I was *sad* and I don't care what they said, Joe made that jump a million goddamn times.
I don't think it was an accident.

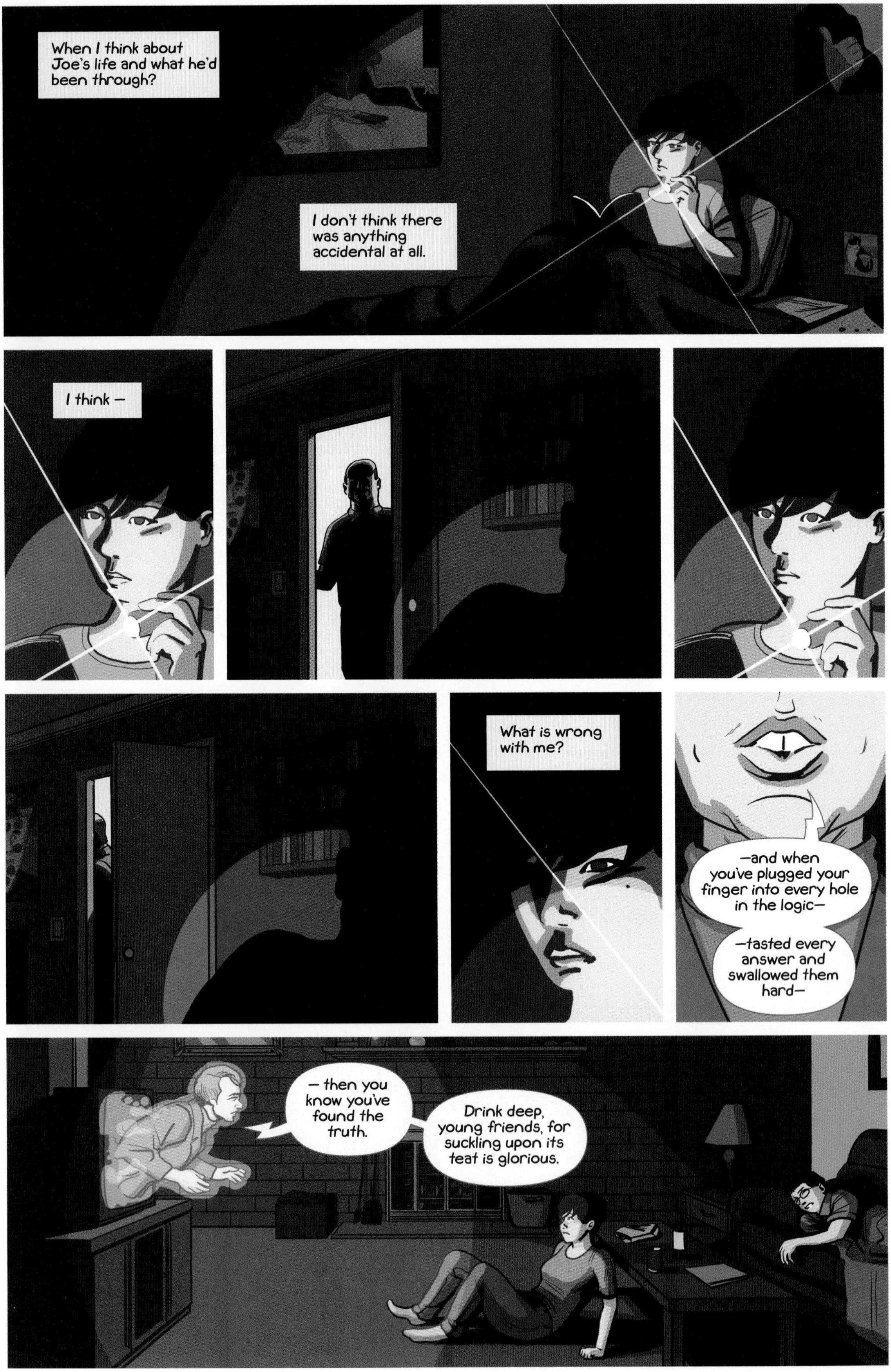
When I think about Joe's life and what he'd been through?
I don't think there was anything accidental at all.
I think —
What is wrong with me?
—and when you've plugged your finger into every hole in the logic—
—tasted every answer and swallowed them hard—
— then you know you've found the truth.
Drink deep, young friends, for suckling upon its teat is glorious.

And then...

...Then I knew.

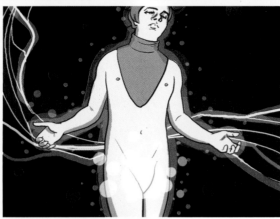

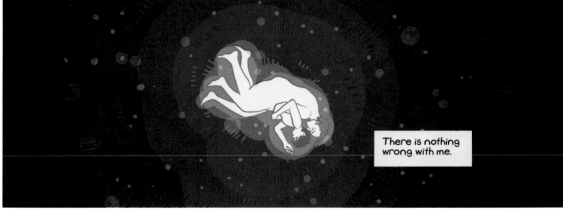

There is nothing wrong with me.

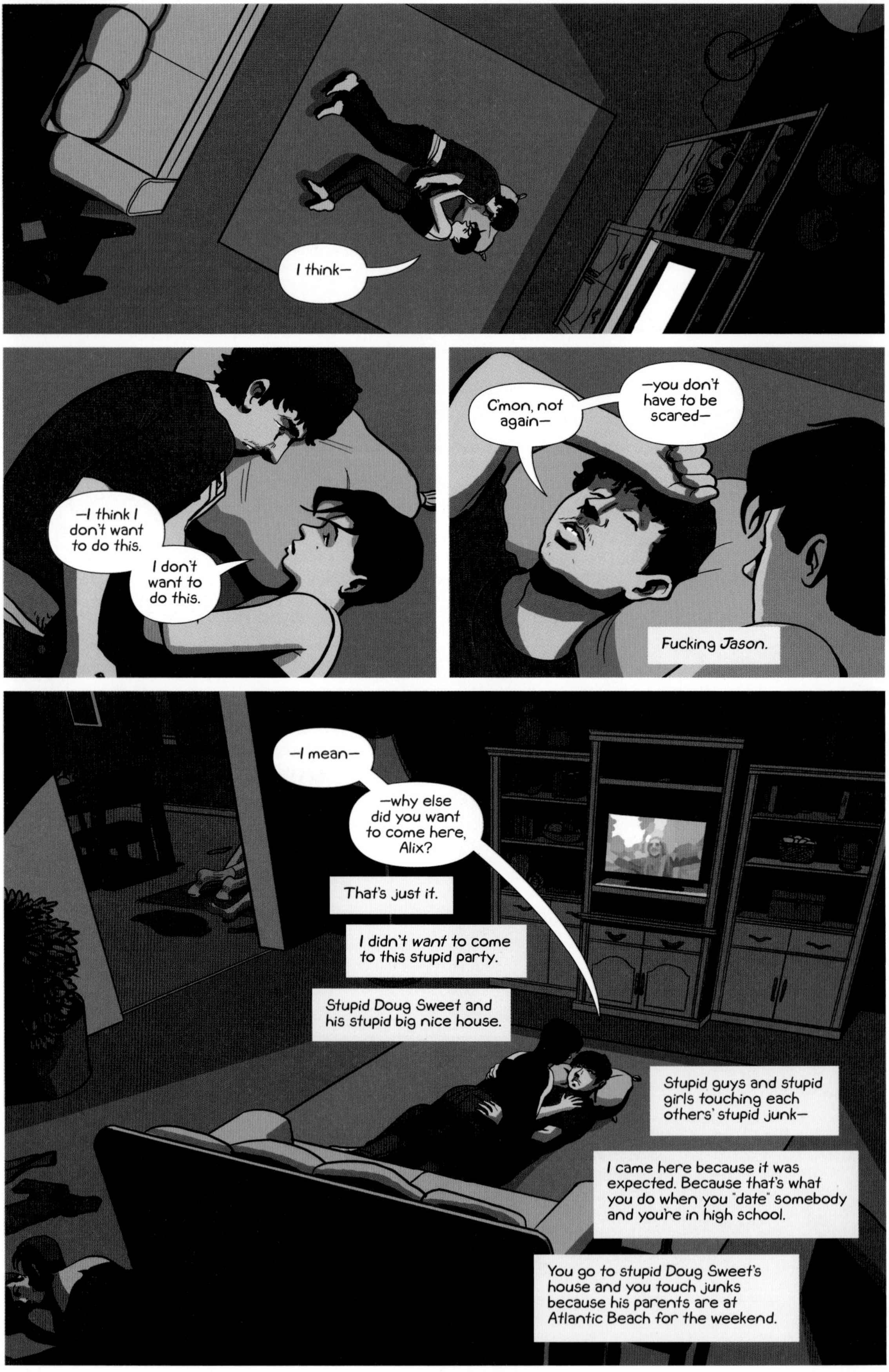
I think—
—I think I don't want to do this.
I don't want to do this.
C'mon, not again—
—you don't have to be scared—
Fucking *Jason.*
—I mean—
—why else did you want to come here, Alix?
That's just it.
I didn't *want* to come to this stupid party.
Stupid Doug Sweet and his stupid big nice house.
Stupid guys and stupid girls touching each others' stupid junk—
I came here because it was expected. Because that's what you do when you "date" somebody and you're in high school.
You go to stupid Doug Sweet's house and you touch junks because his parents are at Atlantic Beach for the weekend.

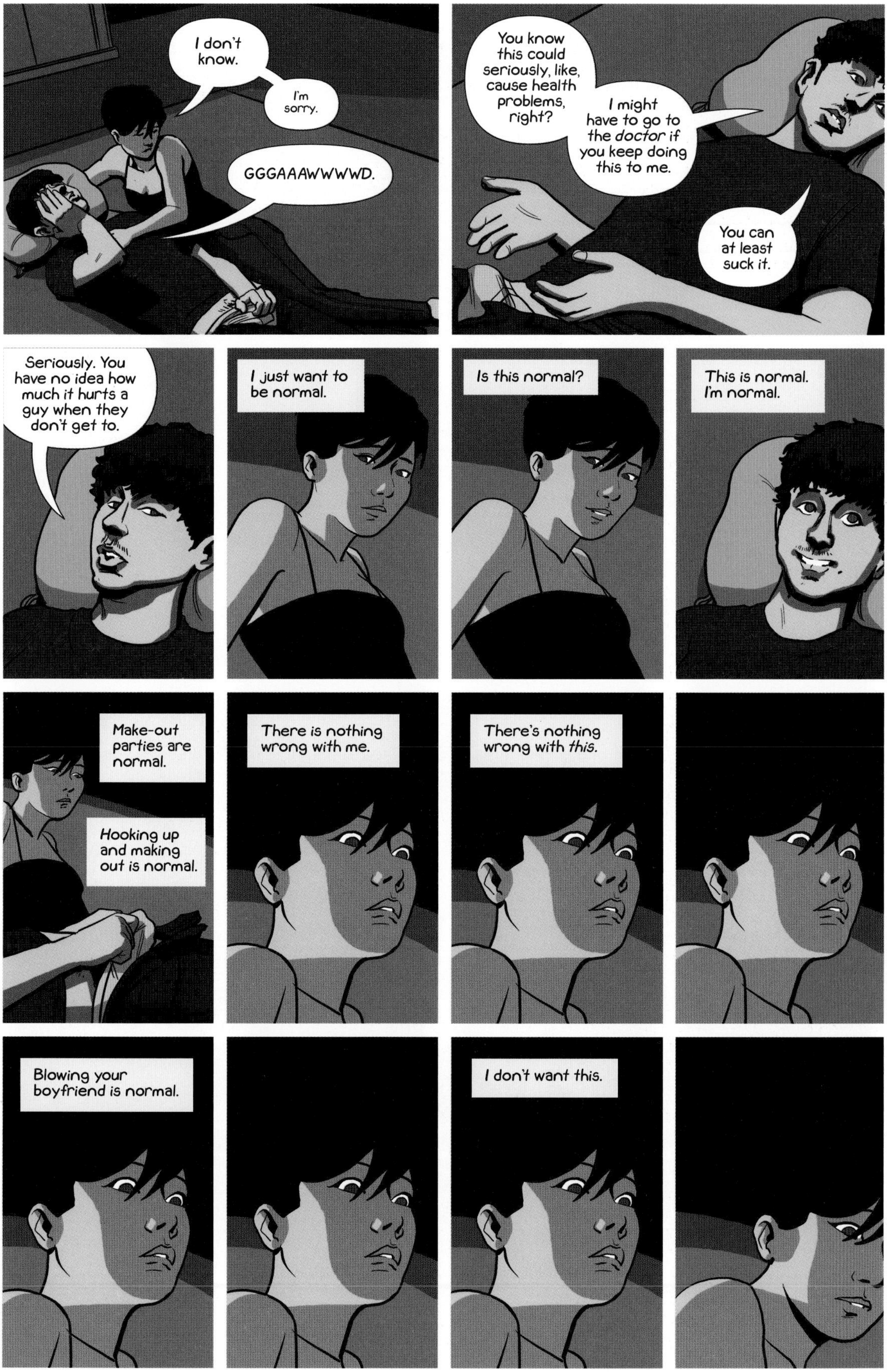
I don't know.
I'm sorry.
GGGAAAWWWWD.
You know this could seriously, like, cause health problems, right?
I might have to go to the *doctor* if you keep doing this to me.
You can at least suck it.
Seriously. You have no idea how much *it* hurts a guy when they don't get to.
I just want to be normal.
Is this normal?
This is normal. I'm normal.
Make-out parties are normal.
Hooking up and making out is normal.
There is nothing wrong with me.
There's nothing wrong with *this*.
Blowing your boyfriend is normal.
I don't want this.

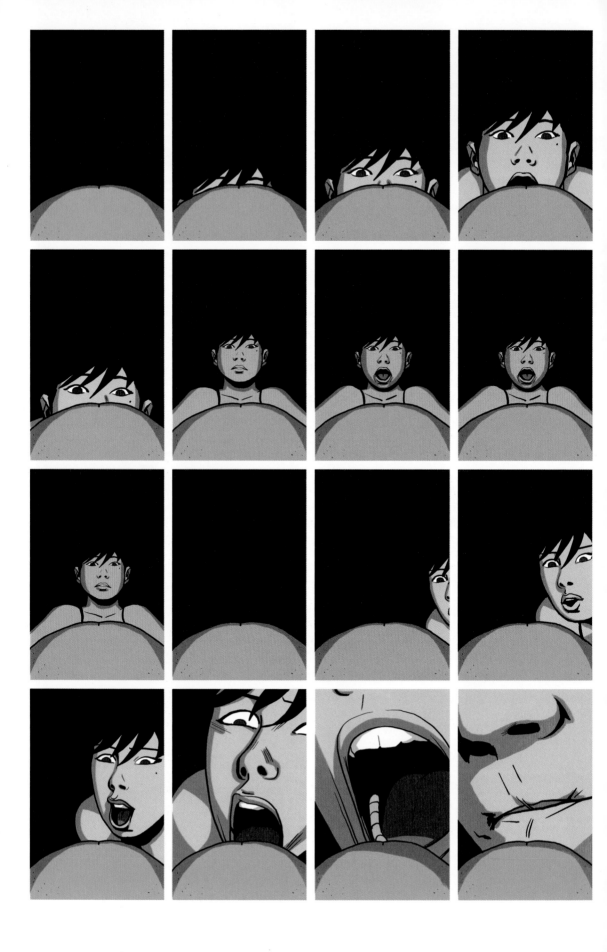

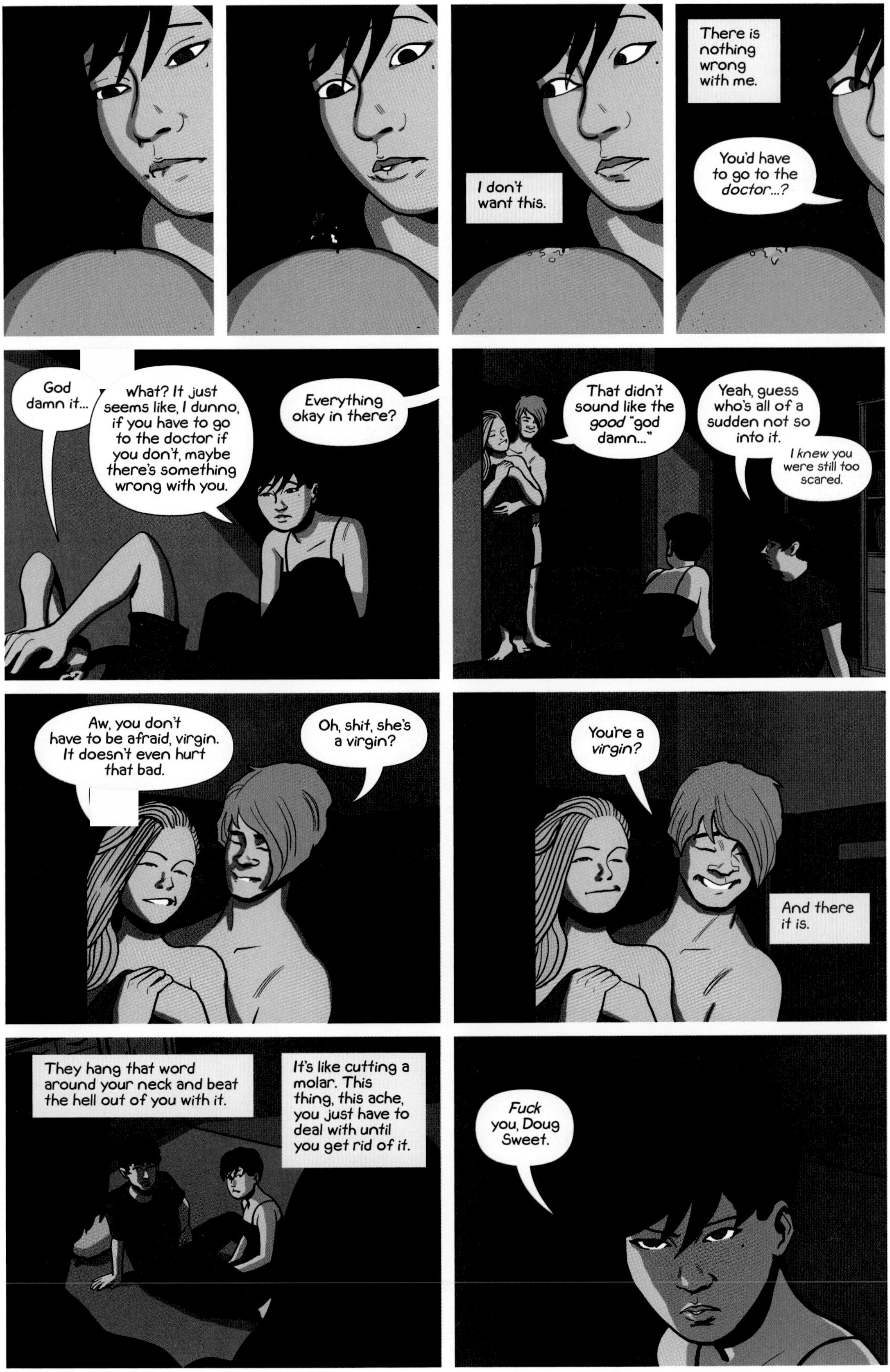

There is nothing wrong with me.
I don't want this.
You'd have to go to the *doctor*...?
God damn it...
What? It just seems like, I dunno, if you have to go to the doctor if you don't, maybe there's something wrong with you.
Everything okay in there?
That didn't sound like the *good* "god damn..."
Yeah, guess who's all of a sudden not so into it.
I *knew* you were still too scared.
Aw, you don't have to be afraid, virgin. It doesn't even hurt that bad.
Oh, shit, she's a virgin?
You're a *virgin*?
And there it is.
They hang that word around your neck and beat the hell out of you with it.
It's like cutting a molar. This thing, this ache, you just have to deal with until you get rid of it.
Fuck you, Doug Sweet.

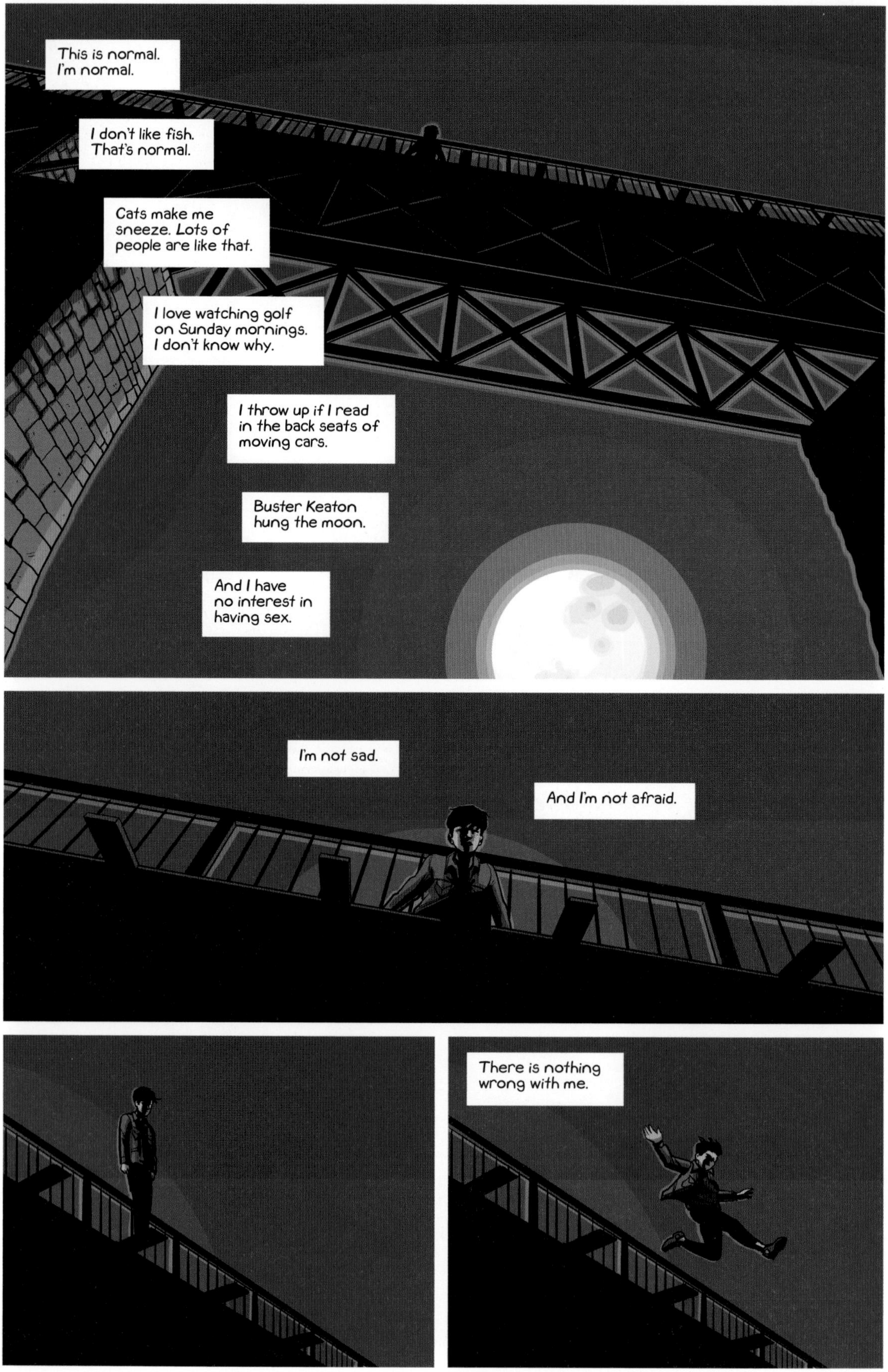
This is normal. I'm normal.
I don't like fish. That's normal.
Cats make me sneeze. Lots of people are like that.
I love watching golf on Sunday mornings. I don't know why.
I throw up if I read in the back seats of moving cars.
Buster Keaton hung the moon.
And I have no interest in having sex.
I'm not sad.
And I'm not afraid.
There is nothing wrong with me.

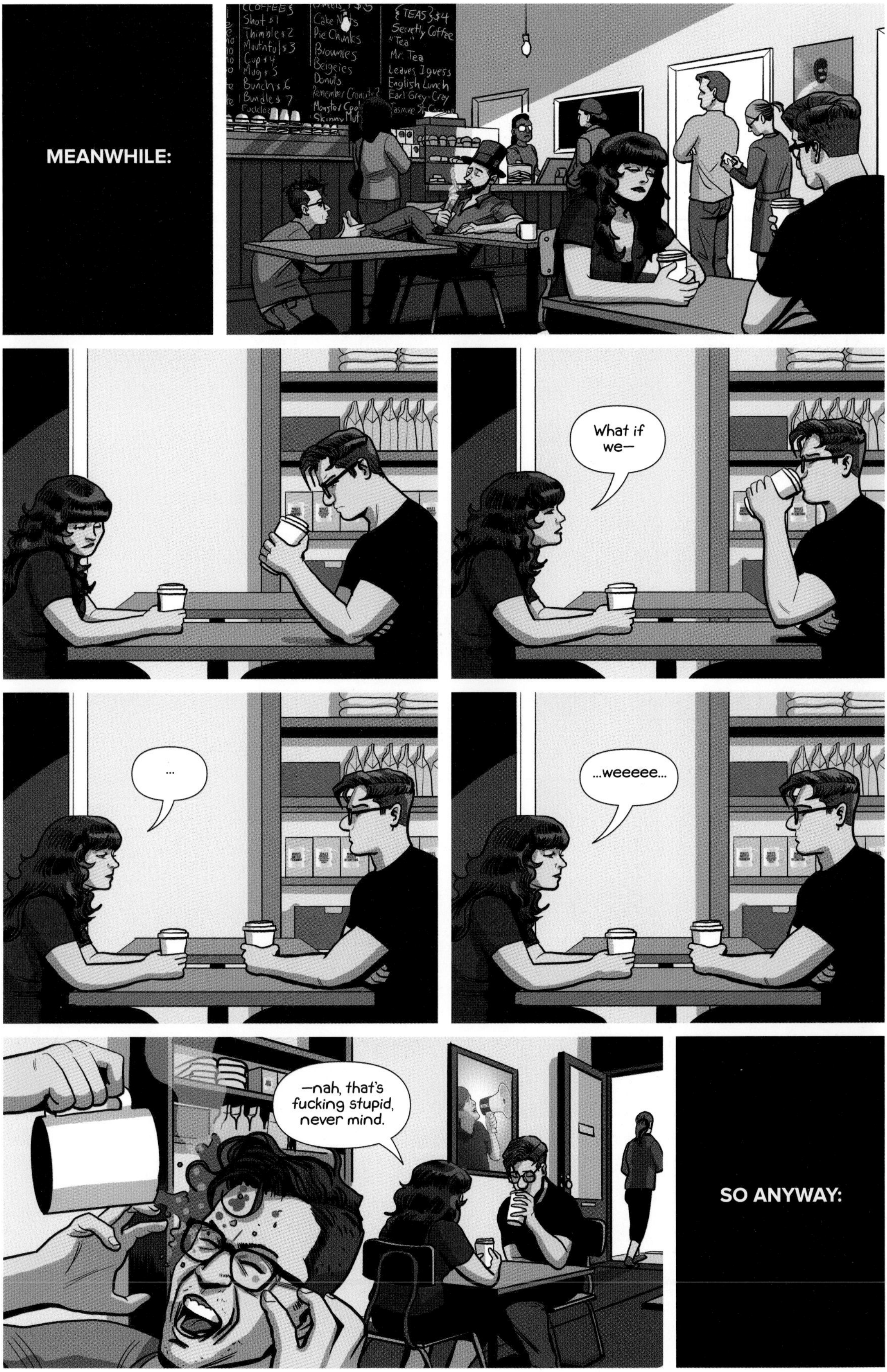
MEANWHILE:
{COFFEE}
Shot $1
Thimble $2
Mouthful $3
Cup $4
Mug $5
Bunch $6
Bundle $7
Pie Chunks
Brownies
Beigeies
Donuts
{TEAS} $4
Secretly Coffee
"Tea"
Mr. Tea
Leaves, I guess
English Lunch
Earl Grey-Cray
What if we—
...
...weeeee...
—nah, that's fucking stupid, never mind.
SO ANYWAY:

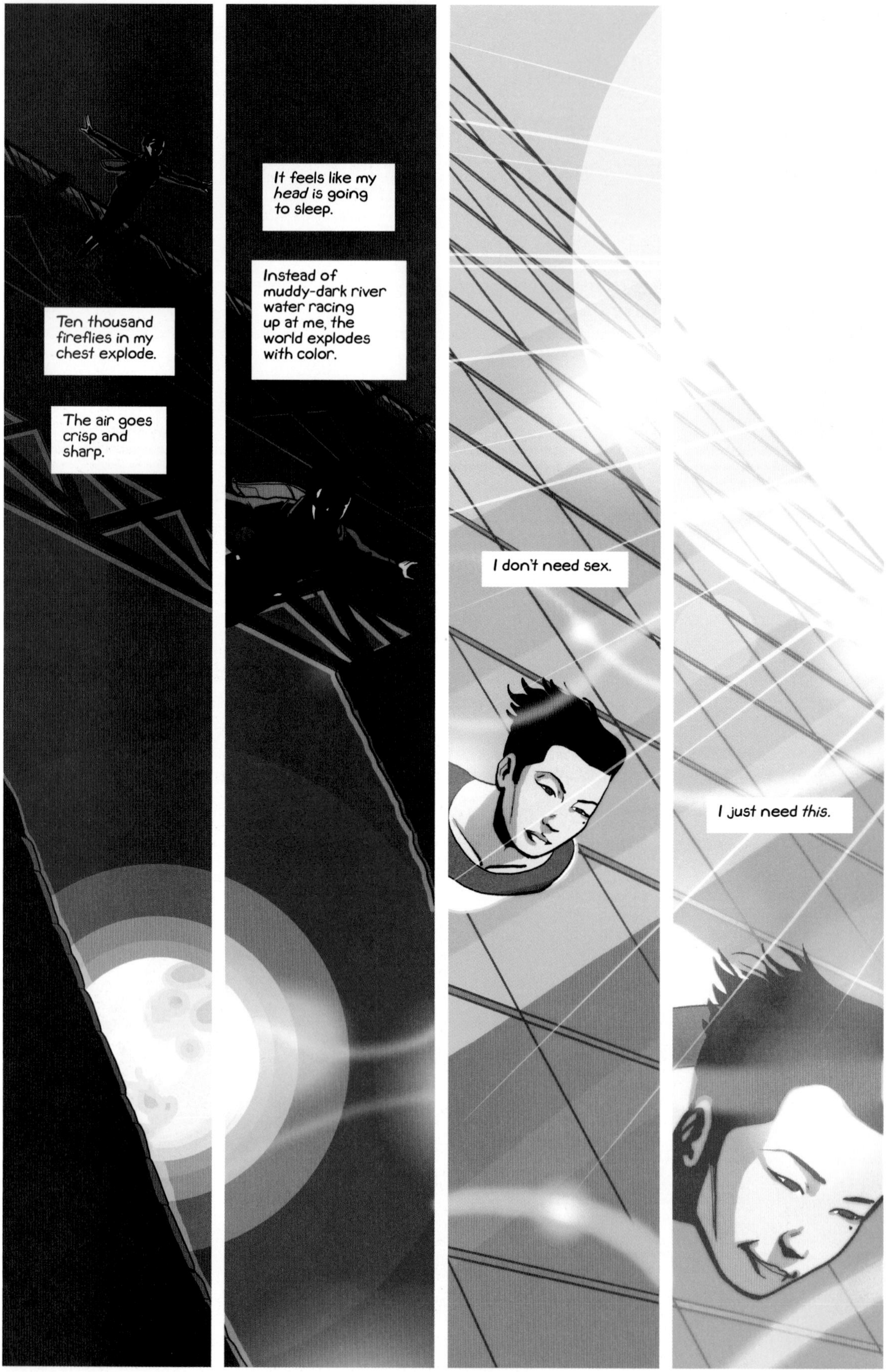
Ten thousand fireflies in my chest explode.
The air goes crisp and sharp.
It feels like my *head* is going to sleep.
Instead of muddy-dark river water racing up at me, the world explodes with color.
I don't need sex.
I just need *this*.

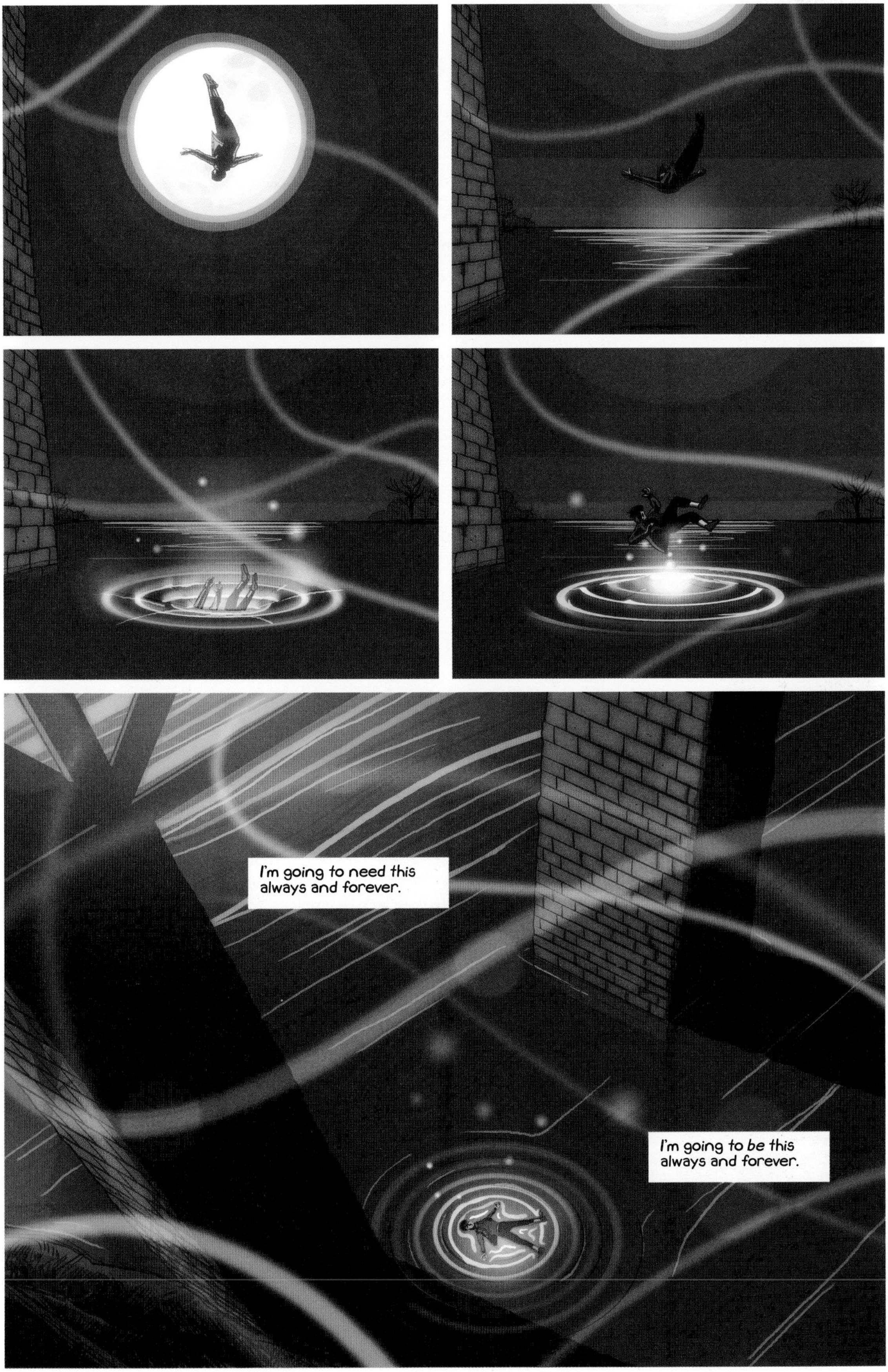
I'm going to need this always and forever.
I'm going to *be* this always and forever.

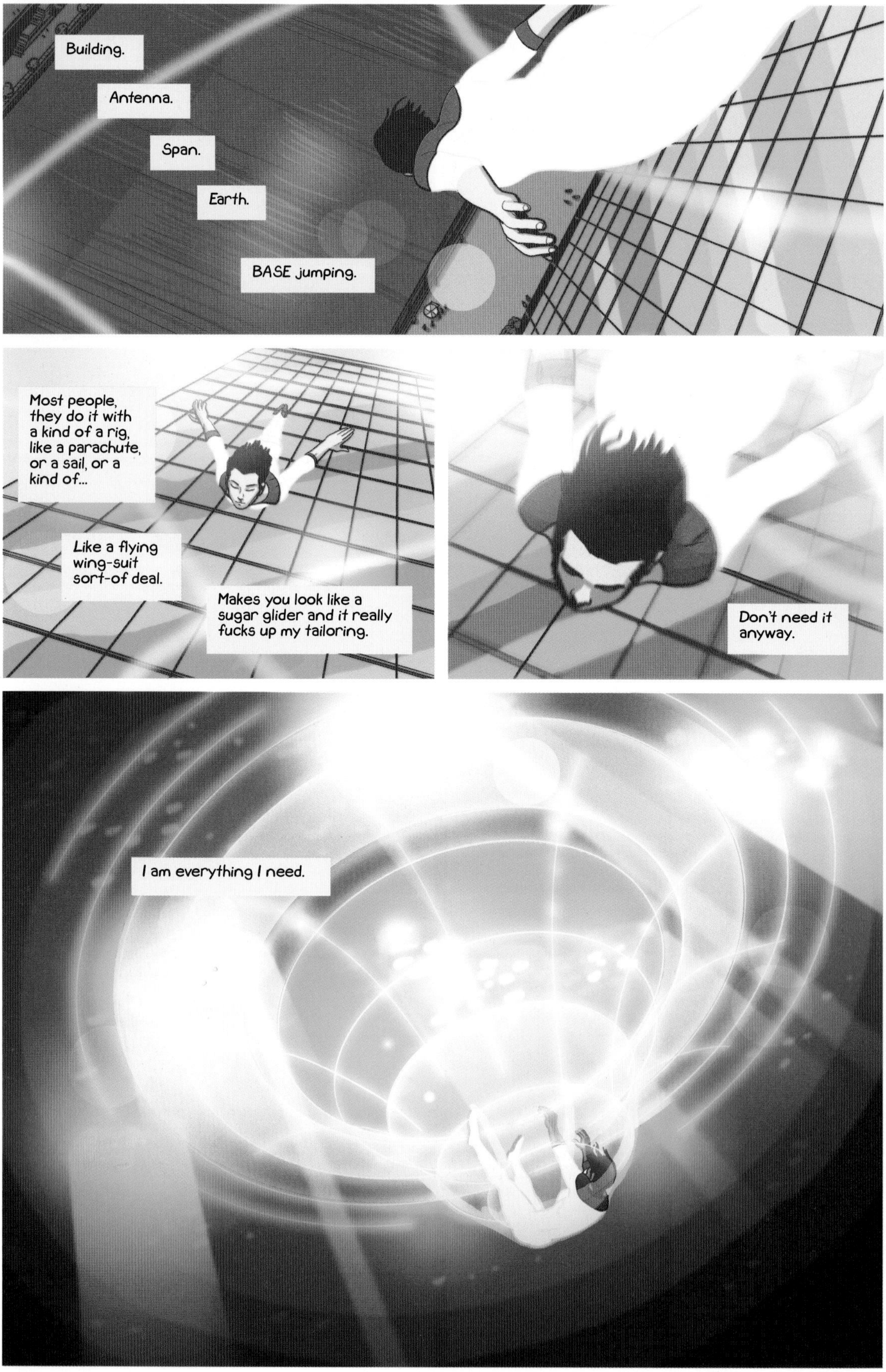
Building.
Antenna.
Span.
Earth.
BASE jumping.
Most people, they do it with a kind of a rig, like a parachute, or a sail, or a kind of...
Like a flying wing-suit sort-of deal.
Makes you look like a sugar glider and it really fucks up my tailoring.
Don't need it anyway.
I am everything I need.

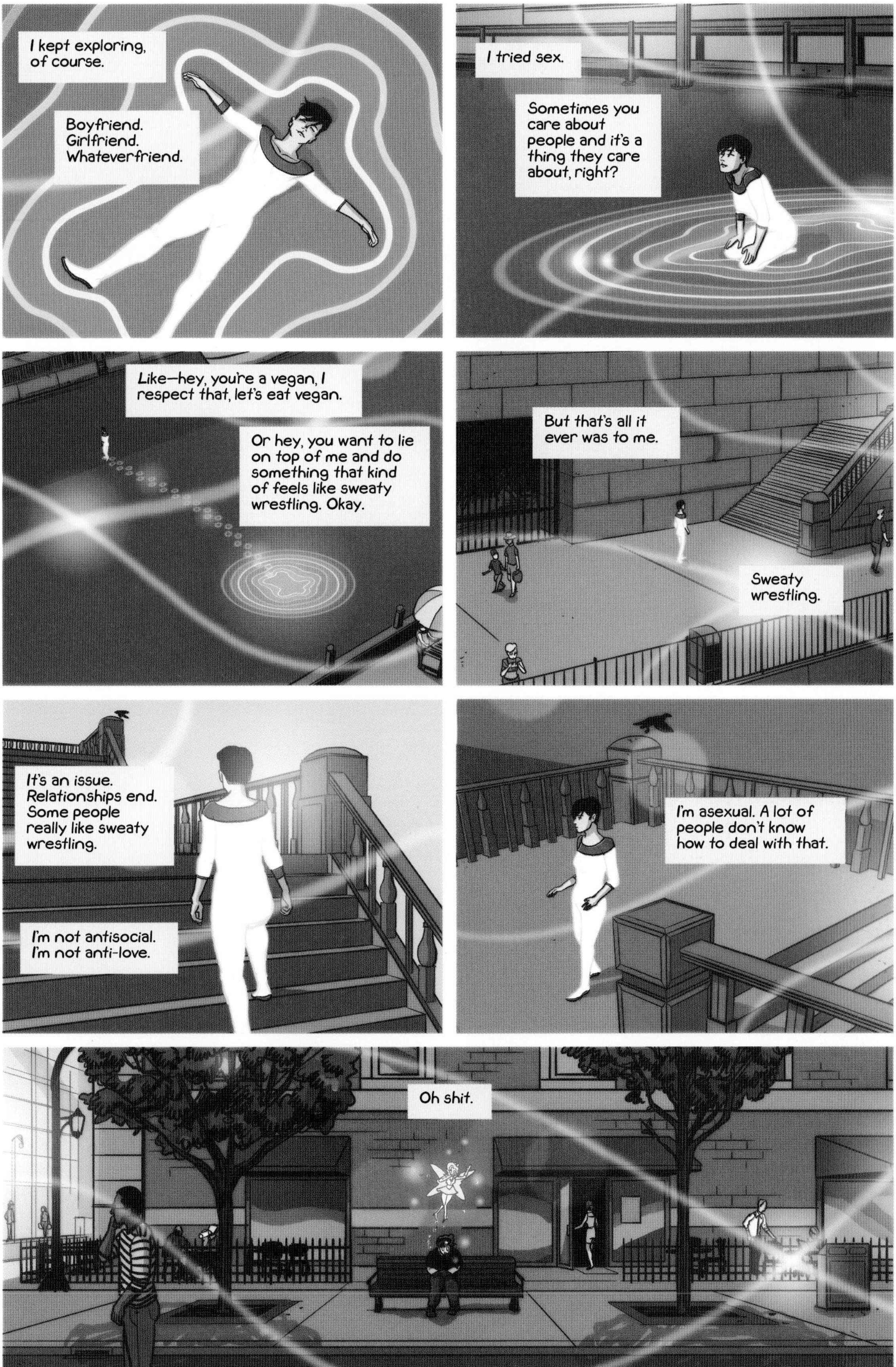

I kept exploring, of course.
Boyfriend. Girlfriend. Whateverfriend.
I tried sex.
Sometimes you care about people and it's a thing they care about, right?
Like—hey, you're a vegan, I respect that, let's eat vegan.
Or hey, you want to lie on top of me and do something that kind of feels like sweaty wrestling. Okay.
But that's all it ever was to me.
Sweaty wrestling.
It's an issue. Relationships end. Some people really like sweaty wrestling.
I'm not antisocial. I'm not anti-love.
I'm asexual. A lot of people don't know how to deal with that.
Oh shit.

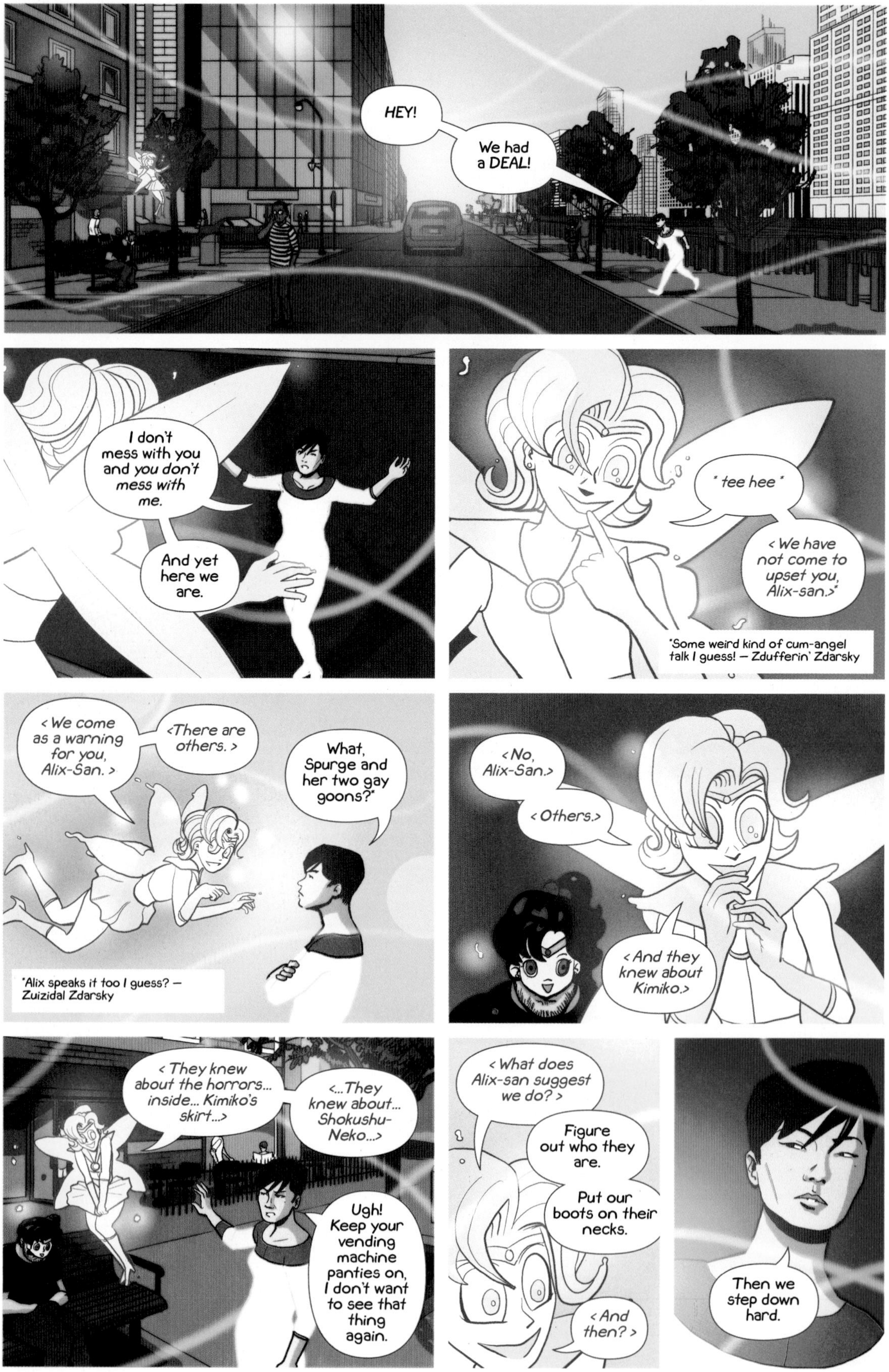
HEY!
We had a DEAL!
I don't mess with you and you don't mess with me.
And yet here we are.
* tee hee *
< We have not come to upset you, Alix-san.>*
*Some weird kind of cum-angel talk I guess! — Zdufferin' Zdarsky
< We come as a warning for you, Alix-San. >
<There are others. >
What, Spurge and her two gay goons?*
*Alix speaks it too I guess? — Zuizidal Zdarsky
< No, Alix-San.>
< Others.>
< And they knew about Kimiko.>
< They knew about the horrors... inside... Kimiko's skirt...>
<...They knew about... Shokushu-Neko...>
Ugh! Keep your vending machine panties on, I don't want to see that thing again.
< What does Alix-san suggest we do? >
Figure out who they are.
Put our boots on their necks.
< And then? >
Then we step down hard.

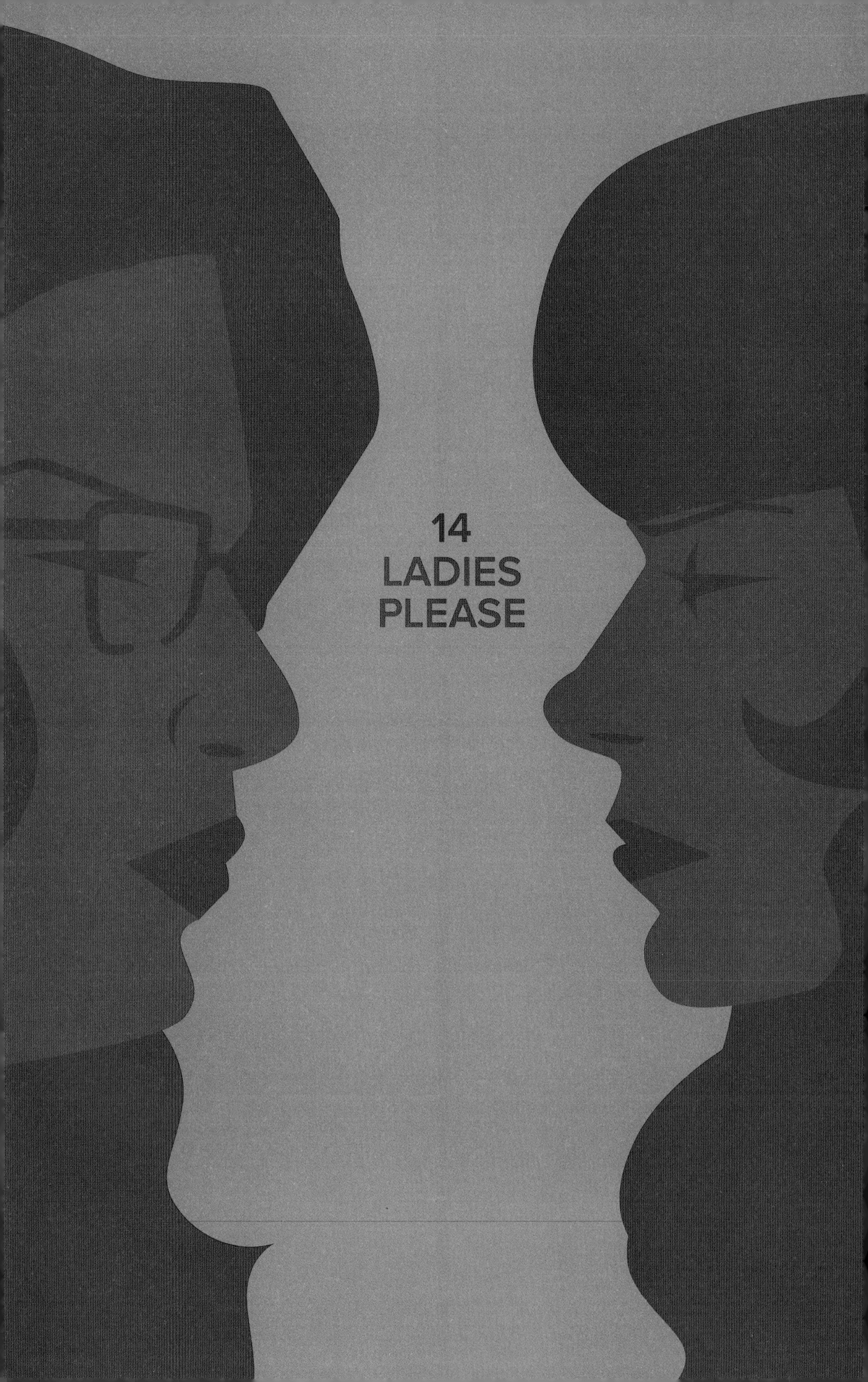
14
LADIES
PLEASE

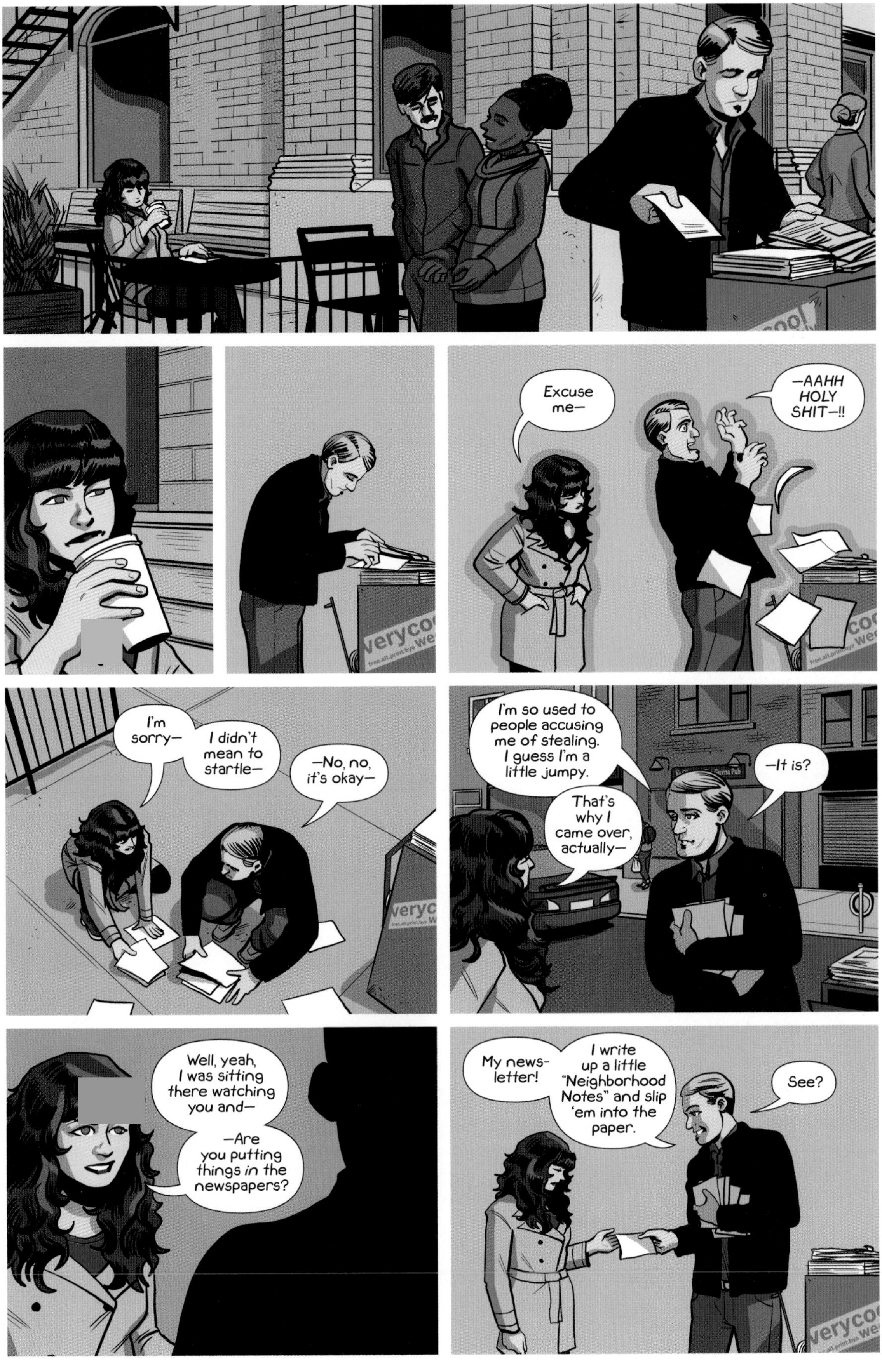
Excuse me—
—AAHH HOLY SHIT—!!
I'm sorry—
I didn't mean to startle—
—No, no, it's okay—
I'm so used to people accusing me of stealing. I guess I'm a little jumpy.
—It is?
That's why I came over, actually—
Well, yeah, I was sitting there watching you and—
—Are you putting things *in* the newspapers?
My news-letter!
I write up a little "Neighborhood Notes" and slip 'em into the paper.
See?

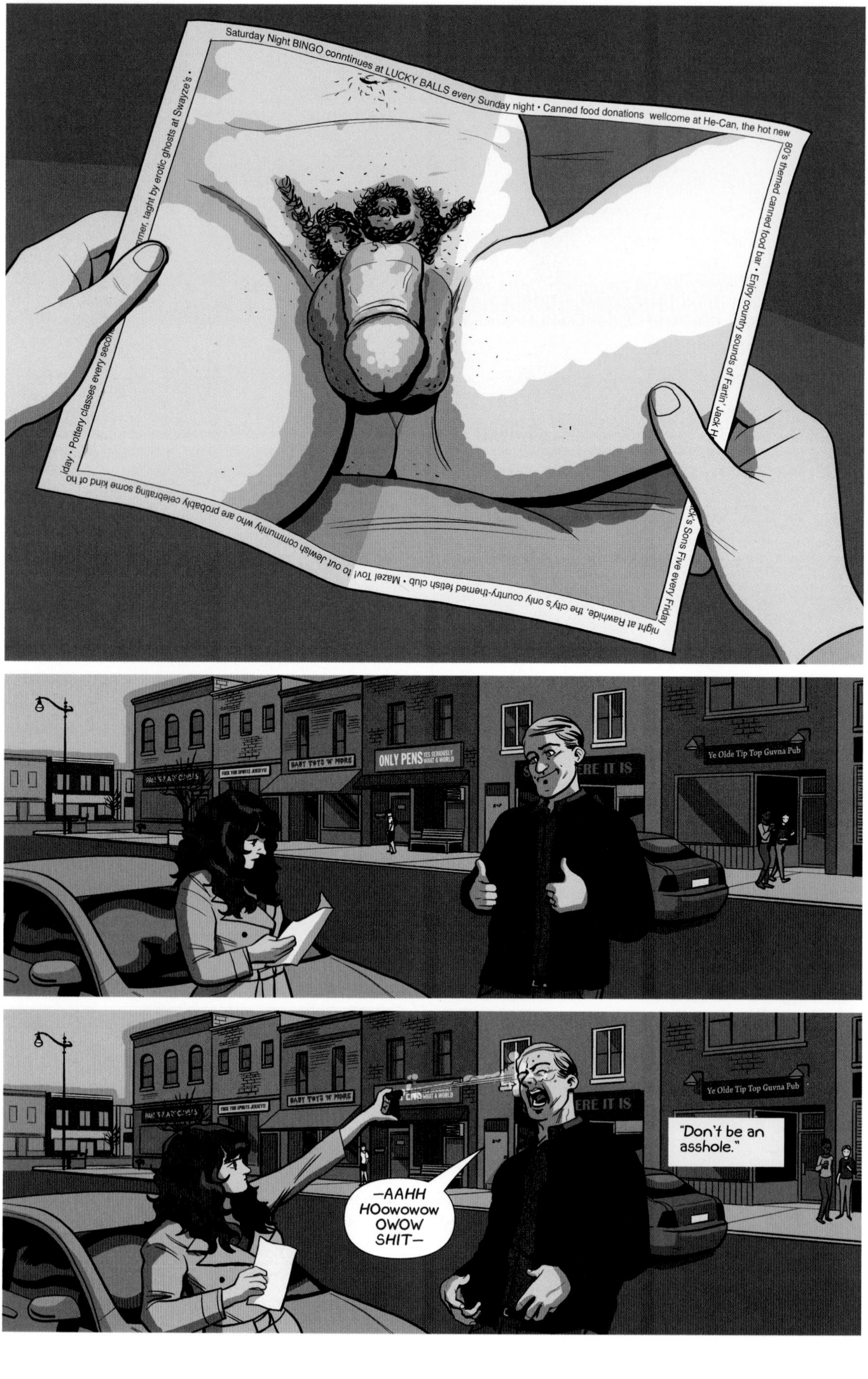
Saturday Night BINGO conntinues at LUCKY BALLS every Sunday night • Canned food donations wellcome at He-Can, the hot new 80's themed canned food bar • Enjoy country sounds of Fartin' Jack H
ck's Sons Five every Friday night at Rawhide, the city's only country-themed fetish club • Mazel Tov! to out Jewish community who are probably celebrating some kind of ho
iday • Pottery classes every seco
omer, taght by erotic ghosts at Swayze's •
ONLY PENS YES SERIOUSLY WHAT A WORLD
BABY TOYS 'N' MORE
Ye Olde Tip Top Guvna Pub
"Don't be an asshole."
—AAHH HOowowow OWOW SHIT—

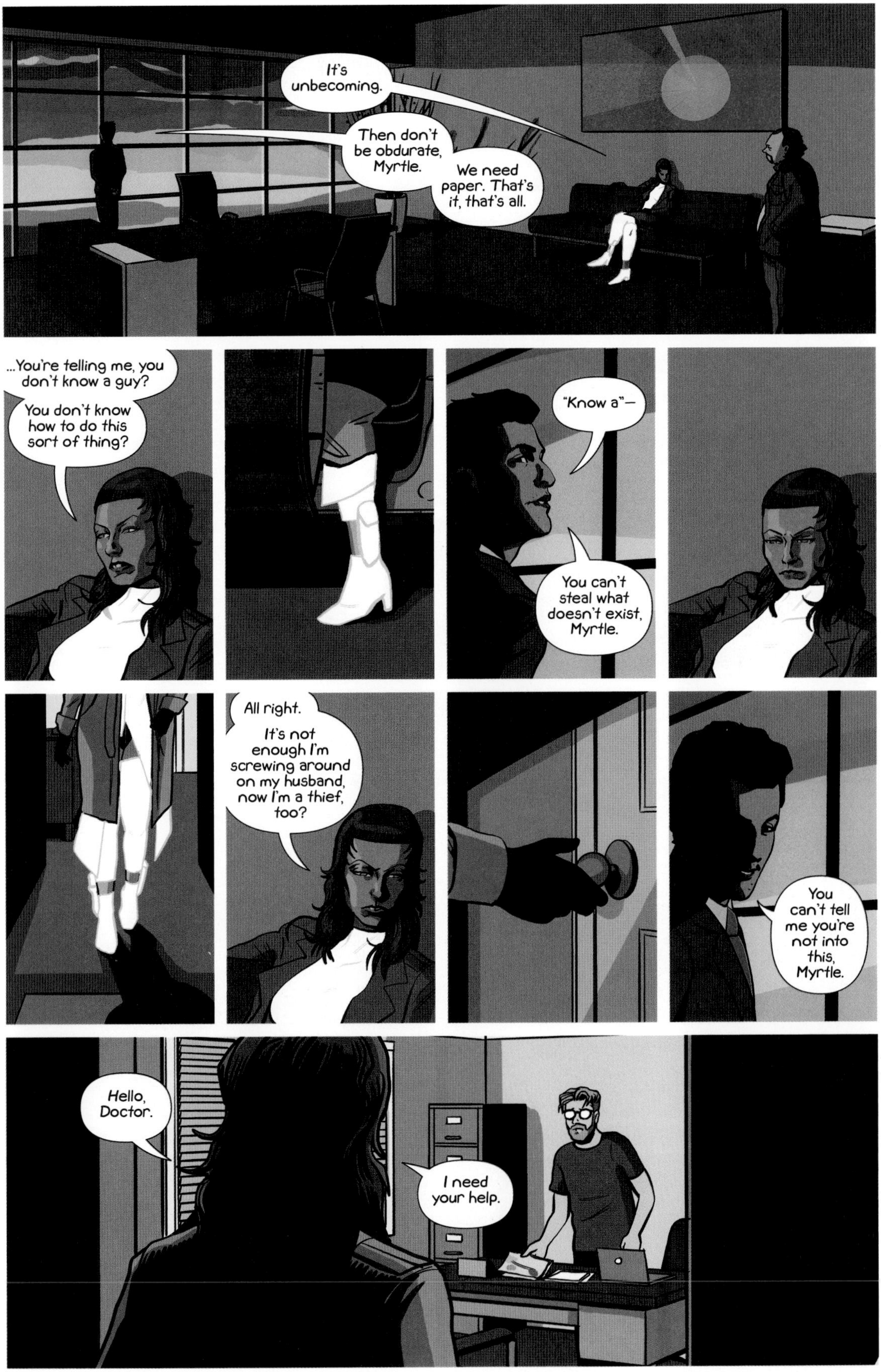
It's unbecoming.
Then don't be obdurate, Myrtle.
We need paper. That's it, that's all.
...You're telling me, you don't know a guy?
You don't know how to do this sort of thing?
"Know a"—
You can't steal what doesn't exist, Myrtle.
All right.
It's not enough I'm screwing around on my husband, now I'm a thief, too?
You can't tell me you're not into this, Myrtle.
Hello, Doctor.
I need your help.

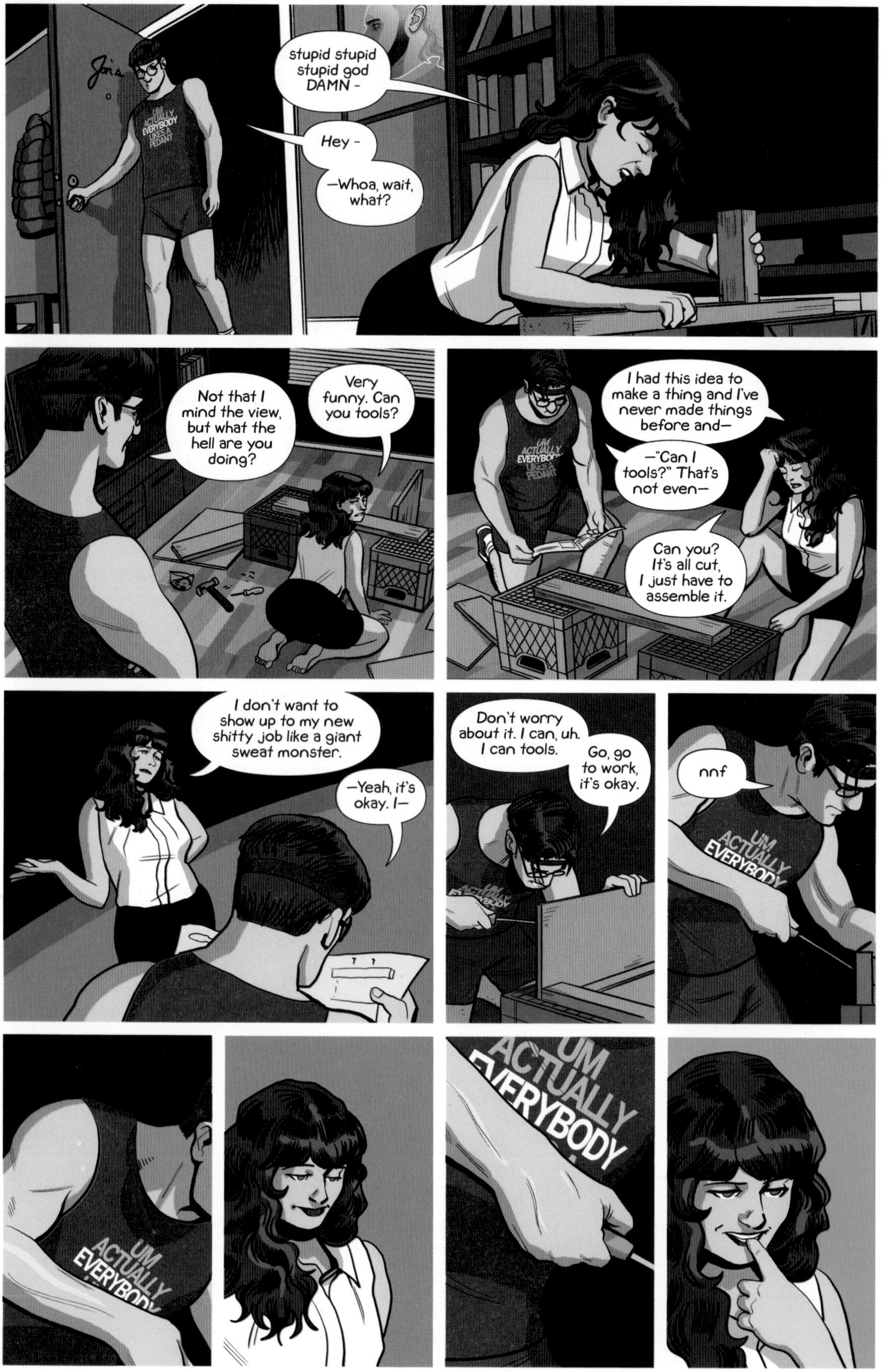
Jon's
UM ACTUALLY EVERYBODY LIKES A PEDANT
stupid stupid stupid god DAMN -
Hey -
—Whoa, wait, what?
Not that I mind the view, but what the hell are you doing?
Very funny. Can you tools?
I had this idea to make a thing and I've never made things before and—
—"Can I tools?" That's not even—
Can you? It's all cut, I just have to assemble it.
I don't want to show up to my new shitty job like a giant sweat monster.
—Yeah, it's okay. I—
Don't worry about it. I can, uh. I can tools.
Go, go to work, it's okay.
nnf
UM ACTUALLY EVERYBODY

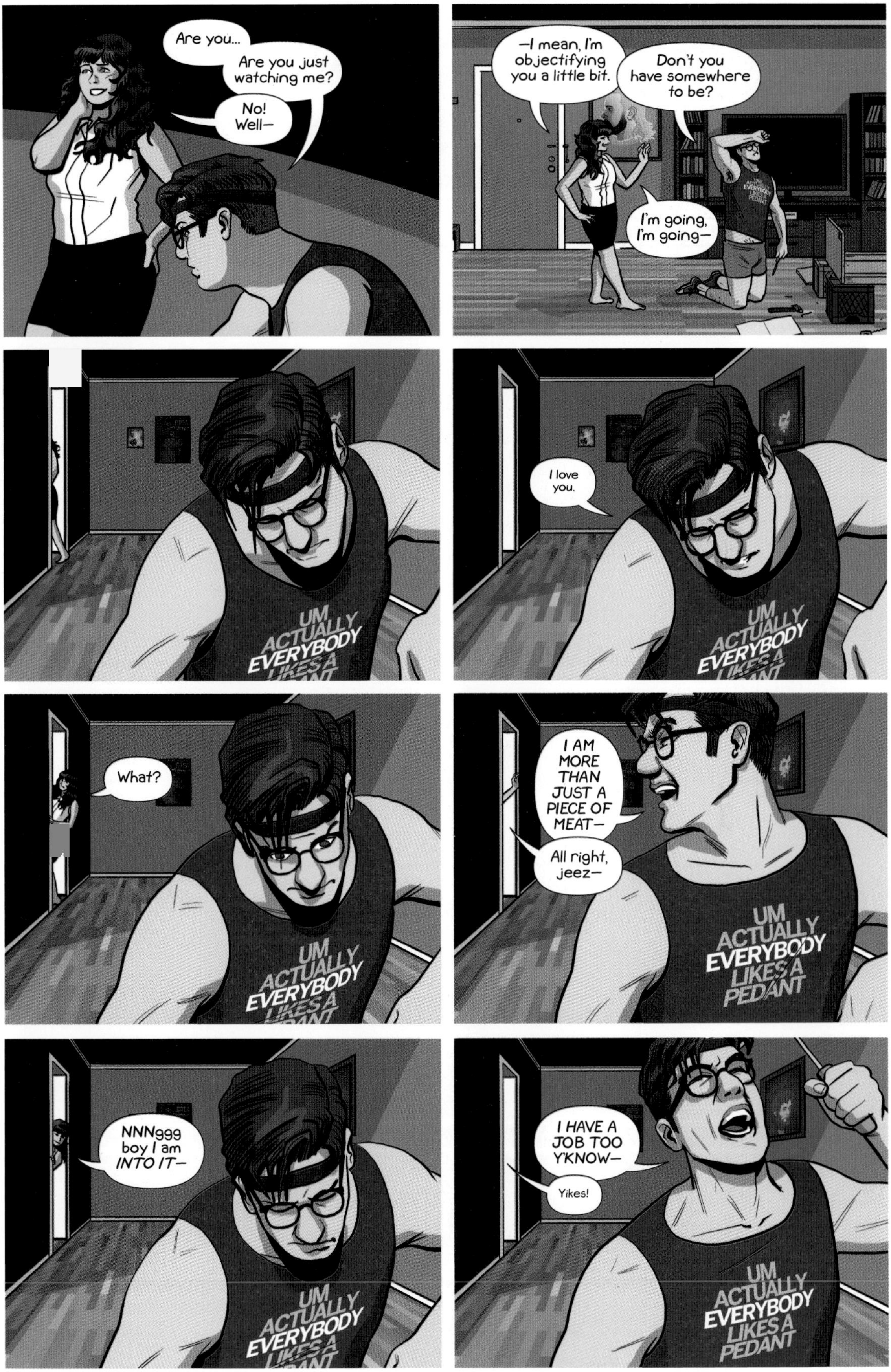
Are you...
Are you just watching me?
No! Well—
—I mean, I'm objectifying you a little bit.
Don't you have somewhere to be?
I'm going, I'm going—
UM ACTUALLY EVERYBODY LIKES A PEDANT
UM ACTUALLY EVERYBODY
I love you.
UM ACTUALLY EVERYBODY
What?
UM ACTUALLY EVERYBODY
I AM MORE THAN JUST A PIECE OF MEAT—
All right, jeez—
UM ACTUALLY EVERYBODY LIKES A PEDANT
NNNggg boy I am *INTO IT*—
UM ACTUALLY EVERYBODY
I HAVE A JOB TOO Y'KNOW—
Yikes!
UM ACTUALLY EVERYBODY LIKES A PEDANT

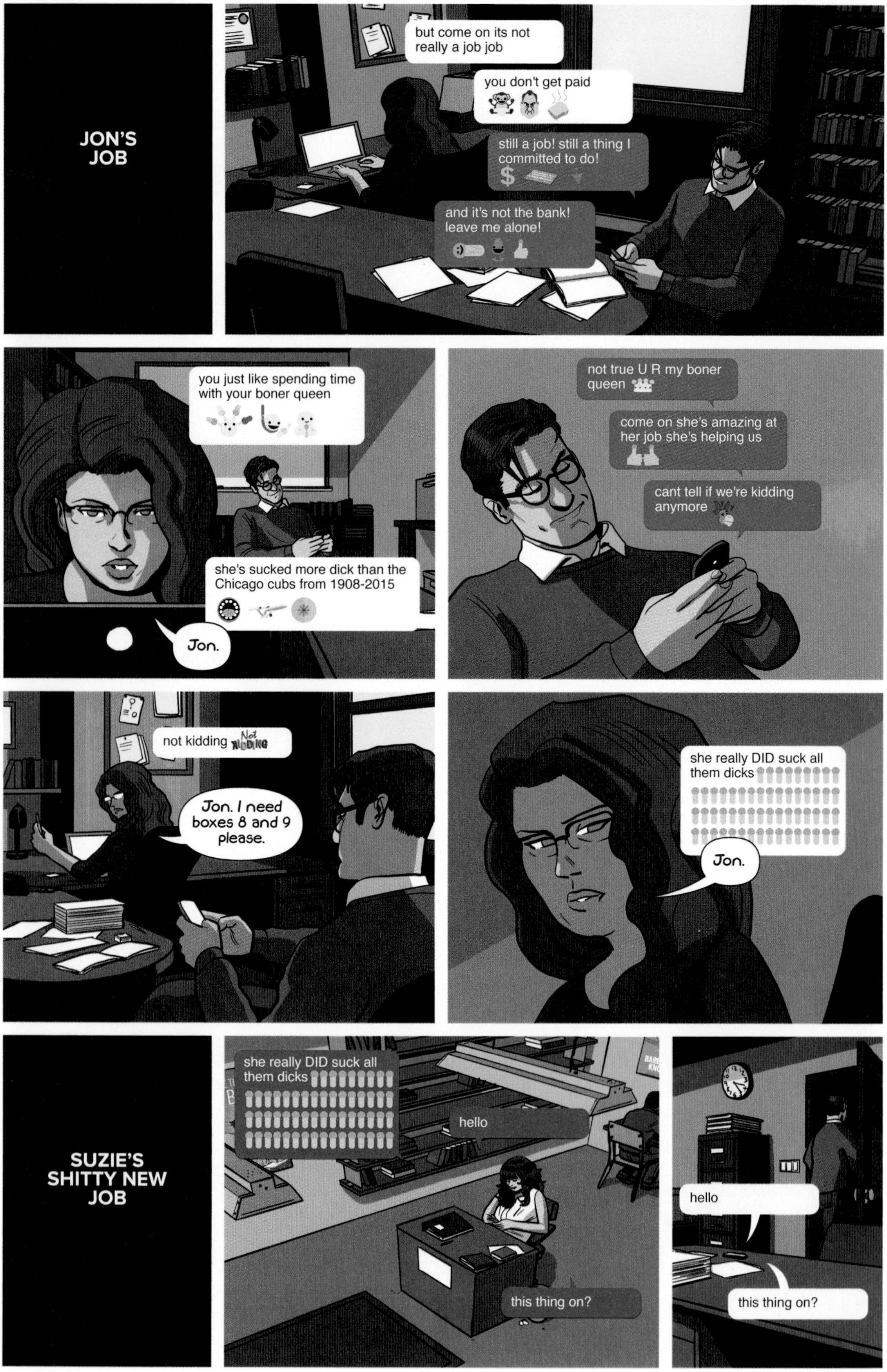

JON'S JOB
but come on its not really a job job
you don't get paid
still a job! still a thing I committed to do!
and it's not the bank! leave me alone!
you just like spending time with your boner queen
she's sucked more dick than the Chicago cubs from 1908-2015
Jon.
not true U R my boner queen
come on she's amazing at her job she's helping us
cant tell if we're kidding anymore
not kidding
Jon. I need boxes 8 and 9 please.
she really DID suck all them dicks
Jon.
SUZIE'S SHITTY NEW JOB
she really DID suck all them dicks
hello
this thing on?
hello
this thing on?

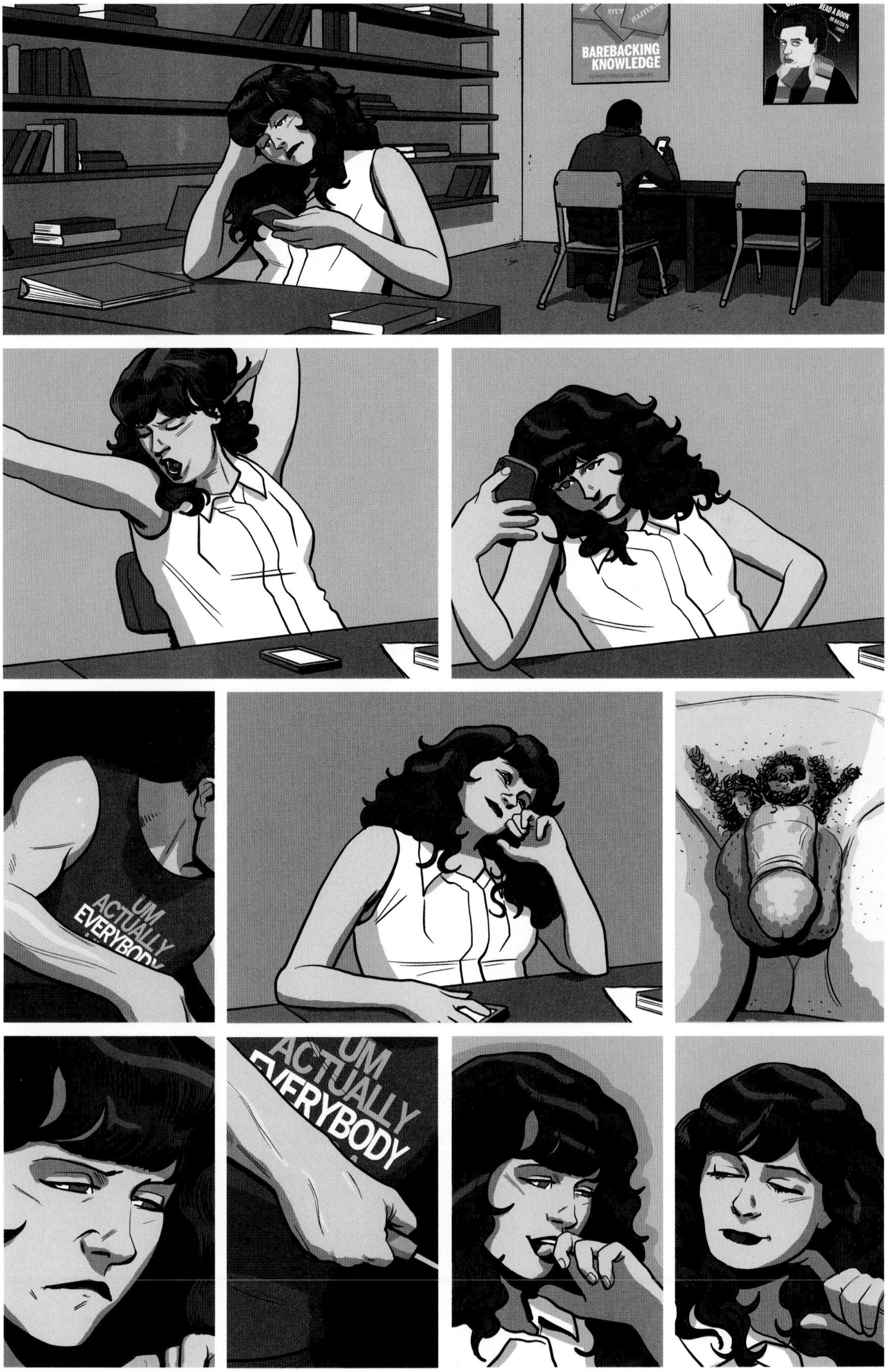
BAREBACKING KNOWLEDGE
READ A BOOK
OR WATCH TV
UM ACTUALLY EVERYBODY
UM ACTUALLY EVERYBODY

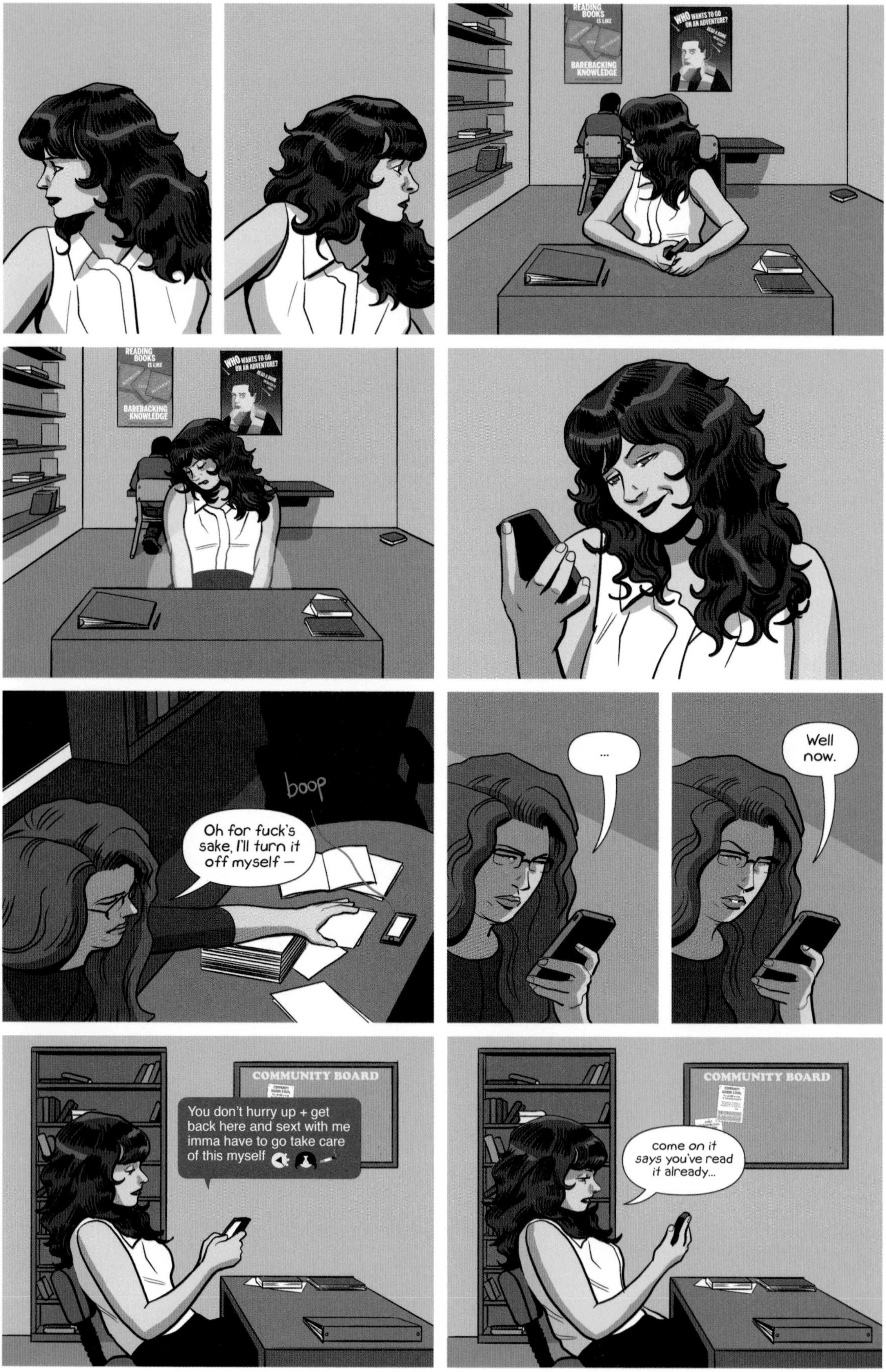
READING BOOKS IS LIKE
BAREBACKING KNOWLEDGE
WHO WANTS TO GO ON AN ADVENTURE?
boop
Oh for fuck's sake, I'll turn it off myself —
...
Well now.
COMMUNITY BOARD
You don't hurry up + get back here and sext with me imma have to go take care of this myself
come on it says you've read it already...

Your loss, pal...
DOIN' THE DEW(EY)
BACK IN 5
UNITY BOARD
UNITY BOARD
lock
lock
Oh god da—

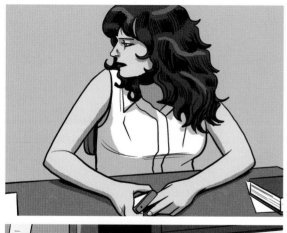

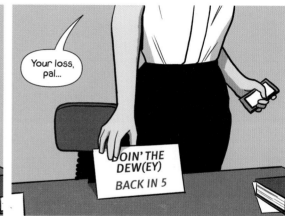

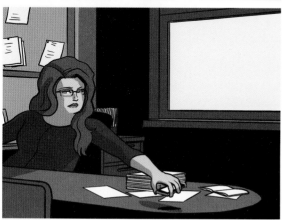

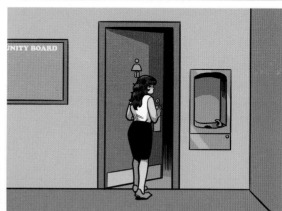

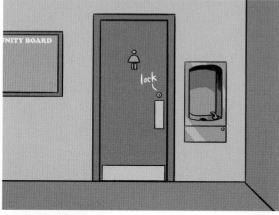

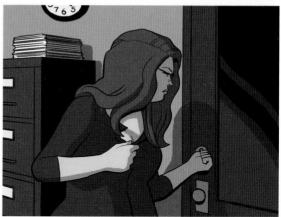

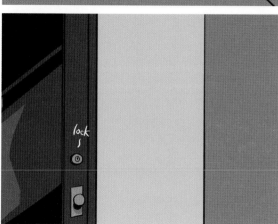

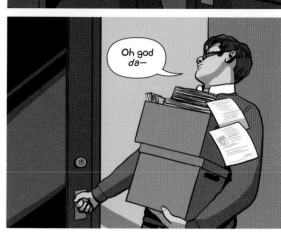

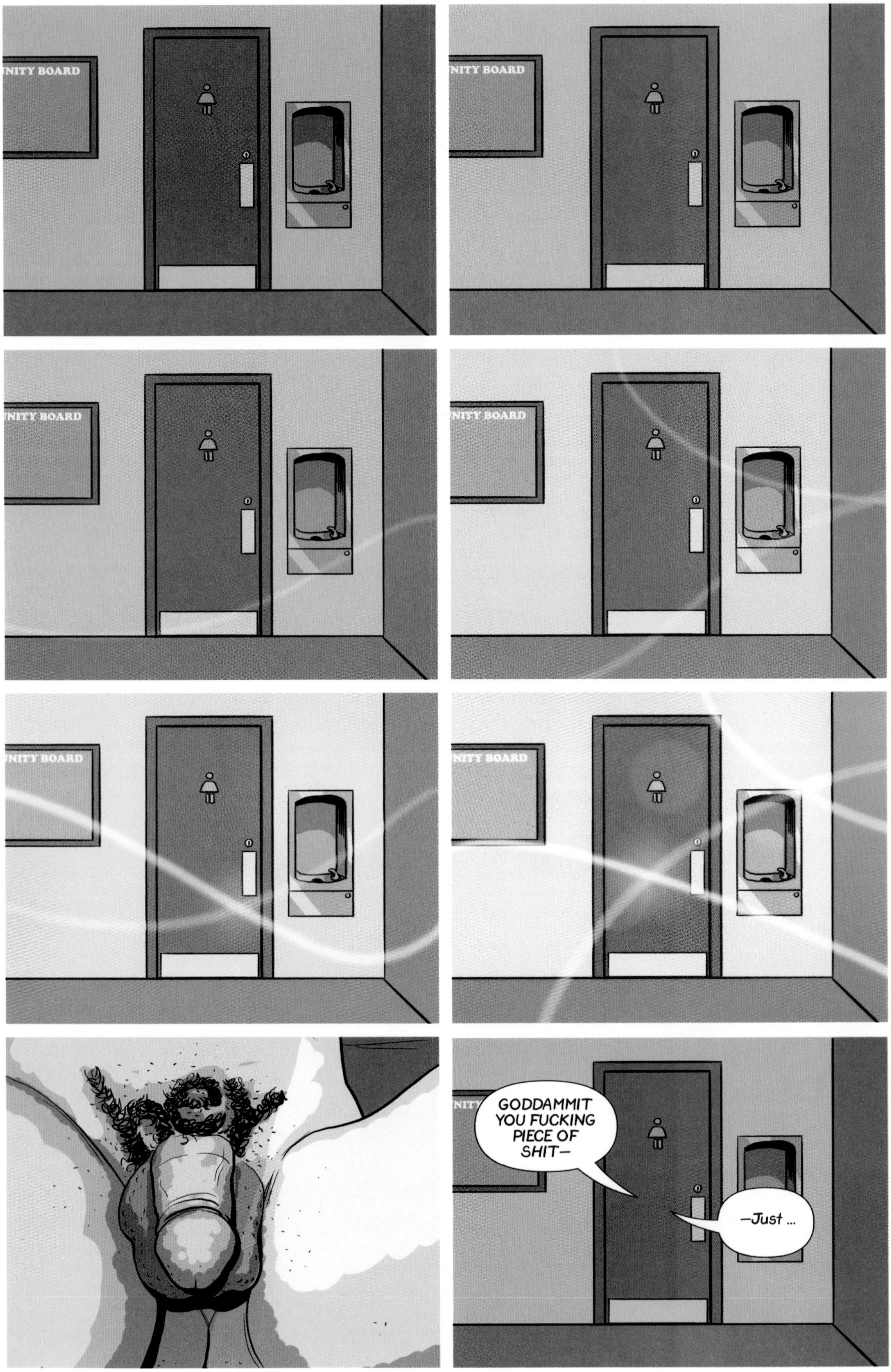
NITY BOARD
NITY BOARD
NITY BOARD
NITY BOARD
NITY BOARD
NITY BOARD
GODDAMMIT YOU FUCKING PIECE OF SHIT—
—Just ...

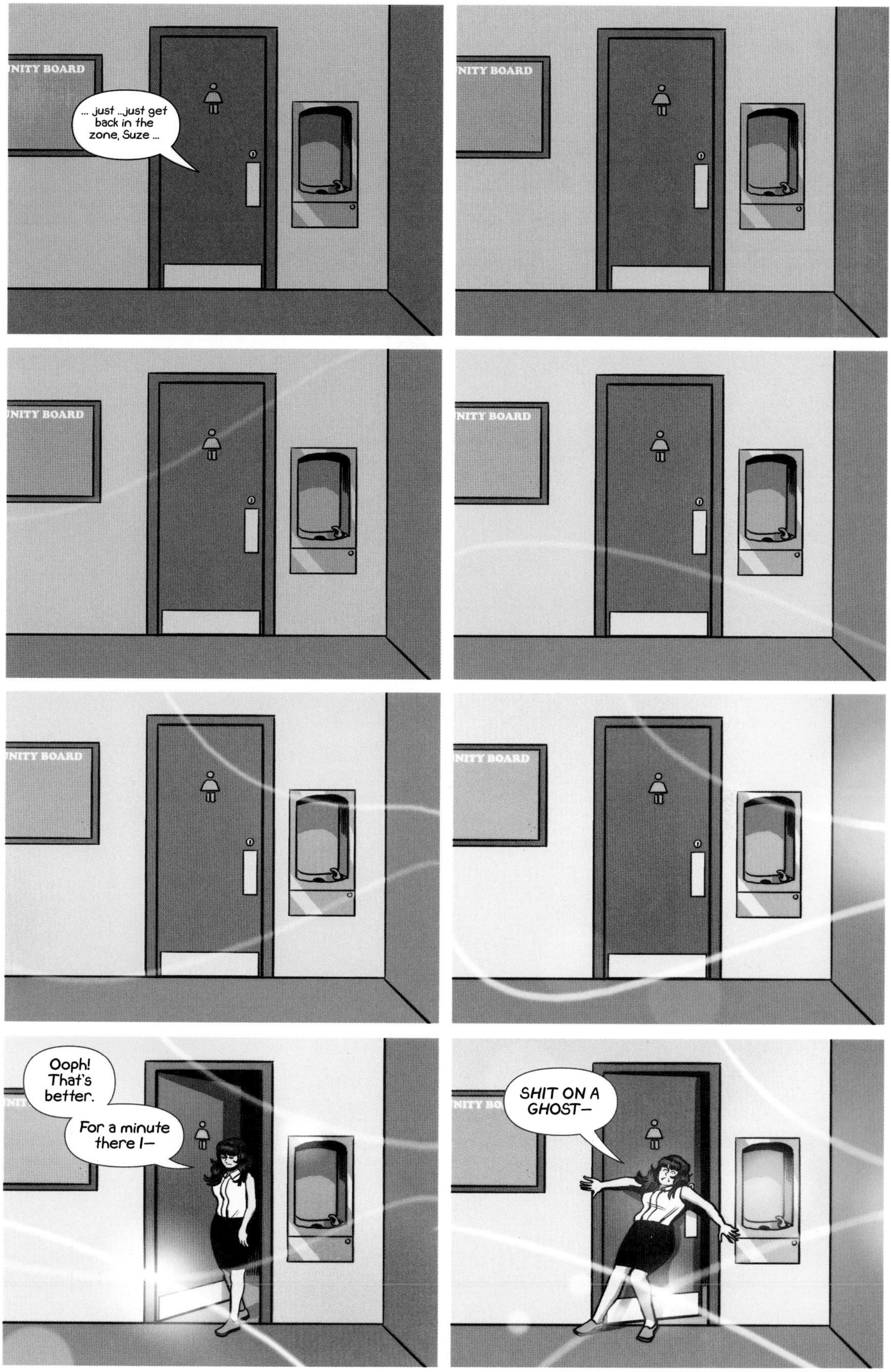

NITY BOARD
... just ...just get back in the zone, Suze ...
Ooph! That's better.
For a minute there I—
SHIT ON A GHOST—

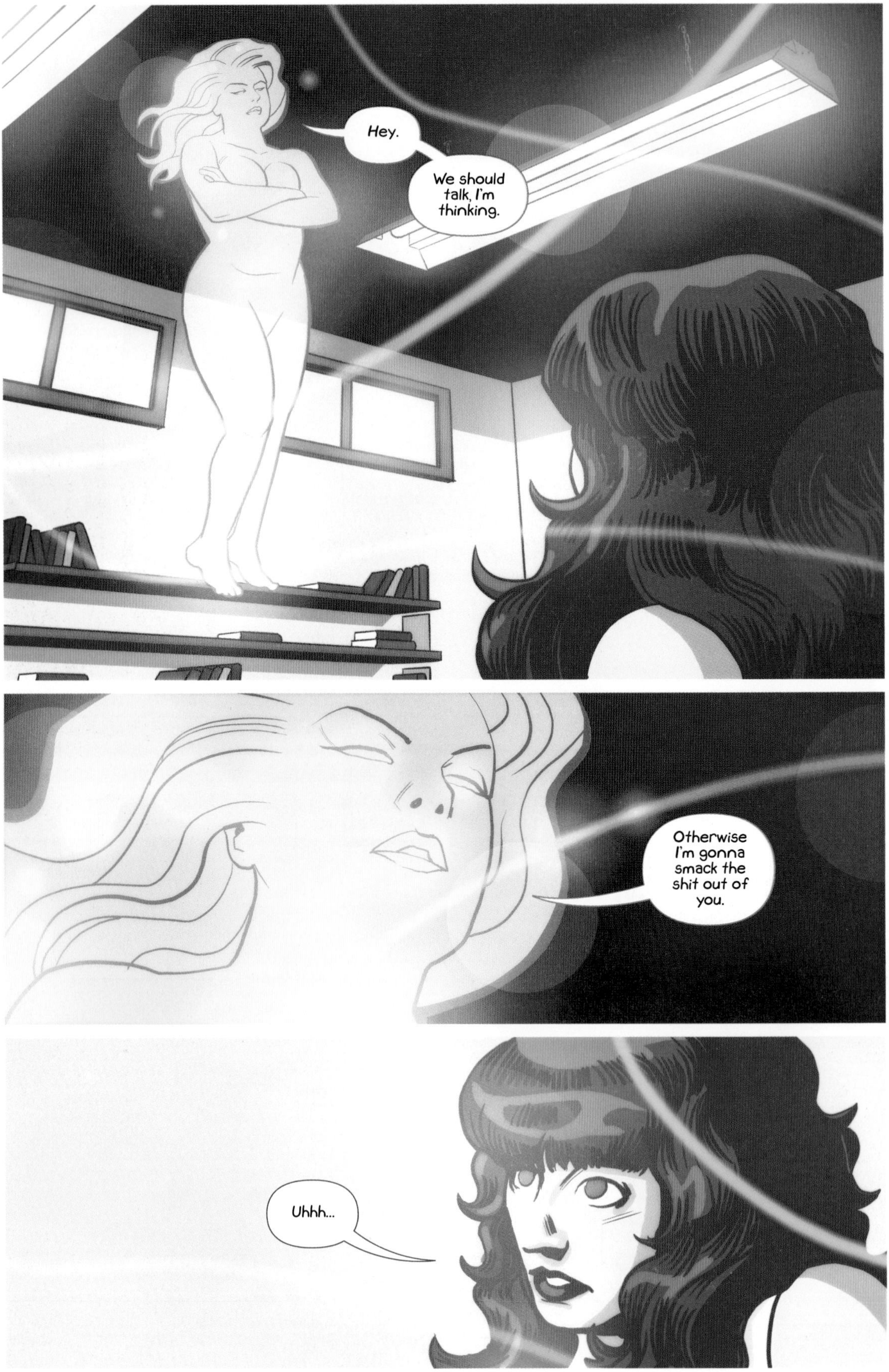
Hey.
We should talk, I'm thinking.
Otherwise I'm gonna smack the shit out of you.
Uhhh...

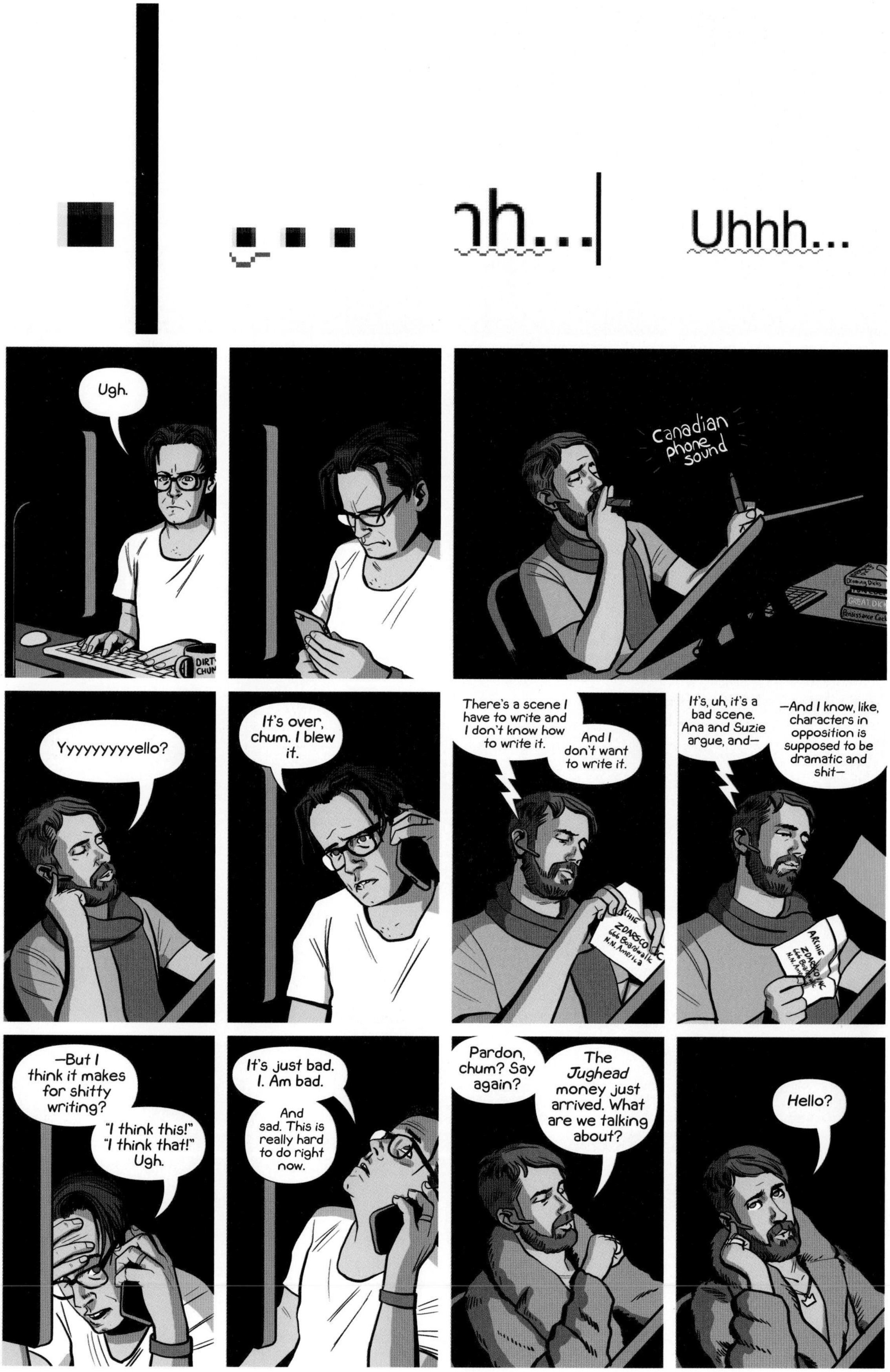

Uhhh...
Ugh.
Canadian phone sound
Yyyyyyyyyello?
It's over, chum. I blew it.
There's a scene I have to write and I don't know how to write it.
And I don't want to write it.
ARCHIE ZDARSCO INC 666 Boardwalk N.N. America
It's, uh, it's a bad scene. Ana and Suzie argue, and—
—And I know, like, characters in opposition is supposed to be dramatic and shit—
—But I think it makes for shitty writing?
"I think this!" "I think that!" Ugh.
It's just bad. I. Am bad.
And sad. This is really hard to do right now.
Pardon, chum? Say again?
The *Jughead* money just arrived. What are we talking about?
Hello?

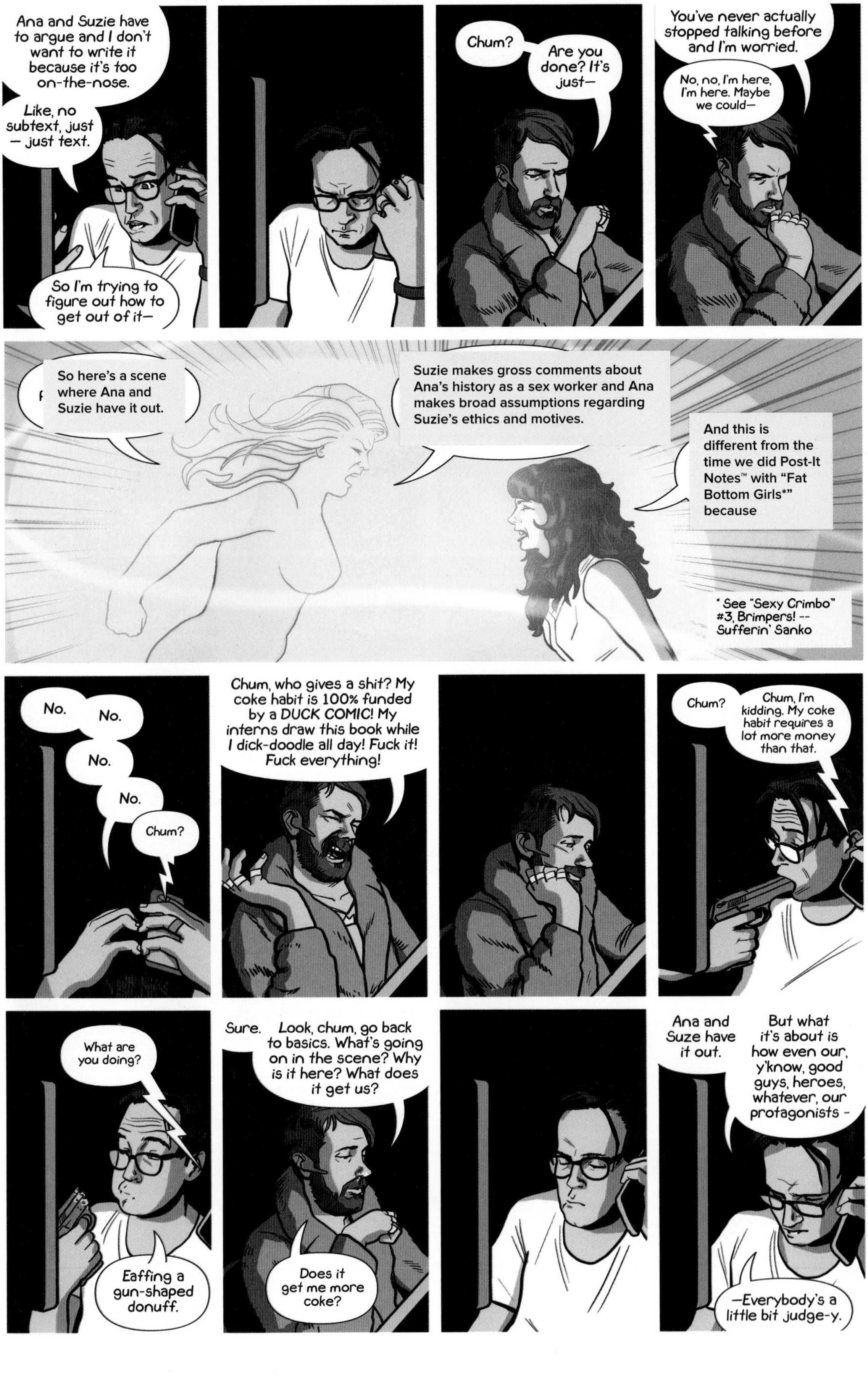
Ana and Suzie have to argue and I don't want to write it because it's too on-the-nose.
Like, no subtext, just — just text.
So I'm trying to figure out how to get out of it—
Chum?
Are you done? It's just—
You've never actually stopped talking before and I'm worried.
No, no, I'm here, I'm here. Maybe we could—
So here's a scene where Ana and Suzie have it out.
Suzie makes gross comments about Ana's history as a sex worker and Ana makes broad assumptions regarding Suzie's ethics and motives.
And this is different from the time we did Post-It Notes™ with "Fat Bottom Girls*" because
* See "Sexy Crimbo" #3, Brimpers! -- Sufferin' Sanko
No.
No.
No.
No.
Chum?
Chum, who gives a shit? My coke habit is 100% funded by a DUCK COMIC! My interns draw this book while I dick-doodle all day! Fuck it! Fuck everything!
Chum?
Chum, I'm kidding. My coke habit requires a lot more money than that.
What are you doing?
Eaffing a gun-shaped donuff.
Sure.
Look, chum, go back to basics. What's going on in the scene? Why is it here? What does it get us?
Does it get me more coke?
Ana and Suze have it out.
But what it's about is how even our, y'know, good guys, heroes, whatever, our protagonists -
—Everybody's a little bit judge-y.

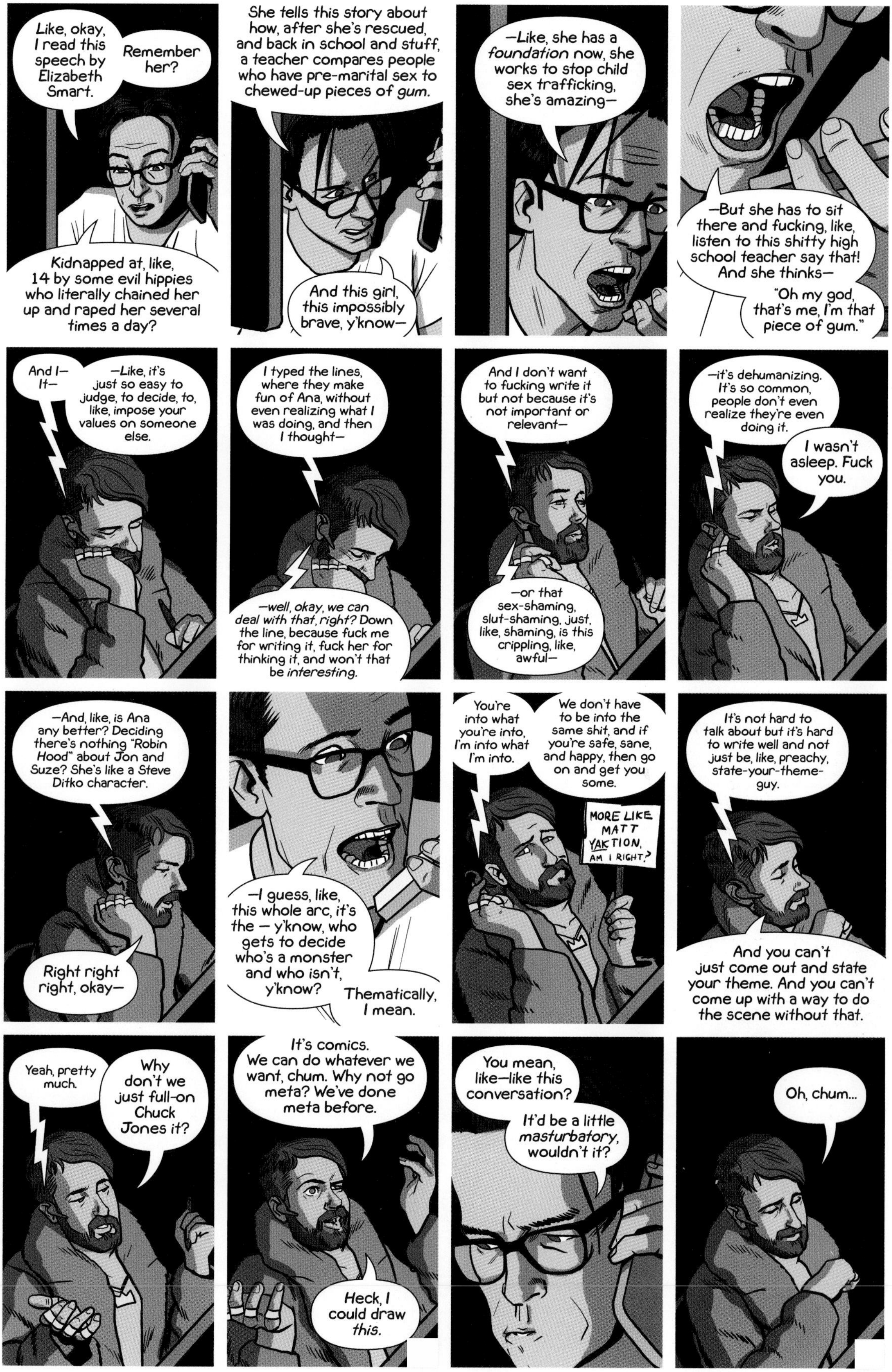
Like, okay, I read this speech by Elizabeth Smart.
Remember her?
Kidnapped at, like, 14 by some evil hippies who literally chained her up and raped her several times a day?
She tells this story about how, after she's rescued, and back in school and stuff, a teacher compares people who have pre-marital sex to chewed-up pieces of *gum*.
And this girl, this impossibly brave, y'know—
—Like, she has a *foundation* now, she works to stop child sex trafficking, she's amazing—
—But she has to sit there and fucking, like, listen to this shitty high school teacher say that! And she thinks—
"Oh my god, that's me, I'm that piece of gum."
And I— It—
—Like, it's just so easy to judge, to decide, to, like, impose your values on someone else.
I typed the lines, where they make fun of Ana, without even realizing what I was doing, and then I thought—
—well, okay, we can deal with that, right? Down the line, because fuck me for writing it, fuck her for thinking it, and won't that be *interesting*.
And I don't want to fucking write it but not because it's not important or relevant—
—or that sex-shaming, slut-shaming, just, like, shaming, is this crippling, like, awful—
—it's dehumanizing. It's so common, people don't even realize they're even doing it.
I wasn't asleep. Fuck you.
—And, like, is Ana any better? Deciding there's nothing "Robin Hood" about Jon and Suze? She's like a Steve Ditko character.
Right right right, okay—
—I guess, like, this whole arc, it's the — y'know, who gets to decide who's a monster and who isn't, y'know?
Thematically, I mean.
You're into what you're into, I'm into what I'm into.
We don't have to be into the same shit, and if you're safe, sane, and happy, then go on and get you some.
MORE LIKE MATT YAKTION, AM I RIGHT?
It's not hard to talk about but it's hard to write well and not just be, like, preachy, state-your-theme-guy.
And you can't just come out and state your theme. And you can't come up with a way to do the scene without that.
Yeah, pretty much.
Why don't we just full-on Chuck Jones it?
It's comics. We can do whatever we want, chum. Why not go meta? We've done meta before.
Heck, I could draw *this*.
You mean, like—like this conversation?
It'd be a little *masturbatory*, wouldn't it?
Oh, chum...

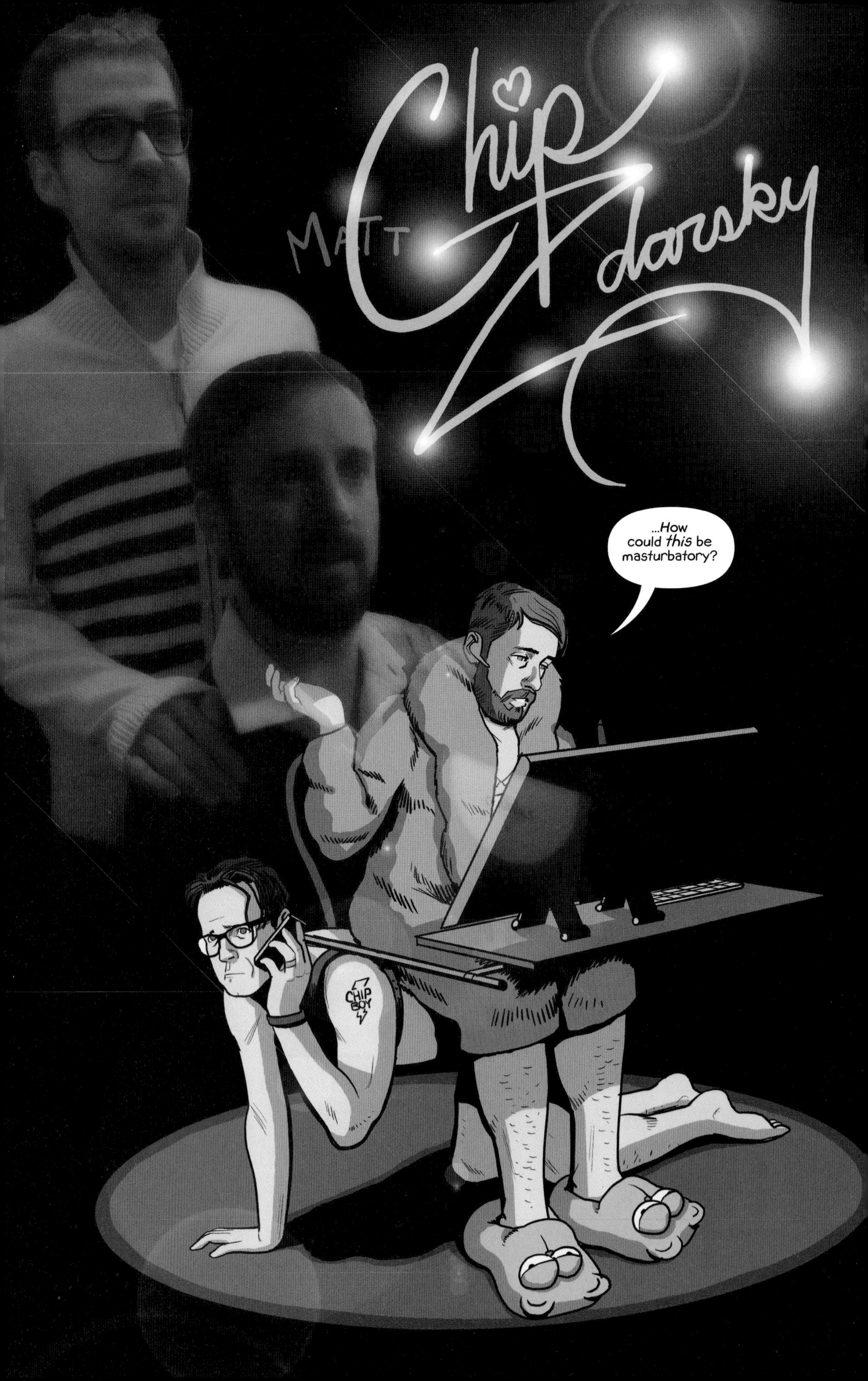
MATT
Chip Zdarsky
...How could *this* be masturbatory?
CHIP BOY

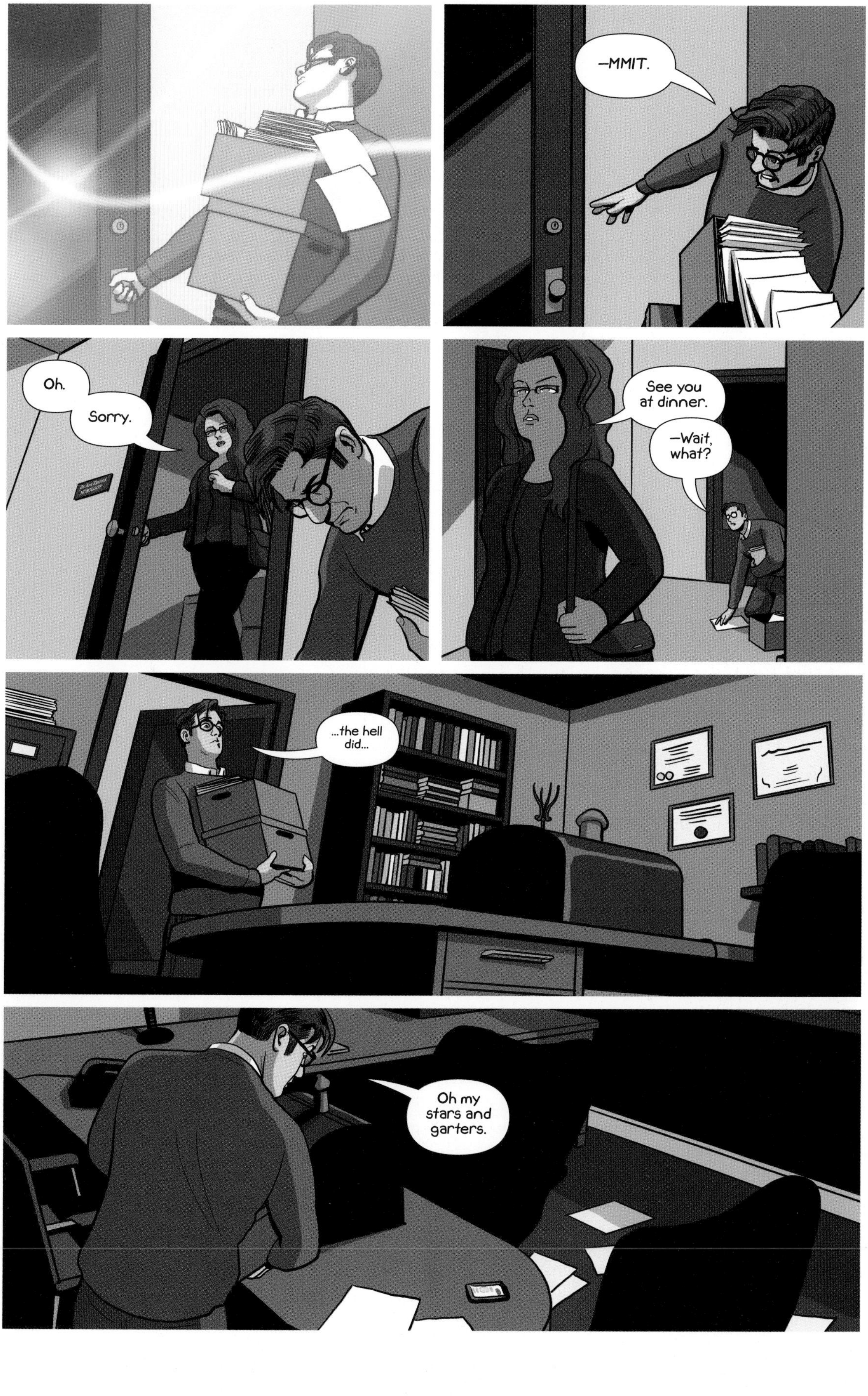
—MMIT.
Oh.
Sorry.
See you at dinner.
—Wait, what?
...the hell did...
Oh my stars and garters.

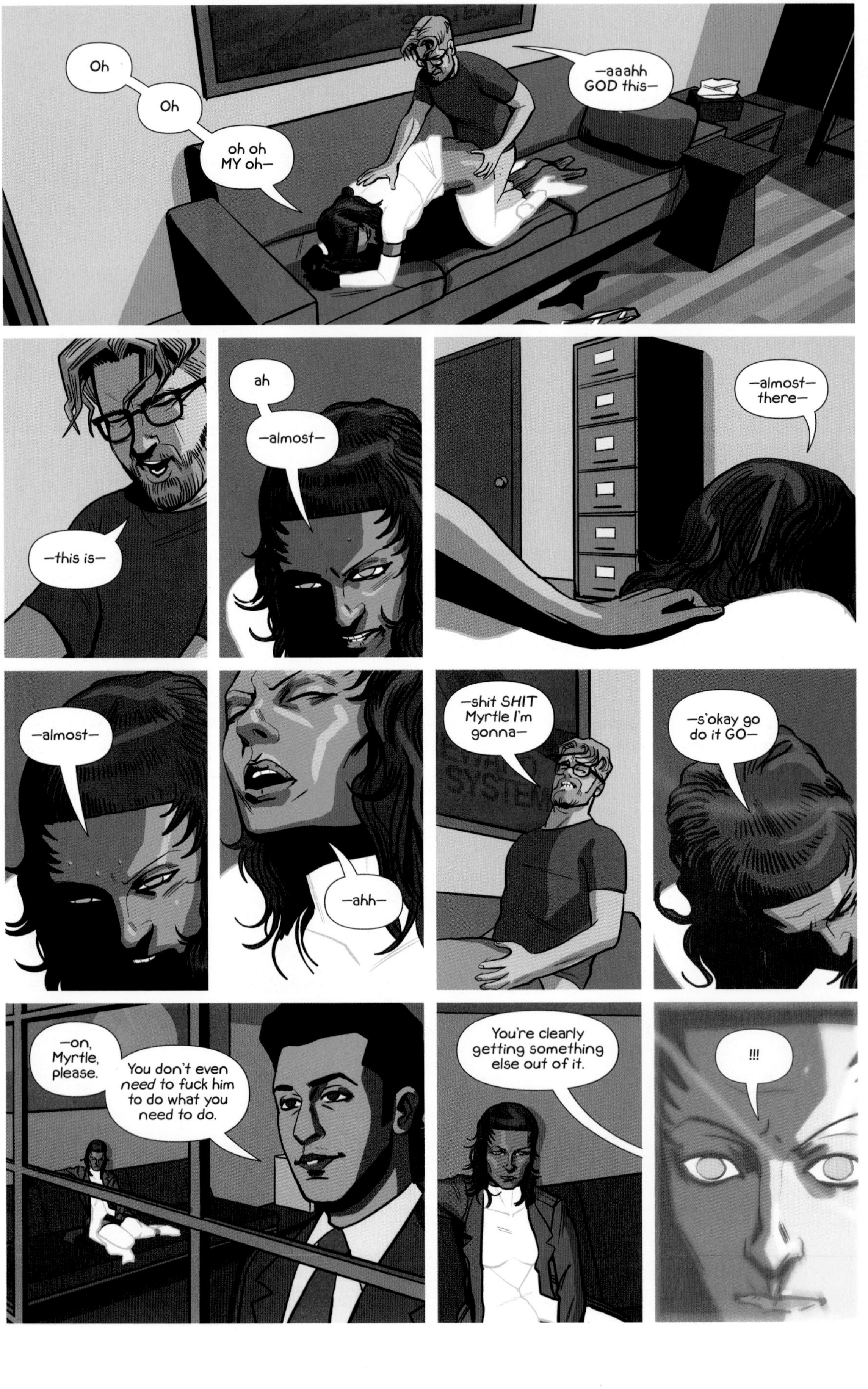
Oh
Oh
oh oh MY oh—
—aaahh GOD this—
—this is—
ah
—almost—
—almost— there—
—almost—
—ahh—
—shit SHIT Myrtle I'm gonna—
—s'okay go do it GO—
—on, Myrtle, please.
You don't even *need* to fuck him to do what you need to do.
You're clearly getting something else out of it.
!!!

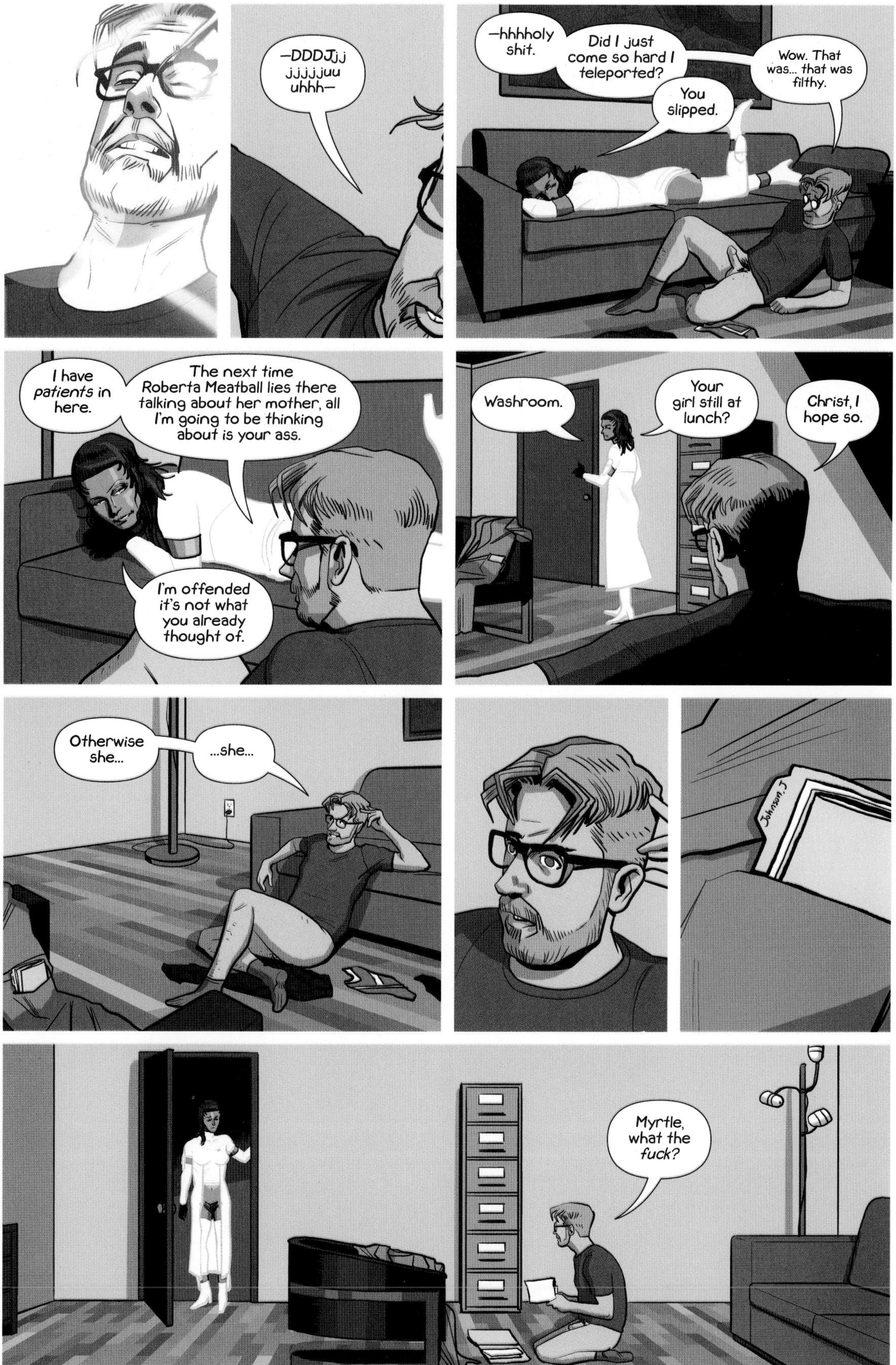

—DDDJjj jjjjjuu uhhh—
—hhhholy shit.
Did I just come so hard I teleported?
You slipped.
Wow. That was... that was filthy.
I have *patients* in here.
The next time Roberta Meatball lies there talking about her mother, all I'm going to be thinking about is your ass.
I'm offended it's not what you already thought of.
Washroom.
Your girl still at lunch?
Christ, I hope so.
Otherwise she...
...she...
Johnson, J
Myrtle, what the *fuck*?

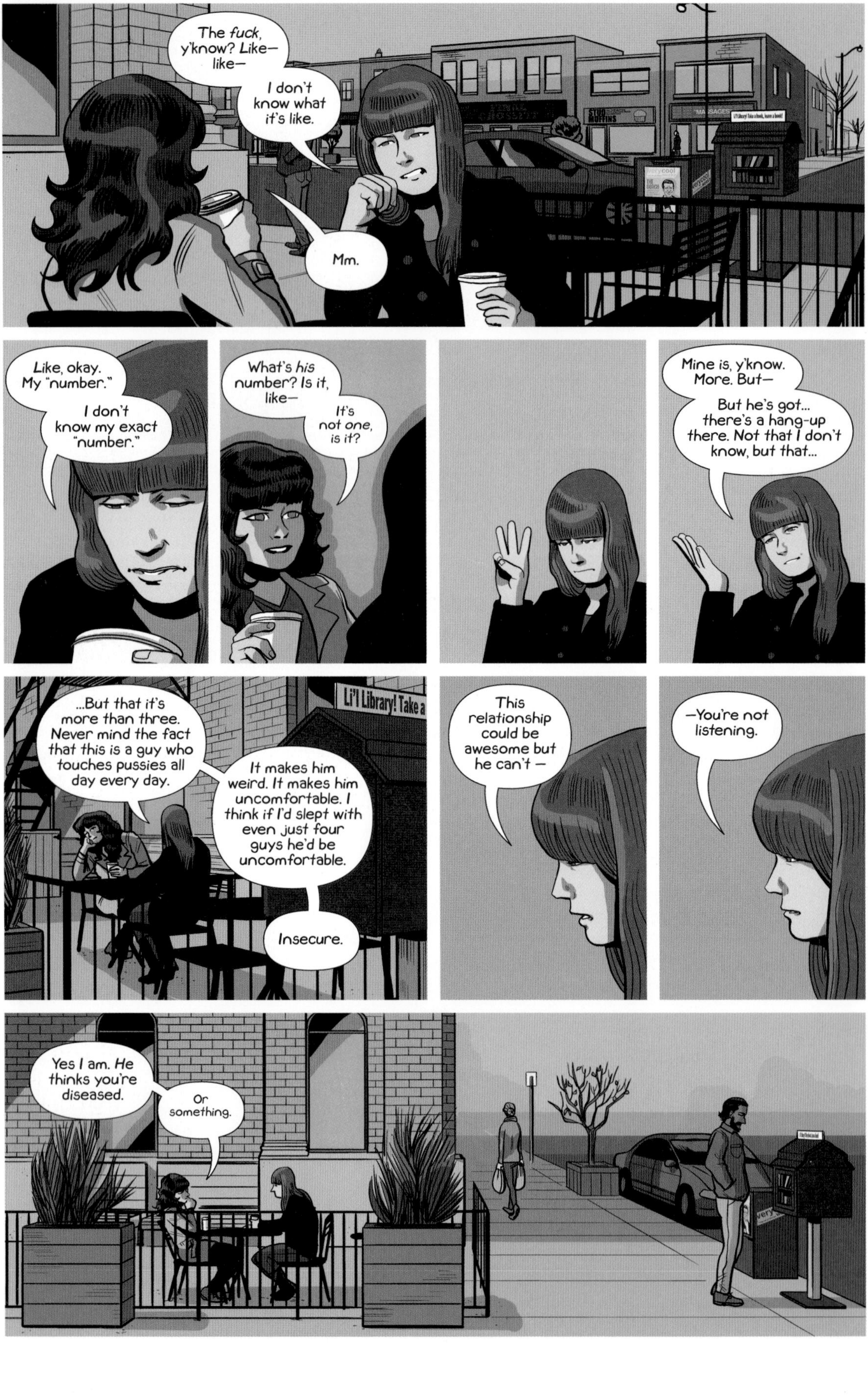

The *fuck*, y'know? Like— like—
I don't know what it's like.
Mm.
Like, okay. My "number."
I don't know my exact "number."
What's *his* number? Is it, like—
It's not one, is it?
Mine is, y'know. More. But—
But he's got... there's a hang-up there. Not that I don't know, but that...
Li'l Library! Take a
...But that it's more than three. Never mind the fact that this is a guy who touches pussies all day every day.
It makes him weird. It makes him uncomfortable. I think if I'd slept with even just four guys he'd be uncomfortable.
Insecure.
This relationship could be awesome but he can't —
—You're not listening.
Yes I am. He thinks you're diseased.
Or something.

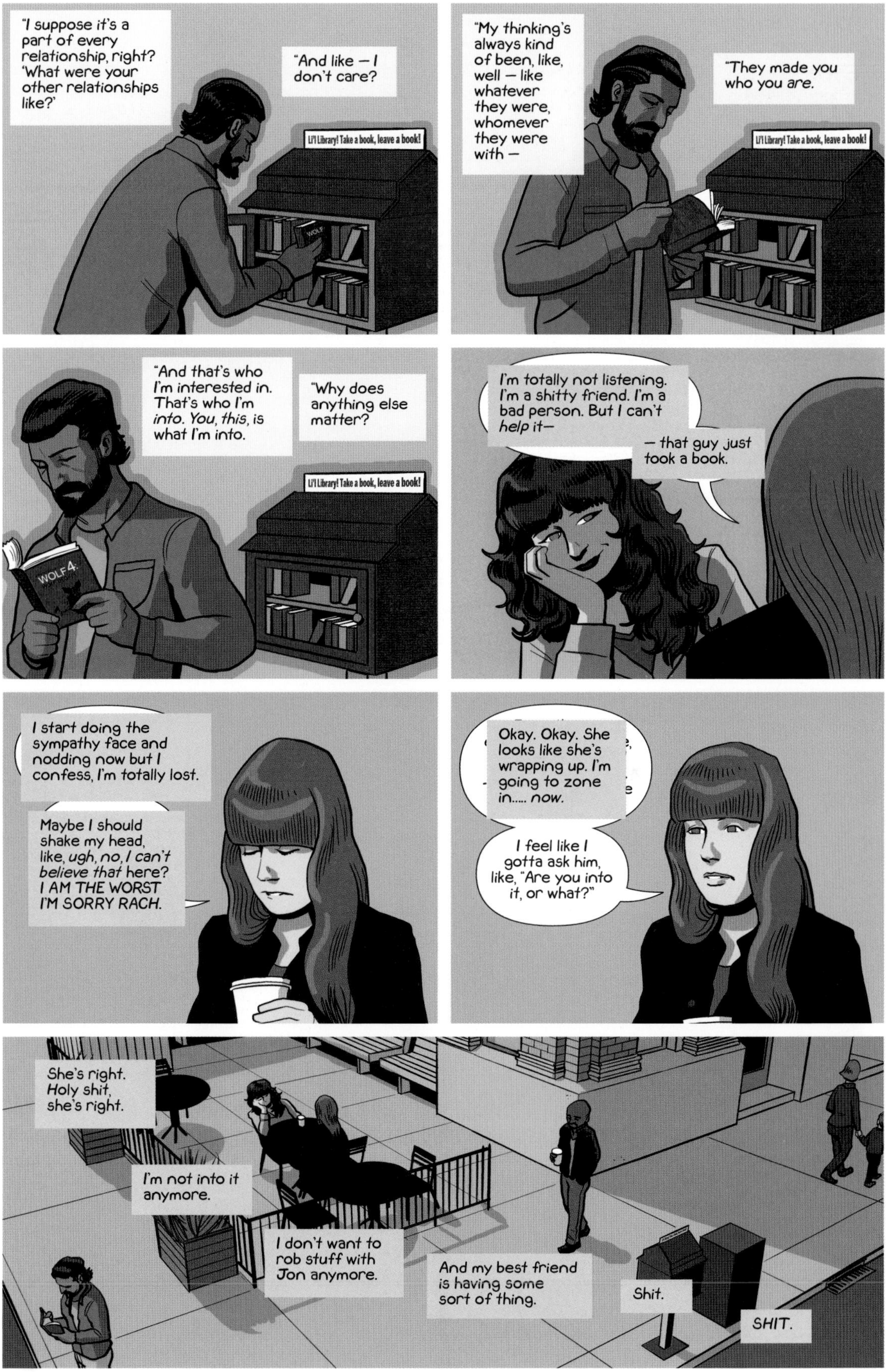
"I suppose it's a part of every relationship, right? 'What were your other relationships like?'
"And like — I don't care?
Li'l Library! Take a book, leave a book!
"My thinking's always kind of been, like, well — like whatever they were, whomever they were with —
"They made you who you *are.*
Li'l Library! Take a book, leave a book!
"And that's who I'm interested in. That's who I'm *into. You, this,* is what I'm into.
"Why does anything else matter?
Li'l Library! Take a book, leave a book!
WOLF 4:
I'm totally not listening. I'm a shitty friend. I'm a bad person. But I can't *help it—*
— that guy just took a book.
I start doing the sympathy face and nodding now but I confess, I'm totally lost.
Maybe I should shake my head, like, *ugh, no, I can't believe that* here? I AM THE WORST I'M SORRY RACH.
Okay. Okay. She looks like she's wrapping up. I'm going to zone in..... *now.*
I feel like I gotta ask him, like, "Are you into it, or what?"
She's right. Holy shit, she's right.
I'm not into it anymore.
I don't want to rob stuff with Jon anymore.
And my best friend is having some sort of thing.
Shit.
SHIT.

15
THE
CREW

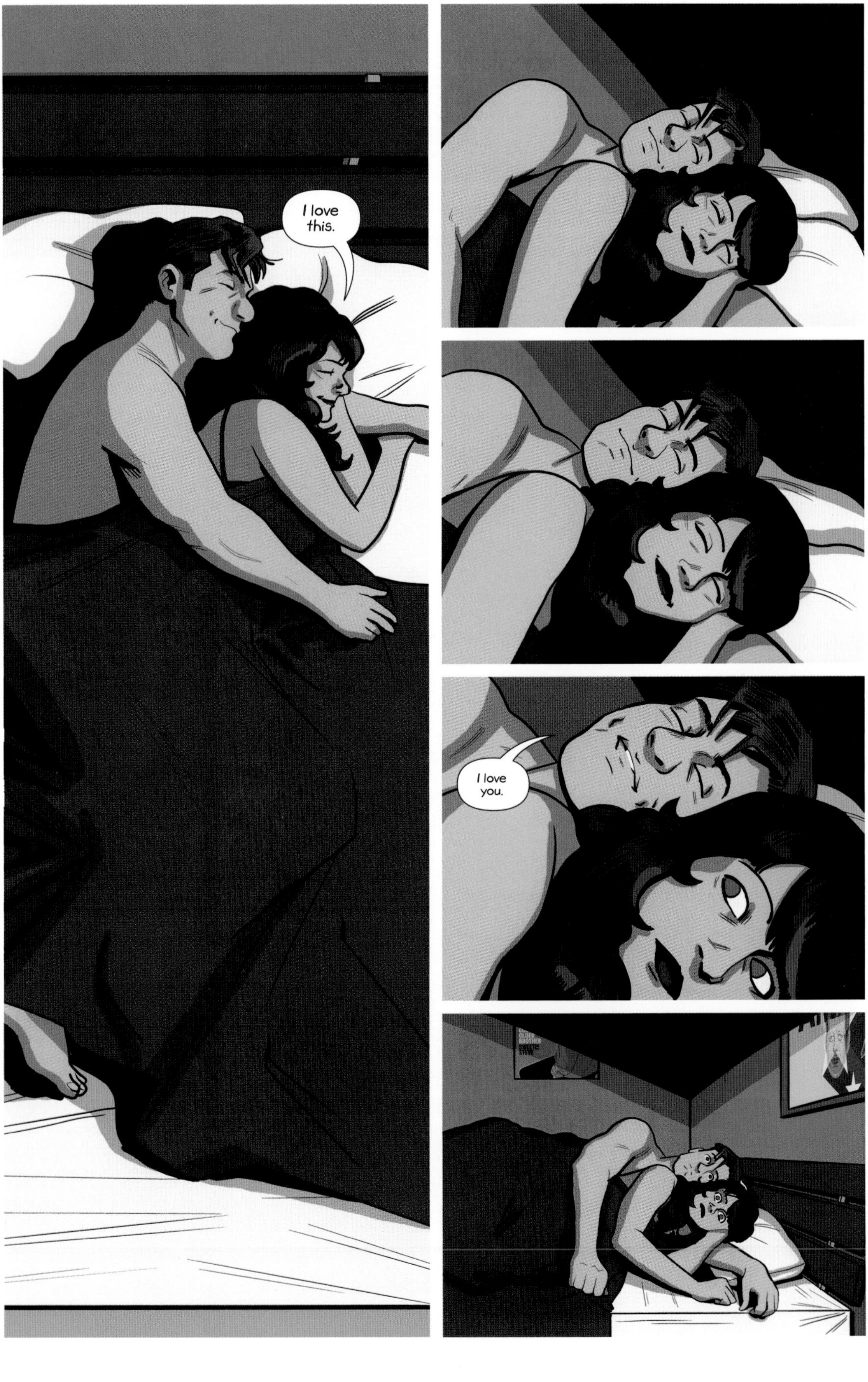
I love this.
I love you.

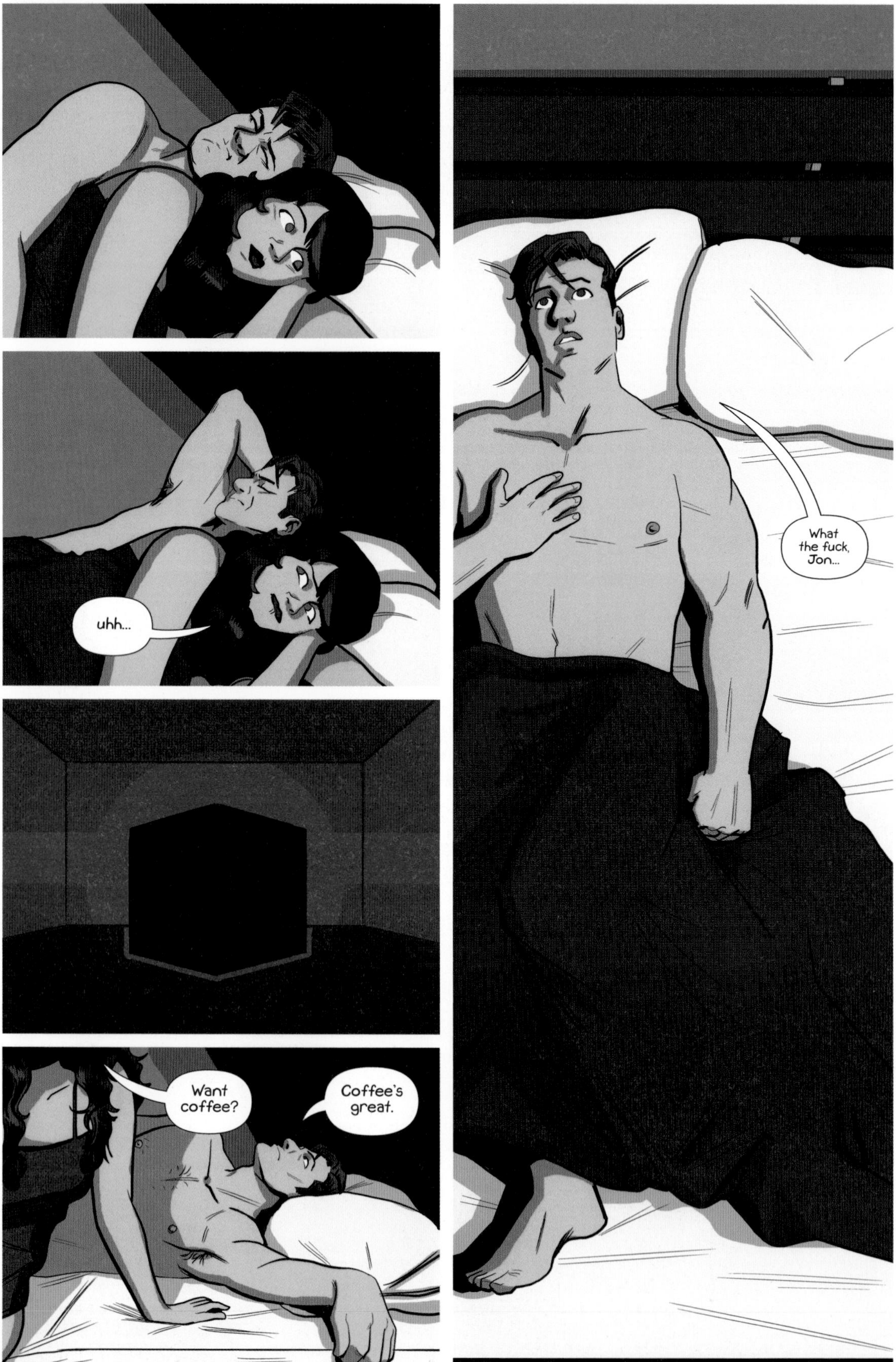
uhh...
Want coffee?
Coffee's great.
What the fuck, Jon...

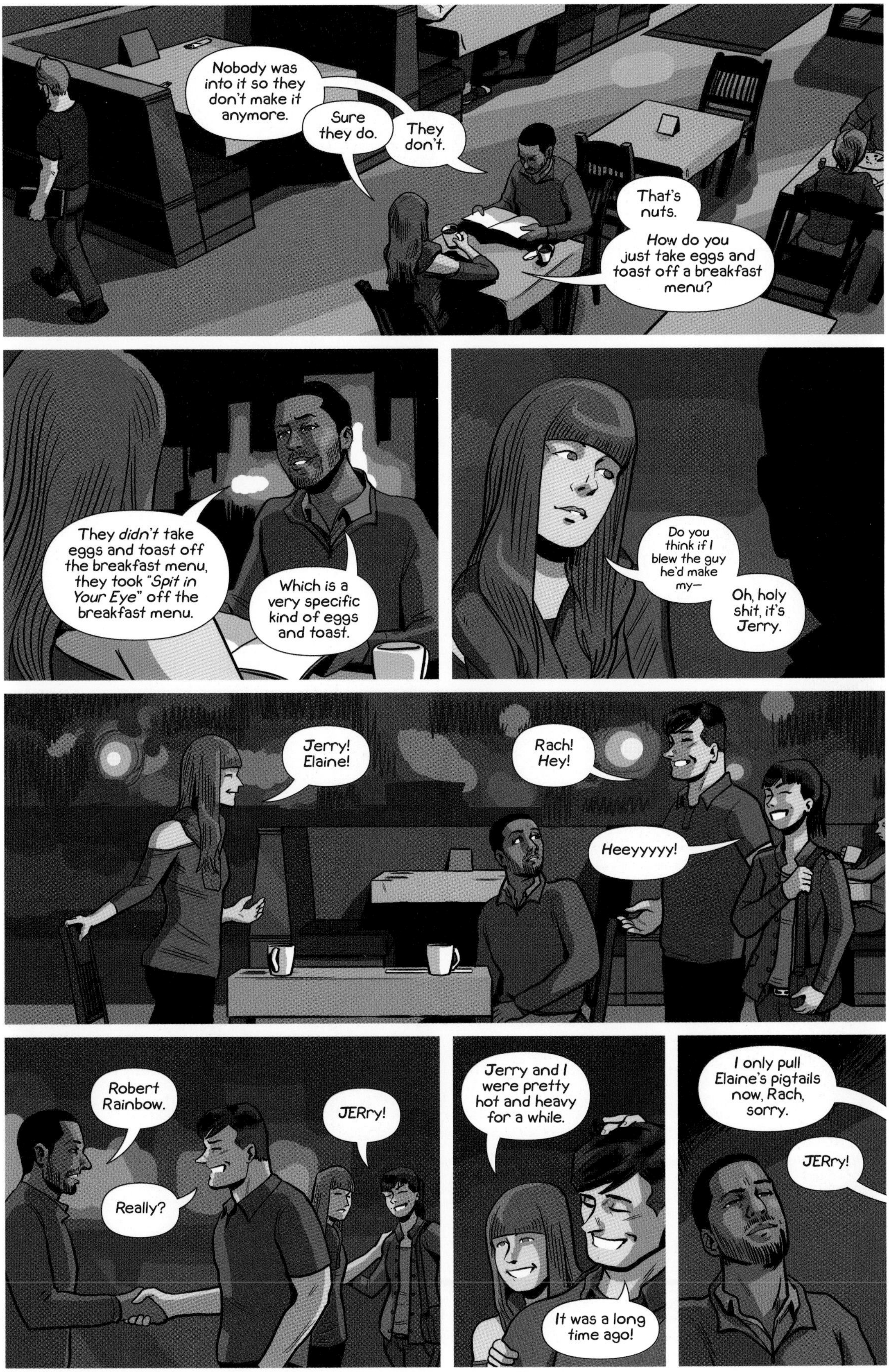
Nobody was into it so they don't make it anymore.
Sure they do.
They don't.
That's nuts.
How do you just take eggs and toast off a breakfast menu?
They *didn't* take eggs and toast off the breakfast menu, they took *"Spit in Your Eye"* off the breakfast menu.
Which is a very specific kind of eggs and toast.
Do you think if I blew the guy he'd make my—
Oh, holy shit, it's Jerry.
Jerry! Elaine!
Rach! Hey!
Heeyyyyy!
Robert Rainbow.
Really?
JERry!
Jerry and I were pretty hot and heavy for a while.
It was a long time ago!
I only pull Elaine's pigtails now, Rach, sorry.
JERry!

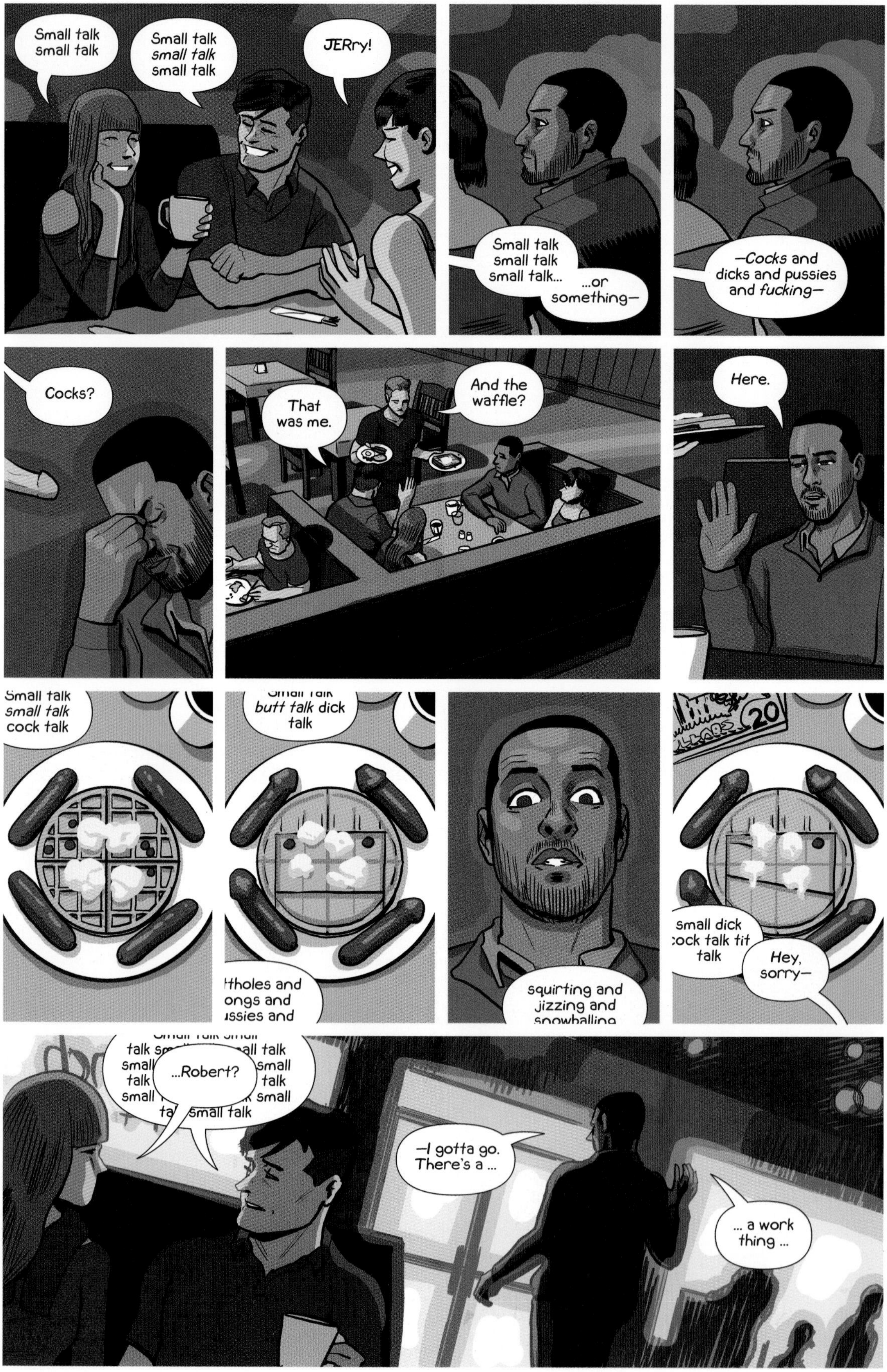

Small talk small talk
Small talk *small talk* small talk
JERry!
Small talk small talk small talk...
...or something—
—*Cocks* and dicks and pussies and *fucking*—
Cocks?
That was me.
And the waffle?
Here.
Small talk *small talk* cock talk
butt talk dick talk
squirting and jizzing and
small dick cock talk tit talk
Hey, sorry—
...Robert?
—I gotta go. There's a ...
... a work thing ...

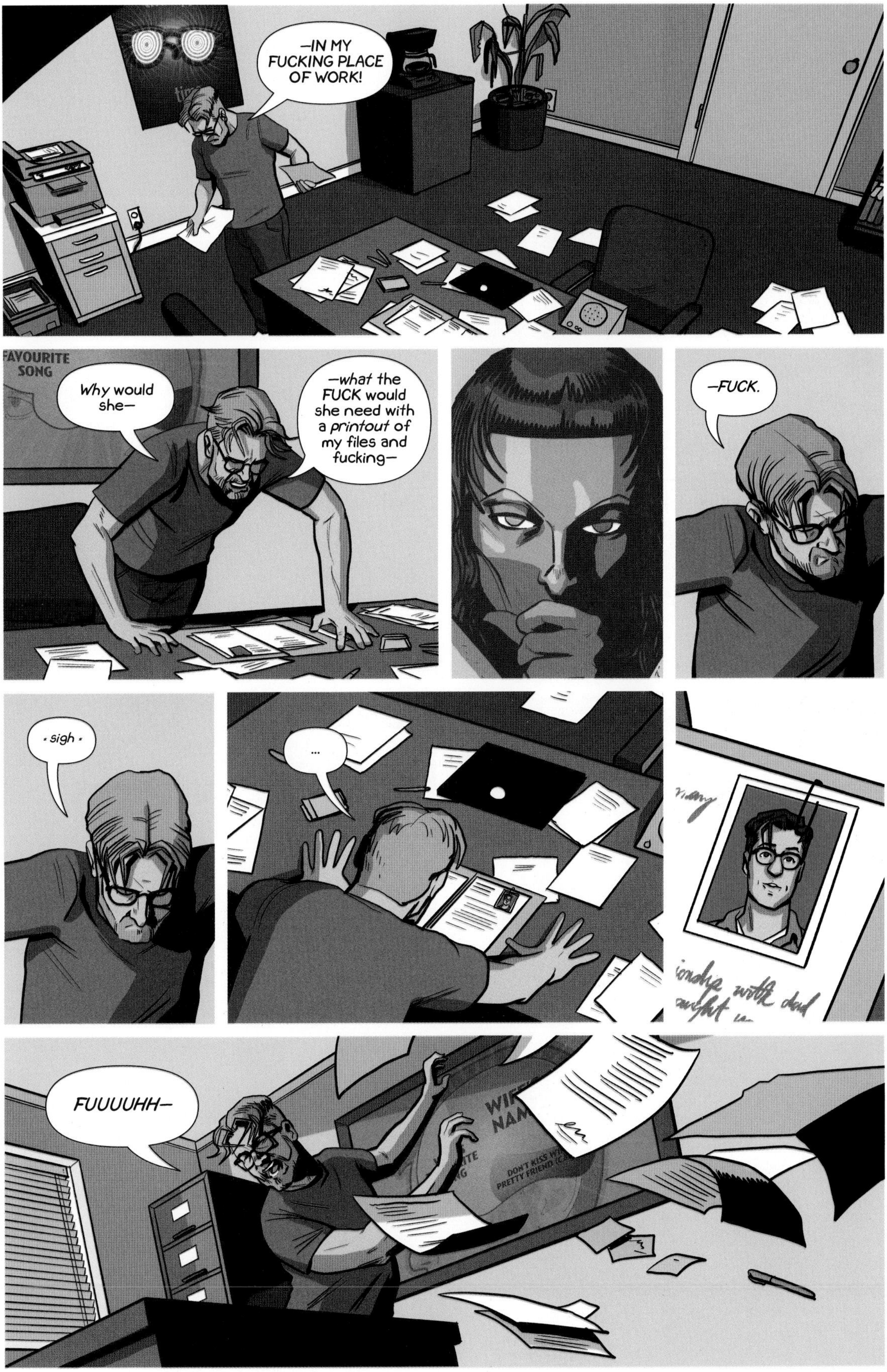
–IN MY FUCKING PLACE OF WORK!
FAVOURITE SONG
Why would she–
–what the FUCK would she need with a *printout* of my files and fucking–
–FUCK.
* sigh *
...
FUUUUHH–

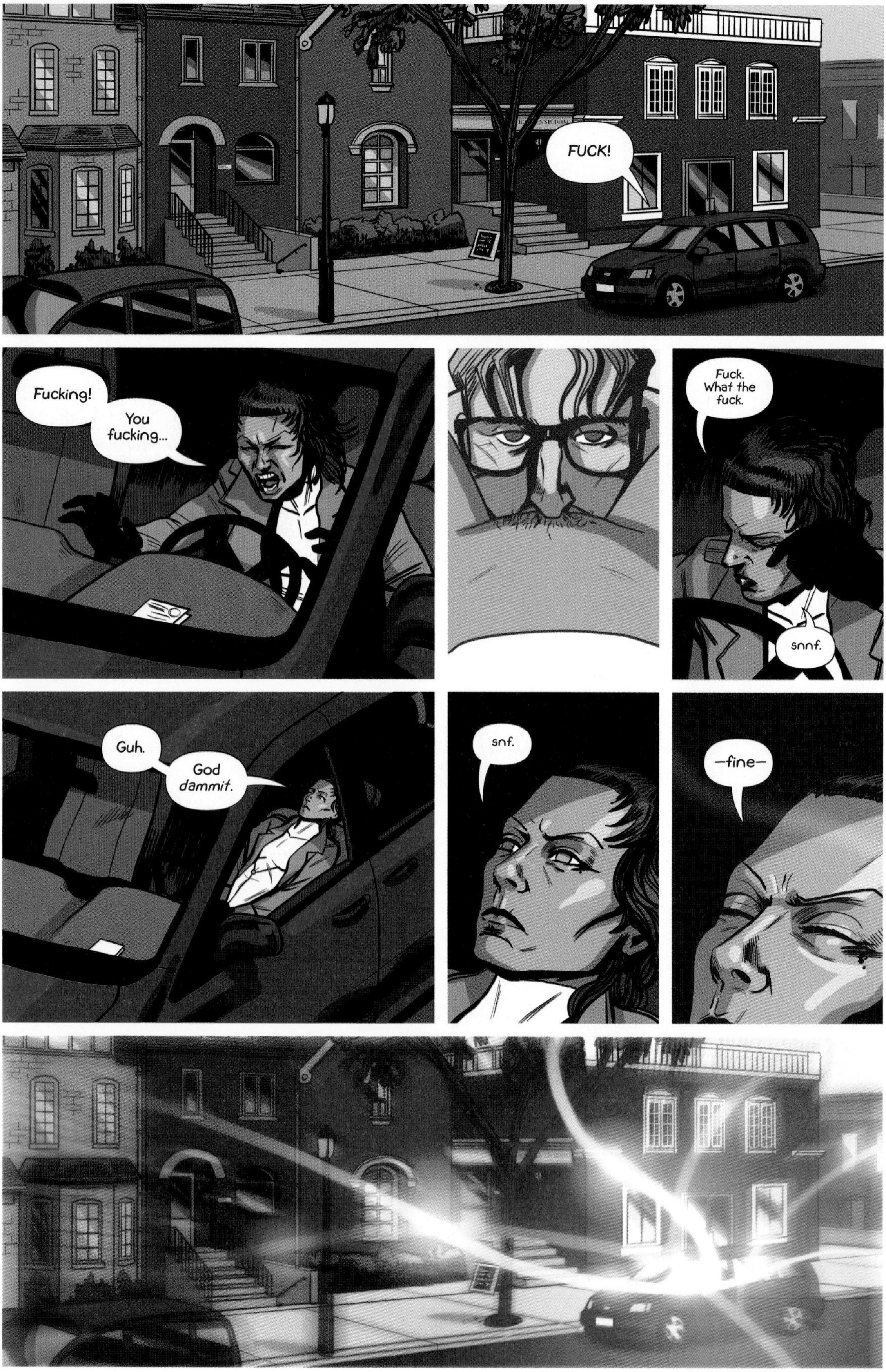
FUCK!
Fucking!
You fucking...
Fuck. What the fuck.
snnf.
Guh.
God dammit.
snf.
—fine—

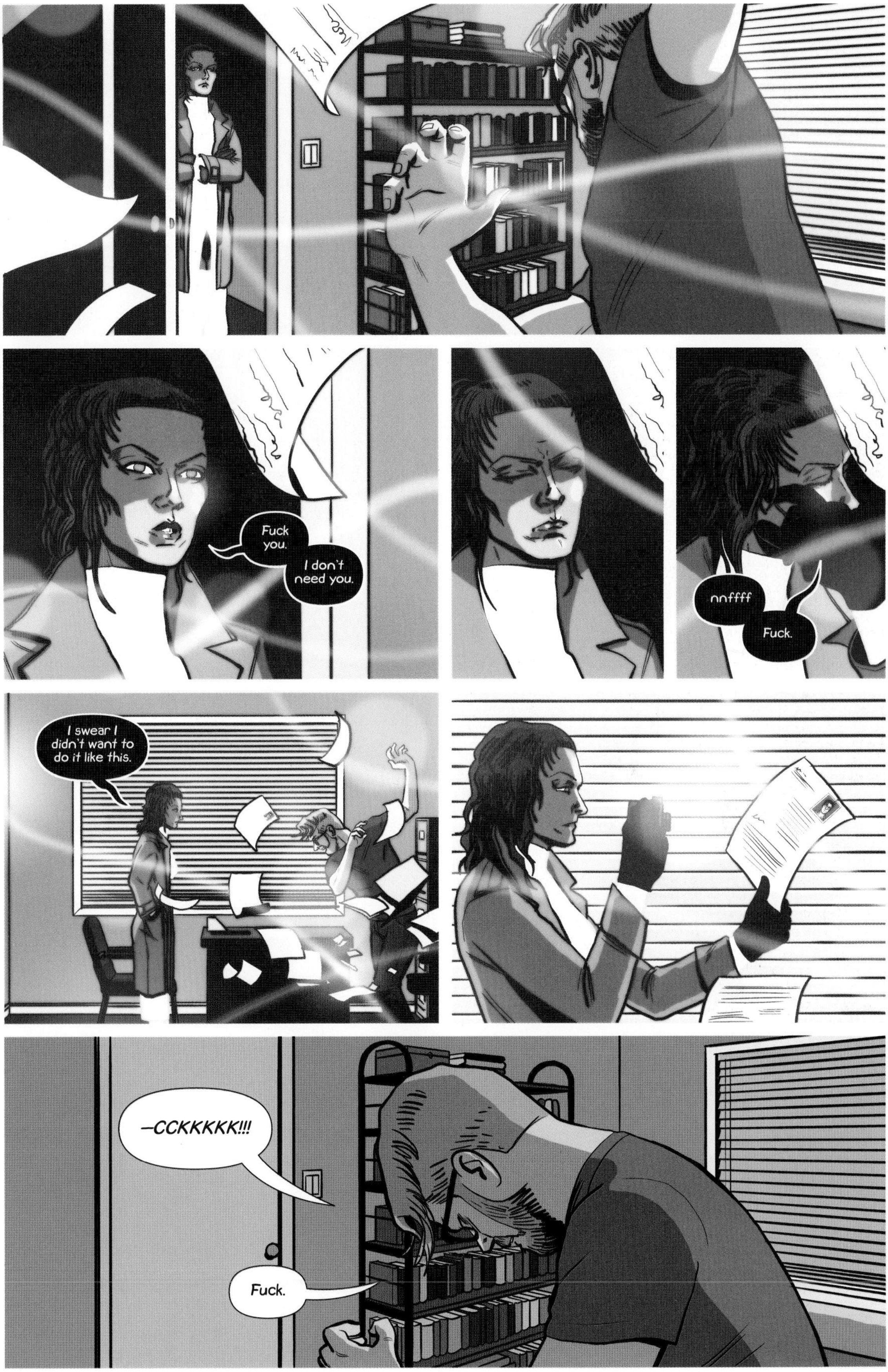

Fuck you.
I don't need you.
nnffff
Fuck.
I swear I didn't want to do it like this.
–CCKKKKK!!!
Fuck.

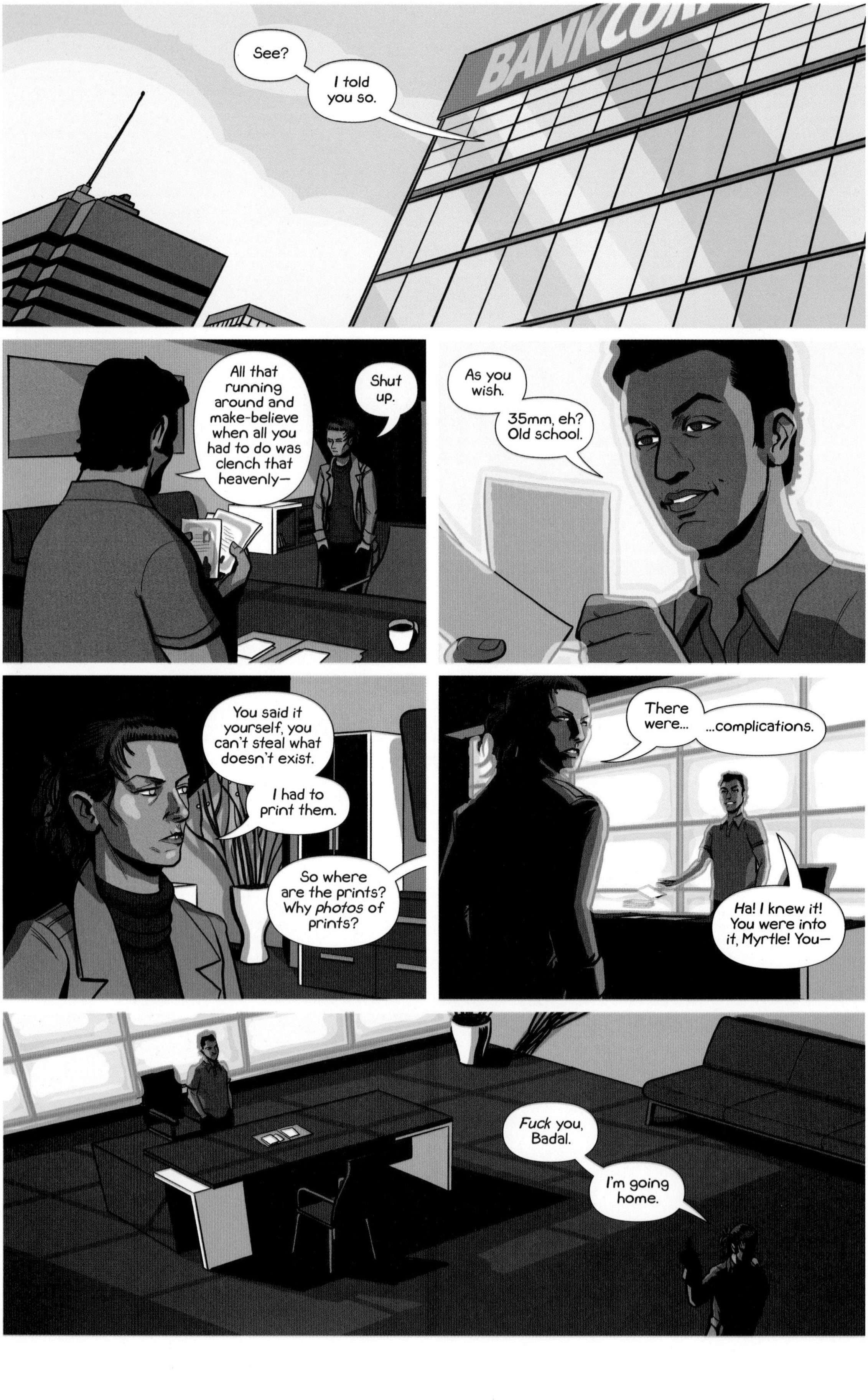
BANKCORP
See?
I told you so.
All that running around and make-believe when all you had to do was clench that heavenly—
Shut up.
As you wish.
35mm, eh? Old school.
You said it yourself, you can't steal what doesn't exist.
I had to print them.
So where are the prints? Why *photos* of prints?
There were...
...complications.
Ha! I knew it! You were into it, Myrtle! You—
Fuck you, Badal.
I'm going home.

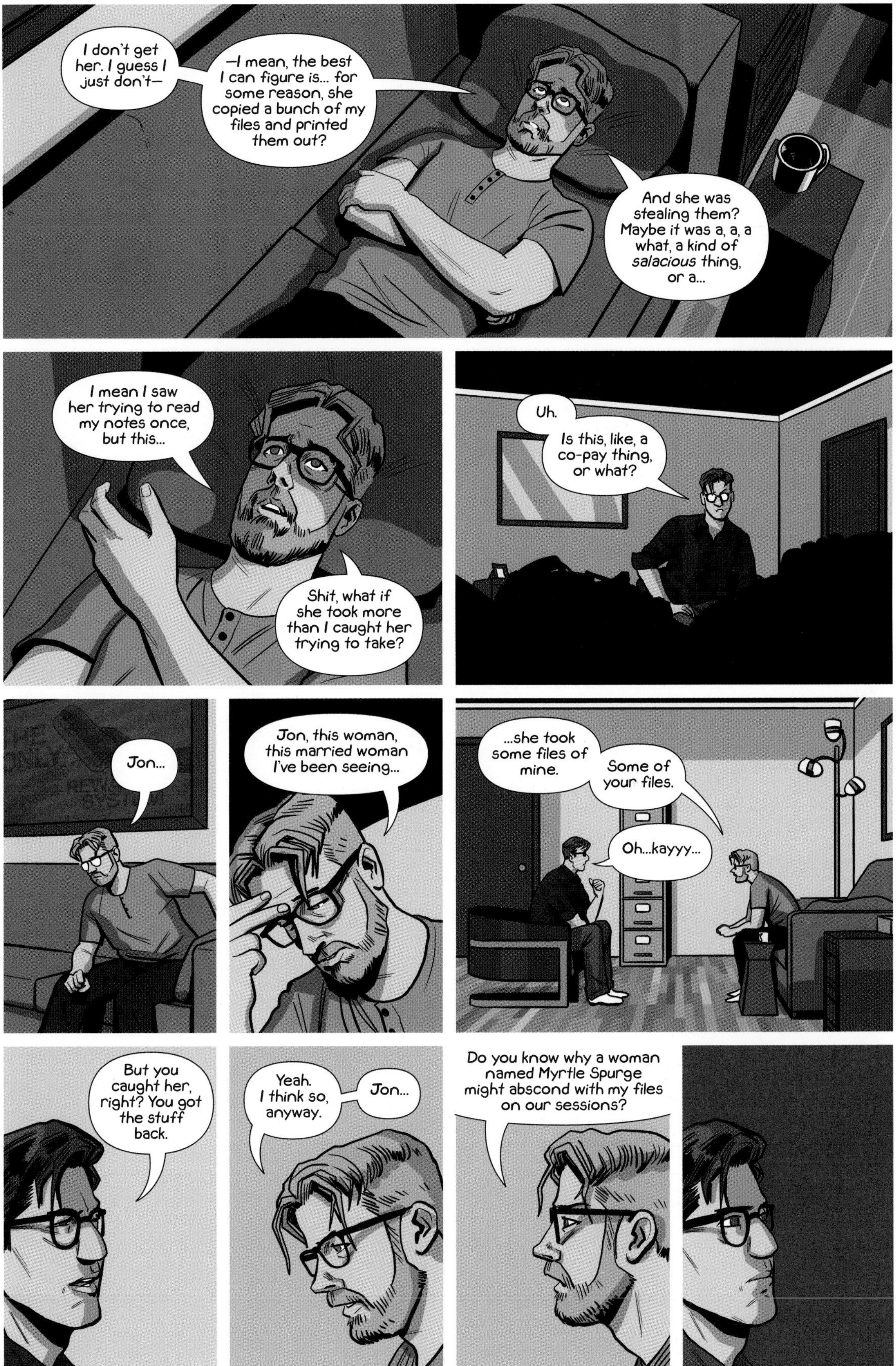

I don't get her. I guess I just don't—
—I mean, the best I can figure is... for some reason, she copied a bunch of my files and printed them out?
And she was stealing them? Maybe it was a, a, a what, a kind of *salacious* thing, or a...
I mean I saw her trying to read my notes once, but this...
Shit, what if she took more than I caught her trying to take?
Uh.
Is this, like, a co-pay thing, or what?
Jon...
Jon, this woman, this married woman I've been seeing...
...she took some files of mine.
Some of your files.
Oh...kayyy...
But you caught her, right? You got the stuff back.
Yeah. I think so, anyway.
Jon...
Do you know why a woman named Myrtle Spurge might abscond with my files on our sessions?

No.

Really?

Because you looked like you shit your pants just then.

Something you want to tell me?

Pshh. Please.

Yeah.

Yeah you shit your pants, yeah there's something you want to tell me, or yeah really?

My files, like—like my, our, our, like—

The stuff we talk about.

Yes.

Like, like, the—my—

Like all the stuff I told you, all the—

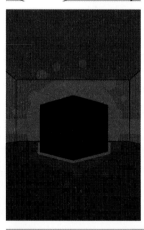

Yes.

She stole my files on all our sessions. Or tried to.

Everything is fine and I'm totally fine.

It's nothing. This is fine.

I am going to leave now.

I am going to go.

Jon, wait—

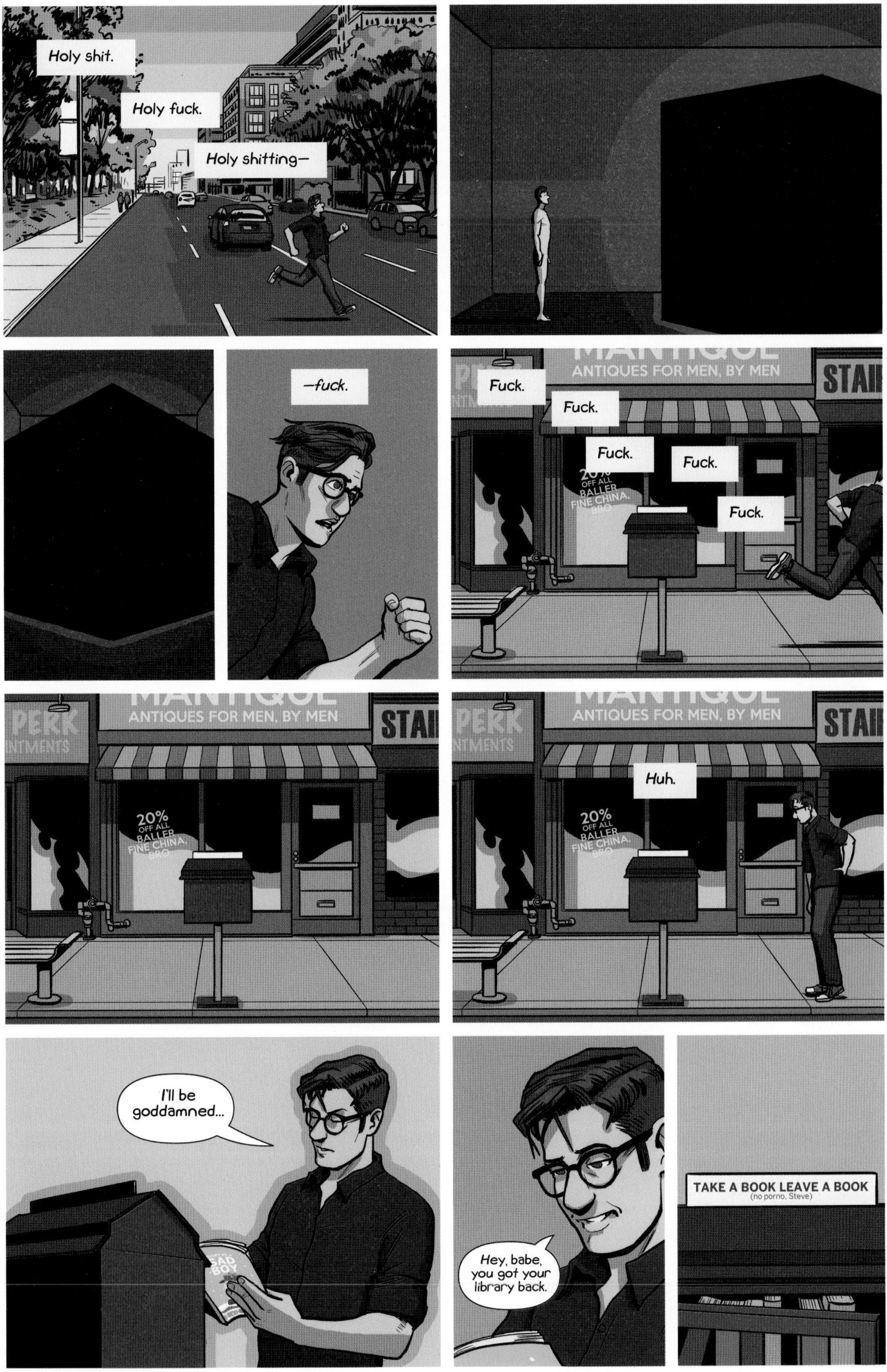
Holy shit.
Holy fuck.
Holy shitting—
—fuck.
ANTIQUES FOR MEN, BY MEN
Fuck.
Fuck.
Fuck.
Fuck.
Fuck.
ANTIQUES FOR MEN, BY MEN
PERK
20% OFF ALL BALLER FINE CHINA, BRO
ANTIQUES FOR MEN, BY MEN
Huh.
I'll be goddamned...
SAD BOY
Hey, babe, you got your library back.
TAKE A BOOK LEAVE A BOOK
(no porno, Steve)

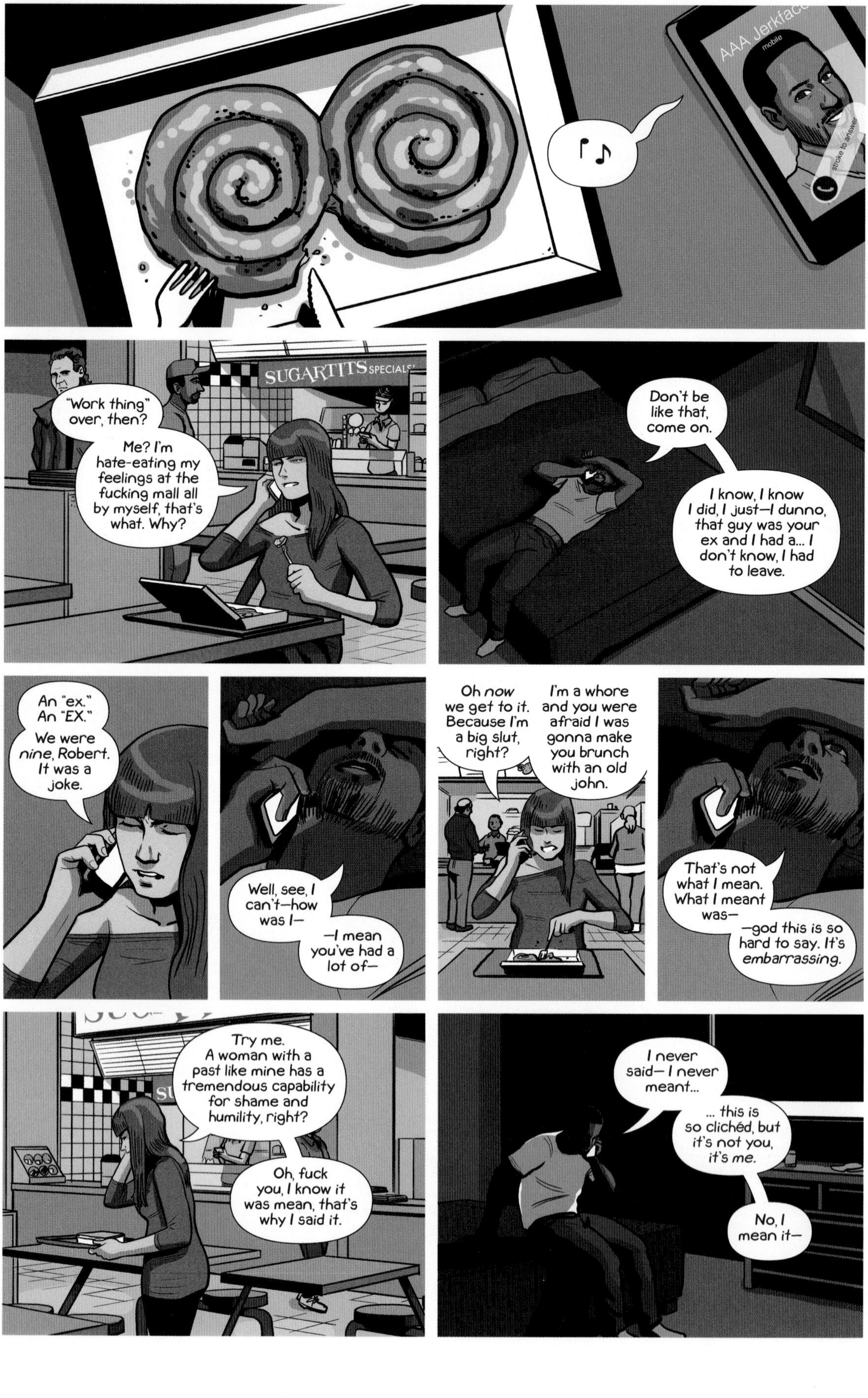
AAA Jerkface
mobile
stroke to answer
SUGARTITS SPECIALS!
"Work thing" over, then?
Me? I'm hate-eating my feelings at the fucking mall all by myself, that's what. Why?
Don't be like that, come on.
I know, I know I did, I just—I dunno, that guy was your ex and I had a... I don't know, I had to leave.
An "ex." An "EX."
We were *nine*, Robert. It was a joke.
Well, see, I can't—how was I—
—I mean you've had a lot of—
Oh *now* we get to it. Because I'm a big slut, right?
I'm a whore and you were afraid I was gonna make you brunch with an old john.
That's not what I mean. What I meant was—
—god this is so hard to say. It's *embarrassing*.
Try me. A woman with a past like mine has a tremendous capability for shame and humility, right?
Oh, fuck you, I know it was mean, that's why I said it.
I never said— I never meant...
... this is so clichéd, but it's not you, it's *me*.
No, I mean it—

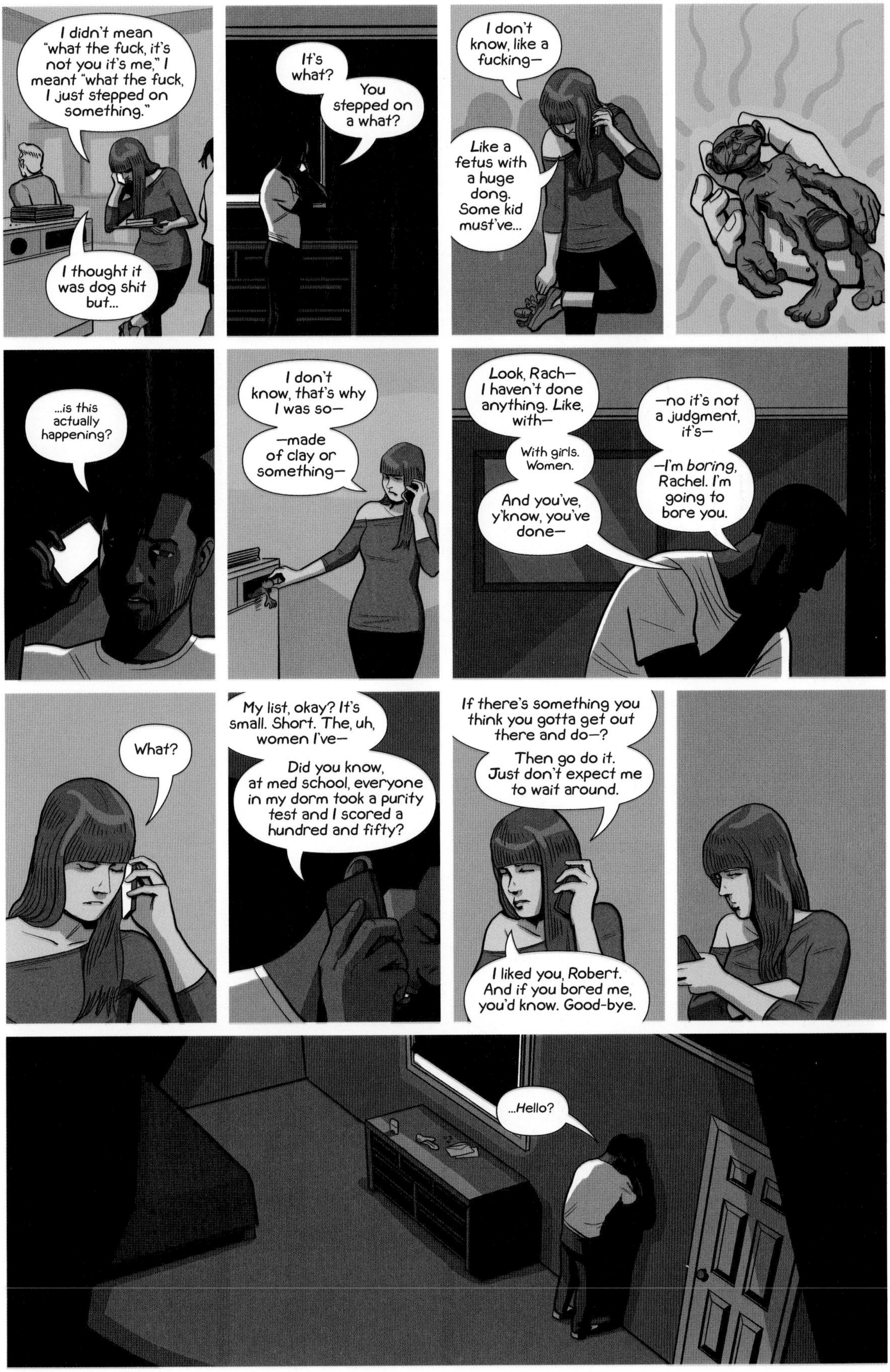

I didn't mean "what the fuck, it's not you it's me," I meant "what the fuck, I just stepped on something."
I thought it was dog shit but...
It's what?
You stepped on a what?
I don't know, like a fucking—
Like a fetus with a huge dong. Some kid must've...
...is this actually happening?
I don't know, that's why I was so—
—made of clay or something—
Look, Rach— I haven't done anything. Like, with—
With girls. Women.
And you've, y'know, you've done—
—no it's not a judgment, it's—
—I'm *boring*, Rachel. I'm going to bore you.
What?
My list, okay? It's small. Short. The, uh, women I've—
Did you know, at med school, everyone in my dorm took a purity test and I scored a hundred and fifty?
If there's something you think you gotta get out there and do—?
Then go do it. Just don't expect me to wait around.
I liked you, Robert. And if you bored me, you'd know. Good-bye.
...Hello?

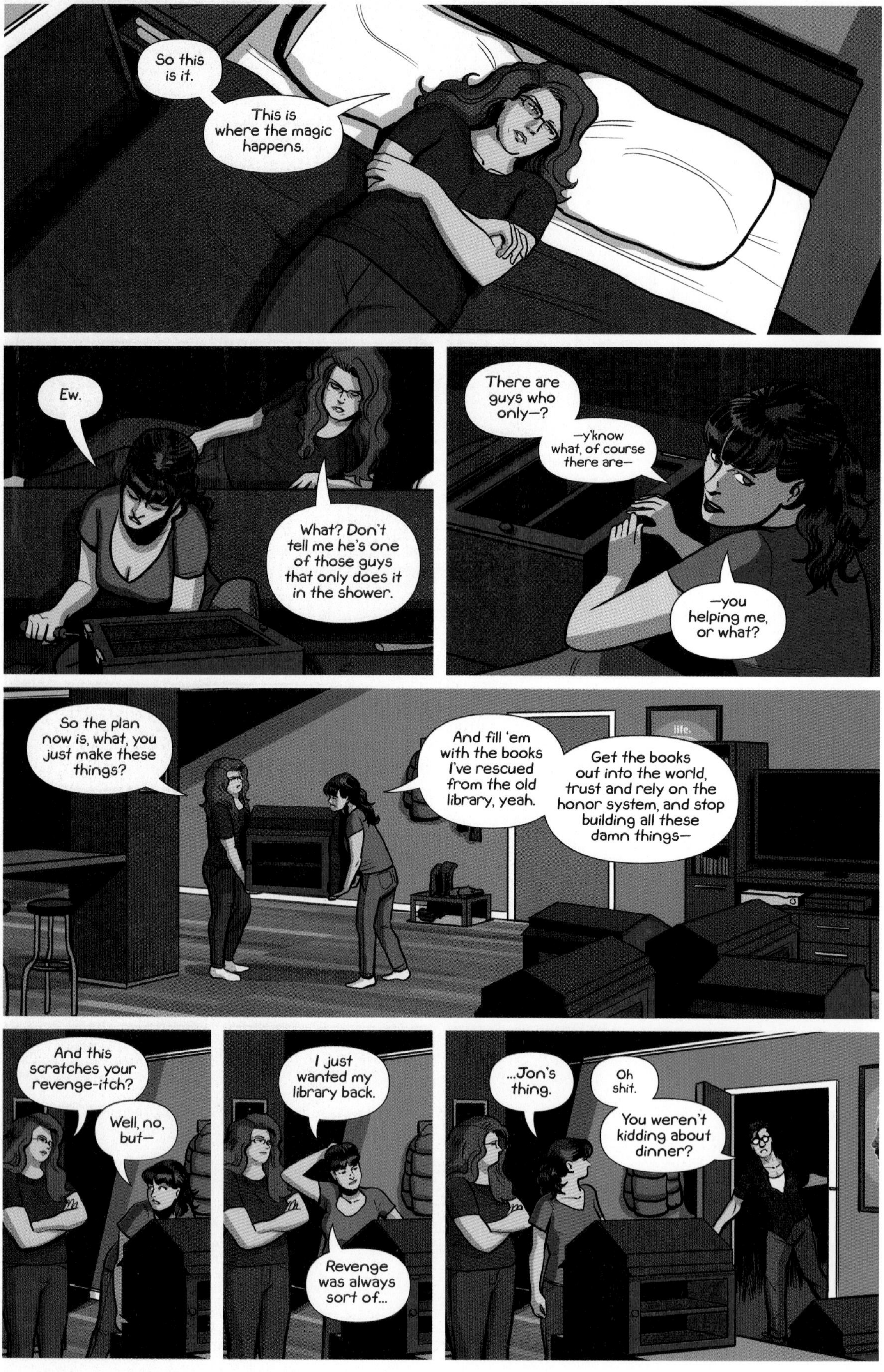
So this is it.
This is where the magic happens.
Ew.
What? Don't tell me he's one of those guys that only does it in the shower.
There are guys who only—?
—y'know what, of course there are—
—you helping me, or what?
So the plan now is, what, you just make these things?
And fill 'em with the books I've rescued from the old library, yeah.
Get the books out into the world, trust and rely on the honor system, and stop building all these damn things—
life.
And this scratches your revenge-itch?
Well, no, but—
I just wanted my library back.
Revenge was always sort of...
...Jon's thing.
Oh shit.
You weren't kidding about dinner?

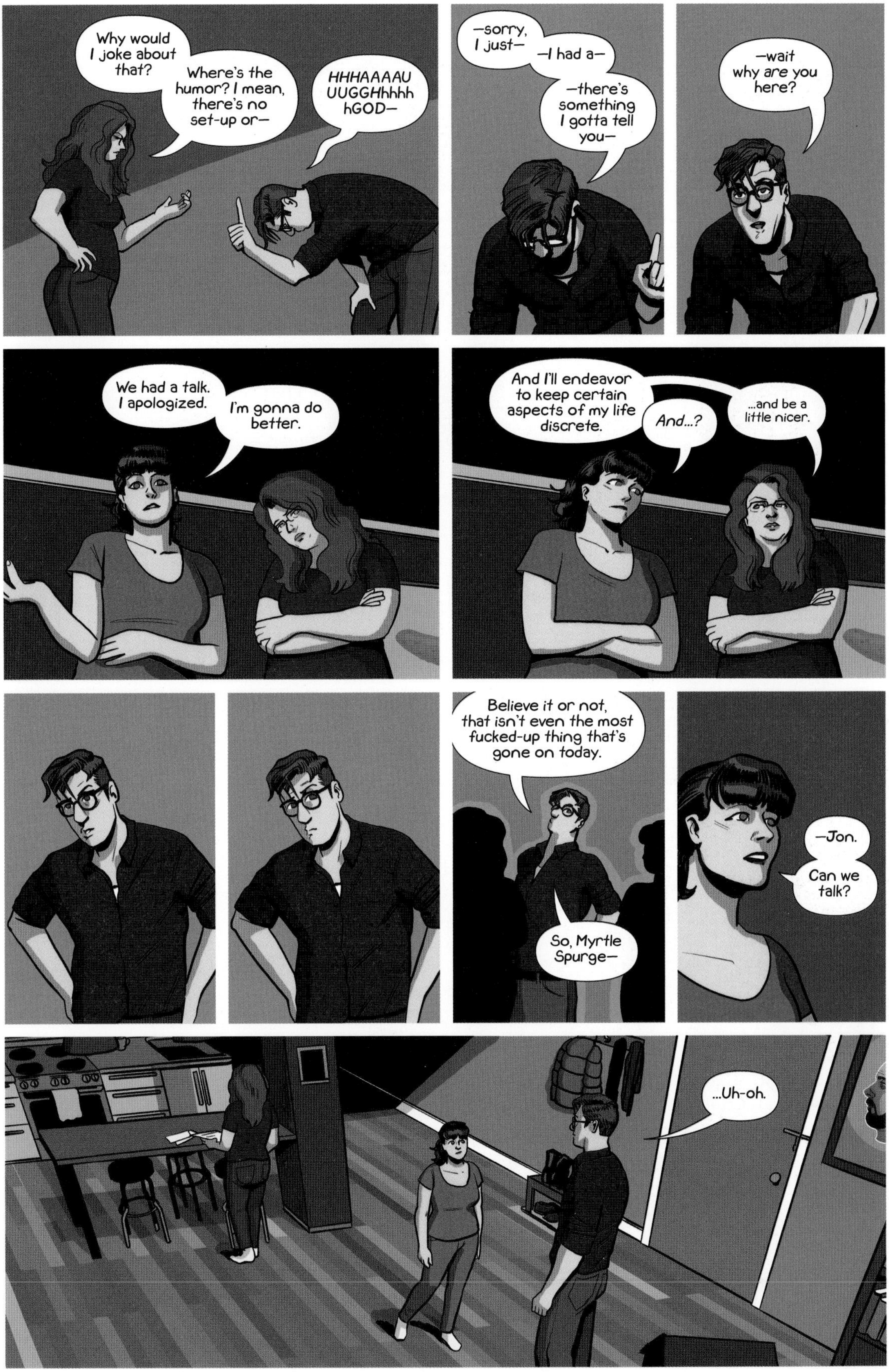
Why would I joke about that?
Where's the humor? I mean, there's no set-up or—
HHHAAAAU UUGGHhhhh hGOD—
—sorry, I just—
—I had a—
—there's something I gotta tell you—
—wait why are you here?
We had a talk. I apologized.
I'm gonna do better.
And I'll endeavor to keep certain aspects of my life discrete.
And...?
...and be a little nicer.
Believe it or not, that isn't even the most fucked-up thing that's gone on today.
So, Myrtle Spurge—
—Jon.
Can we talk?
...Uh-oh.

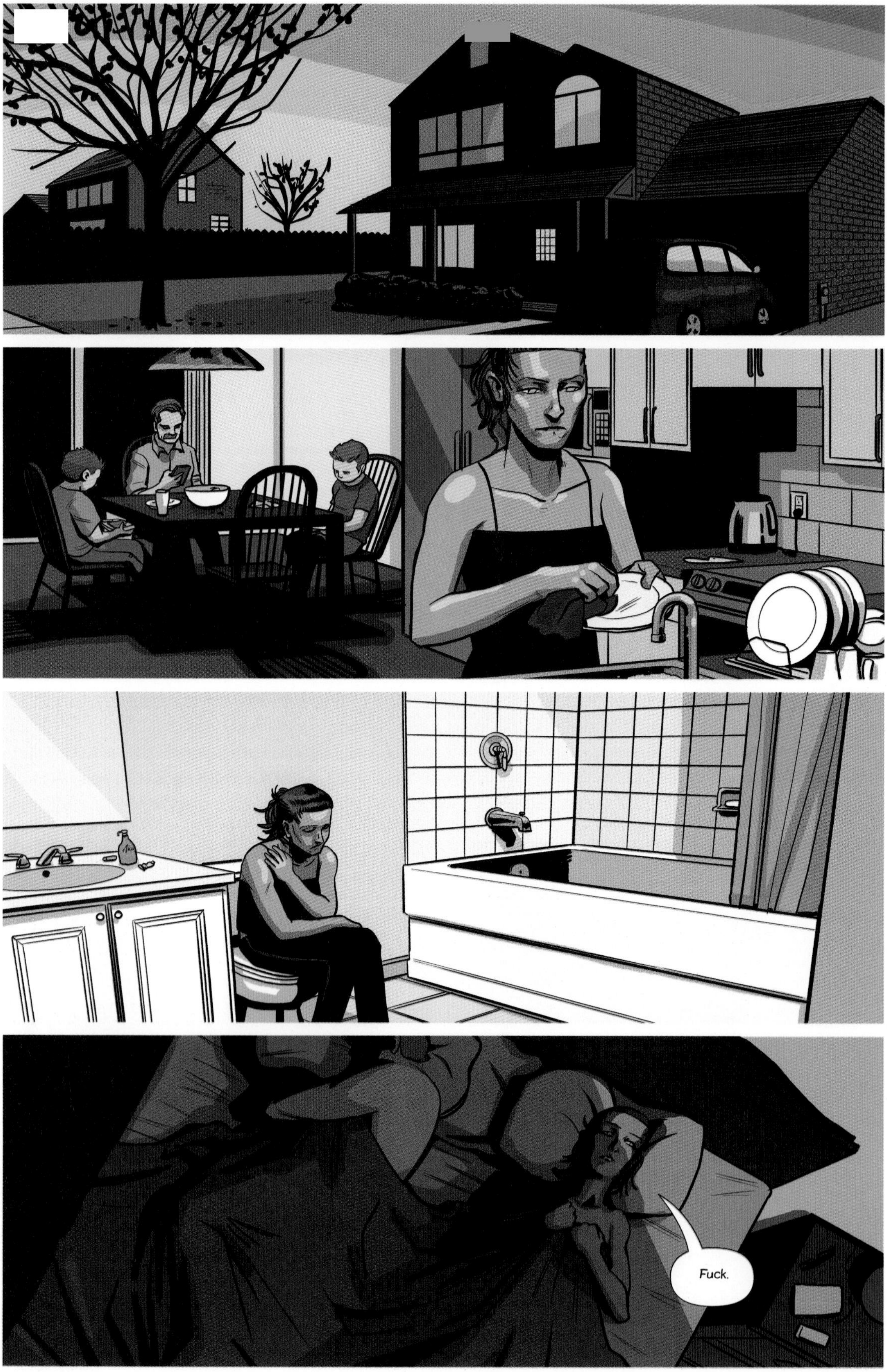
Fuck.

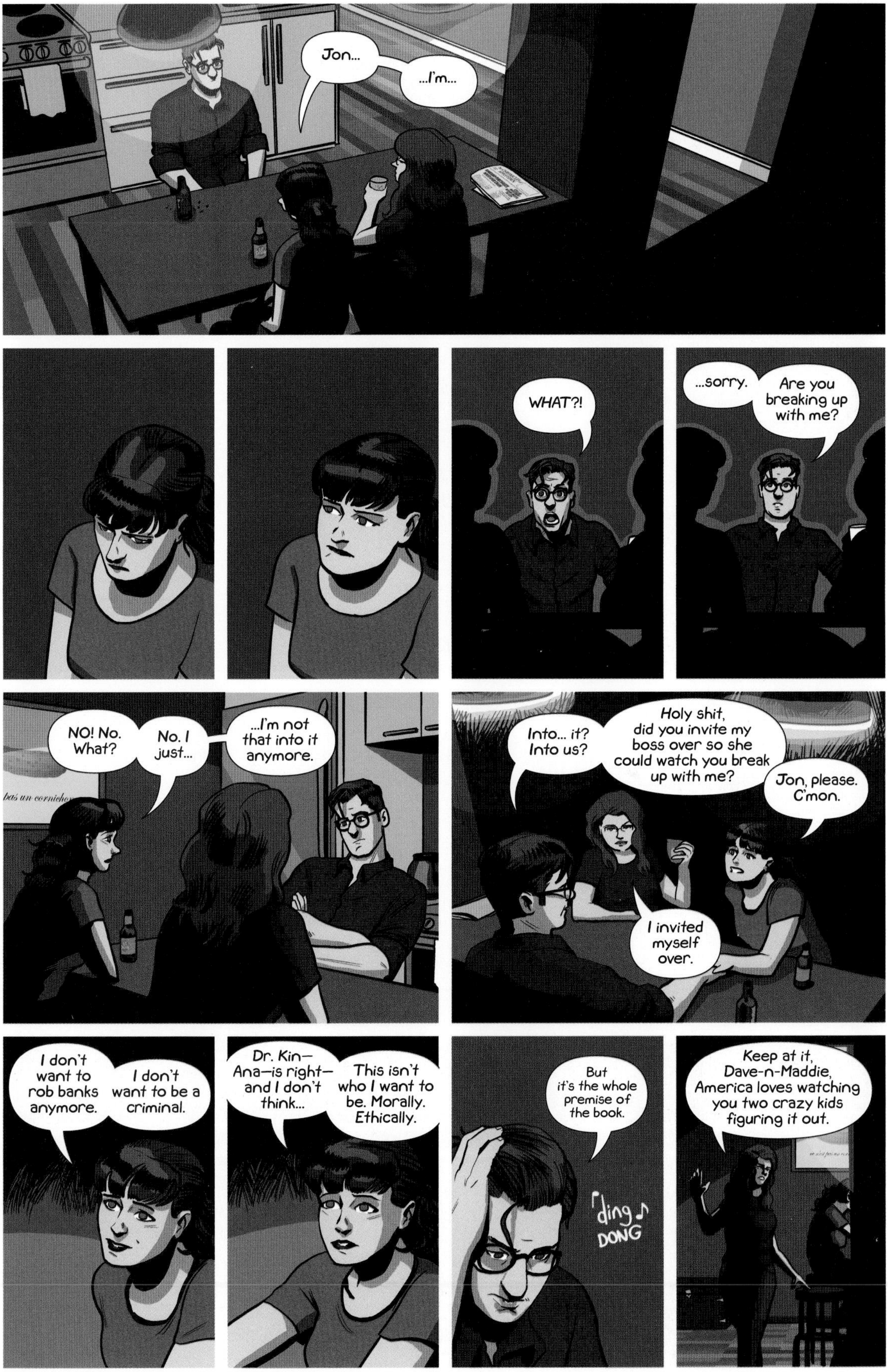
Jon...
...I'm...
WHAT?!
...sorry.
Are you breaking up with me?
NO! No. What?
No. I just...
...I'm not that into it anymore.
Into... it? Into us?
Holy shit, did you invite my boss over so she could watch you break up with me?
Jon, please. C'mon.
I invited myself over.
I don't want to rob banks anymore.
I don't want to be a criminal.
Dr. Kin— Ana—is right— and I don't think...
This isn't who I want to be. Morally. Ethically.
But it's the whole premise of the book.
ding DONG
Keep at it, Dave-n-Maddie, America loves watching you two crazy kids figuring it out.

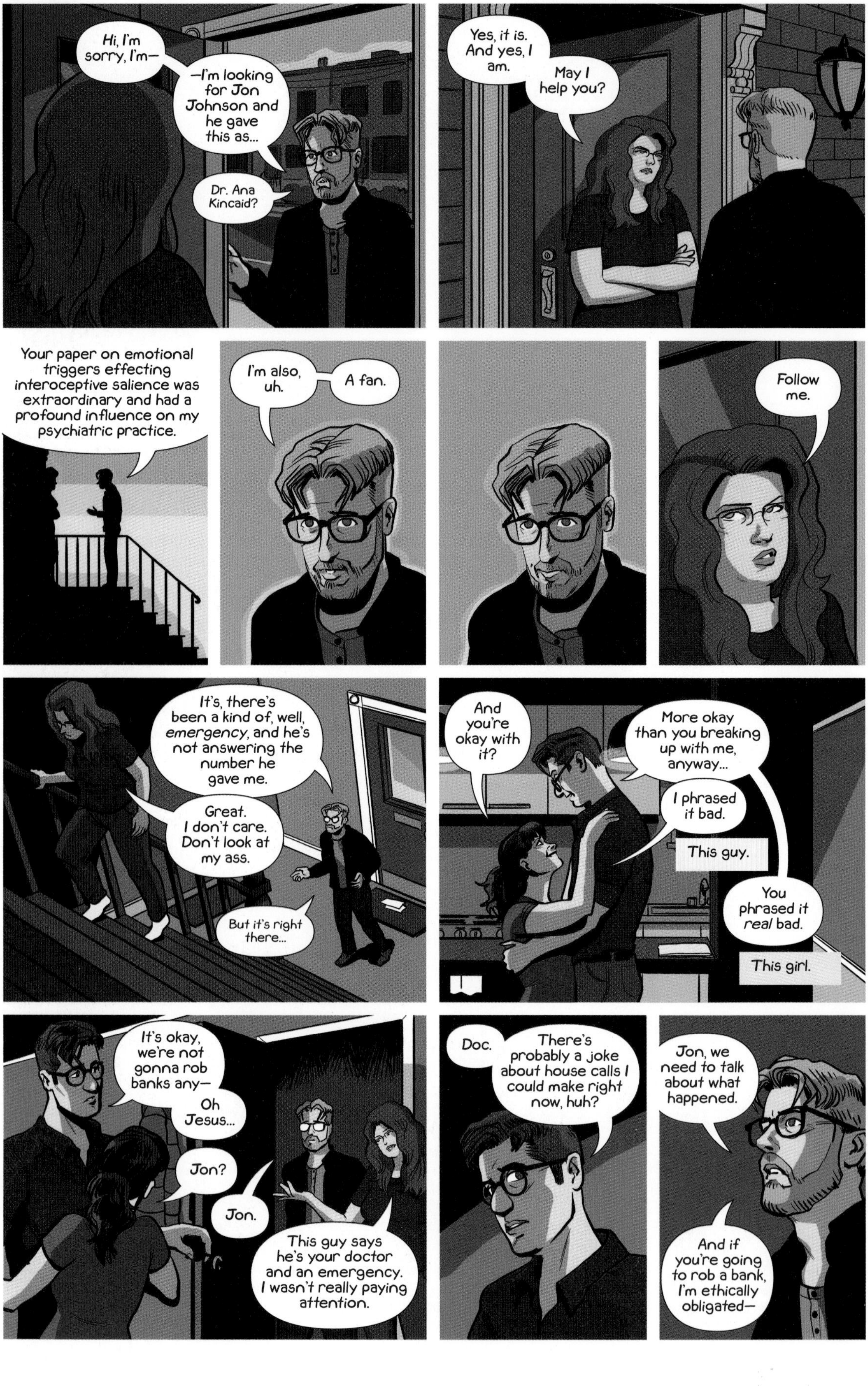
Hi, I'm sorry, I'm—
—I'm looking for Jon Johnson and he gave this as...
Dr. Ana Kincaid?
Yes, it is. And yes, I am.
May I help you?
Your paper on emotional triggers effecting interoceptive salience was extraordinary and had a profound influence on my psychiatric practice.
I'm also, uh.
A fan.
Follow me.
It's, there's been a kind of, well, *emergency*, and he's not answering the number he gave me.
Great. I don't care. Don't look at my ass.
But it's right there...
And you're okay with it?
More okay than you breaking up with me, anyway...
I phrased it bad.
This guy.
You phrased it *real* bad.
This girl.
It's okay, we're not gonna rob banks any—
Oh Jesus...
Jon?
Jon.
This guy says he's your doctor and an emergency. I wasn't really paying attention.
Doc.
There's probably a joke about house calls I could make right now, huh?
Jon, we need to talk about what happened.
And if you're going to rob a bank, I'm ethically obligated—

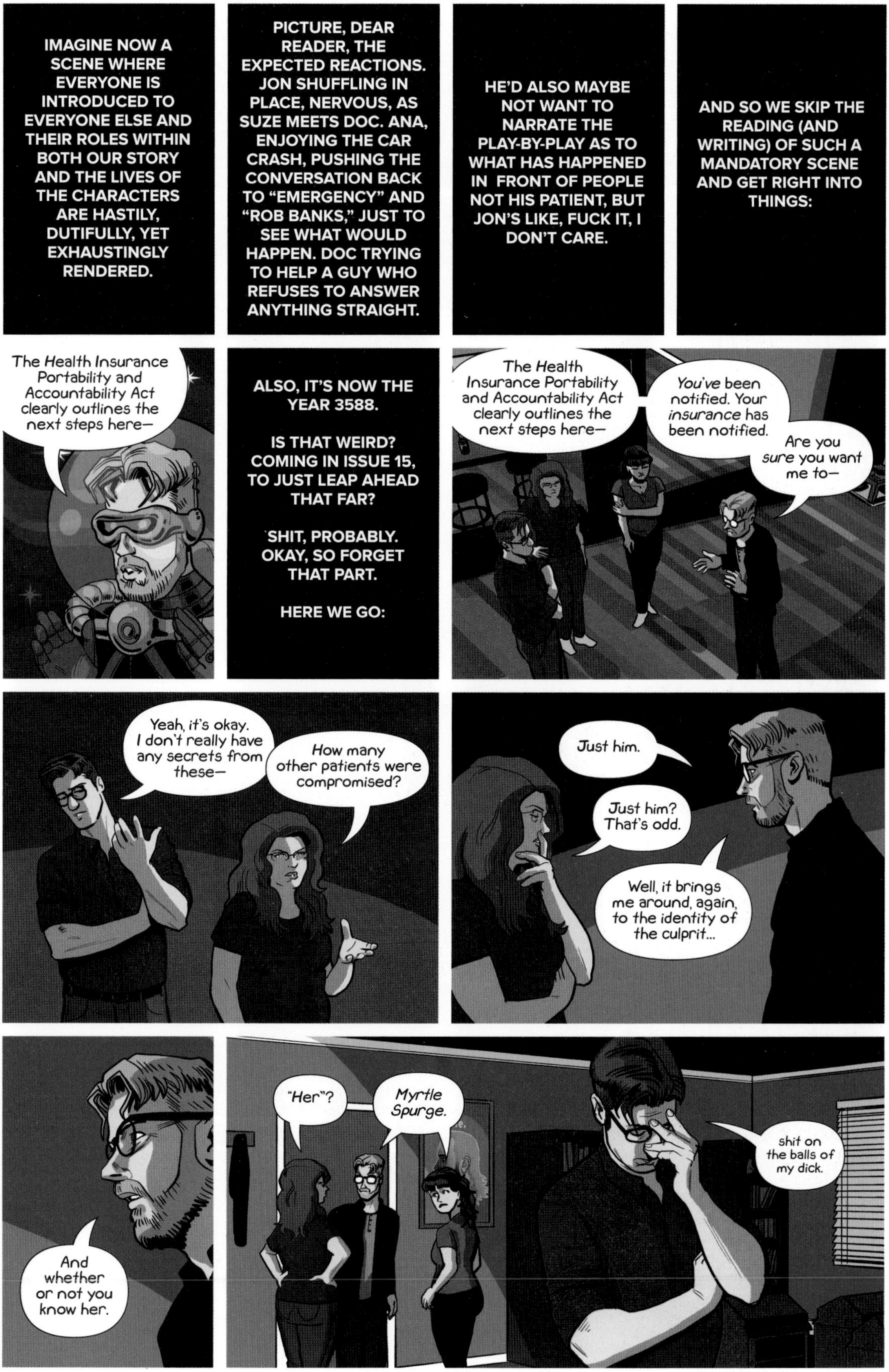
IMAGINE NOW A SCENE WHERE EVERYONE IS INTRODUCED TO EVERYONE ELSE AND THEIR ROLES WITHIN BOTH OUR STORY AND THE LIVES OF THE CHARACTERS ARE HASTILY, DUTIFULLY, YET EXHAUSTINGLY RENDERED.
PICTURE, DEAR READER, THE EXPECTED REACTIONS. JON SHUFFLING IN PLACE, NERVOUS, AS SUZE MEETS DOC. ANA, ENJOYING THE CAR CRASH, PUSHING THE CONVERSATION BACK TO "EMERGENCY" AND "ROB BANKS," JUST TO SEE WHAT WOULD HAPPEN. DOC TRYING TO HELP A GUY WHO REFUSES TO ANSWER ANYTHING STRAIGHT.
HE'D ALSO MAYBE NOT WANT TO NARRATE THE PLAY-BY-PLAY AS TO WHAT HAS HAPPENED IN FRONT OF PEOPLE NOT HIS PATIENT, BUT JON'S LIKE, FUCK IT, I DON'T CARE.
AND SO WE SKIP THE READING (AND WRITING) OF SUCH A MANDATORY SCENE AND GET RIGHT INTO THINGS:
The Health Insurance Portability and Accountability Act clearly outlines the next steps here—
ALSO, IT'S NOW THE YEAR 3588.
IS THAT WEIRD? COMING IN ISSUE 15, TO JUST LEAP AHEAD THAT FAR?
SHIT, PROBABLY. OKAY, SO FORGET THAT PART.
HERE WE GO:
The Health Insurance Portability and Accountability Act clearly outlines the next steps here—
You've been notified. Your *insurance* has been notified.
Are you *sure* you want me to—
Yeah, it's okay. I don't really have any secrets from these—
How many other patients were compromised?
Just him.
Just him? That's odd.
Well, it brings me around, again, to the identity of the culprit...
And whether or not you know her.
"Her"?
Myrtle Spurge.
shit on the balls of my dick.

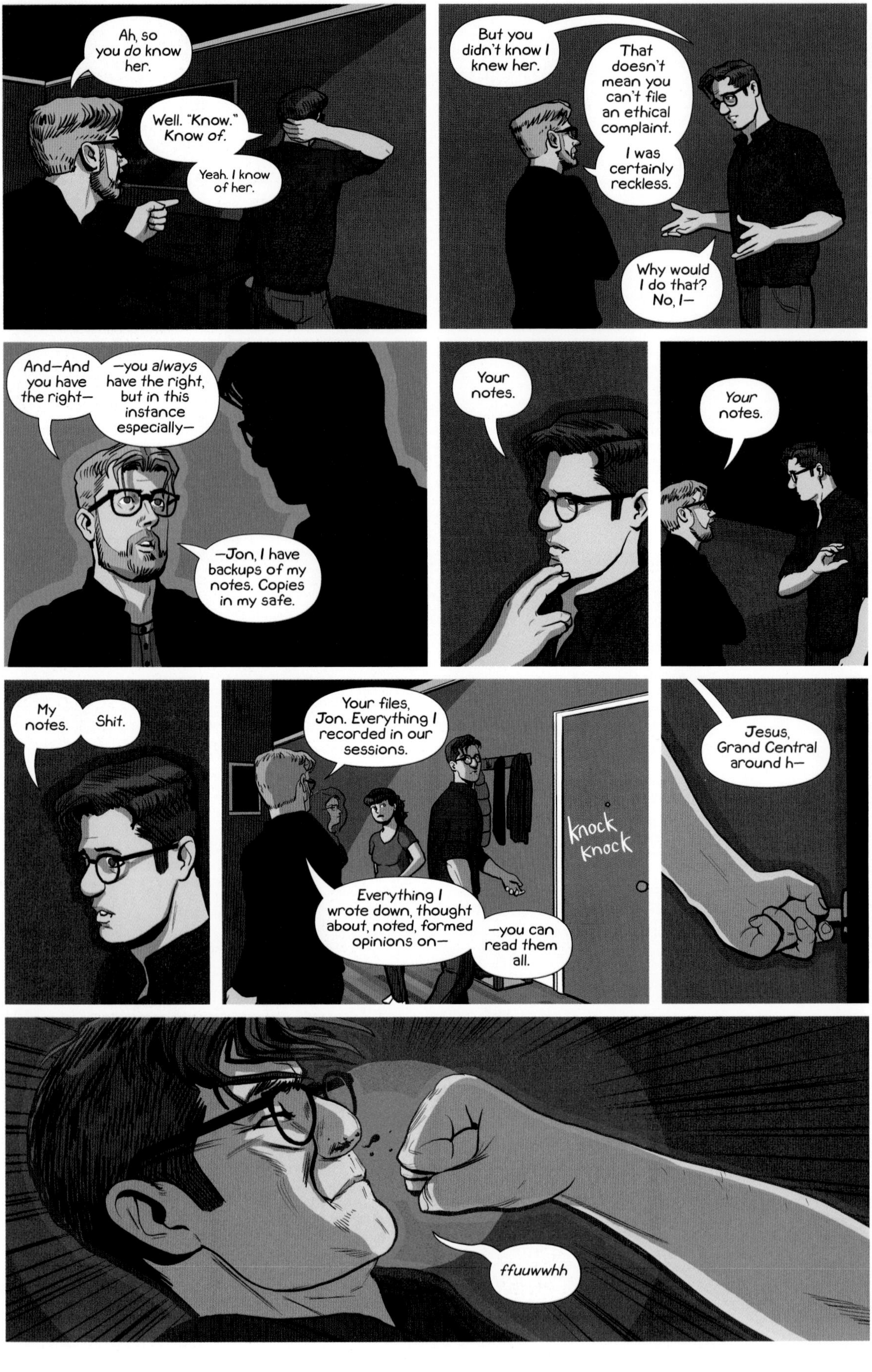

Ah, so you *do* know her.
Well. "Know." Know *of*.
Yeah. I know of her.
But you didn't know I knew her.
That doesn't mean you can't file an ethical complaint.
I was certainly reckless.
Why would I do that? No, I—
And—And you have the right—
—you *always* have the right, but in this instance especially—
—Jon, I have backups of my notes. Copies in my safe.
Your notes.
Your notes.
My notes.
Shit.
Your files, Jon. Everything I recorded in our sessions.
Everything I wrote down, thought about, noted, formed opinions on—
—you can read them all.
knock knock
Jesus, Grand Central around h—
ffuuwwhh

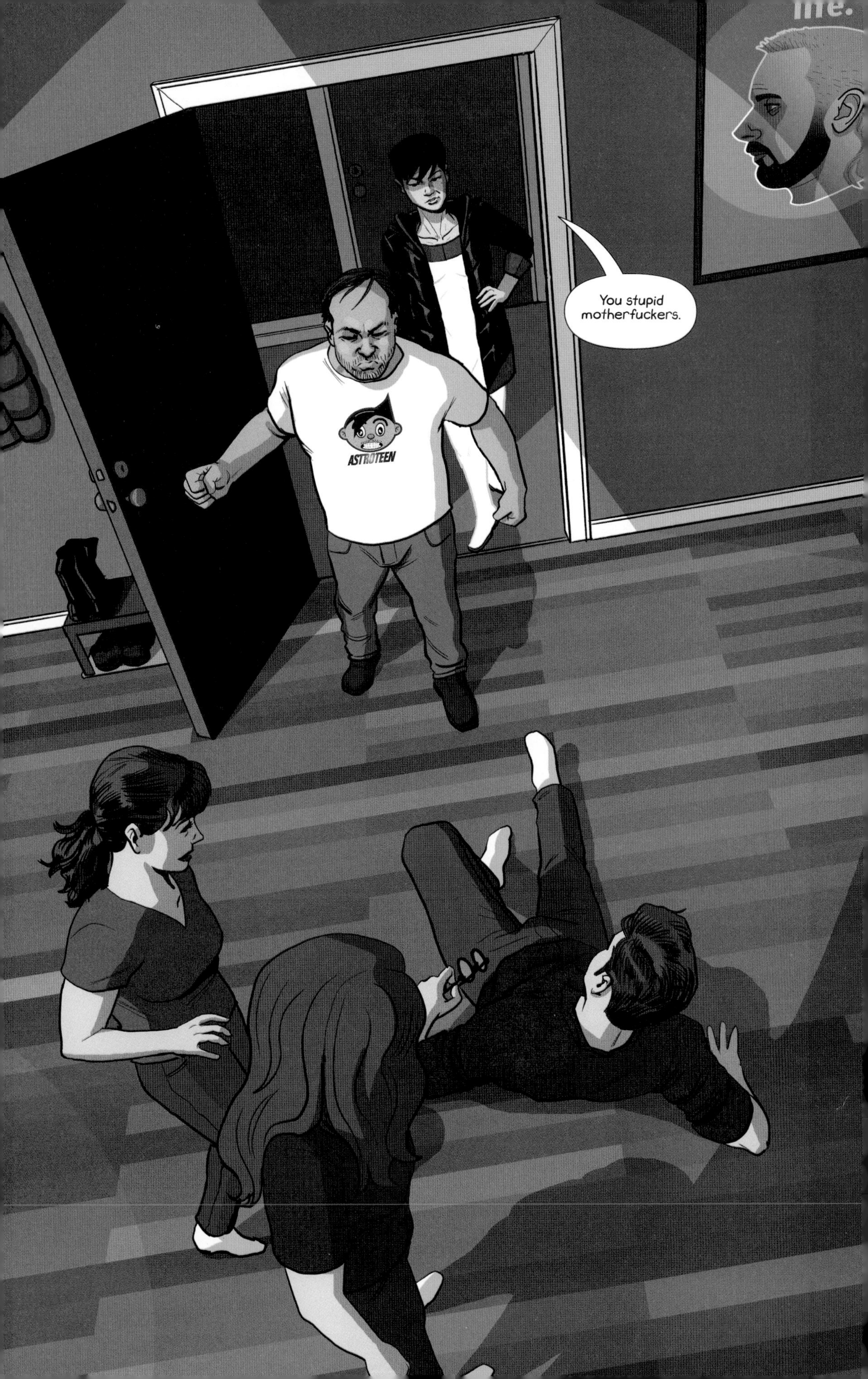
You stupid motherfuckers.
ASTROTEEN

BIG OL' INTERVIEW

TIFFY THOMPSON & ALEX HOFFMAN

Matt interviews the REAL sex criminals, the models and inspiration for Chip and ... a nation?

MATT FRACTION Itsa me, Matt, who makes Chip make you do all those horrible things he photographs and then turns into $$$$$$. Tiffy, let's start with you, because 1) I am a gentleman 2) Alex, ugh, amirite and 3) you are a new mother with a new baby and I want to absorb as little of your time as I can, for I know soon this mewling, barfing shit-machine you've brought into your home will be demanding your time, and your time is actually important.

Chip knew, right away, that you were who he wanted to use as a model for Suzie. Where and how'd you meet Chip, and how, exactly, did he propose such a thing to you? At what point did he mention it was for a comic called SEX CRIMINALS?

ALEX HOFFMAN While I agree that Tiffy's time is more important, as the manager of a comic book store, I should remind you that much of my day is also taken up by mewling, barfing shit-machines.

TIFFY THOMPSON I met Chip through a mutual friend, Zosia, who he worked with at the *National Post*. They met when they worked on a sports story together and ended up handing out $100 worth of pancakes to football fans. She was like, you gotta meet this guy, he's the funniest person alive. Unfortunately, I was living far away in Sault Ste. Marie, and I think he was also slightly terrified of me. I was looking through my old Facebook messages and this is the first one I got from him, before I had met him, in 2008:

•

PAST CHIP *So, I'm working on a Todd Diamond episode where Todd accidentally knocks up a young lady and uses it as analogy for the current financial crisis.*

Would you be that young lady? I would call you "Tiffy" and use a photo from here of your head and animate it.

PLEASE?

Love,
Chip

•

Faced with the possibility of immortalization on the National Post YouTube channel, of course I said yes. I finally met him several years later, after convincing him I was as harmless as any household appliance. The meeting was filled with explosive laughter!

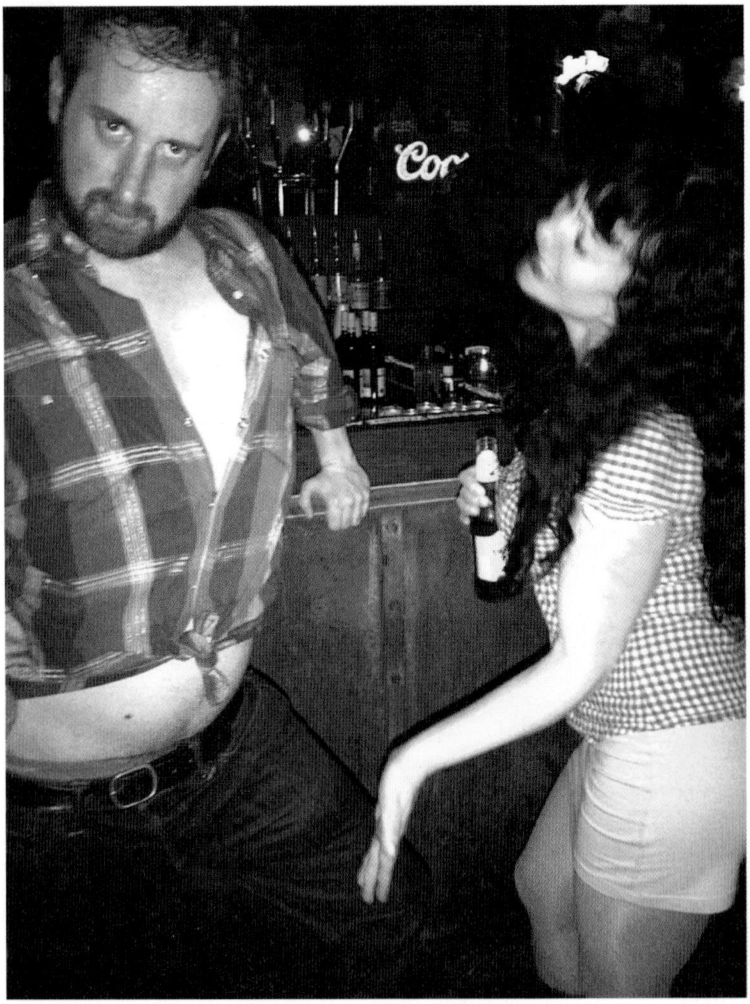
Cor

Sure this photo is gross, but now imagine my hand and arm are actually super tiny instead of farther away from the camera. Happy dreams! -Chip

Then I got this message from him on April 5, 2012.

•

PAST CHIP I mayyy be close to inking a deal to illustrate a comic book series called SEX CRIMINAL about a couple who, when they orgasm, stop time and commit robberies. SHHHH.
I tell you this because I want to make you the model for the main lady character, because you are sexy and look like you could rob a bank.

PAST TIFFY I approve of this with my whole heart, mind and vagina

•

TT I want to add that Chip was the only male invited to my bachelorette party, and his mom baked penis-shaped "cockolates" for the occasion. This is from that night. *(photo to the left)*

MF Wow, he almost got the title right.

Tiffy, Alex, are your parents aware?

And, Tiffy, you got made once in a comic book store, right? Someone recognized you as the model for Suzie?

Alex, what about you? How did Chip approach you? Was it in a men's restroom?

AH I'm not sure exactly when I first met Chip. There's a large and friendly pool of comics people in Toronto, and Chip's been floating in it for ages. I do remember him first mentioning a project called "Sex Criminals," and my telling him it'll never work with a title like that.

My parents are both vaguely aware of SC, but both are so disinterested

Through the magic of art school (one year Graphic Design (dropped out), one year Art Fundamentals, one year Illustration, a year off because of a gun charge, and two more years Illustration), I can turn ANY photo into a happy doodle! -Chip

in comics that I think it's pretty much impossible they'll ever read it. When my mother found out that my store sells X-rated comics, she was astonished to learn that such business is legal. My dad has the wisdom not to try to understand what he knows he'll never understand, so he's barely asked about it. My customers think it's pretty cool. That's something, I guess.

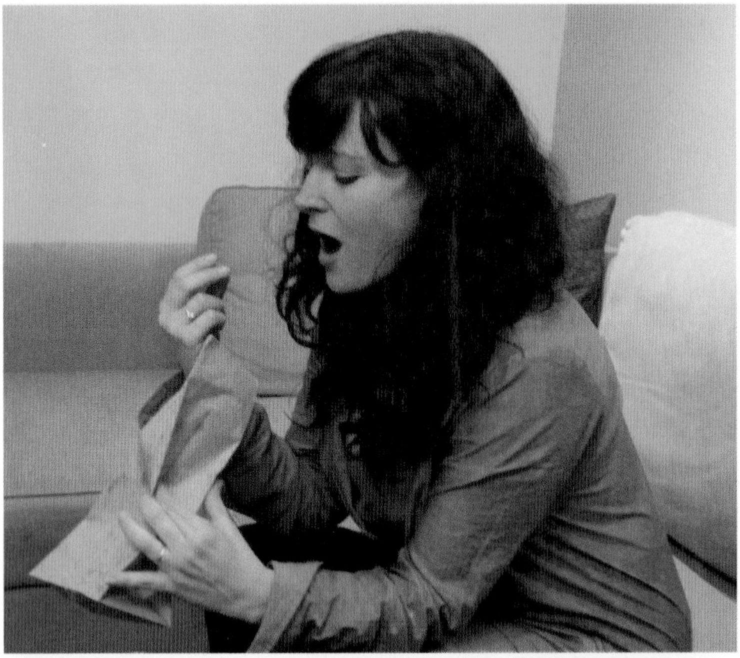

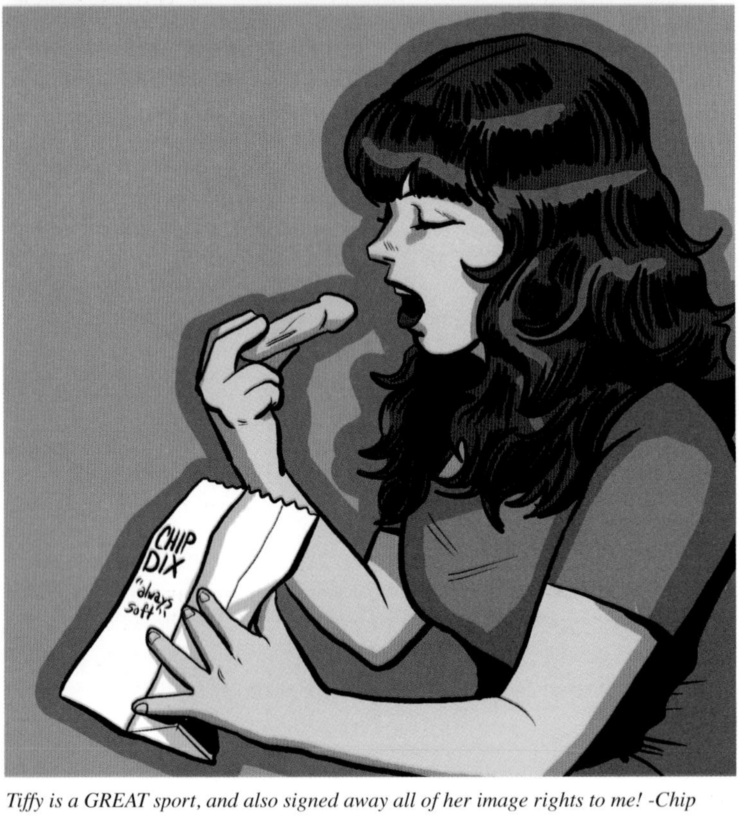
CHIP DIX
"always soft"

Tiffy is a GREAT sport, and also signed away all of her image rights to me! -Chip

TT I was in a comic store called Nuclear Winter in London, ON, and the owner got me to pose for his blog.

My parents are devout Christians, so they were skeptical when I told them I was in a comic called "Sex Criminals." When I brought them back the first issue, my mom flipped through it and said, "That girl really looks like you!" Well, it is me, mom. She muttered something about there being "lots of butts." And then never really mentioned it again.

MF We found out it's illegal to create comics about either sex OR crime in Canada. It's amazing Chip hasn't been arrested.

So, for both of you — walk me through what the first issue was like. Did Chip give you the script to read? Did you just show up cold? Do you bring your own ideas about blocking and stuff to the sessions, or does he treat you like meat puppets? Do you guys actually strip down? How long do the sessions last? Does Chip make it awkward?

TT The first issue, I remember I was nervous, as I had never met Alex and was worried about my breath, simulating intercourse, etc. But it was fine! Chip plied us with chips and drinks, and showed us his storyboard sketches. I think he just threw us right into the scene of getting pounded in the bathroom? Right, Alex? It took a couple of minutes to get into it, but Alex is very charming and fun so it wasn't hard, no pun intended.

We are essentially pliable meat puppets in Chip's hands, but try to imbue it with our own "personality". He perches at various angles (up a ladder once), and takes hundreds of photos, all while urging us on like a soccer mom. He is capturing a series of stills (not video, that we know of!), so it's basically like sex miming.

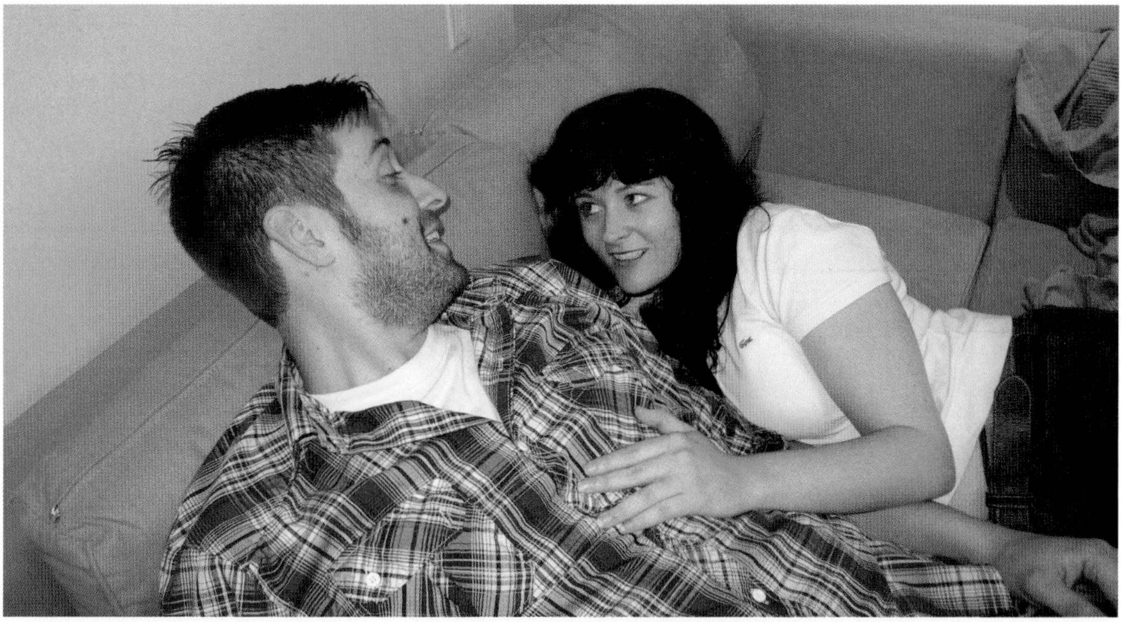

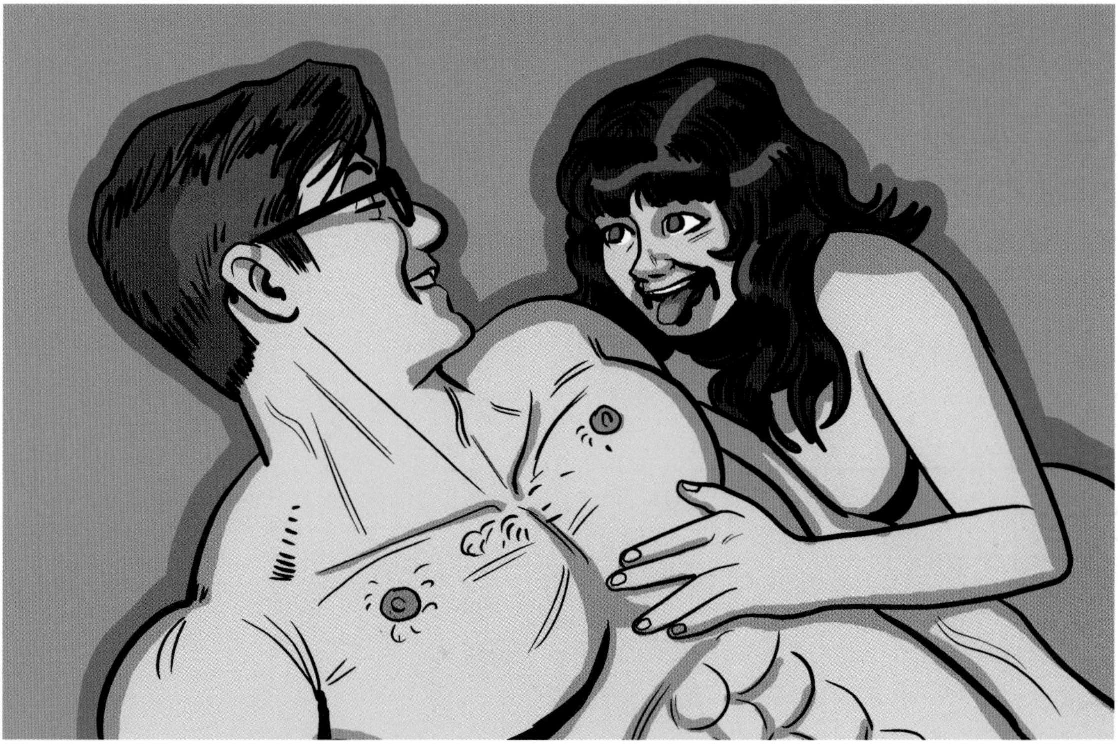

A lot of people think that artists who use photo reference can't actually draw. But the photos aren't the end of my job! I need a VERY thorough understanding of anatomy to bring you the comic content you crave! -Chip

We don't get completely naked, but Chip does, which makes it pretty memorable. The sessions last a few hours and then we get our money and split. We are getting pretty efficient at it; we skim the script and have at 'er.

It was slightly awkward when I was visibly pregnant and Alex felt weird about "crushing the baby," so I tried to make him comfortable, saying "let's crush some babies" as a euphemism for sex. It's a nice little outing for me, I don't get out much these days.

MF Just so you guys know, Chip sends me all the photos and we skype while masturbating to them. Thanks for the "help!"

FIN

Matt Fraction writes comics
and writes TV and lives in the woods
and it's pretty great out here in the
woods I gotta say.

Chip Zdarsky is the award-winning
humorist of such collections
as "I'll Mature When I'm Dead,"
"Boogers Are My Beat," "The Taming
of the Screw," "Homes and Other
Black Holes," "Stay Fit and Healthy
Until You're Dead," "Dave Barry Does
Japan," "Dave Barry in Cybersp—"
—wait a second ... Dave Barry wrote
all of those.

What the fuck has Chip
ever done?

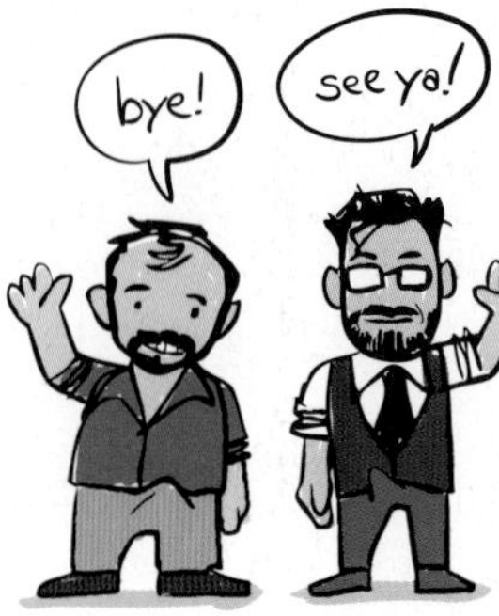
bye!
see ya!